A Blood of Kings

BOOKS BY BRYCE O'CONNOR

THE WINGS OF WAR

Child of the Daystar

The Warring Son

Winter's King

As Iron Falls

Of Sand and Snow

THE GODFORGED CHRONICLES

Shadows of Ivory

WARFORMED: STORMWEAVER

Iron Prince

BOOKS BY LUKE CHMILENKO

ASCEND ONLINE

Ascend Online

Hell to Pay

Legacy of the Fallen

Glory to the Brave

A Blood of Kings

THE SHATTERED REIGNS

II

BRYCE O'CONNOR &
LUKE CHMILENKO

Wraithmarked
CREATIVE

A BLOOD OF KINGS: BOOK TWO OF THE SHATTERED REIGNS

Cover Illustration: Mansik YAM
Cover Design and Interior Layout: STK•Kreations
Art Direction: Bryce O'Connor

Trade paperback ISBN: 978-1-955252-06-5

Worldwide Rights.
1st Edition

Published by Wraithmarked Creative
www.wraithmarked.com

To the Baxter clan!

For being wonderful people,

friends,

and family to me.

PROLOGUE

1076P.F.

I have suffered a blow to my pride on this, my day of coronation. My mother—may she rest well in the Mother's embrace—did her best to prepare me for the moment, but there is only so much even diligent warning can do to brace a man for such an experience. Witnessing that transformation, that revealing which I know now is granted only to the newly crowned sovereign of these great lands, is a thing which would shake even the greatest King or Queen to their core. I have been made to feel small, have been made to feel humble in the presence of such a being, in the knowledge of her existence.

Still, after spending the evening in the creature's company, learning of the truths of Viridian's past, I suspect I will soon be more than a little grateful for her loyalty to me, to my family, and to my throne…

—PRIVATE JOURNALS OF MALYTHUS RETH AL'DYOR, FORMER KING OF VIRIDIAN

"A… A Queen, my Lord?"

First General Makkus Oren's question was not voiced with doubt, per se. Doubt would have been insolent, and—given who the General was addressing—insolence was not something to be tolerated lightly. Still, Cassandra Sert couldn't begrudge the man the waver of uncertainty he spoke with, considering what it was they had just been told.

"*The* Queen, Makkus," Mathaleus Kenus al'Dyor answered evenly, obviously having expected some level of disbelief from his gathered retinue. "The *Endless* Queen, to be precise, though I've little patience for such gratuitous titles at the moment."

The King of Viridian was dressed at leisure—in sharp contrast to the men and women he'd ordered gathered in the great space that was his private study—and was steadily stroking the form of his white cat, Shal, who'd curled herself up in his lap. He wore spun evening robes of black with purple accents, and Cassandra would have been willing to bet a bag of golden levers that his feet—hidden behind the body of the lacquered, gilded desk at which he was seated—were bare. His face—ordinarily bright and warm—was more gaunt than last she'd seen during a similar audience granted not a month prior, and she knew without asking that he was losing weight. The bags under his pale blue eyes, along with the reddish shadow of several day's beard, gave him the look of a man some decade older than his thirty-five years.

Cassandra had not expected Mathaleus to be idle—what with the wereyn hardly two weeks march north of Aletha—but the ruler of men looked to have been long working himself to the bone on little food and less sleep.

There was a cough, and an old, bent man at Cassandra's elbow spoke up wheezily.

"May I be so bold as to ask where you have obtained this information, my Lord?" Kentan Vale, the court's lead historian, queried with a bluntness only age could allow for. "You'll pardon our... confusion... but—to put it mildly—this news is not of an ordinary nature. I can attest to the existence of magic and spellwork in this nation's past, but these are banished arts, cast aside by the wisdom of one of your eldest ancestors. To make mention of it in this day and age is... well..."

He left the suggestion unspoken, trusting the rest of the gathered to follow his thoughts.

Madness, Cassandra finished privately, not wholly disagreeing.

Still...Mathaleus had never been one to play at games.

"I've this intelligence directly from the mouth of a source I would trust my life on, along with that of every man, woman, and child in this kingdom." Despite his appearance, the King spoke with a firmness which belayed his obvious fatigue, still absently running his left hand—index finger glinting with the silver band of the al'Dyor signet—over Shal's ivory fur. "They, in turn, did not share this with me lightly. Weeks have they spent piecing hints together, but there can be no doubt now. Sehranya is a threat the likes of which Viridian has not seen in over half a millennia, and we *must* do our best to prepare accordingly."

Along the left side of the room, a figure stirred among the larger bodies of the men about her. Cassandra cast a careful glance in Sahna Ar'esh's direction, studying the King's spymaster as subtly as she could manage. The old woman, in a plain white tunic and grey robes that might have fit better in a nunnery or farm-hold, was—for once—distracted. Her weathered face was frowning at her Lord and master, dark eyes narrowed warily beneath the short bangs of her cropped silver hair. Cassandra looked away as soon as she'd made her deductions, not wanting to be caught appraising the wily hag.

Whoever Mathaleus' "source" was, they were clearly not a part of Ar'esh's network.

Unsurprisingly, the King had caught the old woman's expression as well.

"Is a sovereign not entitled to a few of his own eyes out in the world, Sahna?" He tried for a tired smile. "Fear not. You and your charges have my faith just as well. There are merely a few family secrets

I've not the right to share, even with you."

Cassandra raised an eyebrow at that. A secret the sovereign of Viridian couldn't share with his most trusted advisors?

Abruptly, she had a great desire to meet this mysterious informant, to know what kind of person could hold such a sway over the kingdom's greatest...

There was a movement in Mathaleus' lap, and Shal lifted her head to turn and take in the room with wide, bright green eyes. Cassandra might have imagined it, but thought the cat's gaze lingered on her for a second longer than the rest.

Then another voice stole her attention back.

"But... how?" Ethena Oren spoke up from behind her older brother. The Third General looked somewhere between bemused and perplexed, clearly straddling the edge of disbelief and confusion. "Magic... A witch who can raise the dead... My Lord, if this is indeed all true, *how* do we prepare for such an enemy?"

"There is knowledge to be imparted," Mathaleus assured the woman with a nod of acknowledgment. "Lessons of the past to be learned, even if they are from an age before the time of our palace archives." He gave Kentan Vale a quick look, silencing the distinct start to an objection the historian had clearly been about to make. "Now is not the moment to share such things, however. I have already given you all much to consider."

"And swallow," Geven Kavel, guildmaster of the Seekers, muttered from behind Cassandra, only loud enough for her and the other company heads to hear.

"For now," Mathaleus continued, "you are dismissed. Be at liberty to discuss what I have said amongst yourself, but *do not* share a word of this with anyone beyond those in this room. Morale would not hold—in the Vigil *or* the populace—if word got out of what we are all facing. Is that understood?"

With diligent dips of their heads, every one of the dozen men and women stated their unified acknowledgment of the decree. No one would be fool enough to let slip so much of a syllable of the conversation, especially not with Sahna Ar'esh present to witness their gathered vow.

There was the *clunk* of a bar lifting, and behind the group Tenet Thrum and Behn Hald—two of the King's six personal guards—pulled open the heavy double doors which led out into the private corridor that would see them back to the main residential wing of the palace. As one the dismissed turned to leave, but before she could take more than a step, Mathaleus called after Cassandra.

"Sert. You and the other guildmasters stay a moment, if you would."

Cassandra stopped short, as did Geven Kavel, Brund Jalys of Stonewall, and Keth Holden of Holden's Guard. Tana al'Von, leader of the Grey Shields, had already been dispatched with her three thousand men as caravan guards for the supply train between Aletha and the gathering Vigil north of Thenus.

There was a moment of shared silence, the five of them waiting for the others to clear the study's threshold. A few of the departing—the Orens chief among them—looked back curiously at the guildmasters but made no objection. The King's business was the King's business, and Mathaleus was not the sort of ruler to need his advisors constantly whispering in his ear.

Once Kentan Vale limped out, leaning heavily on the offered arm of Second General Thurst Lohv, Thrum and Hald closed the study doors again with a dull *boom.*

"Updates," Mathaleus ordered simply as soon as it was quiet again, rising up from behind the desk. Shal made not a sound as she was displaced from his lap, leaping down to the slatted floor with agile dexterity and padding along beside her master while he made for a silver-lined glass cabinet along the right wall.

Cassandra almost smirked when she saw that he was, indeed, barefooted.

"I've received word back from most of the Iron Wind outposts," she answered, watching the King pull open the cabinet doors and retrieve five fist-sized crystal glasses, along with a bottle of what looked like dark wine. "Evacuation of each of the northern cities has commenced, if not without issue."

"Oh?" Mathaleus sounded duly unsurprised while he poured a finger for each of them. "You mean hundreds of thousands of my subject's *don't* wish to leave their homes and flee everything they've ever known with nothing more than what they can carry in both hands? Color me *astounded.*"

Cassandra knew well the bitterness in the King's voice, and understood it. It could not have been an easy decision to make, enlisting the help of the nation's largest mercenary companies and tasking them with the hard job of seeing Ebadon, Ranheln, and Vasteel—along with every small community that could be found between them—forcefully abandoned by their residents. Indeed, as she accepted a proffered glass—each of the three men behind her doing the same in turn—Cassandra tasted a little of that sourness herself.

"They ain't makin' anythin' easy for us, to be sure," Brund Jalys commented in exasperation, the signature slurring of his upbringing in Aletha's slums almost harsh on the ears in the presence of the King. "My boys've been sendin' letter after letter from the coast, tellin' me how the merchant folk've been tryin' to pinch the locals' horses an' carts so they can bring their goods with 'em south outta Vasteel. Never mind the common folk barely got enough to live by as is. Fuckin' pigs." The large man paused, about to take a swig from his glass, remembering his company with a cautious look towards Mathaleus. "Beggin' yer pardon, yer Lordship. Ain't sayin' all rich folk is like that. You've done well enough in my book, if'n it counts for anythin'."

Mathaleus, for his part, gave a tired laugh, raising his own wine in Brund's direction. "Cheers to that, Jalys my friend. To a King who's done 'well enough'."

Cassandra and the others chuckled, lifting their glasses in turn and taking a swallow. The drink burned her throat, warming her from the inside out with an almost acrid sharpness.

It amused her that Mathaleus al'Dyor, to this day, preferred the cheap swill of the back-alley taverns to the fine distillations of his noble vintners.

"Will you manage, though?" Mathaleus asked once the alcohol had settled, returning to the topic at hand. "Do I need to reassign the Grey Shields, or part of the Vigil?"

Cassandra glanced back at the three behind her, who all looked between themselves before shrugging in dismissive unison.

"Nay," she finally told the King with a grim smirk. "We'll manage, just the four of us. The rabble might put up a fight, but the silver lining of the wereyn coming off the Tears everywhere is that no one can deny their presence anymore. They'll bitch and moan about it, but we'll get them all moving. If we need more hands, we can tap the smaller companies. It'll be faster deploying them than a contingent of the army anyhow." She tilted her drink at her sovereign. "We'll be sending you the bill, of course."

Mathaleus waved the comment away with a casual air only a man who had not once in his life had to count his lehts and levers could achieve. "Yes, yes, so be it." He sighed, letting his hand fall and resting his chin on the edge of his glass. Under him, Shal wove her way through his legs, arching her back against the soft cloth of the man's black-and-purple robes. "The lower cities are preparing to take in whoever they can. I've sent envoys to the borders of the Vyr'en, too, hoping to warn them of the evacuation, but Graces be damned if the Matriarch will ever receive them."

"W-won't that cause its own troubles, m-my Lord?" Keth Holden asked tentatively. He was the youngest of them by far, having only recently taken over the guildmaster's position following his grandfather's retirement hardly four months gone, and this was only his second time before the King, and first addressing him directly. "I-if the *er'enthyl* see this mass movement towards their border a-as threatening in any way…?"

"War with the elves isn't a concern," Mathaleus said with a shake of his head, not looking at the man while he continued to stare at the ground. "This Queen, though… Sehranya." He gave a frustrated exhalation, lifting his eyes to the ceiling as though the answer waited among the sculpted oak panels of the arched study. "*She* is going to be trouble. What in the Mother's good name we're going to do about a witch like that, I've not even the faintest…"

Cassandra and the others said nothing, to a one understanding that the King was less speaking to them than he was voicing his own worries and unease. Indeed, after several seconds in which Mathaleus continued to stare upwards, he seemed to remember himself.

"Apologies." He gave a polite cough, meeting their gazes again. "I find my mind wandering more and more frequently in these last few weeks."

"Understandable, my Lord," Cassandra said with a dip of her head. "I doubt you'll hear any of us claiming we can imagine the sort of pressure you are under." There was a mumbling of genuine agreement from the others, and Mathaleus nodded distractedly.

"Indeed…" he murmured distantly, lingering on some thought a moment more. Then, with another sigh, he gestured towards the study entrance. "I thank you for the information. See yourselves out, if you would." He looked around them, towards his personal guard. "Thrum. Hald. You're to take leisure as well. I've need for a bit of solitude, I think."

With a collected nod and bow, all did as they were commanded. The guards opened the doors and stepped smartly out, followed by the guildmasters. Cassandra was the last to leave the chamber, but as Thrum and Hald sealed the room off behind her, she heard Mathaleus al'Dyor still muttering quietly.

"Do I think they believed me? Ha… We can only hope…"

Then the doors *boomed* shut at her back, and as she and the other company heads moved quickly down the corridor, Cassandra frowned to herself in concern. It did not portend well for Viridian if their King had taken to talking to himself.

Then again, perhaps that boded more favorably than the chance the man had been speaking to his cat…

CHAPTER ONE

Common men cannot fathom to the power of dragon. Even the lesser beasts—subordinate to their primordial line—are terrifying to behold. Massive creatures as they are, however, it is less their physical form that one need concern themselves with, and more the magics they wield at will. It is the commonly held belief of the educated that, even as hatchlings, dragons lack any need for the arduous training of the mankind's mages and the occassional of the elven races who show a potential for the art. Rather, they are born knowing, born understanding their race's instinctive talent for drawing upon the leylines of the world, and the subsequent destruction they can reek is mostly myth for a very simple reason: one does not tend to witness it and survive.

More frightening still, however, is that one trembles to consider what sort of creature the Mother above would allow into being to balance such a presence...

—*In the Dragon's Den*, author unknown, c. 250p.f.

Ryn knew only vaguely that he was falling.

It was a secondary concern, inconsequential compared to the pain, fury, and ferocity of the fight he had more directly on hand. In his great talons the drey thrashed, almost small despite its five-foot broad chest and some nine feet of height, but for all their difference in size the creature was a match for him. Viciously-clawed hands tore at his scales, and each time a hoofed foot caught Ryn in the chest it was like being struck across the ribs by a battering ram. The thing's leathery wings whipped about his face and eyes, obscuring his already-limited vision, and the broken juts of its uneven fangs shone bloody in its elk's head. Ryn's neck throbbed, a searing agony boiling through his shoulder and back from where his opponent had just ripped a mouthful of flesh from the place just below the curve of his jaw. He was paralyzed by the pain, and through the haze of it he realized that *this* was why he was falling, *this* was why he was hurtling down, down into the dark to be swallowed by the abyss beneath the earth.

Schlunk!

Ryn roared as he felt something long and thin, like the blade of a sword, tear into his side. The drey had taken further advantage of his moment of incapacitation to sink the cruel barb of its jointed tail as deep as it would go.

Still, with this new shock came clarity, and so it was with a blink or two of his white-gold eyes that Ryn's spirit returned to the battle with a vengeance.

CRACK!

With a slashing of one front leg, Ryn struck the thing across the side of the head. Any other creature would have been decapitated by such a blow, but the drey's doubtlessly-imbued bones held firm, and only an antler snapped off to spin away into the whirling black. With a screech it returned the treatment in kind, tearing and slashing at him. They fell and tumbled and sank deeper, deeper into the dark, faster and faster until the air screamed all around them. Blood and scales and fur were cut and ripped away, each of the pair taking it in turn to roar or scream in alternating pain and victory. First Ryn had the upper hand, then the drey, then Ryn again, this cycle repeating as endlessly as the emptiness that was engulfing them. Nothing existed to each but the other, as well as the firm, clear knowledge that one sole victor would have a prayer of walking away from this exchange alive.

When the moment of advantage came, therefore, Ryn didn't hesitate.

Sacrificing a front shoulder to a series of long, clawed gashes, he managed to wrap a hand about the drey's abdomen. It keened again, writhing under the pressure of his talons piercing its gut, pounding at his forearm with enough force to break the trunk of a small tree. Ignoring the hammering ache of each blow, Ryn managed instead to get his other front hand around its chest, finally pinning it somewhat steadily before him. Together they continued to tumble endlessly through the air, but finding itself before his great head, the drey changed tactics, scrabbling and slashing at his face instead of his arms, trying and failing to get at his eyes.

With a thought, the magics in Ryn's blood flared to life, heat building in his throat and chest, and the blackness all around them fled when his mouth began to glow white with the building of ivory fire.

Unfortunately, the drey were as intelligent as they were savage.

Forgoing its attempt to slash at him, the pinned beast instead reached down with both hands and took him by the bottom jaw. With a strength that belied its slighter frame, the thing wrenched Ryn's entire head up and away with a piercing scream. Unable to hold back the fire already roiling between his fangs, Ryn was forced to release the magic through teeth clamped shut by the restraining angle. The flames sprayed out in a tumbling fan around them, spilling by and across the pair of them in their plummet. It seared even Ryn's own hide, splashing across his black scales painfully and scorching the more delicate membranes of his wings. It was not for nothing, however, that he had been gifted with primordial blood. The power in his veins repelled the broiling heat, refused it with the absolute firmness of a mountain unmoving in the lashing of a winter storm. The pain pulsed, then ebbed, fading as the fires ran their course, streaming off him like water over oiled cloth.

The drey was less fortunate.

Despite saving itself the greater calamity of taking the dragonfire full in the chest, the spilling of the magic was not so kind to its form, made more widely of fur and skin. It screeched and thrashed, letting go of Ryn's jaw in favor of scrabbling at its own hide, trying to bat and claw away the flickering white of the clinging magic. It managed it, barely, but not before half its face had all but melted away and its broad wings became nothing more than useless sheets, tattered with holes that smoldered and widened with the stink of burning skin.

Ryn took his chance, then.

He'd not had great opportunity to fly in the last seven of his eight centuries, and so it was with some difficulty that he struggled to get his bearings. Through the pain he did his best to focus, the confusion of his swirling direction not helped by the spinning tumble into the abyss. Ryn's mind battled with gravity as the pair of them twisted, trying to capture which way was up. He failed again and again, and in his grasp the drey's attention had turned back to him, and Ryn saw the thing's cruel tail swing around and stiffen in preparation again.

Forgoing his hope for better timing, Ryn flared his wings wide with a *snap* of catching air.

Luck—or perhaps the deity Declan and his forefathers called "the Mother"—must have been on his side this day, because it turned out he'd been in the middle of spinning right-side-up when the broad membranes caught. His wings jolted and strained in the upward rush, like catching the winds of a gale, and Ryn gave an unbidden grunt when the corded muscles of his back were wrenched by the jarring impact of cutting his momentum with a twisting jerk. The movement, though, slung the drey off of him as its own impetus continued to pull it down. With a keening scream that echoed in the ocean of emptiness it plummeted away, and Ryn could only listen to it fall, hearing for a long few seconds the flapping sound of its ruined wings fighting uselessly to keep it afloat.

Then even that faded into the black, and Ryn was left alone, suspended in limbo.

At once he sagged, the pain of the hard-won fight pulling at him, dragging him down. The slow beat of his wings stuttered, and he dipped a dozen feet before he caught himself. Though he couldn't see it, he could feel blood streaming along his chest and legs, spilling particularly nastily from one back foot, below where the drey's tail had punched into his side. His neck, too, ached dreadfully, acutely so when he lifted his head to blink up into the black.

There, far, far above him, a distant, single point of light marked the cavern from which he'd fallen.

Hold on, Ryn said to no one in particular, pushing his wings to beat a little harder. Once. Twice. On the third he started to gain momentum, and soon he was ascending with gathering speed.

Hold on.

CHAPTER TWO

"I have seen a minor officer of the er'endehn take on five trained soldiers of the Vigil and come out the easy victor.

When I share that story, though, you might be surprised how often I fail to mention that the elf was the only one in the fight to start out unarmed..."

—Tryvean Morne, First General of Aletha, c. 310p.f.

Declan Idrys was not a man unaccustomed to danger. In his relatively short life of some twenty-five years, in fact, one could argue that he had come across most every threat a man of the blade was like to face. Between a near-decade spent under the firm rule of the mercenary guilds of Aletha—the great capitol city of the human kingdom of Viridian—then three more years on the road as a hired sword for his more personal gain, not so long ago Declan would have been comfortable claiming he had seen it all. Pirates along the eastern coast, come off of Borel's Sea. Rebellions in the west, among the townships beneath the shadows of the Reaches, furthest from the authority of the King's justice. Beasts, murderers, highwaymen and common thieves, the latter of these not infrequently being so bold as to cause trouble on both sides of Viridian's southern border, shared with the Vyr'en, the sacred forest of the *er'enthyl* wood elves.

Unfortunately, more recently, Declan had discovered that his understanding of danger was not only limited, but severely lacking within the spectrum of what the world had to offer. He had, in the course of the last three months or so, had the misfortune of crossing steel with dead men, clashing with the chimeric nightmares of old that were the drey, and learned that his greatest companion was not simply *not* a horse, but in fact a dragon of a lineage akin to royalty among his kind.

And yet, despite the incredible reality of each of these facts, Declan couldn't recall a single time he'd felt closer to death than in the moment he sat on the damp stone of that cavern beneath the mountains of the Mother's Tears, staring up the wet length of a glassy black blade.

The sword was held to his throat with such unmoving precision, it might have been the decorative weapon gripped in the fist of a stone statue. It didn't so much as shiver, held with a steely confidence in the slim fingers of the woman before him, her figure clad in smoke-darkened armor of bound leather and light metal plating burnished gold around the edges. An open-faced helmet sat upon her head, from the top of which the long tail of a black plume hung loose down her back. Her skin was similarly only a few shades lighter than the shadows that had swallowed Ryn and the drey he'd been battling only a few moments before, and glistened with sweat.

But it was the woman's eyes that spoke most absolutely to Declan, the cool danger of her narrowed gaze—like fire made ice behind the white irises, teasing at red around their edges—that sent fear crawling up his spine.

Yl vas ah'ren, veht? the dark elf had asked of him. He did not speak her language—it was a curved, twisted dialect of a tongue in which he only knew a handful of words as it was—but the question was not lost on him all the same.

It was, after all, written in the threat of the blade at his throat.

What are you doing here, human?

Declan tried to speak, tried to answer, but found himself instead mouthing uselessly at the air. He was frozen, and not only by the paralyzing gaze of the woman before him and the wet gleam of her sword, still slick with the acidic blood that refused to catch on the strange, crystalline material from which it been forged. To his right he could hear Ester yr'Essel breathing only shallowly, thrown from Orsik's back as Declan had similarly been when the drey *they'd* been battling had caught them a massive swipe of its tail. Further to his left, he could barely make out Orsik himself wheezing and gasping, the warg largely unmoving on his side some dozen yards away where he'd been sent flying with a kick. Beyond the elf before him, the very creature responsible for the scene was lying in a crumpled heap against the slight incline of the cave's plateau, a half-dozen figures in the same armor as the woman standing motionless all around it, swords and spears held with silent confidence at their sides. Another of theirs lay dead, her head crushed to a pulpous mass in the twisted metal of what had been a helmet, the only casualty of the exchange that had downed the foul thing.

Yes. Declan had reason aplenty to have lost his tongue, he rather thought.

"Heys, veht!" The sword shivered a hair closer as its owner grew impatient with his silence, her stare boring into him with the same intensity of a drawn bow. *"Yl vas ah'ren?!"*

Again, Declan thought he could catch the gist of the demand.

Speak, human! What are you doing here?!

At last he fell back into himself, instinct working well to tear away the momentary shock as he realized there would likely be no third chance to answer. Declan opened his mouth with every intention of responding, but he stopped before he could get the words out.

How *was* he to answer? What was the likelihood the elves spoke the tongue of men? If Ryn and Bonner were right, then the *er'endehn*—the dark elves of Eserysh—had deliberately secluded themselves from

Viridian and its people for well over six hundred years ago. Would they have bothered to keep up with a language so useless to them? The spoken word of a people they had purposefully cut themselves off from?

In the end—and with the elf's white teeth starting to show as she bared them in final warning—Declan decided he at the very *least* had to make the attempt.

"We mean no harm," he said as steadily as he could manage with the sword at his throat, raising both hands in what he prayed to the Mother and her Graces above was a universally acknowledged sign of surrender. "We are not your enemy. Only travelers."

Unsurprisingly, the only response he got from the woman was a blank stare as she too, it would appear, realized the discrepancy in their situation. She spat something quietly, sounding like a curse, and Declan decided to take advantage of her uncertainty and try again a different way.

"Se'av," he said gently, hoping against hope that he had correctly recalled the elven word for "friend" as he lowered his left hand—around whose middle finger the silver signet of the al'Dyors gleamed—to indicate he and Ester not far to his right. Slowly, he worked to get his legs underneath himself, aiming to stand. "*Se'av*... uh... *Se'av as*—"

CRACK!

The blow came so fast Declan thought he'd blinked and missed it. The woman had stepped forward and retracted her sword—originally so close to his throat and face—only to bring it around with the snapping precision of a snake, catching him a blow in the temple with the weapon's pommel. Declan was knocked sideways to half-crumble to the stone again, too dazed even to think to bring his hand up to the side of his head. Through the stars in his vision he strangely could only appreciate that the elf hadn't struck him with the flat of her blade.

A splash of drey blood in the face felt like the only thing that might possibly have made their situation any worse.

Through the ringing of his ears following the blow, Declan heard his aggressor lay into him with a furious tirade, and he guessed his mistake had likely been to try and stand. He shook his head, attempting to clear his vision, and he realized he was looking down on Ester's bloody face, her eyes closed, her face wet and red from a nasty gash across her forehead. His heart skipped a beat for fear, but it brought him back to his senses.

Just as it reminded him that he and the half-elf were far from alone in this exchange.

CRUNCH! BOOM!

As though on cue, there was a spray of shattering rock, and a fissure appeared in the slick slope to Declan's left, crumbling away from him while dust and wet stone disintegrated and streamed into the widening mouth. He heard the elf curse again, and looked around in time to blink through his still-blurred vision at the form of the woman dancing back. Shapes chased after her, pressing her further away, and it took Declan several seconds to comprehend the rigid outlines of a dozen stone spikes, longer and narrower than the ones that had briefly held the drey in place during their fight. They were cutting diagonally out of the fissure, like fangs of an underslung jaw, and stopped growing once the woman had been pressed a fair ways in retreat.

And there, approaching from beyond the elves with a slow care that Declan found almost frustrating in the desperateness of their situation, Bonner yr'Essel sat atop Eyera—Orsik's female sibling—with both hands in the air, each of them glowing a verdant green.

The hood of the old mage's robes was thrown back, revealing his clean-shaven head and the careful braiding of his beard. The light in his fingers—dancing with shimmering runic characters that faded in and out of existence like flames—reflected in the emerald of his eyes and off the white and grey fur of the warg between his legs. His face was calm—calculating, almost—and Declan even thought he saw the man hush Eyera when the animal bared its teeth at the elves.

"*Mytos...*"

The word was a hiss. It slipped off the lips of the dark elf who'd held him at sword point, and despite her having her back to him now—facing the challenger who'd chased her away with his stone skewers—Declan could see the tension ripple through her body. There was fear, there, to be sure. A deep-seated, terrible fear.

But more than that, there was anger.

Abruptly the elf barked something at the rest of her retinue, and like shadows made liquid the black forms surrounded Bonner and Eyera with a precision Declan had never imagined was possible. He'd spent more than a year as a higher officer in the Iron Wind, assessing and training the mercenary recruits under Cassandra Sert's guiding influence. He'd even had the occasion to be graced with a glimpse of the surgical escort that formed the personal guard of Mathaleus al'Dyor and his queen, Syla.

Not a one among them—not among his own men, or the best of the royal couple's—had shown half of the methodical exactness these dark elves moved with despite not exchanging a word between themselves.

Bonner, for his part, looked largely unconcerned. Indeed, after glancing with only mild interest at the entourage of black blades that encircled him, he dropped the spells he'd weaved with both hands, letting the green light fade to nothing before looking over the narrow chasm he'd formed to address Declan.

"You all right, boy?" Bonner half-shouted, his voice echoing eerily in the vast hollow of the cavern. It reverberated in Declan's ears and did nothing to chase away the lingering ring the dark elf's blow had left him with.

"Aye," Declan grunted back once he'd squinted away the ache. "Ester's in bad shape, though. Losing blood. And Ryn... Ryn fell..."

Though he kept his composure, the mage's face shifted subtly at that, which was impressive in and of itself. Though they'd known each other only some weeks now, Declan would never be able to imagine Bonner as anything but supremely protective of his daughter, and knew he considered the dragon a great friend.

It seemed, for whatever reason, that the old man was being careful to give away as little as possible to the figures surrounding him.

"Do what you can for her, for now," Bonner said as steadily as he could manage, his green eyes now shifting again to the *er'endehn* who hadn't yet made any move against him. "I'll see to her once I've settled things here."

Declan opened his mouth to protest, to tell the mage of the anger he'd seen in the bearing of the woman, but he shut it just as quickly again. For one thing—judging by the old man's countenance around the elves—he suspected Bonner was already far more aware of the tensions than he was.

For another, the mage had already started speaking to the soldiers that encircled him in the fluent, twisting syllables of their kind.

For the first time there appeared the briefest pause in the confident bearing of the group. Declan even caught a few pairs of pale eyes exchange looks of subtle surprise through the slats of their open helms, but just the same not a blade moved, not a spear or sword was lowered. The hesitation did not go unnoticed, too, because the women with her back towards him—this strange unit's leader, Declan thought he could safely deduce—snapped something at the offending lessers, and all eyes locked on Bonner once again.

"Urrgh..."

The sound of groaning from his right made him start, and Declan cursed his distraction, looking around in time to catch a glimpse of Ester's eyes—as brilliant green as her fathers—fluttering open. He half-twisted to press himself near to her, feeling his left knee—which had been caught by the strike of the drey's tail that had sent them all flying—straining and protesting at the abrupt motion. Ignoring the discomfort, he reached the half-elf just as she came further too.

"Aaaaah...," she moaned when she tried to lift her head, one hand coming up to her face as a wave of obvious pain paired the motion. "What... What happened?"

"Don't move," Declan told her, his words instinctively quiet as Bonner continued to speak—and hopefully plead their case—to the dark elves. "We took a hit. The bastard sent us flying a good way."

This did nothing to quell Ester's apparent confusion. Pulling her hand down, she blinked several times in lack of understanding at the blood coating her fingers. "W-what? How...?" Her eyes went wide as understanding clicked into place, and Declan got a hand on one shoulder just in time to keep the woman from trying to sit bolt upright.

"Stay down. It's alright. They downed the drey. We're safe, at least for the moment." Without thinking he took the cuff of his sleeve and start gently wiping the red from her face.

"'They'?" Ester repeated, still squinting at him as he tried to clean away the blood and grim, though she ceased in her struggles. "Who's 'they'?"

Declan opened his mouth to answer, but before he could get the words out, Bonner's voice was cut off to his left.

The unit leader had interrupted the mage, lifting one gleaming sword to point at him accusingly. Her words were slow, as though in consideration of what must have been Bonner's imperfect speech, but all the same there was no warmth, there, no care or empathy. Indeed, the dark elf spoke with clean hostility, like one lacking all trust or faith in the person they addressed. Declan supposed he could understand the woman's hesitation. If the e*r'endehn* were even half as long-lived as their wood elf cousins far to the south, then their memories were likely to be measured in centuries rather than years.

And the last time the dark elves of Eserysh had crossed blades with a wielder of magic could hardly have left them with any pleasant tales to tell their young…

At his side, Ester gave a hiss of surprise when she made out the elvish words, confusion crossing her face first, then realization. With difficulty she turned her head to peer in the direction of the conversation, but Declan knew her view would be obstructed by the long spears of stone Bonner had summoned to their aid. Just the same, the half-elf seemed to understand.

"*Er'endehn*?" she asked quietly of no one in particular.

Declan stopped working on her face, choosing instead to press his bloody sleeve over the still seeping gash across her forehead. "Can you understand them? I can't make out a word in ten, if that."

Slowly, Ester nodded. "They're… accusing Father of trespass? I'm not sure… The language is a bit different from the southern dialect. They want to know what our kind are doing in the mountains…and where a mage learned to speak the elven tongue."

Her brows furrowed, concerned as Bonner answered calmly only to have *several* of the dark elves raise their voices in anger at his reply. When Ester translated, Declan understood their alarm.

"He's told them our hope is to reach Ysenden. That we are fleeing the eye of the Queen."

The elves' agitation was kept brief by a short order from their leader. The woman with her back to them was no longer leveling a sword at Bonner, but the tension in her bearing had redoubled. When her subordinates were quiet again, she spoke, and for once Declan understood the simplicity of her statement without assistance.

"*Teyth'e, Sehranya.*"

Serhanya is dead.

There was a moment of quiet, the silence clinging to the emptiness. The absence of noise made Declan fear again for Ryn, but before he could look to the gaping hole at the base of the incline, Bonner spoke again.

This time, Ester translated his words directly.

"Whether dead or alive, it does not change the fact that the Queen is taking actions in the lands of men."

There was more, but the rest of the mage's statement was drowned out by further shouts from the elves. They appeared *truly* angered, now, baring white teeth at the old man, and beneath him Eyera bared fangs right back. Two of the *er'endehn*—tall male figures of a matching height bearing mirrored black spears with curved, heavy blades—turned their weapons on the warg silently. They alone had maintained all composure throughout the conversation, and even as a growl built in Eyera's throat, the pair stared her down impassively.

"*Ythe*!"

The leader's order for silence—for it could have been nothing else—cut across the noise so abruptly it might have been a knife. At once the others stilled and quieted, their answer to the command so abrupt it was almost mechanical. The elf woman, for her part, wasn't actually looking at Bonner anymore. Her head had turned, her pale eyes now on the corpse of the drey, and Declan thought he could just make out the hint of concern in what little of her face he was able to make out from a side view of her helmet. He watched as she trailed the outline of the creature with her gaze, taking it in from the crowning horns of its ram's head to the barbed tip of its segmented tale. Eventually her eyes lifted, and Declan suspected she was looking along the incline of the cavern to the other body laying facedown at the far end of the cave, near the shadows left untouched by the floating orbs of light Bonner was still holding suspended among the stalactites above their heads. *This* drey the dark elves had slain before Declan and the others had even known they were nearby, and despite its smaller stature, it did not change the fact that two of the creatures had been lurking within the mountains in such close proximity to each other.

Nor that a *third* had tumbled into the blackness of the abyss down the slope from them, dragging Ryn along with it.

It took the elf a long moment to come to her decision, not looking away from the corpses as she obviously contemplated Bonner's words. At last she turned to take the mage in, and was silent for another few seconds, whatever choice she was deliberating not an easy one to wrestle with.

Finally, she spoke again, a single word, and Declan felt Ester stiffen in alarm under his arm even as the ring of dark elves closed in as one of the old man and the warg.

"There will be no seizing of anyone, *thank you very much*!" Bonner shouted, the fingers of both his hands twisting into a rapid series of runes Declan didn't have a prayer of following despite the time he'd been studying under the mage's care. Quick as thought the spell formed, and the elves were only feet from him, blades aiming for Eyera on all sides, when Bonner thrust his arms out like a man sweeping aside a curtained door.

WHOOM!

The blast came as a wave of energy erupting outward in all directions. It was visible as a distortion of the air for only the briefest moment, picking up dust and pebbles and moisture from the slick floor of the cave, but it slammed into the offending elves with the same result they might have had had they been running full tilt at a solid wall. In combat the *er'endhen* were silent, as silent as they'd been when fighting the drey, but discipline did nothing to keep their swords and spears in hands, nor their boots underneath them. As Bonner's magic caught them all together, they were knocked onto their backs or thrown away, tumbling outward from the mage like the falling petals of a black, blooming flower. Armor crashed against stone and weapons were sent scattering. Only the leader was far enough away so as to keep her feet, and even she was forced back three full steps, nearly impaling herself on the stone spikes that still flanked her. She kept her blades, however, and while her lessers scrambled to gather themselves, she regained her balance, then shot forward with breathtaking speed.

That was when the sound of wings reached Declan's ears.

There was a *whoosh* of churning air, and in the corner of his vision he saw a massive shadow rip upward from the emptiness beyond the ledge of the stone slab. Then his mind registered the details of the colossal black shape, and Declan choked out a cry of relief as Ryn made himself known, the black dragon tucking his wings and slamming down onto the stone with his front legs flanking Bonner and Eyera on either side. Though the warg bristled and whined in fear, she did not bolt as the mage brought a reassuring hand to the animal's neck. Ryn, for his part, bent his neck down, his body arching over the pair so that his head came flush to the ground, directly in the charging dark elf's path. With a breath of shock that betrayed her discipline, the woman did her best to stop herself, sliding dangerously across the slick rock.

She came to a halt not a foot from Ryn's exposed fangs, just in time for the dragon to open his maw...

... and *roar*.

In the enclosed confines of the cave, the sound of the primordial's anger was a sundering force, vibrating through still air and hard stone. Declan had to bring his hand away from Ester's face to cover his ears, and lying beside him the half-elf did the same with a yell of pained surprise. The world itself felt like it was shaking, and as the roar slowly faded away there came the quiet pitter and clacking of dust and pebbles falling to the floor, shaken loose from the rough ceiling above them.

Caught more directly in the blast, the dark elf had dropped both her swords to bring her hands to either side of her helmet in a vain attempt to protect her ears, and all the same she was brought to her knees. By the time Declan could shake the ringing in his head enough to look around, the woman was shivering, kneeling before the dragon, who had reared up once more, apparently satisfied with the outcome of his entrance. All around them, every one of the other elves—including the pair of stoic spear-wielders—were standing slack-jawed, Ryn's bloody, twenty-foot-tall presence in their midst apparently more than enough to wipe away whatever self-control had been left to them after Bonner's announcement.

NOW—Ryn's voice was like a hammer on steel through everyone's head while he stared down on the half-crumpled dark elf before him—*if you are all done with this folly, shall we restrain ourselves and discuss this complication LIKE CIVILIZED PEOPLE?*

CHAPTER THREE

Whether it was shock, fear, or some other uncertainty, Declan didn't know, but for whatever reason the dark elves made no move against Ryn, nor any more towards Bonner and Eyera. Two of them—the spear-wielders Declan was rather sure were brothers, if not twins—started at last to step forward after several moments, lifting their fingers from the haft of their weapons in a mirrored gesture of peace when the warg snarled at them. Reaching the woman still kneeling before the dragon, they each took her under one arm, hauling her to her feet and kicking her swords back towards the others with a tinkling clatter before retreating away again.

Better, Ryn rumbled approvingly, narrowing his eyes at this group once the two men had made sure the woman was able to keep her feet. *Tell the rest they will lower their blades as well, or I will personally ensure not a one of you make it out of these mountains as anything more than ash on the wind. I am injured, I am tired, and I have arrived to find you* attacking *my companions without need or cause, as far as I am aware.* He snorted, lowering his head again to eye the leader in particular, who seemed to be steadily composing herself again. *I had thought better of the er'endehn of Ysenden, truth be told.*

Ryn did indeed appear the worse for wear. He had returned to them bloodied and battered, with a number of injuries leaking wet even as he spoke. The dark scales of his neck glistened like black glass under a great hole that had been ripped from the flesh beneath his jaw, and Declan could make out his back right leg shaking under the strain of holding the dragon upright. A puncture wound had been punched into the side above the involved haunch, and crimson wept over the massive curves of Ryn's hip, knee, and clawed toes.

Still, even mangled as he was, the dark elves appeared hardly fool enough to think themselves any match for the dragon, who in weight alone likely outclassed any of the felled drey by ten times at least.

The others turned inward, looking to their leader, and despite a continued tremor in her hands the dark elf stood taller, lifting her chin proudly. She began to answer, and it was as she spoke that Declan realized with a bit of a start that the woman appeared to have understood the dragon perfectly. It wasn't all that surprising, of course. Ryn, after all, did not communicate via any spoken tongue, but rather through a connection of thought Declan had only recently heard the dragon and Bonner call "mind-speech." It was strange to consider, but with the mastery of cerebral magics Ryn's kind were best known for, it was hardly a daunting possibility that the language of dragons was a more universal communication than the simpler, vocalized words of men and elves.

And yet, despite this fascinating revelation, what intrigued Declan even more about the exchange happening between Ryn and the dark elf was the lack of fear, the absence of astonishment.

There had been shock in the first instances of Ryn's return, yes, but watching the pair now Declan had to assume it had been more surprise at the dragon's abrupt reappearance than any unexpected occurrence. Indeed, Declan couldn't bring himself to believe the elves had missed him when they'd first arrived, as Ryn had been having it out in the air over the chasm he'd then plummeted down into along with the drey.

And still they're calm... he thought in puzzlement, studying the faces of the other *er'endehn* he could see, all of them indeed watching

Ryn now with careful interest as opposed to any fright or suspicion.

"Seven hundred *bloody* years, and the bastards still haven't gotten over their grudge. Dragons are fine, are they? Oh of cooourse they are… Never mind that the overblown reptile could belch them all into dust before I likely had a chance to summon up so much as a damn *spark*."

Declan blinked and looked around. Bonner, it transpired, had taken advantage of Ryn's preoccupation of the *er'endehn* to slip with Eyera from between the dragon's front feet. He'd rounded the top of the narrow fissure that still separated Declan and Ester from the others, and was in the process of sliding off the warg's back, still muttering to himself. Landing with a *thump*, he looked around to pat Eyera's shoulder even as the female half-turned away with a whine.

"Yes. Go see to your brother. I'll be there as soon as I've fixed up this pair."

With permission given, Eyera bounded off at once, lopping towards Orsik's still-wheezing form. As she left, Bonner made his way closer to Declan and Ester, already eyeing his daughter critically.

Declan gave him a tired grin as the old man settled down before them to peer more carefully over Ester's wounded head. "Complain all you like. You seemed to have held your own just fine from where I stood."

Bonner snorted in answer, his bald head gleaming in the light of the orbs high above them. "I hope I've not fooled you into thinking me unconquerable, boy." The mage started poking and prodding at Ester's forehead, making her wince and grunt in pain. "While I can certainly handle myself, the odds were *not* in my favor, had that little altercation escalated."

Declan opened his mouth to argue, but paused. Indeed, he supposed he *did* have trouble imagining Bonner yr'Essel as anything other than untouchable. He'd seen the man's magic throw off a drey, seen him summon the vitality of the earth with titanic efficiency. He'd witnessed Bonner pull both he *and* Ester from the edge of death, and known him to have grown back lost fingers and flesh claimed by the cruel claws of Sehranya's wights.

And yet...

Declan glanced back to where Ryn was still hearing out the dark elves as they pleaded their case, the injured dragon listening impassively and without looking away. The way they had moved... Declan had never seen anything like it, and could feel his heart picking up in pace as he rewound the fight in his head, thinking again of how the *er'endehn* had danced around the drey, ducking and darting and striking with such precise intent it had been like watching the choreographed ballets of one of Aletha's royal companies. There had been no playing with the creature, no toying or teasing it as they cut away its life. Rather, it had merely been a battle carried out with calm confidence the likes of which Declan doubted he would ever know...

Yes... He supposed even *Bonner* could die, if cut down a thousand ways from a dozen swords that could bring even a *drey* to heel with near-perfect ease...

"No fractures, no displacement," the mage announced quietly, sounding a little relieved, and Declan looked back again in time to see him stick a finger into the blood that coated Ester's forehead. Scrawling a trio of complicated runes into the wet red with the same ease Declan might have signed his name, Bonner leaned back with a sigh as the symbols flashed once, then seemed to vanish into the half-elf's skin. "That's done." The mage's green eyes turned to Declan. "Now you. Anything broken?"

Declan had to tear his attention from the wound on Ester's head, which was stitching itself together as the woman's face relaxed in relief.

"You're *sure* you can't teach me that?" he asked of the old man, only half-joking.

Bonner managed a dry chuckle, taking it upon himself to move and grasp Declan's left leg—which he'd been guarding fairly obviously—in both wizened hands. "Auramancy is not a discipline you have much talent for, boy," he replied tactfully while Declan inhaled in pain when he knee protested the sudden manipulation of the limb.

"'About as much talent as a rock,' I think was the exact phrasing," Ester joined in, managing a twisted smile through whatever ache remained as she started to sit up with only mild difficulty, clearly feeling much for the better.

"Yes-*ergh*-I recall, thanks," Declan grunted in answer, having trouble appreciating the teasing in his vulnerable circumstances. Bonner was bending his leg without tenderness, clearly intent to do what he could and move on now that he knew the pair of them were in no significant danger.

"Nasty sprain," the mage muttered to himself. "Torn inner ligaments. Not to worry, not to worry." He let Declan's knee settle, taking the joint into both hands. There was a building glow of green light, and at once Declan started to feel the pain of the insulted limb fade. Some fifteen seconds later, Bonner pressed himself to his feet with a huff, dusting his ever-clean hands off as though by habit. "You two take it easy. You'll be fine, but I'll not have you pushing yourselves while the lesser healing sets in." He looked Declan and Ester over one final time. "Any other injuries?"

When the pair of them shook their heads, he gave a brief nod of satisfaction, then turned on his heel and started towards where Eyera's was licking at her brother's quivering form.

"Where we'd be without your Father, Graces only know," Declan breathed after a moment, testing his knee before starting to climb to his own feet when he found it lacked all but the mildest protest at the motion. Standing up, he grimaced as he found his leg less-pleased with the sudden acceptance of his weight, but he turned to help Ester just the same. Taking his hand, the woman allowed herself to be pulled up, blinking a little at what must have been some lightheadedness.

"Been saying the same since I was a girl," she got out after the bout ended, looking up at him. "You're filthy, by the way."

Declan snorted. "You're one to talk. Hold still." He took her by the shoulder, using his cleaner sleeve to rub at the half-elf's face again. Whatever magic Bonner had imbued into her skin had dried the blood he hadn't managed to wipe away earlier, and so the remainder flaked off easily enough, leaving only a hint in her hair and around her ears that she would have to take care of later.

"Can you walk?" he asked once he was done. The dark elves had gone silent, which made Declan think Ryn was having a more-private exchange with the leader of the unit. "I don't trust this ridge Bonner's left us on."

Ester pondered the bare four feet of ground between them and the magic-made chasm. Before answering, though, she turned, scouring the ground where they'd been huddled against the flat slope of the stone that led up into the larger cavern they'd left behind only some ten minutes prior. With a curse she pulled away from Declan and moved unsteadily a few yards along the base of the incline, bending down to grab a pair of items from the ground.

When she stood and turned around again, she held Declan's sword in one hand, and her bow in the other.

Her splintered, useless bow.

"Damn," Declan echoed her disappointment. He was no archer, but even he could tell there would be no salvaging the weapon. It had cracked along the body, and one tip was snapped clean off, leaving the string to dangle limply.

"I doubt it matters," Ester tried to sound light-hearted, handing over his sword before reaching back to pull her quiver around herself and peering in. Sure enough, most of the arrow hafts were clearly snapped in two or more pieces, and the ripped fletching of those that had miraculously survived said they would be hardly good for any kind of straight flight.

"And Orsik was carrying the spares," Declan groaned, sheathing his blade on his hip after a quick inspection told him the steel had survived the tumble largely unblemished. "I'm sorry. If I'd been paying more attention…"

Ester looked sadly down at the damaged bow for a moment more. Then she shrugged, letting the weapon fall to the ground with a *clatter*, and started making her way to where Bonner was hunched over Orsik. As she passed Declan, she lifted a hand, almost reaching his face before hesitating, then patting him gently on the chest instead.

"Against that *thing*, I think we did the best we could." She let her fingers linger on his shirt for a moment as she indicated the fallen drey with a dip of her head. "And we're alive. All of us."

"Not without help," Declan grumbled, turning with her as Ester began walking again.

The half-elf was about to answer, but was interrupted when one leg partially gave out beneath her. Declan managed to catch her before she could fall, grunting as his own knee expressed displeasure at the abruptly-added weight.

"Thanks," Ester breathed, standing herself up again. "I think that answers your earlier question about whether I can walk…"

Declan chuckled darkly, bending to bring one of her arms about his shoulders, then looping his own around her waist. She voiced no protest for once, and soon they were limping together towards Bonner and the warg, Orsik whining and wheezing with every breath, Eyera pacing nervously at the mage's back.

"How is he?" Declan asked once they reached the odd trio, easing Ester down beside her father before hobbling around to the male's head. Orsik's eyes were closed and blood was bubbling along the warg's lips with every breath, but one ear flicked up half-heartedly when Declan managed to kneel beside him and run a rough hand through the hair of the animal's neck.

"Not out of danger, unfortunately," Bonner said, clearly distracted. His hands were wide, fingers splayed as he ran them over the male's broad, upturned side. "More broken ribs than I care to count, and almost certainly a punctured lung. We'll be here a few hours, if I'm to see him on his feet again."

Do it. Commander ay'ahSel tells me their purpose in the mountains is completed. They are returning to their forward camp, and will lead us out.

Ryn, it would seem, had completed his conversation with the dark elves. He was turning towards them, each fall of his clawed feet landing with a crunching shake that made the slab beneath them quiver ominously. Beyond him, the *er'endehn* had not moved from their gathered position, though the leader—"ay'ahSel", if Declan guessed correctly—had been returned her swords, the black blades now hidden in plain, matching leather sheaths at her hips.

Bonner scoffed without looking up from his charge. "Ryndean, I would kindly point out that without your timely intervention, I would likely be slung over the shoulder of one of their number and Eyera would be dead, most likely along with these three." He waved one hand between Declan and Ester, the other working on a number of circles in the stone before Orsik's weakly rising chest. "You can't possibly think I'm heavily inclined to join them so easily, even if they give us an apology."

Ryn, for his part, gave a grunt and started to shrink before their eyes. As the titanic presence of the dragon's true nature contracted into the tall, lithe form of his *rh'eem*—his dragonling's form—he answered.

You misunderstand, Bonner. There will be no 'joining'. We are to be prisoners.

A true five seconds of silence followed this statement, in which Declan and Ester could merely stare at Ryn while Bonner's astonishment was displayed in his freezing mid-crafting of the runic circle he was putting together.

"*WHAT*?"

All three of them made the exclamation in the same moment, Declan and Ester both even trying to leap to their feet, she failing and falling back down to sit by her father, he managing to do so only barely.

"Ryn, you can't be serious?!" Declan demanded of his friend, gaping up at the white-gold eyes like he expected to make out some hint of a jest in their reflection. Of course he found nothing, and so his incredulity bloomed into true anger. "Bonner has the right of it. You weren't here. You didn't see. If he hadn't intervened when he did, I'm fairly sure my head would be tumbling down into the dark right now." He gestured in the general direction of the abyss down the incline from them.

It is a temporary measure only, Ryn assured them. *I've explained our situation. They seem doubtful, but Commander ay'ahSel is choosing to see us as something to be handled by her superiors. We are to be escorted to a nearby camp, where she says someone will have a better sense of what to do with us.*

"*Aside* from skewering us in our sleep, I hope?" Bonner asked dryly, having returned to his work.

Ryn gave him a sharp look. Despite the transformation, his wounds had remained—if in a lesser form—and he had one clawed hand pressed to the open puncture that now bled over his right hip. *I would remind you that this* particular *leg of our thus-far rather* eventful *journey was none other than* your *idea, Bonner.*

Bonner was silent at that, feigning focus as he pressed his magic into the finished circle of power. It flashed, then faded, and all around Orsik the stone began to stir and tremble.

"You don't think they took you for your word a bit too quickly?" Ester asked calmly, clearly attempting to defuse the tension of the conversation. "It's not a trap? Or something of the like?"

Ryn hesitated at that, and the pause was enough to tell Declan that the possibility had not been lost on the dragon.

I had considered the same, he confirmed a moment later, dipping a head in acknowledgment towards Ester as behind her Bonner's stone ribs started to extend like claws out of the ground to encase Orsik. *But their confidence in me seems... genuine?* He made a face before glancing over his shoulder at the dark elves, who had gathered about the single fallen among their number, apparently giving their final farewells. *I can't place it. They did not fear me as they should have...*

"Did you ask after Arrackes?" Bonner spoke up from his place on the ground where he was now scrawling more runes into the growing arches of rock. Within them, Orsik began to still, his wheezing and snuffling lessening into slow, steadier breathing. "Perhaps they are more familiar with your kind than we could have hoped for...?"

Ryn considered again, then shook his head. *Perhaps, but I did not. I left how best to monitor the* er'endehn *to his discretion, as I did with Shaldora and Tylvenar with their charges. If Arrackes has been in hiding all this time, I did not want to risk putting him in danger.*

Bonner gave an absent nod of accent, not disagreeing. Declan, for his part, had momentary trouble imagining how a dragon would be hard to spot in a place like Ysenden—which sounded like the single central hub of an entire people—until he ventured a guess that this "Arrackes" had likely taken on a less-conspicuous form for the last centuries. Declan had known Ryn as nothing more than a horse of peculiar gifts for the better part of twenty-five years, and therefore could imagine another of his kind standing silent guard over the dark elves as some sort of bird, perhaps, or domestic animal. He shivered, not liking the consideration of how lonely such an existence must have been over hundreds of years.

"Poor bastard must be a wreck," he mumbled to himself, easing down to sit beside Orsik's head again as Bonner's magics began their long, slow work. Fortunately no one else appeared to hear him, so he settled on eyeing Ryn's injuries while he started to pet the warg through the stone ribs the mage was still drawing symbols into. "You're practically in pieces, friend."

Raz grunted like he was only again feeling the pain of his injuries, and the hand that wasn't held to his side came up to dab with clawed fingers at his neck. *Evil thing didn't make it an easy fight. Their imbued, I'll stake my line on it.*

"I have a feeling that's a reality we'll have to accustom ourselves to," Bonner said while he worked, and Declan saw the mage glance sidelong to eye the dragon as well. "Will you hold up until I'm done with Orsik?"

Ryn nodded, wincing as the motion didn't agree with the injury to his neck. *Likely. The bleeding is not so great in this form.* He half-turned to take in the body of the drey that wasn't more than a handful of meters from where they lay. *They're a different sort of challenge altogether, like that. If* I'm *to have so much trouble with even one at every encounter, I shudder to think what sort of fight the lesser of my kind will face, if it ever comes to it.*

"Then let's pray it doesn't," came Bonner's low reply.

Ester, however, was looking between the two of them curiously. "Is this so rare? Were the drey of the war not imbued?"

Ryn grimaced like the question brought forth too many unpleasant memories. *Some were. A few, in the first encounters. They were the root cause of our initial decimation, at least before we learned to take them on in groups. Tyrannus and I could manage an imbued as a pair with relative ease, but for a beast to claim the exclusive attention of a single primordial, much less the* both *of us...*

Declan nodded along, for once understanding. For the greatest among the dragons to have been so involved in a single class of enemy during a war in which mages, monsters, and men both living and dead sought to tear them from the skies could only have been disastrous.

"If we assume each of the others is equal to the one you faced, then we have a problem, Ryndean." Bonner was clearly listening to the conversation, but spoke without looking around from his work. "That would imply our enemy is stronger, this time around… *much* stronger."

Ryn nodded gravely, but caught the questioning look both Declan and Ester were alternating between him and the old man.

During the war, one in fifty of the drey were so empowered, he explained as behind him the *er'endehn* were rising from their vigil over their fallen comrade, the slain elf's sword held reverently in both the leader's hands. *Such magic is fiendishly complicated. Certainly beyond me, and likely beyond Bonner, though I prefer to assume that is merely for lack of study.* The dragon glanced over at the mage, who offered only a noncommittal shrug that had Ryn continuing quickly. *Imbuing is a weave that requires not only immense power, but complicated materials and the care and time to see it done to perfection. If* each *of the four we've faced has been so blessed by the Queen's hand…*

"Then we need to assume she has been at work for a long, long time," Declan finished for his friend with a groan, shutting his eyes in understanding as he heard Ester curse in elvish from where she was still seated beside her father.

Exactly, Ryn confirmed, looking around when the sound of leather boots over wet stone reached them. *For the time being, we should assume this fight will only get harder before it gets easier.*

Declan nodded, but said nothing more, choosing instead to join the dragon in watching the elves close the distance between them. The consideration was heavy in his chest—he'd stopped counting the number of times this battle with their intangible enemy had already very nearly claimed all of their lives—but there was hope, too, in Ryn's words.

So long as the primordial of the dragons had not given up on this shadowy war, Declan supposed he had no reason to himself.

The elves stopped some distance from them, fewer of their number than Declan might have expected eyeing Ryn's new transformation with anything more than mild interest. They were more invested in the magics they could witness coming to fruition before them, pale gazes wide—and suspicious—while they took in Bonner's work.

"*Kay vyth, dregun*?" the leader of the unit asked of Ryn, not looking away from the stone ribs extending up and over Orsik's massive body. She had removed her helmet, holding it by the lip in one hand while in the other she grasped the sword of her fallen subordinate, blade bare to the glimmering light. Her hair was bone-white and long, plated into a flat braid not so different from Ester's style, and the tight pull of it revealed the slenderness of her pointed ears. She might have made a spitting image of the wood elves of the Vyr'en, were it not for the near-black of her skin.

It is a spell of healing, came Ryn's answer. *Nothing to be distraught over. It will run its course in an hour or two, at which point we will be fit to move again as you desire.*

Declan hadn't understood the question, and was grateful for the context the dragon's response provided. From the elves, on the other hand, there was an unhappy murmuring, though whether due to the magics or the length of their execution Declan couldn't deduce. One among them—the left of the spear-wielding duo he was almost *sure* were twins, now—even said something brief and firm.

Ryn snorted at the comment, narrowing his eyes at the offender. *Prisoners we may be, but do not press your luck. You and I both know it is in name alone, and I do not recommend leaning so heavily on your decorum in my presence.*

That silenced the man, and Declan could have sworn he saw the elf's brother hide the shadow of amusement on his face by turning his head and pretending to examine the body of the drey not far away.

Either to spare her officer further embarrassment or merely adhering to some strict protocol, the leader of the unit stepped forward smartly. With a sweep of her helmet she indicated Declan, Ester, and Bonner as she spoke to Ryn, lifting the sword in her other hand as though in example. The dragon, for his part, rolled his eyes before looking around at them again.

Commander ay'ahSel politely *requests*—he said the word with a note of sarcasm—*that we surrender all weapons we might have on our persons.*

The elf had clearly not missed his tone, because she added something terse that said in no unclear terms the dragon was pressing his own luck with her. Ryn, of course, appeared as though he couldn't have cared less, and didn't turn back to so much as bother acknowledging that the woman had spoken to him before translating.

She has asked that I clarify that should her superiors deem us in no way a threat to the er'endehn, *our possessions will be promptly returned with apologies.*

"In so many words," Ester grunted from beside her father, clearly having understood the dark elf without any trouble. It made Declan realize Ryn was very likely turning the commander's words for his sole benefit, and he felt simultaneously grateful and embarrassed by the prospect.

Then again, it didn't look like they were about to suffer a shortage of free time in the coming days, so maybe he could convince the yr'Essels to spare some of the journey on improving his handling of the tongue.

Declan. Your sword. Knife, too.

Ryn's private voice startled Declan, who'd momentarily fallen into considerations of the language difficulty. Raising a brow at the dragon in displeasure, he handed over his bastard sword before reaching down to pluck his long knife from his belt, where it had hung much more frequently now that he typically fought with a firestone in his off hand. Ryn accepted the blades, then handed them off to the dark elf leader, who again passed the weapons to one of her lessers at her back. Declan watched with growing resentment as the soldier took the steel in with an amused look, like a learned man might examine the stone tools of some long lost civilization. Beside him, one of his companions was doing much the same with Ester's saber, though this elf woman's mouth was downturned behind the opening in her helmet, clearly finding the weapon wanting.

"Done."

Bonner's tired announcement managed to drag Declan's attention from his irritation towards the elves, and he turned in time to see the old man stepping away from Orsik's healing cage and dropping his hand. He seemed exhausted—as he always did when completing any significant magic—but looked doggedly to Ryn. "It's not as meticulous as I'd like it to be, but it will do the trick in a couple hours. For now, that bleeding looks like it needs more attention."

The dragon didn't argue, nor voiced a word of protest when the mage approached to peer up at the underside of his jaw, then the hole over his right hip. Declan could hear Bonner muttering to himself, but clearly the damage was less involved, because after several seconds the man turned to look at him.

"Declan, water from Eyera's bag, if you would. I'll have to replenish his blood."

He didn't have to be told twice, but Declan's legs felt sluggish as he turned to do as instructed. His knee throbbed and almost gave in under the weight of his first step again, and he grunted as he caught and steadied himself on one of the stone ribs of Orsik's cage. The healing magics thrummed pleasantly under his palm, but Declan snatched as hand away as quickly as he could, afraid of interrupting the delicate cycling of the weave. The runes shifting in the rock continued their dance unperturbed, however, and he breathed a low sigh of relief before starting to move again, making for Eyera.

The female didn't so much as glance at Declan as he dug through her saddlebags for their waterskins, too intent on her brother to even growl in displeasure. With a bag in each hand, Declan turned away from the warg and limped to Bonner, handing the first of the pouches over. The old mage accepted the water with hardly a glance away from Ryn's neck, in turn shoving it against the dragon's chest so that his patient was forced to catch it with his one free hand.

"Drink," Bonner said simply. "It will make this job much easier."

Uncapping the bag, Ryn did as instructed, tilting it back to guzzle down the contents. After days of careful rationing, Declan had to suppress a jolt of alarm at seeing the liquid vanish so quickly before his eyes, particularly when the dragon drained the first of the skins and offered it as a trade for the full one. There was nothing for it, though, and—with the elves beyond them seeming unconcerned about the loss of provisions—Declan handed the second bag over dutifully.

A minute or so later, Ryn stood before them much less rigidly, fingering the newer, less-ordered scales under his neck that marked where a jagged rending of flesh had stood only shortly before.

"Anything else?" Bonner asked. Despite standing tall before the dragon, he sounded exhausted. Declan couldn't blame him. Between the fight, the healing of Orsik in particular, and now the tending of Ryn's wounds, the mage had very likely expended more magic in a single go than Declan had witnessed since after their very first encounter with the drey, back at the yr'Essel's woodland cottage hidden away in the heavy woods of Viridian's western forest.

Ryn shook his head, dropping his hands from his neck to eye the elves again over one shoulder. *Nothing time and some rest won't handle on their own.* Indeed, Declan hadn't missed the smaller scratches and cuts around his friend's snout, face, and shoulders. *The latter of which we could* all *use, if I had to guess.*

There was no argument to the contrary, especially not with the dragon, too, looking nearly ready to keel over, which was hardly unexpected. After weeks of intense study in the basic principle of the arcane, Declan understood better now the kind of toll transforming from a lesser form—like his *rh'eem*—was likely to take on Ryn.

Still… The idea of dropping their guard now, of all times…

"I know we're not likely to move for a couple of hours, but is it a good idea to sleep here?" Declan asked quietly, pointedly gazing past Ryn when the dragon and Bonner looked around at him, towards the dark elves now standing some dozen yards away. The lot of them were apparently examining the remains of the drey, and discussing amongst themselves.

Ryn nodded slowly. *Abrasive they might be, but I don't sense we're in any danger of being 'skewered in our sleep', as someone put it…* he gave the old man at his right a sidelong glance, which Bonner pointedly ignored. *If anything, there's the argument to be made that we're safer now than we were an hour ago.*

Not so convinced, Declan only shrugged. He'd had nothing but unpleasant interactions with pure-blooded elves in his own life. Those had come from the *er'enthyl,* sure, but thus far his experience with the *er'endehn* had borne with it no confidence that the dark elves harbored any less distrust or distaste for outsiders.

In the end, though, it was hardly his call to make with Bonner and Ryn both of the verge of falling asleep on their feet, and so with only moderate resignation Declan joined the other two in returning to Ester and the warg, feeling naked absent the familiar weight of his sword and knife pulling him down to the stone when he sat beside the woman. Ester had shifted closer to Orsik's head so she could run her hand over the rough grey-white fur of the sleeping beast's neck, but she looked around as Declan groaned against the twinging of his knee while he eased himself down.

"How's Ryn?" she asked gently. Her other hand was resting atop the crown of Eyera's head. The female, having curled about the half-elf, snuffled and whined quietly, dark eyes not leaving her brother's slumbering form.

"Fine. Tired." Declan finally managed to get comfortable, the damp stone under him having been carved out into pits and lines by what could only have been centuries of condensation and runoff. "I think he and your father are going to get some sleep while they wait for Orsik to heal."

Ester frowned at that, pausing in her stroking of the male. "Is that a good idea?"

"I asked the same thing. Apparently they're not worried, though." Declan tilted his head to indicate Orsik's other side, and Ester craned a little to look over the warg and his cage. Ryn, sure enough, was already laid out—having not even bothered to change out of his dragonling's form—while Bonner looked to have just finished drying a patch of ground for himself to do the same.

"Lucky bastards," Ester muttered, sitting back again.

Declan gave her half a grin. "Sleep, if you want to. I'll keep any eye out for trouble."

The woman raised an eyebrow at him and cocked her head. "Declan Idrys, how in the name of *any* god do you expect me to sleep soundly in the presence of people who can do *that*—" she lifted one had to point "—to a monster you, me, *and* my father together were having trouble taking down?"

Declan followed her finger, and took her meaning to heart at once. In death the great form of the ram-headed drey was hardly less terrifying than it had been in life, and from the slow current of blood trailing down the incline of the stone Declan could just barely make out the subtle *hiss* of acid eating at the rock.

He swallowed and looked around at the dark elves even as he nodded in understanding of Ester's fear, and unbidden his right hand lifted to the breast of his jacket.

Then his heart slipped into his stomach.

Oh no…

"What? What is it?"

His alarm—or sadness, rather—must have been plain on his face, because Ester was suddenly looking at him with grave concern.

"The firestone," Declan hissed, forcing himself not to shift too abruptly as he turned towards the fissure in the earth Bonner had rent to save them for the wrath of ay'ahSel. "I've lost the firestone your father gave me. When the drey hit us."

Ester blinked at him, like she didn't understand.

"… And? What of it?"

Declan frowned at her. "I've only been practicing for a few *weeks*, Ester. Without it *and* my sword? What use am I?"

To his surprise, Ester gave him a lopsided smile.

Then, before he could ask her what was so amusing, she reached down and—from the scattered options offered to her by the destruction wrought in the wake of the drey's attack—plucked a single, sharp pebble about the size of Declan's thumb from the ground.

"Here." She held up the rock, still grinning. "Found it."

Declan frowned at her, not understanding even as he held his hand out to accept it. "What are you on about? This isn't—"

Ester, though, cut him off.

"No, of course it isn't the same one, Declan. But it doesn't *need to be.* Those stones aren't anything special. They come and go as my father needs them, and he certainly doesn't carry them with him as he travels. It's not the stone that matters, Declan."

"It's the magic."

Declan was the one who finished for her, and he might have smacked his palm to his face had he not thought Ester was close enough to bursting with laughter already. He had seen Bonner do exactly that, hadn't he? Thrown a firestone away like it was nothing once it ran the course of its use? Several times, in fact.

And he had also seen the old mage make them anew.

Talking the pebble more firmly in hand, Declan closed his fingers about its jagged surface and focused. Though he didn't know *exactly* the method by which he was supposed to go about it, the concept couldn't be all that different from infusing the ground with energy, something he'd been doing ever since they'd fallen into these infernal tunnels. He was careful, *so* careful. He'd been struggling as it was to throttle his King's blood whenever he and Bonner had been practicing without a vessel, and Declan had no interest in seeing what would happen if the stone took in so much magic it exploded in his palm. Calmly he focused, pressing his will out of himself, down his arm and into the rock. He could feel the now familiar tingling, the prickling flow of energy up his arm...

"Oh."

Ester's quiet exclamation had Declan blinking and looking up. He didn't even remember closing his eyes, and almost had to shut them again against the sudden blaze shimmering before him. Between his fingers, light danced in undulating white-red rays, casting an orange glow so bright about them even Eyera's attention was finally stolen away from her brother.

"Woah..." Declan muttered, drawing his will back even as he opened his scarred hand. For a second or two more the light was well and truly blinding, causing all of them to avert their eyes.

Then it faded, and Declan looked around again, a jolt of victory leaping in his chest.

Though the stone was a little bigger and sharper than the one Bonner had originally given him, it glowed with dim fire, like an ember left to the air too long. The light within it danced, shimmering outward across the jagged surface of the stone, and the warmth of it was palpable on his face even though it didn't burn his hands.

"I did it…"

The disbelief in his own voice had Declan barking out a laugh, which Ester joined him in. Reaching out, she held her slender hand briefly over the firestone, feeling the heat of it for herself.

Then she moved to close his fingers about it.

"Don't sound so surprised. If *I* had dragon's blood running through my veins, I damn well hope I could do a sight more than make a pebble glow."

Declan was too stunned, however, to run with her humor. He continued to stare at his hand. It no longer glowed—the excess of power he hadn't quite managed to hold back receding now as his resonance with the pyromancy took over the balance of power—but it amazed him all the same. He'd created with his magic before, in a way. Heat. Fire. Even that outward eruption of force which had twice now saved him, first when they'd fallen into the mountain, then again against the drey.

But this was different…

Whereas those spells had flashed and flared out in an instant, here before him was the first true *weave* as Declan had imagined them. Tangible. Solid. Lasting. In his hand, incandescent and warm, was something real. Something *he* had made.

Taking in the jagged rock, Declan suspected he would not be losing *this* particular firestone as easily as he had the one Bonner had given him.

"Declan, put it away."

Ester's tone, a moment ago excited for him, was suddenly stiff. Declan snatched the stone closer to himself, slipping it into the breast pocket of his jacket instinctively. Needing no explanation as to the trigger of Ester's abrupt shift in character, he couldn't stop himself glancing over his shoulder. At once, though, he snapped his head about again, pretending to be interested in Orsik's now-steady breathing.

He hadn't missed, though, the icy stare of Commander ay'ahSel, the dark elf's white-red eyes having been in the process of sliding up from where he'd just been holding the magic to take him in with cold realization.

CHAPTER FOUR

Magic as we know it is not something to be feared. Respected, yes. But not feared. The spellcraft you will be taught in these initial courses will be the foundation of what should eventually be a broad and encompassing understanding of the arcane arts, an education which will—hopefully—supply you with the tools, weapons, and defenses to protect yourselves and the subjects of Viridian from any known threat.

By the end of your tenure in this school, it is the hope and prayer of we, your instructors, that the only real danger to your lives once you step beyond these walls will be the sorts of magics the world should never have cause to know…

—Transcript from an introductory course of the Alethan Magical College, c. 150p.f.

The Endless Queen did not scream as her drey fell. She did not rant and rave. There was anger, yes—a seething, blistering anger that felt like a fire in the confines of her empty chest—but centuries of life did not come without the development of an inhuman patience.

Her rage would have to wait.

Two of her stitched beasts were dead. The third was only hardly less so, half-buried as it was in the rubble of shattered stalagmites at the bottom of the abyss it had so nearly dragged Ryndean down into.

It was unfortunate, but ultimately it mattered little. Only the dragon's fire would be able to dispose of the bodies, and the Queen had little doubt the damned creature wouldn't be looking to take his true form again anytime soon.

No… No. She would get the bodies back. She would gift the drey with life again. She needed only be patient.

Be patient, and think on how to try once more…

It was apparent to the Queen, now, that she had been a fool not to take care of the *er'endehn* when they had first broached the slopes of her secret kingdom. She'd thought little of the elves, and any action against them now might well complicate her coming plans for their people. Still, the decision had been to her loss in the end, because whatever level of alert the *er'endehn* might have been put on by the loss of their hunting party would hardly have been any meaningful price in exchange for the deaths of the group they had saved…

There was a harsh, grinding sound as the Queen clenched her timeworn teeth, her focus lingering on the youngest of the companions, the one of King's blood. She'd not opened her eye on them since the four and their beasts had been climbing the southern slopes of Karn's Line, having not missed Bonner Fehn's catching of the spellwork. Her hand was already too apparent in the bloody mess of the drey's failure, and she couldn't risk the old man being ready to track her the next time she spied on them. So, instead, she was left with only the extension of her senses, the broadened understanding of the world fed to her by the magics she'd long since woven into the mountains.

It was more than enough, though, to take note of the spark inside the young man. The flare of magic that had grown even in just the week since the group had entered her domain.

That was a fire she could not allow to thrive. It was bad enough the man—the *boy*, really—was shielded by the likes of his more dangerous comrades.

If he was allowed to harness his *own* power in addition…

Then the Accord may hold eternal, the Endless Queen thought with irritation.

There could be no such allowing that.

Making her decision, the Queen pulled her senses back, away from the cavern high above her and the strange ensemble of characters now resting there. When her focus was retracted, she sent it promptly out again.

This time, though, she went down.

Down, down into the earth, seeking, searching. She'd not forgot where the creature lay, had not forgot where she'd discovered it, long dead and half-rotten among the icicles and frozen lakes of the caves miles beneath any known world. Her kingdom was vast, however, and it took her some time to reach the thing, for her power to touch the pallid flesh of its time-ruined form.

Time, though—and death with it—meant as little to the Queen's subjects as did a passing breeze.

"Rise," she whispered aloud to the emptiness of her chamber, feeling the command shiver along the tethers of her magic. For a long moment, nothing happened.

And then the world began to shake.

CHAPTER FIVE

"There world is vast, Elalyn. No matter how many years you spend exploring it—no matter how many miles you travel—do not fool yourself into thinking you ever know all its secrets. There will always be new wonders to behold even for those who walk these lands for centuries.

Wonders, and terrors..."

—Amherst Sehren al'Dyor, to his daughter, Elalyn

In retrospect Declan suspected that Bonner had very deliberately made no attempt to rush the process of Orsik's healing, and he had no qualms with the delay. It was satisfying, for a time, to watch the irritation build in the posture of the dark elves after one hour turned into two, then three. They were masters of impassivity, their expressions largely blank as the promised time of departure came and went, but their impatience was given away by the grinding grips of black-armored hands about sword hilts, and the stiffness of certain sets of shoulders.

At last, however, as their *fourth* hour spent resting beneath the distant illumination of Bonner's faint lights approached, it seemed the old mage felt the elves had suffered enough for their aggression.

"Up, you two."

Declan started, blinking awake as beside him he felt Ester come to in much the same sudden fashion. He cursed privately as he pushed himself up from Eyera's side where the pair of them had apparently dozed off shoulder-to-shoulder despite their earlier reservations.

The fight had been more exhausting than he'd thought, Declan realized.

The first thing he noticed was once again the sad absence of his blades about his hip. Shoving that annoyance aside, however, he looked around to find Bonner standing over Orsik, the animal wide-eyed and breathing easily at long last.

"Oh *there* he is." Ester's delight as she clambered forward to greet the warg with a hand on his scarred snout was beaten only by Eyera's happy keen, the female scrambling across the wet stone to get to her brother so quickly she buffeted Declan about the head with her tail as she passed. Snorting at the lot of them, Declan nonetheless pressed himself up, testing his knee only briefly before he, too, joined the celebration. Bonner was in the middle of retracting the stone ribs—runes and all—back into the shelf beneath them. The moment he was able, Orsik kicked himself off his side and onto all fours, cracking several of the slender arms that hadn't yet pulled away completely to bound free and join his sister in play.

"Hold on you bloody big furba—oh, never mind."

Bonner, while still a bit the worse for wear, sounded much more like himself than he had after the fight. Indeed, he waved at the excitable beasts with a dismissive "bah" as he turned to Declan and Ester, a smile playing about his beard.

"It's time we get moving, We've left the *er'endehn* stewing long enough, I suppose."

Ester snorted. "Orsik would have managed fine with two hours in that weave and you know it."

Bonner shrugged, but it wasn't he who answered the woman.

It's fine. Let the elves squirm a little. I get the impression they have yet to understand the formality of our situation.

From the other side of what was left of the shattered stone cage that had housed the warg, Ryn, too, was getting to his feet, wincing only slightly as he rubbed at the new scar in his side.

"I'm not sure *I* have either," Ester said, crossing her arms irritably. She looked like she felt out of place without her bow and curved saber at her side as Declan did. "Prisoners 'in name only'? Easy for you and father to say, Ryn. Declan and I are hardly more than a walking waste of provisions without our weapons."

"Not true. One of us has to be the pretty one," Bonner answered his daughter, stretching and rolling his neck as he continued to watch Orsik and Eyera tussle about in celebration of the former's recovery. Then he looked over his shoulder at Ester. "Not sure what purpose that leaves *you* with, though, dear."

Declan and Ryn both managed to cough out a laugh at that. It felt good, even if it was at Ester's expense. For a moment things felt like they were sliding into place again, their usual banter returning despite the gravity of their circumstances.

Then reality returned with the cool snap of alien words.

"*Ys vohn, dregun*?"

Unable to stop himself, Declan whirled. Completely undetected by any of them, Commander ay'ahSel had approached to come to a stop not five feet from him, flanked on either side by the taller, spear-wielding twins.

Ryn's lip curled in annoyance.

Yes, Commander. We are ready. Had you given us even half a minute to do so, we would have told you ourselves.

The dark elf seemed to have regained her composure in their respite, because she didn't so much as blink at the dragon's tone. Instead, she slipped immediately into a series of rapid-fire statements that Declan—even without understanding the language—could tell were orders.

At his right, Ester stiffened, still with her arms crossed over her chest.

"'Not to speak'?!" she demanded, like she were repeating something ay'ahSel had said. "How are we supposed to communicate, then?!"

"Ester, quiet." Bonner's order was firm, the sort of tone he only took when something serious was at hand. He hadn't looked from the dark elf officer, either, and his faint smiled had faded quickly into a frown.

Ester shut her mouth, though she still seethed, and Declan leaned over to whisper to her.

"Are we not supposed to speak? Why?"

The woman grit her teeth as ay'ahSel continued to speak as though there'd been no interruption. "*Apparently* sound carries in the tunnels, and they don't want to attract trouble."

"The tun—Wait. How long are we 'not to speak' for?"

Ester's irritation deepened. "The entire time."

Declan almost groaned at that, but a warning glance from Ryn had him holding his tongue. Still… They wouldn't be allowed to speak? It was clear they wouldn't be granted their weapons back until some superior said—or *didn't* say—otherwise, and Declan would bet on the Graces that Bonner wouldn't be allowed to train him in spellcraft for the duration of their trek.

To put it bluntly for himself: they were about to spend days—if not longer—in the dark and cold, without distraction or conversation.

Shortly after, ay'ahSel quit her orders, and Bonner and Ryn only nodded together to affirm they understood. She didn't move after this assertion, however, and so it was with a roll of the eyes that the old mage and dragon turned to the other two.

You catch any of that? Ryn asked of the pair of them.

Declan shook his head even as Ester nodded.

"We're not to converse while in the tunnels," Bonner started to summarize for him, already moving to gather their things from where he'd stripped Orsik of his harness before casting the healing weaves. "Additionally, there's to be no light apart from what the moonwing lanterns provide. We're to share what provisions we have, and the elves will do the same. Between their causalities and extra rations, we shouldn't have much trouble reaching the exit."

"Moonwing lant—?" Declan began to ask, but Ester interrupted him.

"What about Orsik and Eyera? What are they to eat?"

Whatever we do, Ryn answered, moving to take the packs from Bonner as the old man grunted when he picked them up. *Apparently the Vyr'esh isn't far from the north slopes of the mountains. Once we're free of these caves, they'll be able to hunt for their own game again.*

That didn't seem to completely satisfy Ester, but—seeking to avoid any more potential arguments—Declan beat her to it, this time.

"The Vyr'esh?" It was less a question than a statement. Declan could guess on his own what the title had to mean, given the Vyr'en—the dense woodlands of the *er'endehn*—stood titanous and omnipresent far to the south, beyond Viridian.

Just the same, Bonner saw fit to translate for him.

"The northern forests." The mage whistled, calling Orsik and Eyera back to them. "You'll see. Or do you still think Eserysh nothing more than a wasteland of frost and snow, boy?"

Rather than address the jibe, Declan followed up with a more immediate curiosity.

"More importantly: what in the Mother's name are 'moonwing lanterns'?"

◆

Moonwing lanterns, it transpired, were a breathtaking contraption of the dark elves' making. About the size of a man's head, the main body of the device was a delicate cage of carved wood, each wall an intricate layer of curved spindles chiseled *just* close enough together to keep entrapped the contents of their enclosure. Within each cage, a single large moth around the size of Declan's hand batted slowly at the air, sometimes resting on the bottom, other times fluttering about or clinging to the sides or top. Each lantern was suspended from an iron loop at the end of a long, polished handle not unlike the haft of the spears some of the elves carried. Had that been *all* the contraptions were, though, Declan might have thought them nothing more than some odd display piece for an eccentric collector.

What made the lanterns fascinating, however, was that—rather than flickering with firelight—they *glowed.*

The light was faint, very nearly not enough for him to see by—at least not for the first few minutes they spent descending back into the tunnels. Still, it was present, emanating in a constant pale wash of white from thick lines along the wings of the moths in their cages. It helped, too, that there were three of the lanterns, divided equally along the line with Commander ay'ahSel at the head, leading the way with one in hand. The other two—Declan was unsurprised to find—were carried by the twins, one in the middle of their group, and one trailing at the back of the line, accompanied in silence by two of the remaining elves.

In silence...

Everything was in silence, now. Or nearly so. It was eerie, not speaking as they took the faint incline of the tunnels down, heading sometimes north, sometimes east or west. All was quite except for the echoing crunch of their descent, and—making it that much worse—Declan and his companions were the *only ones* producing any such noise. While he'd always been made to feel like something of an oafish brute when compared to Ester's nimble movements, it was apparent from the moment they'd left behind the dead drey and the great cavern that even her elven grace was as nothing to the training and intuition of the their *er'endehn* "captors". The moment they were among the narrower tunnels of mountain caves, what was *truly* unsettling about their trek was the fact that Declan felt suddenly like the four of them were traveling in the company of ghosts, spirits of air and shadow. When the dark elves moved, it was without sound, without even a whisper of leather on leather or of loose stone crunching underfoot. Every step was quick and yet so, *so* cautious, avoiding the scattered pebbles and pools of water they occasional passed with deliberate precision. More than once, Declan found himself, Bonner, or Ryn on the receiving end of icy glares from one elf or another when they accidentally kicked a rock or caught a crack in the ground that had been hidden in the dark.

Even Ester did not go unscathed from this disapproval after she misjudged a patch of smooth stone and slipped ever so slightly, her hiss of surprise jarring after some half-hour in the dark.

The silence of the elves was so impressive, in fact, that Declan soon found his irritation with the unit for their earlier assault fading away, to be replaced by keen interest. The exactness with which they moved with their weapons sheathed was no less astounding than had been their armed assault on the drey, sweeping out of the black like they had to cut down the beast in what couldn't have been more than ten seconds. Declan, despite himself, found that he could not stop from studying them, from trying to discern their secrets, the tells in their steps and motion.

He became so focused on his analysis, in fact, that when a voice cut across his thoughts he had to stifle a hiss of surprise.

All's well back there?

The astonishment came twice over then, and Declan blinked several times in confusion until Ester—walking at his left in front of where Orsik and Eyera trailed them in single file—started much as he had. He'd long deduced that mind-speech could only be performed either aloud to all present or to a single person individually, but it wasn't the fact that the one who'd reached out had clearly addressed him and the woman one after the other that shocked him.

It was that the voice in his head hadn't been *Ryn's*.

Looking ahead, it only took a few seconds for Declan to catch Bonner turning to glance over his shoulder at the two of them, half-grinning like he knew exactly what sort of confusion he had just caused the pair.

Oh, don't gape like that, the voice spoke up inside Declan's head, and this time he distinctly caught the old man's tenor in the tone. *You knew Ryndean and I spoke like this already, did you not?*

That he had, Declan had to admit to himself when Ester blinked beside him, clearly getting addressed in turn with what was likely the same treatment. He'd witnessed the dragon and mage communicate in silence several times, in fact, in situations where speaking aloud wasn't an option or optimal. First in the hilltop clearing, where they'd been assaulted by wights, and then again as they'd ascended into Sehranya's great storm along the southern slopes of the Tears.

Still, this *was* the first time Bonner had addressed *him* in such a manner—and Ester too, judging by the look on her face—so Declan thought the scowl the pair of them mirrored in that moment was fairly deserved.

If Bonner noticed, he didn't make any indication of being bothered by it, turning forward again.

We are merely discouraged from using our voices, not communicating as a whole. Ryndean and I have been talking, and we thought this might be a perfect opportunity for you two to learn to mind-speak, wouldn't you say?

That had Declan's frown vanishing, and he felt the firestone in his breast pocket thrum with warmth to match his elevated heartbeat. A new magic. Something outside the realm of basic arcane law and pyromancy that had been the focus of his lessons these last weeks.

Ryn had already implied that he should learn the art once, he recalled, but being presented with it now was more than just exciting. It was relieving. Maybe they *wouldn't* be so stuck in the dark and silence as he'd thought…

There was a dull grunt from his right, and he turned to Ester to find the woman looking dubious—and deliberately ignoring the scowl one of the *er'endehn* soldiers shot her at the sound. There was a brief pause of silence, and the woman's expression softened a little, making her look suddenly a little more hopeful.

Ester has doubts about her ability to master the craft, Bonner's voice returned, explaining, and Declan had to appreciate the man's effort. It had to be tedious to switch back and forth like this between the two of them. *She's afraid her lacking talent for weaving will be a hiccup.*

Will it? Declan thought automatically in reply, only to feel foolish a few seconds later when Bonner's voice didn't answer him.

Obviously there had to be a lot more involved with the magic than the desire to have one's thoughts heard.

Click-click.

The sound, coming from behind Declan, Ester, and the warg like little more than the light patter of some falling dust, had an instantaneous effect on the *er'endehn.* In step with each other the elves halted abruptly, to a one looking over their shoulders. In front of him, Declan saw Ryn and Bonner nearly run right into the backs of the soldiers who had been escorting them, the former's clawed feet stopping him in time while the latter barely suppressed a curse to his gods that echoed eerily in the silence.

Following the eyes of the elves, Declan and Ester, too, turned to look behind them. The sound, it seemed, had come from one of the spear-wielding brothers, because the elf had tucked the shaft of his moonwing lantern under one arm to free a hand, the fingers of which he was now twisting through a rapid pattern that Declan couldn't make out in the faint light. At first he thought the elf was crafting some sort of physical rune—not unlike the symbols Bonner sometimes formed with his own hands in combat—but the thrill of alarm this brought on was quickly quelled when Declan realized some of the movements seemed to be indications, gestures and pointing.

Specifically gestures and pointing at him, Ester, and Bonner in particular.

Signing, he realized, impressed. *He is signing silently.*

Viridian had its own language for the deaf and hard of hearing, though those fluent in it were few and far between given only the wealthy could afford to send their children to schools or tutors who could teach such communication. Still, Declan had witnessed it not a few times in and around the bustling market streets of Aletha, and so while the motions were alien to him, the act was not.

A voice, somewhere beneath a snarl and a whisper, spoke up in the strange language of the elves, and Declan found himself turning once more. Commander ay'ahSel had—in her fashion—looked to have stormed down the line until she stood before Ryn, where she appeared to very distinctly be berating a *dragon*. Once again Declan found himself astonished by the gall of the elves—the woman in particular—in Ryn's presence. Had any human been present to see the *rh'eem*—much less the dragon's *true* form—it was unlikely they would have been willing to be caught within miles of such a creature. And yet there ay'ahSel stood, as close to nose-to-nose with Ryn as their discrepancy in height would allow, hissing at him under her breath like he was truly just some insubordinate prisoner.

You said only that we could not speak, *Commander*, the dragon seemed almost amused at the elf's obvious annoyance. *You have no instruction that we not* communicate.

The elf barked out an order, which had Ryn raising an eyebrow at her.

No. I don't think we will stop, thank you. We've agreed to your terms. Twice now, in fact. We've bowed to your fear that voices carry, but I should point out that you *are the only one speaking aloud right now. Should my companions and I seek to converse via other means, then it is no different than your soldier's language.* He waved a clawed hand at the tall elf man at the tail of the line.

Soldier's language?

Declan frowned and looked around as the spear-wielding *er'endehn*, who in turn frowned right back at him. Like ay'ahSel, he had white-red eyes that glimmered dangerously from beneath his visor in the glow of the lantern tucked under his arm.

Was that what the signing had been? A method of communication that allowed the soldiers of the *er'endehn* to speak even when silence was necessary? If so, not only was the fact that the dark elves possessed such a means impressive, but it also meant that—despite their silence—Declan, Ester, and Bonner had been caught in their once-sided exchange.

Silent, deadly, and astoundingly observant, Declan thought, unable to fathom the rigor it must take to achieve such mastery of such a broad range of the arts of war.

There was a final sharp word, and Declan looked around in time to see ay'ahSel stalking away from Ryn without a sound, leaving the dragon looking smug. The moment the commander was at the head of the column again they started moving, slipping once more deeper into the dark. After several seconds of silence more, Bonner's voice started up again.

It seems we will be allowed our communication, the mage said brightly, though he didn't turn around this time as he addressed Declan. Likely he wasn't keen on the observers behind them catching onto the discussion again, even if it had been allowed. *Which means we will need to turn this into a conversation, rather than a lecture. First and foremost, I will need you both to review your knowledge of the Six Essentials of the Arcana, focusing most heavily on Primary Three, which, as you know—*"

Unable to help himself, Declan groaned, earning himself a curious look from Ester.

Then her father's attention must have switched to her, because she, too, made a face like she'd just been asked to lick the damp stone beneath their feet.

CHAPTER SIX

On the one hand, learning to mind-speak came about as naturally to Declan as had his rapidly developing pyromancy. It made sense, if he stopped to think about it. His King's blood—*Ryn's* blood—was what artificially heightened his affinity to fire in the first place, so it stood to reason that he would have a knack for the second thread of the dragon race's strengths: mind magics.

Unfortunately, on the other hand, it turned out that Declan had just as much trouble controlling the flow of his power through thought as he had channeling it into heat and flame.

"*Gah*," Bonner only barely managed to stifle a groan of discomfort, one hand jerking up to clutch at his temple.

"Sorry!" Declan hissed instinctively. "I'm so sor—!"

He caught himself, though, noting the attention of *both* elven sentries on either side of the tunnel from where they sat, cold eyes warning him.

It's nothing, Bonner's voice assured him as the man's other hand waved his concerns aside. *If anything it's encouraging. Better to have trouble* throttling *your ability than suffer a struggle to procure it.*

This isn't like mastering flame. Ryn—crouched beside the mage opposite Declan—seemed to be thinking along the same lines, though he couldn't have heard Bonner's private communication. *That firestone can't help you channel this magic.* He gestured to Declan's paired hands, which were clutching the glowing red rock between his fingers like his life depended on it. *You are without a vessel in this. It's understandable that you would have trouble tempering your strength.*

Declan grimaced, forcing himself to loosen his grip on the firestone. It was warm in his hands, comforting and familiar. Ryn and Bonner both had denied ay'ahSel when she'd attempted to confiscate the enchanted object from him on their first "night" among their present company, an act for which he couldn't have been more grateful. It may have proven useless as a channel for mind-speech, but it still helped him focus in its own way, helped him concentrate.

And concentrate he had to, these days.

With a sigh Declan looked around, taking in the grim darkness all about them. Four days. Four days now they had been descending into the earth, with little change to their surroundings other than the occasional cavern and the fact that Declan could *swear* it was getting colder. That part of the journey didn't bother him, of course. Though he had to make a conscious effort every time he drew the thing out not to call upon its light, the firestone provided him with ample warmth throughout their trek. Bonner—impressed when he discovered that Declan had created a new one for himself—had even taught him his first rune, a basic mark of channeling that allowed him to draw some measure of heat from the stone as he slept.

But the dark... The dark, and the unchanging, endless passages of damp stone and glistening walls brought with them a sort of exhaustion, particularly when combined with the silence with which they moved. Despite Ryn and Bonner keeping up a steady commentary—very likely to try and bolster the groups' spirits—and these soundless lessons that accompanied every rest, Declan had been feeling his mood blacken by the day. He and Ester never got to exchange a word, for one thing. They'd grown close these last months—closer than Declan had realized—and having their banter silenced with the finality of the guillotine seemed to be as hard on her as it was for him, judging by the tired half-smiles that were all she seemed to have anymore. With Ryn and Bonner, too, there was no exchange, everything being one-sided except for the rare occasions where Declan slipped up, as he'd just done. He was trying to learn, *trying* to master mind-speech with at least some shadow of the same speed with which he had gotten a grip on the basic principles of pyromancy, but channeling his power through thought indeed required a completely different practice than fire.

A practice which, if his two teachers were to be believed, required that they suffer something not unlike standing directly under the largest waterfall in the world all while palace trumpeters sounded off a royal arrival directly into their ears.

Declan sighed, feeling the weight of everything as he slid the fire-stone into his pocket. Bonner and Ryn, seeing this, exchanged a glance.

Shall we try again? the old mage asked. *You* are *improving, even if it doesn't feel like it. A few more nights of practice and you may well have the basics down enough to—*

Bonner stopped short, though, when Declan shook his head and let his chin fall to his chest. He wasn't all that tired, but the culmination of their discomforts was getting to him.

For now, even just for a little bit, he wanted to be alone.

Ryn—ever knowing him best—clearly gathered as much, because Declan thought he saw the dragon put a clawed hand on Bonner's shoulder and shake his head before the old man could insist. Sure enough, a few seconds later the two of them were getting to their feet and walking away, leaving their charge to his thoughts.

Once they were gone, Declan looked up again, breathing a sigh of relief at the solitude.

They were resting for the evening—if it indeed *was* evening—in the belly of one of the larger tunnels they'd come across over the course of their four days together. Nearly perfectly tubular in shape, the walls of the place were rough-hewn and wet, extending away and over them some thirty of forty feet above their head, while beneath him the stone was only dry because he and Bonner had taken the time to treat a wide line along the bottom of the cave with heat.

Funny how the elves didn't seem to mind *that* particular magic, when they'd realized what it did.

At the thought of the *er'endehn*, Declan looked in the direction he was fairly sure was north, towards the front of the line. There, in a scattered grouping, a majority of the dark elves had taken to the ground, having lain down where they'd stood like they needed nothing more than ay'ahSel's silent command to sleep. Only two of their number were still awake, standing sentry at either end of the "camp", each bearing a moonwing lantern borrowed from the officers, with the third on the ground among their sleeping companions.

Between Declan and the elves, Ryn and Bonner had seated themselves, their shifting expressions telling him they were carrying on a private discussion of their own. Not far away to his right, Ester was resting, too, though judging by the crease between her eyes and the sweat that lined her brow she was dreaming of nothing pleasant. Per usual she'd curled herself up between Orsik and Eyera, their fur and warmth very likely a better insulator than even Declan's paltry weave. Apparently sensing his gaze, the male's dark eyes opened a crack, and he shifted his head to fix Declan with a hopeful look.

A hopeful, hungry look.

It broke Declan's heart a little, and did nothing to spark his ever-dampening spirits. While the warg hadn't gone completely without, Commander ay'ahSel had apparently not counted on the ravenous nature of the animals in her calculations, and so Orsik and Eyera's daily meals had become a fraction of what they were accustomed to. Indeed, beneath the male's ragged fur and scars, Declan was starting to see ribs again, and he was reminded all-too-unpleasantly of the state in which they'd first found the pair, beaten and half-starved by their wereyn masters.

Sorry, boy, was all Declan could manage privately, feeling a stone build in his throat when Orsik seemed to sense his hopes were in vain and turned away again to tuck his nose beneath his sister's back leg for warmth.

Mother's Graces, we need to get out of here...

Crunch.

The light sounds of shifting dust and stone had Declan glancing around, surprised when he found Ryn on his clawed feet, looking like he'd stood up suddenly. The dragon's white-gold eyes were set southward, back along the direction they'd coming, and he was frowning even as his ears spread to their extent. There was a moment of silence in which the oppressive nature of their surroundings had Declan's thoughts in a fog, not registering more than his annoyance that *Ryn* didn't seem to get much of a rise from the elves when *he* made noise.

Then, though, long years of experience and a mercenary's instinct took over, and Declan was shoving himself to his own feet in alarm.

What is it? he wanted to ask, but thought better of it. Not because of the orders of the *er'endehn*, but because Ryn was standing unmoving, as though straining to make out something either very quite or very far away. Declan waited, watching his friend as Bonner, too, eased himself up carefully, like he'd also registered Ryn's stillness.

Whatever had caught the dragon's attention, though, seemed to pass, because his humanoid shoulders relaxed and he took a low breath that *might* have been tinged with relief. Catching Declan's eye, Ryn waved for him to sit down again with a clawed hand, shrugging apologetically.

Sorry. It's nothing. I thought I felt something.

Declan cocked an eyebrow at him, then brought a hand up to point first at his ear, then at his head, hoping the dragon would understand. Though Ryn's senses weren't as sharp as Ester's—and therefore likely the dark elves', too—his ears were still several times keener than that of a man's. It wasn't his hearing, though, that Declan suspected.

Ryn, like all of his kind, possessed a singular knack for knowing the details of the world around him. *His* ability in particular was potent—courtesy of his lineage in the primordial line of his kind—allowing Ryn to extend himself, of a sort, to press out his senses until he could fathom every detail of every nook and cranny and hidden secret of the land all around him. As far as Declan had ever been able to deduce, this skill extended in nearly a half mile in every direction when it was engaged, with some lesser ability a quarter mile beyond that.

Ryn seemed to catch his meaning, because he shook his head as he answered.

No. My senses aren't worth a damn in these tunnels. The rock muffles everything. That, or the magic Sehranya has very clearly been weaving into these mountains for longer than I care to think about.

Declan suppressed a shiver at the thought, and pointed at his ear again.

No. I meant it. I thought I felt *something. Like the ground was shaking. Obviously I was wrong, though. Can you imagine if something could make the mountains shiver from far away enough for me not to* hear *it?*

The dragon offered something of a tense smile at that, which Declan tried and failed to return. Despite his friend's attempt at levity, there was just no improving their situation.

On the other hand, in the next moment Declan got the unfortunate impression there was ample room for it to worsen.

Click-click.

The sharp sound, familiar now, echoed only once in the tunnel before Declan's hair stood on end. He, Ryn, and Bonner all snapped about to look south, up the space, where the *er'endehn* sentry there had given warning and—for some reason—lifted his gaze to the barely-perceptible ceiling above them. At Declan's back there was a flurry of quiet movement for once, and despite their near-silence he knew the sleeping elves were all on their feet, to a one likely grabbing weapon hilts in anticipation. For the moment, though, he had other things to pay attention to, much like the dark elf sentry.

Such as the fact that it had, somehow, started to rain…

For a second, Declan couldn't grasp the event, flinching as several drops of icy water struck him about the head and shoulders. Before him, Ester stirred briefly as the wetness pattered her face, and then in a breath was snapping up onto her own feet with green eyes wide, slim hands darting instinctively to the empty scabbard at her hip. But even for her Declan had no eyes, squinting instead up at the ceiling in confusion.

And then he felt the tremor, and the flecks of water—condensation shaken loose from the pocked stone above them—turned to a scattered shower of dust and rock.

Move! All of you! We need to move!

Ryn's mental shout, after so long spent in nothing more than quiet instruction, felt like it vibrated in Declan's head. Indeed, as he whirled about he caught several of the elves wincing where they stood, and every eye beneath their black-and-gold helmets snapped to the dragon. From their center ay'ahSel stepped forward smartly, snarling something in quiet elvish that Declan didn't have a prayer of catching.

Ryn was having none of it.

No! Enough of the charade, Commander! Something is coming! WE NEED TO MOVE!

CRACK.

As though on cue, there was another shower of dirt, and this time the budding form of a small stalactite came tumbling down one side of the tunnel to scatter into broken chunks about their feet. What was more, Declan could feel it now, could actually *feel* it.

Under his boots, the earth was trembling.

"What in the Mother's name…?" he hissed, looking down at the ground. Sure enough, the fractured pebbles and stone were just barely moving, trembling along in a minuscule dance around and about themselves.

"Declan!"

A hand took him by the elbow. Ester was suddenly beside him, looking up the tunnel, and Orsik and Eyera had bounded up to circle the two of them to growl with teeth bared in the same direction. There seemed no concern for sound anymore, because ay'ahSel was all but shouting now, and he thought he caught the words for "fight" and "defend" among the scattered phrases.

Ryn thundered over her once again.

NO! he roared. *RUN! NOW!*

Whether it was the volume of his voice, the alarm in the command, or the fact that a *dragon* appeared to be displaying even the faintest hint of fear, it was enough to make ay'ahSel hesitate. Her dark complexion paled ever so slightly, and she looked uncertain.

It was enough for Bonner.

"YOU TWO!" he bellowed at Declan and Ester. "RUN!"

Neither of them needed telling again.

Taking hold of their scabbards to steady them, they bolted, barreling by the elves with Orsik and Eyera hot on their heels. The *er'endehn* made no move to stop them, for once seeming completely undecided as to what it was they should be doing. Their loss was understandable, to be certain, but it was still frightening to see in the faces of the soldiers who'd until that point been nothing less than iron and steel.

Whatever was coming, it was enough to bend that mettle.

Even as he sprinted into the dark, Declan could feel the tremors growing worse beneath him, could feel the thing's thunderous approach. Whatever it was had to be massive, because by the time he'd pulled out the firestone and willed its light into life to see by, the pattering of water and grit had turned into a dusty shower of crumbling rock. Small chunks of stone began to pepper them in truth, and Declan was forced to lift one arm to shield his head, feeling the debris bounce off the limb painfully. Several steps ahead of him, Ester was doing much the same, with the warg now loping along on either side of them.

That was when Declan finally heard the beast.

The thing itself made no sound, whatever it was, but it was near enough now that its passing through the tunnel could be made out over the cacophony of showering stone. The rumbling, crushing approach was still distant, but the destruction of its passing was evident, and that alone was enough to send a lance of fear through Declan that even Ryn's yelling hadn't been able to illicit.

It sounded almost as if the thing was so big, it had to tear the tunnel apart to make room for itself…

A suspicion of what was coming for them suddenly itched at Declan, and he couldn't stop himself from turning briefly to look over his shoulder, searching in vain for any sign of the creature. Instead, not as far back as he might have thought, he saw the bouncing glow of the three moonwing lanterns illuminated the running form of the elves. Between their two groups, Bonner was *on* Ryn, who'd taken to his wolf's form, the mage in the process of trying to summon up what looked like more lights for them as the dragon closed the distance fast.

The sight tempered Declan's alarm enough to focus.

"Orisk!" he yelled, and to his left the male warg's ears flicked in the orange glow of the firestone as the beast looked around at him. Declan reached out with his free hand, and Orsik seemed to understand, because he slowed down at once and drew himself closer. Declan made a wild swing and just managed to catch the widest strap of the warg's carrying harness. With a grunt and a leap, he swung forward and caught a satchels with one foot, giving him the leverage he needed to haul himself properly onto the animal's back. As he got situated there was a flare of white, and abruptly the tunnel before them grew brighter even before the flickering, butterfly-like orb's of Bonner's spell darted by to light their way. Stowing the firestone again, Declan pointed.

"Ester! Get me to Ester!"

Never again would he doubt that the warg were vastly more intelligent creatures than anyone had ever given them credit for. At once Orsik's loping gait shifted slightly even as he dodged more falling debris, and within a few second they were alongside the woman. Noticing them, Ester only had time to look around with wide eyes before Declan leaned down and took her by the back of her shirt and blue half-cloak. With a heave and a strained prayer to Her Graces that the harness he was holding onto wouldn't slip or break, Declan hauled her off her feet, gracelessly pulling her up onto the warg's back with him. The half-elf yelped, arms and legs flailing as she landed awkwardly across his thighs, but with all the agility of her mother's people it wasn't a moment before she twisted and righted herself to sit with her back against his chest, taking fistfuls of Orsik's hair for handles.

"Thanks!" Declan heard her shout over the thunder of the tunnel that was now well and truly crumbling around them, but he didn't have time to answer.

Escape. They had to escape. Whatever was following them was coming fast, *too* fast, and there seemed to be no standing one's ground against it if *Ryn* had been the first to advocate that they run. Again Declan couldn't help but think he knew what it was that might be chasing them, and if he was right then they were less looking for a way to get away from the creature and more in need of a means of slowing it down long enough to be free of the mountains altogether.

A chunk of rock the size of Declan's head slammed into the ground between them and Eyera running beside them, shattering into a hundred pieces. Flinching at the near miss, Declan refocused on the tunnel, the foremost of Bonner's scattered orbs of light now keeping pace with them a dozen yards ahead and above them. Their passing glow sent shivers of shadow flickering over the wet walls, and when a particularly wide patch of darkness passed, Declan had an idea.

"A tunnel!" he shouted out at once. "Ester! Look for a side tunnel! As small as possible!"

Ester glanced over his shoulder at him in confusion for only a second, but appeared to trust his instinct because then she looked to be scanning the walls around them. Unfortunately they seemed to have chosen a particularly long swath of undisturbed passageway, because it was nearly half a minute of running all-out—with the world shaking more violently around them with every passing second—before the woman finally pointed abruptly ahead of them.

"There! To the left!"

Declan couldn't make out what she saw yet, but that was hardly surprising, and so just the same he tugged hard on the strap looped about Orsik's neck, hoping to guide the male in the promised direction. The warg, though, either didn't understand or was too preoccupied with fleeing whatever was coming to notice, and didn't so much as flinch from his path.

Declan was about to curse when Bonner's voice called out.

"Let me!"

The mage was there, then, pulling up between them and Eyera in a flash atop Ryn's lumbering black form. He must have heard Ester's shout, because with a quick slashing motion of one hand Bonner's lights fell from the sky ahead of them, regrouping in a twisting spiral that dove and cut left, directly into the mouth of a side passage so narrow Declan was impressed even Ester had seen it. Following the light instinctively, Orsik and Eyera both shifted left as Ryn pulled ahead to lead the way into the passage. Last to enter behind the other two, Declan had to duck atop the male to keep from smashing his head against the suddenly-low ceiling.

They didn't stop for several seconds, driving deep into the shaft at what turned out to be a steep incline. Though the trembling of the earth didn't cease, it did fade a little the further they ran, confirming that whatever it was that had the mountains shaking had been very distinctly following the tunnel they'd just been trekking.

It was Ester, at last, who stopped them.

"Wait! What about the *er'endehn*?! What about the elves?!"

It took a few seconds more, but at their head Ryn finally started to slow, then stopped, turning to Declan and the woman.

Ester, there's no time. Whatever it is that's coming down that passage is—

"We can't leave them!" the half-elf protested.

"We can, and we will." Bonner's voice was firm, but not without a slight shake, as though he didn't like saying the words. "We can't risk going back and—"

"Yes, we can." Declan spoke up. Now that the walls weren't falling in around them, his breath came a little easier, and he found himself stoically on Ester's side. "We owe them, after the drey, *and*—" he pressed on quickly, seeing Bonner open his mouth to protest "—if that's not enough, then remember that they're also our way out of here."

We can find our own way, Ryn argued. *We did for the first days.*

"And if we'd followed that logic through, we'd be at the end of our provisions by now." Declan didn't back down. "They've been leading us along the straightest path they know, and it's still been four days. There's no guarantee we're near the exit. Are you willing to risk us starving in this place before we get out?"

That seemed to hit Ryn and Bonner both hard, because they exchanged a frown.

Then both of them looked around again.

"Fine," the old man said stiffly. "But if we get eaten for playing the heroes, boy, I'll be blaming *you*."

◆

It didn't take them long to return to the mouth of the tunnel, the stone around them shaking more and more violently with every step taking them closer to the larger passage. Once more Bonner's lights led the way, with Declan, Ester, Orsik, and Eyera following behind, running in the order they'd entered the narrower shaft. Crowding together as best they could at the mouth, none of them ventured into the wider tunnel itself.

Only a fool would have braved the slow collapse of the space that was happening before their eyes.

In larger and larger chunks the passage was coming down, whole sections of the wall sloughing off in cracking sheets while hunks of rocks of every shape and size rained down. Only Ryn just barely stuck his head out of the shielding overhang to look down the way, drawing it back again as a stone the width of Declan's thigh struck the ground not a foot from where his snout had been.

I see their light! Bonner, guide them!

Bonner took action at once, swiping at the air again with a few more complicated gestures this time. His orbs of light poured from the smaller tunnel where they'd been hovering around the group, looping out until they formed a trail five or six feet apart from each other that led directly to the mouth they sheltered under. As the magics swept away from them, Declan noticed that a second small tunnel opened up on the other side of the passage, a half-dozen yards back up the way they'd come. Judging by the angle it looked to be a latter end of the very shaft they now stood in, missed as they'd run due to the angle of the entrance.

"There they are!"

Ester's exclamation brought Declan back, and he leaned around the woman just enough to brave the briefest peek around the edge of the wall to their right. Sure enough, several dark figures had made their appearance among the tumbling debris, looking as though they'd cast aside their moonwing lanterns as Bonner's light proved more efficient. After a second more, though, Declan suspected the total loss of the lanterns was less voluntary than it might seem.

Of the eight elves who'd survived the slaying of the drey, only four remained, now dancing and darting through the terrible rain of death even as they fought to keep moving forward.

Ester, in front of him, sucked in a breath of shock at the sight, and Declan might have joined her had Bonner's yell not cut him off.

"*ES! ES, ER*!"

Here, Declan understood for once, the simple words common enough. *Here, elves.*

At once, he joined in the call, waving both hands in an attempt to get the attention of the *er'endehn.*

"ES! ES!"

Ester added her voice, too, and then the three of them were all screaming and waving, only Ryn holding his silence, his mind-speech of little use in the endeavor at hand. Through the cacophony, Declan thought he heard a shout, and at once the elves—now more-fully in view—made a line for their little hole.

"Back! Get back!" Bonner ordered even as Ryn started to retreat beneath him. "Make room!"

Declan dug his heels into Orsik's sides at once, coaxing the male into an awkward withdrawal. Eyera came with them, backing away from the mouth of their small tunnel just as a trio of dark forms reached them, diving into the space to join their little group.

A trio…?

"Where's the other one?!" Declan demanded, re-counting the three—two of whom were the spear-wielding brothers. "Where's the fourth?!"

His shout seemed to alert the *er'endehn* to the discrepancy, because the twins in particular were already looking around as they clambered to their feet.

"Lysiat?" one of them asked in the eloquent flourish of the tongue, then again with more urgency as he spun on his heels to face the tunnel. *"Lysiat?!"*

Declan, too, looked out.

And found her.

Fallen among the tumbling rubble, the form of an elf woman was on her knees, one hand clutching at the side of her helmeted head, the other on the ground, looking to be barely keeping her from falling flat on her face. She tried once to get up, but staggered sideways, clearly disoriented.

"*LYSIAT*!" the elf who had screamed repeated, making it barely a step towards the tunnel before the other two grabbed him and held him back

"Ny! Ny, Tesied!" the elf's brother shouted, looking stricken even beneath his plumed helmet.

No. No, Tesied.

"AWAY!" Bonner bellowed as the shaking of the ground became so violent beneath them that Orsik staggered under Declan and Ester. "AWAY FROM HERE! QUICKLY!"

Ryn was already moving, and with what looked like a mighty struggle the two elves dragged the third away, the *er'endehn* fighting so fiercely to reach the stranded woman in the passage that he let his spear fall to the ground. From the right, the sounds of the creature's approach peaked, and Declan suspected that whatever it was, it was only moments from reaching them.

That was when he made his decision.

"Oomph!"

Ester made a sound like the wind had been knocked out of her as Declan shoved her from Orsik's back, sending her tumbling to the ground.

"Ryn! Take her!" Declan yelled back, trusting that the dragon would see the wish through.

And then, sure that Ester was free and clear of his foolishness, he reached for the power in his blood and dug his heels into Orsik's sides even as every voice among his friends shouted in alarm.

Whether out of surprise or because he'd grown braver since the battle with the drey, the warg responded at once, streaking from the cover of the side tunnel into the collapsing body of the larger passage. Before so much as a pebble managed to strike them, however, Declan found the magics, and without a vessel to help temper his need the heat and force he'd been seeking exploded outward in a searing wave. It was excruciating, and Orsik's keen of pain was coupled with a stumble that nearly sent them both to the ground, but the momentum was already behind them. Together the pair careened at an angle across the space, the blistering shield of power holding as Declan grimaced, fighting to keep the defenses up. He felt more than saw the rocks strike and break away from them, shoved aside by the tangible layer of heat he'd gathered and solidified largely over their heads. As they closed the gap between themselves and the elf woman, the weaker sides of the barrier hit her, too, sending her tumbling backwards in a heap before passing through and into the boiling air within. That worked just fine for Declan.

It would be a few steps less he'd have to carry her.

As they neared the woman, he didn't tell Orisk to slow. Instead, he leaned over the side, trusting the harness more after it had held both him and Ester's weight already. The moment the *er'endehn* was in reach, he snatched at her, not risking missing his one chance by aiming for a feebly kicking leg. Gathering up a fistful of cloth in his swordsman's grip, Declan braced.

Then he was dragging the elf along the stone-strewn bottom of the tunnel, hauling her through the mess as Orsik hurtled the short distance across the way.

It was in that breath of time, in those few seconds as they crossed through the deadly hail of the crumbling shaft, that Declan's eyes lifted, his gaze drawn from the task at hand by movement up the passage from them. For a blink he didn't understand what he was seeing, confused by the tumbling fall of rock and the sight of the thing itself. It was so bizarre, so foreign to him that his mind didn't immediately register what it was he was looking at.

And then, as he watched every edge of the tunnel exploded inwards under the passage of the great beast, he understood.

What he was witnessing was a moving wall of teeth.

"ORSIIIIK!" Declan bellowed, eyes wide in disbelief, but the warg needed no coaxing. In another heartbeat they were through, hurtling into the shaft of the narrower tunnel that had been opposite the one they'd all fled along originally. Still dragging the elf woman, Declan held tight as they dove into utter blackness, the light of the mouth behind them suddenly obscured as the massive *thing* at their backs blocked out the glow of Bonner's magic. With a thought Declan drew back the blistering force of his will, desperately refocusing it instead on the firestone in his breast pocket. Responding to him, the stone blazed into life, the energy within pouring out as light, so bright it glowed a brilliant white even through the fabric of his jacket. It was more than enough to see by, illuminating their way so that Orsik could continue to run, loping in a terrified scramble away, away from whatever it was that had been pursuing them. Instinctively Declan turned his gaze from the blinding light, finding himself looking back up the narrow passage, up the direction they'd come. Even as the mouth of it drew further away, his stomach leapt into his throat when he saw not darkness at the entrance, or even the passing bulk of the beast.

Rather, a hundred great teeth, organized in concentric circles around a gaping throat he could only barely make out, roiled at their backs, tearing into the stone in a clear attempt at pursuit. It might have been nothing more than shadows, but Declan thought the flesh of the thing looked blackened, the shifting skin and muscle about the teeth rotted a putrid grey.

It didn't matter, though.

All that mattered was that they had to go faster.

With a strained growl Declan heaved on the strap of the harness with one hand and the leg of the elf with the other, praying to the Mother and all who would listen for strength. While no god answered his need, Declan felt an odd pulse from his breast pocket, washing across his body and into his limbs in a tingling wave. The next thing he knew, he was back atop Orsik with the now-limp woman half in his lap, the weight of her body coming up to join him so swiftly he nearly found himself tumbling over the warg's other side. Not pausing to dwell on the odd event, Declan wrenched one-handed to situate the *er'endehn* more securely, catching a glimpse of her face as he did. Blood leaked from beneath the right side of her helmet and her eyes were closed in unconsciousness, but there was no mistaking the woman.

It was ay'ahSel.

"Guess I know your name now, Commander," Declan grunted.

Then he dug into Orsik yet again, leaning as low as he could over the elf, unwilling to brave a look back to see if the beast behind them was gaining ground. His plan had been simple: force the thing to move through as much stone as possible by fleeing through the narrowest shaft they could find. After all, he was certain of it, now:

Whatever was chasing them, Declan had no doubt it was the very creature that had carved this great web of tunnels through the mountains in the first place.

CHAPTER SEVEN

Even if he'd wanted to, Declan didn't think he would have been able to convince Orisk to stop running until the warg collapsed from exhaustion nearly a full twenty minutes later. By the time the male finally began to stumble, his breath coming in panting heaves and his every inch trembling beneath Declan's legs, they had to have traveled some eight of nine miles down into the earth and taken at least twice that many turns, all at the animal's whim. Declan couldn't complain, though. It seemed Orsik's instinct aligned with his own deduction of the situation, because every twist or bend the warg took led into narrower and narrower passages, up to the point that Declan was eventually ducking low as much to keep from hitting his head on the ceiling as he was to secure the still-unconscious ay'ahSel hanging across his knees.

Still, even the warg had limited endurance, and it was at long last that fatigue seemed to overcome fear. Orsik first slowed, then staggered to an uneasy stop.

"Woah!" Declan exclaimed, barely managing to throw a leg off the animal and slide himself and the *er'endehn* clear of the male's bulk before Orsik collapsed onto one side to the cool stone, gulping in billowing pants of air.

Unable to help himself, Declan eased ay'ahSel down at once, then rushed to kneel at the beast's side quickly. After a brief inspection, he was relieved to find nothing of concern aside from the gasping, and he put a calming hand on Orsik shivering neck.

"Calm," he said in as soothing a voice as he could manage. "Caaaaalm. You did well, boy. *Really* well."

It was true. As the warg's trembling eased little by little, Declan lifted his head to listen. Nothing but the sound of Orsik's breathing reached him, and the ground beneath his knees, too, was still. He even scoured about for pebbles and small rocks, but those few he found were still, not even twitching. They were, for the moment, safe.

Whatever the creature was, it hadn't been able to follow them.

Breathing a sigh of relief—and sure the warg wasn't in any danger—Declan shoved himself up and moved quickly to ay'ahSel again. Unlike Orsik, the elf was more the worse-for-wear. She lay where he had placed her, head lolling to one side and a hand cast over her chest. The first thing Declan did, kneeling over her, was put an ear to her mouth, and with another leap of gratitude to the Graces he made out a low, steady breathing.

He would have felt even more the fool if he'd separated them from Ryn, Bonner, and Ester for no reason whatsoever.

As it was, even as Declan pulled the firestone from his breast pocket—putting the palm of his other hand flat to the ground beside ay'ahSel—he felt like kicking himself. What had he been *thinking*?! Would it have been terrible to leave the elf woman to her fate? Yes. Of course. But what had this brash act gotten them, in the end? Lost. Lost in the tunnels beneath the Mother's Tears once again, with limited light and even more limited food.

"Idiot," Declan muttered aloud before distracting himself by pouring heat into the stone beneath his hand.

As with every repetition of the weave, it came the slightest bit easier this time, and within a minute or so the ground was dry and warm enough to at least keep the limp ay'ahSel from freezing to death. It took him three tries, but he even managed to char the rune of channeling Bonner had taught him into a flat part of the rock near the center of the spellwork, allowing it to continue without his direct attention so long as he didn't stray too far from the markings.

This essential done, Declan turned his attention to the elf again, this time with a more scrutinizing eye. The metal-bound leather of her armor had done much to negate the abuse of being dragged some two hundred feet across rough stone, but the initial injury that had gotten them into this whole mess was a different story altogether. Given that she was still alive, the falling rock could only have clipped the elf, but it had been a hell of a hit all the same judging by the massive scrape along the side of her black-and gold-helmet, originating from a sizable dent in the metal above her right eye. Not hesitating, Declan stowed the firestone again to undo the buckled strap under the elf's chin and pull off the helm as delicately as he could, wincing when it came free with the sound of drying blood breaking.

ay'ahSel—*Lysiat* ay'ahSel, he suspected now—was not unlike Ester in her frame of delicate beauty. For the first time taking her in from so close, Declan could see more clearly the gentle features of the elven kind. A small nose. High cheekbones over a tapering chin. Even her elongated ears were similar to those of the few pure-blooded elves of the Vyr'en he'd ever had to deal with during his time with the mercenary guilds. Of course, where the dark elf differed, she differed greatly. Her near-black skin shone with sweat along her forehead and cheeks, and blood had caked in her bone-white hair, dying it red in a thick patch above her eye. Trying not to think of the commander's sharp gaze snapping open as he leaned over her again, Declan studied the injury carefully.

"Maybe I should disarm you before you wake up and skewer me on principle," he muttered into the quiet, only half-joking as he shifted his knee slightly to move aside one of the paired swords that still hung from the woman's hip.

The wound itself—a sloughing of skin that had torn free of her brow—was firm to the touch, which Declan could only be further thankful for. He'd seen shattered skulls before, and even those who survived rarely came out the other end the same person. Still, the elf was hardly out of the woods. The torn skin bled profusely—as scalp injuries were want to do—and there was always the danger of harm he couldn't see, of swelling or outright damage to her brain, or any number of other unpleasant complications. Not for the first time Declan cursed his lack of talent in the arts of auramancy. Previously this annoyance had only been directed at his inability to tend to his *own* wounds, but suddenly absent the trusty healing abilities of Bonner yr'Essel left him realizing the price of his inability was greater than he'd realized. His budding skill with fire and heat was useful, to be sure—it would keep them from wandering blind and freezing through the dark, after all—but it left him with few options for treating ay'ahSel other than basic first aid and a lot of patience.

Making up his mind, Declan picked himself up off the ground and moved once more to Orsik, who—though still on his side—was breathing much more-easily now. Giving the male a grateful pat on one large shoulder and a few more words of praise, Declan began rummaging through the satchels the animal wasn't actively laying on. They'd scavenged for food and warm clothes in the wereyn-ravaged ruins of Elghen shortly before their ascent into the Tears, but with Bonner around they hadn't bothered with medicines and bandages, so Declan was forced to make due. Finding one of Ester's spare shirts, he tugged it free of the rest of the bag's contents and looked around, eyes drifting immediately to ay'ahSel's swords. Hesitating only briefly, Declan moved to the dark elf once more.

Within a minute, one of the commander's swords was loose of her belt, sheath and all, and Declan was drawing the blade with near-reverent scrutiny.

It seemed almost blasphemous, as he pulled the glassy black weapon free of its simple leather scabbard, to consider using it for something as mundane as cutting fabric. Indeed, though Declan couldn't begin to guess at what the weapon was actually made of, he could tell at a glance that he'd likely never seen a finer sword, much less held one in his hands. Despite the clean sheen of the blade, the thing was a great deal heavier than he would have expected, like it were carved from incredibly dense stone rather than glass. What was more, there didn't seem to be so much as a nick or chip in the fine, razored edge despite the fact that Declan had witnessed this very weapon cutting into the scaled hide of the drey not a few days before.

Whatever the sword was made of, it was more resilient than any steel he'd ever known…

Whistling softly to himself, Declan wedged the weapon between his knees and set about cutting the spare shirt into long strips. Despite his assumption that the blade would be incredibly keen, he still almost managed to slice a thumb off when the cloth parted over the edge with no more effort than water might have.

More resilient than steel, and sharper too…

Shaking his head in disbelief, Declan finished his work quickly, then set about bandaging ay'ahSel's head as best he could. He had enough experience in battlefield dressing to hopefully make a difference, but it made him nervous when the elf didn't so much as twitch even as he dabbed the wound clean with a cloth, then replaced the torn flap of skin and bound it all together tightly in several layers of wrap. Still, it made him feel better when he stood to look down on the *er'ehdehn's* now-clean face and bandages, so he was a bit more at ease when he returned to Orsik, tying the re-sheathed sword to his belt as he did.

He didn't think the commander would be missing it anytime soon, and his own weapons had likely been lost with the slain elves in the chase.

Declan shivered at the recollection, unable to completely shake the memory from his head, that image of hundreds on hundreds of curved, rotting teeth clawing outward from a hole-like mouth. He still couldn't fathom what the thing was, but he knew he didn't want to encounter it again.

"Which means we need to get out of here..." he muttered aloud, reaching for Orsik.

There was no going *back*, he knew. Even if the threat of the hunting creature wasn't lingering in the direction they'd come, there was no means by which to trace the path they had taken. To go back was to walk straight into the waiting arms of a terrible death, either quick in the clawing bite of those terrible teeth, or slowly at the mercy of starvation.

No. There was no going back.

It took some coaxing—as well as a nibble of what little dried meat they had left among the packs—but Orsik eventually rolled himself up and onto his feet, all four legs shaking a little as he did. Seeing this, Declan decided he could risk not mounting the beast just yet, and instead elected to haul ay'ahSel up, then lay her across the warg's back as gently as he could. It was hardly the best position for the woman's head injury—drooping over the animal with her arms and legs dangling off his sides—but it was the best they would manage in the short term. Luckily the tunnel was just wide enough to walk two abreast, so Declan wasn't forced to strap her down, instead electing only to hold onto the elf with one hand as he pulled the still-glowing firestone out of his pocket with the other.

A thought, and a tiny whisper of flame flickered up Declan's finger, dancing at once forward, down the tunnel, in the direction they had already been heading.

With a prayer to the Mother that he hadn't doomed the three of them to a slow demise, Declan gave a gentle word, encouraging Orsik to start padding unsteadily forward, and together they slipped further down into the dark.

◆

What felt like a full day passed, and ay'ahSel continued to show no signs of waking. Orsik, fortunately, had recovered quickly, not leaving Declan to walk long before he allowed himself back up onto the warg's back along with the woman. In that time, the chasing beast had made no further appearance, and so Declan let himself start thinking of other things aside from being ever-vigilant for the feeling of trembling stone.

As it turned out, their supply situation was better than he'd originally feared. Orsik had been carrying half of their provisions since they'd started the climb up the mountains, meaning that—while the apples and other delicates the warg had rolled over in his exhaustion the previous day were all but pulp, now—they had more than their share of food for the time being. ay'ahSel, too, had a few meager rations of some sort of dried bread and cheese in a thin pouch strapped under the hilt of the sword he'd left her, but Declan decided he wouldn't be touching those until he started to starve, or the elf succumbed to her injuries. The commander was already missing a blade.

If she came to and found herself robbed of her food as well, Declan doubted he'd have a chance to get a word in edgewise before she liberated him of his head in recompense, injured or not.

It was ay'ahSel's condition, too, that assisted their provision situation. She'd not woken since the previous day, and while Declan managed to coax a little water down her throat now and then from the pouches he refilled out of the occasional small pools they crossed, he never managed to get her to swallow anything more. Even the mashed paste of apples and other fruits seemed to sit on her tongue, and after the third attempt to feed her failed, Declan gave up. She wouldn't starve to death anytime soon—not in her current condition, at least—so he thought it best to conserve what food he could.

Their path, too, seemed well set, their guiding flame always firm in a direction whenever they came to a split crossways, so it was easy for Declan not to dwell too frequently on the potential trouble they were in. All he had to do was keep them moving.

Keeping moving, and berate himself for lunacy.

"I don't know why I did it," he grumbled for the fifth time in the last day, leaning around the wet tip of a low-hanging stalactite as they moved. "Yes, I *know* it was stupid, but what were we supposed to do? Leave her there? She was all of ten feet away!"

Beneath him Orsik was managing the lesser forms of a bed of stalagmites with ease, his clawed feet sure in the ample light provided to him by the firestone held in the hand Declan wasn't using to secure ay'ahSel to his chest. The warg didn't make any more response than a quick glance back, taking Declan in with a black eye only briefly before turning his attention forward again.

"You could do a better job at making me feel better," he muttered to the warg. "I know I'm not Bonner and his fancy magic animal-talk, but you understand more than you let on, don't you?"

Not even a twitch or a snort this time, and Declan tilted his head back with a sigh.

I'm going mad already, he thought to himself.

As a means of distraction, he reached a little higher with the fist that held the firestone, taking a slow swipe at another low stalagmite. For the hundredth time, as his hand struck the wet stone, he reached for his power, sought the tingling sensation he'd experienced as he'd fled the "the tunneler"—as he'd taken to calling the horrid creature that had chased them into the dark. For the hundredth time, nothing more than a flaring of the firestone occurred, and Declan grunted more in annoyance than pain as he hit the stalagmite with hardly anything more exciting than a wet grind of grime and dust.

He had—he was sure of it, after hours of dwelling and experimenting—tapped into a different kind of magic as they had run from the tunneler. Declan was strong—his broad-shouldered frame of well-over six feet in height lending well to his physical ability—but pulling himself and a limp, *armored* ay'ahSel up onto Orsik's back from where he had been dragging her along the ground had been a feat no man he knew of could have achieved, even as desperate as he'd been to save them both. It wouldn't have been possible without outside assistance.

And Declan thought he knew exactly what sort of "outside assistance" he had received.

It had been Bonner who'd told him of the stories, on the night the mage and Ryn both shared the truth of Viridian's history, the nature of Declan's lineage and line. When they'd spoken of Amherst al'Dyor's evolution under the influence of the dragon's gift of blood, Bonner had described the past existence of battlemages and warmancers, spellswords who wove their magics into their very flesh in order to draw inhuman strength and speed from their bodies. Amherst, the old man had claimed, had managed something much like that, after what would become known as the "King's blood" had awoken in him.

Like that, and more.

"Probably a bit better at controlling it, though?" Declan mused aloud, reaching up to swipe at another tail of rock with no greater success. "Seems damn useless if it only kicks in *when it wants to.*"

That wasn't fair to him, though, and Declan knew it. While Elysia al'Dyor—the older sister of his ancestor, and crown princess of Viridian at the time—had been the greater talent of the two when it came to spellcrafting, Declan knew that Amherst had still had *years* of magical training by the time he'd been forced to wield his power on any true battlefield. If Bonner had been there, Declan had small doubt the mage would be *oohing* and *aahing* at even his brief—and completely inadvertent—success in imbuing his limbs with magical strength. Declan smiled a little at the image of the old man, wide-eyed with excitement, tripping over himself to explain the method of the magic and the potential it held. Ryn would be standing nearby, a little more nonchalant about it all, but brimming with pride in his own subdued way.

And Ester…

The smile slid from Declan's face slowly. While it was Ryn who had been his closest companion and greatest confidant for as long as he could remember, it was not the dragon Declan worried for when he thought of his friends. Ever since he'd revealed the true nature of his being, Ryn had always seemed untethered from the more fragile world of men, of the laws of mortality and finality. Bonner, too, possessed this quality, and so Declan just couldn't bring himself to believe that either the dragon or the mage would be dying in these tunnels even if they had to wander for weeks to get out.

But Ester…

Declan swallowed, feeling a pit open in his stomach. He hadn't looked back, after he'd bolted into the tunnel to save ay'ahSel. He'd been too focused, too intent on his cause. Just the same, he needn't have seen Ester's face after he had pushed her to the ground to know what it must have looked like. Confusion would have come first, then realization.

Then the fear would have arrived, as she'd watched him drive Orsik into the crumbling passage, take up the injured elf woman, and vanish again into the narrow shaft opposite them just as the thunderous form of the tunneler would have likely blocked them all from view.

"She probably thinks I'm dead," Declan grumbled, berating himself for the hundredth time as he tried to shake Ester's stricken visage from his thoughts.

A moment later, though, her face was gone, because—for the first time since fleeing down into dark—another sound answered his musing.

"U-urgh…"

In Declan's looped arm Commander ay'ahSel—mostly limp for the duration of their descent—stiffened and shifted the slightest bit. With a start Declan brought Orsik to a halt with a quick "Woah", and as soon as the warg had stopped moving he slid off the animal's back, carrying the elf down with him carefully. He landed in a shallow pool of dirty water, the puddle having collected among the budding stalagmites that lined the floor of the shaft they'd been traveling for several hours now, but he didn't care. Watching his footing, Declan moved as quickly as he could, feeling the woman moving more and more firmly in his grip as he did.

"Hold on," he said quickly. "Just hold on. Just a minute."

His words, unfortunately, seemed to have the opposite of their intended effect. At the sound of his voice ay'ahSel started shifting in truth, fighting from what seemed to be a half-consciousness against what likely—to her mind—could only have been some kind of restraint. Fortunately the nearest wall wasn't too far, and reaching it Declan let her slide slowly to the ground with her back to the rounded stone, stepping away again the moment she was sitting of her own accord.

The *er'endehn's* eyes, for the first time, were flickering under the bandages he'd replaced twice now. The ring of red about her pale irises flashed once in the glow of the firestone still in Declan's hand, then again. She mumbled something, her head coming up to rest against the wall at her back. Declan thought better than to approach her. It wasn't like he would have understood the elf either way, but he couldn't help but think that, even in the state she was in, Lysiat ay'ahSel was half again as dangerous as any swordsman he'd ever met.

Sure enough, as her eyes flicked once more, staying half-open this time, the woman's right hand lifted shakily from her side, going for the spot on her hip where her swords usually hung.

Unfortunately, she'd opted to seek the blade now strung off *Declan's* belt.

Then again, finding herself absent the weapon—even in her state of semi-delirium—very clearly did more to rouse the dark elf than anything else.

At once ay'ahSel's eyes snapped open, the fingers of her right hand clawing at the empty space where her second sword should have been. With a hiss that was half-pained, half-shocked her grip moved at once to her other hip, and when she found the hilt of her first weapon she relaxed visibly, if only for a moment.

That, after all, was when her sharp gaze fell on Declan, taking him in in a single sweep, stopping only to stare at the borrowed weapon at his side.

"*Ys, veht*?" ay'ahSel snarled at once, wincing at the sound of her own voice. Clearly she was fighting to stay focused, to stay calm. Declan couldn't blame her. Even for the most hardened of soldiers the situation she found herself in could only be confusing, waking up in the partial dark with nothing but him and the warg as company, when before they'd numbered over a dozen souls.

Fortunately, her first question was one Declan thought he understood.

What is this, human?

Hesitating only briefly, Declan decided first and foremost that he had to put the woman at ease. Placing the firestone on the ground between them, he twisted to start unfastening the sword from his hip, working hard to keep his fingers from twitching nervously. After a few seconds, the sheathed blade came free of his belt, and with deliberate care he offered the weapon to ay'ahSel again. She blinked, a rare look of surprise passing over her face.

Then, just as slowly, she reached up to accept the sword, taking it up in both hands and pulling it from Declan's grip to bring it cautiously to her chest.

The act left Declan feeling naked and exposed, but the moment the thing was securely in the elf's possession again, he knew it had been worth it. ay'ahSel's stare was no longer piercing, no longer murderous. She looked, if anything, curious, the confusion of her situation now coming to the forefront.

Taking advantage of it, Declan began struggling to put to use what little elvish he knew, hoping the dialects weren't so different that the two of them would be left with no avenue of communication whatsoever.

"*Hurt*," he did his best to enunciate in the tongue of the *er'enthyl*, pointing first at ay'ahSel's forehead, then tapping his own brow above his right eye. "*You. Hurt.*"

The commander frowned, clearly not understanding. After a moment, though, his meaning seemed to dawn on her, because she lifted one hand from where she was still hugging the sword to her breast to feel below her hairline. Her eyes went wide as she touched the fabric of the makeshift wrappings, pressing around gently at first, then more firmly. Finding the location of the injury, she started and let out a barely-stifled groan of pain.

"*Stop*," Declan said with a quick shake of his head before repeating the pointing. "*You. Hurt.*"

The elf grunted in—if he wasn't mistaken—sarcastic agreement, as if to say "obviously." Then, though, she looked at him again, hand not leaving the wrappings.

"*Kaya sev?*"

Declan looked at her blankly for a solid few seconds, completely at a loss. His vocabulary was already limited to what little the old quartermaster of the Iron Wind had taught him, years past, and the enunciation of the dark elves was different from that of their cousins, a tad harsher, more rigid.

Eventually ay'ahSel gathered that he hadn't comprehended, because with a grunt of frustration she resorted to miming. Pointing first at her head, she then indicated the place where her sword had been hanging on Declan's hip, then Orsik, who was standing a ways back from them sniffing here and there at the ground. If he had to guess, it was almost like she wanted to know…

"What happened?" Declan asked, feeling it click.

It was the elf's turn to stare, but it didn't matter. Getting to his feet, Declan moved back to the warg, rummaging through the packs only briefly before returning with two items in hand. One was the bundle of loose cloth he'd made from Ester's shirt.

The other was the commander's own helmet, which he'd kept for just such an occurrence.

Handing the latter over, Declan did his best to explain with nothing more than gestures, some few helpful words he knew, and even the occasional sketch drawn into the damp dust of the floor. The elf appeared to follow along, eyes wide from the moment she'd taken in the dent and scrape that had marred one side of the helmet. By the time he finished his rough recounting, she'd started nodding along, and Declan felt a lessening tightness in his chest that he hadn't realized was there.

At the very least, it seemed like the two of them would be less than enemies in this bid to be free of the mountains.

As though following the same train of thought, ay'ahSel turned her eyes on Declan again, frowning now as she studied him. After a moment her gaze drifted down to the firestone still sitting between them, and while she made a face at the thing that said very plainly she still held no more love for the magics within than before, it seemed like the elf's harshness of the last half week had lessened somewhat.

Then again, that could just have been lingering grogginess from what *had* to have been severe concussion…

Eventually ay'ahSel looked up again, and after a second's pause she made an odd motion with one hand. Bringing all five fingers together into a sort of point, she touched them to her lips, staring at Declan pointedly.

"Errr…" The only thing Declan was sure of was that he was supposed to be gleaning some meaning out of this gesture, but he was as much at a loss as he might have been had the *er'endehn* spoken her intent aloud. Still, the commander seemed to have faith that he would eventually understand her, because she repeated the motion a little more slowly.

Then, just as Declan was about to shake his head and try to explain that he didn't understand, the woman's stomach growled so loudly he could have sworn the sound actually *echoed* into the darkness on either side of them.

"Oh!" Declan exclaimed, understanding at once and even repeating the motion back at the elf, touching his fingers to his mouth. "'Food'! This means 'food'! You're hungry!"

Silence answered him, but Declan was confident enough in his epiphany that he got up at once. He returned with one of their less-damaged apples, holding it out for the elf. Judging by the way she snatched it up—so quickly she actually winced in discomfort as the motion jarred her head—he knew he'd been right.

"Your provisions are still in your pouch, just so you know." He said it even as he repeated the sign for "food", then pointed at ay'ahSel's belt, where he'd never touched her rations. The elf, though, ignored him, ripping into the apple like it held the nectar of the gods. It gave Declan a moment to consider.

Maybe there *was* a way they could communicate…

Again he went to Orsik, and again he returned, this time with one of their waterskins in hand. By the time he kneeled before the elf again, she had finished with the apple and was already eyeing the bag in his hand eagerly. Before handing it over, though, Declan pointed at it, then again made the sign for "food", trying for a quizzical expression as he made to convey the question he wanted answered:

Did "water" and "food" have the same gestures?

He suspected the concussion was slowing ay'ahSel down significantly, because it took three more attempts with various expressions and urgencies before she caught on. With a shake of her head—a *slow* shake of her head—she brought the *knuckles* of her hand to her mouth instead.

"Water," Declan repeated, echoing the motion even as he handed the skin over, mind already racing as ay'ahSel snatched it up and began to drink greedily. Learning each other's traditional tongues would likely be nothing but a fruitless endeavor—at least for the time being—but this language of the soldiers....

While he expected there were very likely nuances and layers to the signing that would take a lot more than a few quick lessons to grasp, Declan also knew that such a method of exchange would be a LOT easier than one or both of them attempting to wrap their head around the pronunciations and enunciations of their respectively utterly-foreign languages.

Settling on the matter, Declan felt better as he watched ay'ahSel interchange gulping down water and gasping for air. They could do this, the two of them. They had enough food to last them several days, and he'd been under the distinct impression their little party had been approaching the end of their journey through the mountain before being split up. They had a breeze to guide themselves by and enough food and water to last them days, if not more. If he, ay'ahSel, and Orsik kept to the smaller shafts and avoided coming across the tunneler's path again, they could do this.

Declan took a slow, steadying breath, feeling the pressure of fear and panic he'd been holding at bay only barely both lessen slightly.

The commander appeared to sense his relief, as minimal as it was, because she frowned slightly. Wiping her mouth with the back of one hand, she held the waterskin out for him to take, looking to either side of them as he did. The frown deepened when she took in the low stalagmites and narrow passage, and she seemed uncertain.

Sure enough, turning her attention back to him as Declan stood up before her, she cast her hand first to the left, then to the right, holding her own quizzical expression.

"Which way are we going? Hopefully the right way. Hold on."

He spoke out of habit, knowing the *er'endehn* didn't understand him, but he wanted both hands free if he was going to help her stand. Replacing the skin among their things—Orsik huffing impatiently at him as he did—Declan returned and bent to pick up the firestone, suppressing a low laugh as ay'ahSel retracted from him ever so slightly.

"If you want to get out of here, you're going to have to get used to this," he said quietly. "Here. Look." With a raised finger and a thought, the guiding flame he'd been using all of the last day flickered into being, and at once it bounced and danced, leaning gently to his left, down the shaft in the direction they'd been taking.

"We go that way," he pointed unnecessarily, because ay'ahSel's eyes had already widened in understanding, gaze flicking from the flame to the darkness down the tunnel from them. If she had reservations about the magic, she repressed them, because after a few seconds she nodded.

Then she tried to stand.

"Oy!" Declan exclaimed, bouncing forward just in time to catch the woman by one shoulder as she promptly swayed before she could so much as get both feet under herself. She flinched at his touch, but didn't pull away, instead squeezing her eyes shut and letting out a groan threaded heavily with what sounded *distinctly* like a multitude of elvish curses. Declan held her there for a while, assisting her as they waited for whatever wave of dizziness or discomfort must have seized her to pass, and when ay'ah'Sel opened her eyes again she seemed resigned. Though she still held firm to the sword with one hand, using the other she gestured once again. First, a pulling sort of motion, open hand closing as she brought it from in front of her to her chest.

Then two fingers, almost like legs, split to point down at the ground.

"Need?" Declan thought aloud. "You need to stand? Sure. I could have told you that. And I could have told you to wait for me to help, too."

Before the elf could frown at him again he took her under the arm with both hands and started to lift her as carefully as he could. She was light, reminding him once again of Ester, and even in her armor he had her up on her feet soon enough. The commander let out another groan, and Declan paused, giving her a second to steady herself.

Only when she nodded did he start pulling her carefully towards Orsik, whose impatience seemed to have subsided a little as he took in the injured woman.

Despite her lucidity, ay'ahSel was still in worse shape than Declan would have liked, proven by the near minute it took to help her the ten feet to the warg. Her footing was unsteady among the budding stalagmites and damp ground, and more than once she caught a toe or ankle on one of the swells and dips in the rock. It was a far change from the typically flawless grace of her kind, and she even looked a little queasy by the time they reached the warg.

"Here, hold on," Declan said, peeling her free hand off where it had been instinctively clutching at his sleeve for support and guiding it to one of the harness straps. Still she swayed, and he knew she wouldn't be able to manage mounting while clutching at the sword he'd borrowed.

"You should give that to me." He pointed at the weapon in ay'ahSel's other hand. At first, she hesitated, brow furrowing it what was either discomfort or distrust.

"You won't be able to get on him holding onto it," Declan said gently, hoping the elf would at least read the intent of his words, if not the meaning. "Give it to me. I'll hand it back as soon as you're on him."

It took a moment of silence—Declan holding out a hand expectantly and meeting the elf's eyes in an attempt to make her understand—before ay'ahSel finally succumbed to the logic she didn't need language to understand. She passed the sword over, fingers lingering about the scabbard as Declan accepted it, like she didn't want to let go. Resting the weapon against the largest of the stalagmites within reach, he immediately knelt and looped his finger over one knee.

Half a minute later—and two failed attempts that nearly ended with the commander's ass in the mud—and the elf was situated as best the two of them could manage over Orsik's back. At once the warg bent around to half-snort, half-growl at ay'ahSel's boot, displeased with the unfamiliar rider.

"You'll have to deal with it, sorry, boy," Declan told the warg gently, patting him between the ears before moving to retrieve the elf's sword. "She can't walk, and I'm not leaving her here. As soon as we're free of this damn place, I'll make it worth your while. I promise."

Orsik appeared content with Declan's assurance, because with a grunt he looked forward again, clearly ready to keep moving. Declan couldn't blame him, and so as soon as he had the sword in hand he held it up to the waiting elf, expecting her to take it so they could start their descent once again.

He was more than a little surprised when ay'ahSel—rather than accept the weapon—unsteadily palmed its pommel to push it back towards him before gesturing once more.

A finger at him, then the sign for "need" again, and finally a thumb traced from her hip to her navel, almost like she were drawing a blade.

"I need a sword?" he asked, unsure if he'd caught the meaning this time.

In answer, the elf only pushed the hilt of the weapon towards him again. The motion brought her body a little too far to the side, and with a scramble of hands Declan once again had to help catch her as she started to slide.

"Okay. You're in bad shape, and I'm the only one who can swing a sword properly right now. Got it."

The elf didn't nod this time, eyes shut tight against another bout of pain or nausea as he assisted her in resettling. Once she was balanced, Declan debated climbing aboard behind her, but thought better of it. Orsik had earned himself a break after a full day of carrying them both, and he didn't think he'd won himself enough trust just yet for the dark elf to feel comfortable riding with her back against his chest.

Taking ahold of the lip of ay'ahSel's boot to help steady her, Declan looked to Orsik.

"All right. Let's go."

CHAPTER EIGHT

I have lost count how many times I have desired to strangle that man. My betrothed is not a fool, but fools aren't the only people who don't always think before they act...

—PRIVATE JOURNALS OF ESTERIA YR'ESSEL, C. 1080P.F.

Anything?

Across from Ryn, Bonner shook his bald head slowly. He was standing with his back to the rest of them, both hands glowing green as he pressed them against a flatter section of the narrow tunnel they'd been traveling along for more than two full days. At every rest they took, he had performed the same ritual, enacted the same weaves to extend himself into the earth, reaching as best he could in all directions in what little time these short breaks allowed him. It was easier to press his mind through the solid stone than the living verdure of the world above, he had said.

And, yet, all the same, like every time before, it looked like he'd found nothing.

"*Not within the extent of the spell, no,*" the mage confirmed in elvish a moment later, drawing his hands from the wall even as the glow of power faded from his fingers. "*Not since that first day, when we felt them heading east.*"

Ryn sighed, then nodded, crossing his broad arms across his chest. *What about our exit? Is it as close as they think?* He tilted his head up the tunnel a ways, where the three elves who were all that remained of their escort were standing expectantly, frowning as they were addressed. They'd all stopped because the *er'endehn* had claimed that the air was getting cooler, promising of the open sky soon enough.

"*It's as they say*," Bonner answered, brushing his hands off on his multi-colored robes, the stain of grime and dirt vanishing at once into the enchanted cloth. "*We're not far. The earth starts getting drier a mile up this tunnel.*"

"*Meaning what?*" Ester, standing next to Eyera to Ryn's left, demanded. "*We leave Declan behind?! We leave the tunnels?!*"

There was a stirring from the elves at this—from the two spear-wielders in particular—and Ryn had to quell the knot that formed in his stomach at Ester's words even as Bonner turned to try and calm his daughter. With Declan and Lysiat ay'ahSel gone, the need to translate everything to the common tongue had been abandoned as quickly as the general order for silence. Suddenly finding themselves outnumbered—by a dragon and a mage, no less—the remaining dark elves had taken to treating what was left of their party rather more reasonably over the last few days.

Particularly after Bonner had been able to deliver word to Aliek and Tesied ay'ahSel—the commander's *brothers*, it transpired—that their elder sister had survived the arrival of the great beast that had nearly brought the tunnel down on their heads, thanks in whole to Declan's actions.

His foolish *actions*, Ryn thought privately, feeling the knot tighten.

No. He forced away the concern, forced away the fear. When it became clear whatever the colossal creature had been was not after them, Bonner had been able to weave his magic into the mountains quick enough to sense Declan and ay'ahSel fleeing eastward and down, opposite their own current trajectory of upwards and west. The speed at which they'd been moving had Bonner convinced that Orsik had survived as well, which had been a source of almost equal relief to Ryn. If the warg lived, that meant the supplies the beast had been carrying had likely made it, too.

Declan had food, water, and a mount. He had his wits, as well as Bonner's teachings, brief as they may have been. Even Ester's education on tracking and forestry would come in useful if he survived the mountains, and—assuming ay'ahSel, too, had made it in one piece as well—Declan was in the company of an experienced *er'endehn* officer who owed him her life.

Ryn forced himself not to worry, forced himself to meet Ester's gaze, though it was admittedly difficult. For reasons he was beginning to suspect, she had taken Declan's disappearance the hardest of all of them, and had barely eaten or slept since.

We do leave the tunnels, but we do not leave Declan behind, he told the woman as steadily as he could. *He is hardly without advantages, and the fact that we near an exit other than the passage by which the elves entered the mountains is proof already that there is more than one way in and out of this maze. Their base camp is near. Once we reach it, we will enlist the assistance of the* er'endehn *to scour the slopes. We* will *find him, Ester.*

To her credit, the half-elf didn't say anything more. Ryn knew what she was thinking, of course. They were *all* thinking it, even the two ay'ahSels who desired to see the return of their sibling. They *all* wanted to gather whatever might the dark elves had brought to the foot of the mountains and enter the caverns again, searching the tunnels. Unfortunately, that was impossible.

So long as that creature "lived"—for Ryn wasn't entirely convinced it had been a breathing thing—none of them, not even him, would be setting foot within these caverns again.

Recalling it, recalling the roiling, pulpous mass of the thing he had barely been able to sense through the stone as they'd fled, Ryn looked away from Ester in the hopes that she wouldn't see him shiver. Again the knot formed, and again he pressed it away. It was more difficult this time, though. They had run. They had run from the beast and they had not been chased.

Because as he, Bonner, and Ester had all agreed in whispered conversations in the hours after their flight, it was Declan the creature had turned to go after.

It was Declan that the thing had followed into the depths.

CHAPTER NINE

"Talent and skill, our kind have aplenty. It is bred into us, bred into our bodies and minds. Perhaps it is a harsh thing to admit, but the weak among us do not propagate, do not produce those few children who are the future of our race. Often they cannot find a pair, and those that do frequently take measures to ensure their frailties are not passed on even then. As a result, talent and skill, our kind have aplenty.

But a desire to learn—a need to grow, to become stronger... That is not something that one is so easily born with..."

—Zyl'eht Yrhst, High Chancellor of Erraven, date unknown

No. Left. We go left.

Declan frowned hesitating at ay'ahSel's insistent gestures. They had come—hardly for the first time—to a split in the tunnel, but on this occasion the little flame that had been their guide was proving to be deceptive. It danced and bounced on the tip of his finger, angling first to the right—which led up and looked to bend gently northward—then left—which continued to lead downward, twisting in the same direction. Declan, for his part, had wanted to follow the right path, thinking that as the mountain rose, it tapered, meaning the northern slopes they were trying to find would be reached sooner.

ay'ahSel, on the other hand, seemed to have a different plan in mind.

Left, she repeated in firm silence, her gestures casting shadows on the ceiling above them from where she sat atop Orisk over Declan's shoulder. *We go left.*

Over the course of three days, Declan's grasp on the soldiers' signs had improved significantly—or at least as significantly as could have been counted to in that little time. It had taken many repetitions and not a few misunderstandings, but eventually he'd come to know the essentials well enough to communicate the most basic concepts. Directions. Food. Rest. Halt. All in all, it made for disjointed—if ever-improving—conversation, but conversation all the same.

With the hand not holding his flame and firestone before him, Declan made his own gesture. It was—as far as he had come to understand—actually the sign for "more", but once he'd grasped that the pair of them had been using it to roughly equate to a request for explanation, for "more" information, if it could be allowed.

Without hesitating ay'ahSel opened her mouth to touch her finger to her tongue before sticking it up in a whirling motion, the sign he'd come to understand meant "air" or "wind". While he didn't know the first gesture, the context was enough to guess at its meaning.

"You can *taste* it on the air?" he asked incredulously.

The elf, of course, stared at him blankly, clearly less than thrilled at his slip back into the common tongue. Though Declan still wouldn't have bet the *er'endehn* was ready to swing a sword, she'd improved markedly over the last two days. It hadn't been too long before Declan had trusted her balance enough to let her ride on her own, allowing them to pick up their pace through the tunnels as he led their little train rather than awkwardly plodding along at Orsik's side. The morning after she'd woken up, ay'ahSel had insisted he let her walk, which he'd granted so long as she held onto the straps of the harness. While she hadn't lasted more than five minutes, it was still a significant gain for the woman who hadn't been able to stand on her own the day before, so when she'd asked again a few hours later, he'd given in much more readily.

Now, three days after her rise from unconsciousness, her stoicism seemed to be returning, and Declan admitted himself relieved to see a bit of the hardened officer he had known her as prior to the blow to her head.

Chewing on his lip a moment more, Declan once again looked to the left, then to the right, weighing his options. On the one hand he thought his logic made sense, but on the other, ay'ahSel likely had decades—if not centuries—of experience on him.

In the end, it wasn't too hard a decision to make, and with a gesture to the left he continued to lead Orsik downward.

He felt better about the choice as the tunnel indeed started to bend northward, but he tempered the excitement, just as he'd had to temper it a hundred times already in the four days they'd been on their own. For every loop towards the slopes he knew they couldn't be far from, there was a double-back, or a dip that took them so far down it felt like they would soon be walking under the very surface of the world. ay'ahSel, though, never seemed to worry about this possibility, which made Declan breathe a little easier.

But only a little.

The truth was that they were starting to cut it close. They had eaten the damaged fruits and the like as soon as possible, then immediately started rationing their other foodstuffs, with Orsik getting the largest portion of their dried meat. Between the three of them, though, even careful distribution had dug quickly into their supplies, and a rough calculation told Declan they had another day of food, maybe two. They'd be able to continue for a bit after that, obviously, but if they didn't find the surface soon, they would be in dire straights. The warg, theoretically, could provide for him and ay'ahSel for a while if needed, but the idea was as impractical as it was upsetting. Aside from the fact that Declan had grown more and more fond of the beast, there remained the fact that Orsik was the only reason they were making any sort of decent headway, carrying the injured elf and their supplies as he was. If the warg was felled, ay'ahSel was very likely just as dead, and Declan would be left on his own to wander.

The idea made his stomach turn.

Suddenly in need of a distraction, Declan looked over his shoulder, finding the *er'endehn* squinting around at the wet walls of the tunnel they were plodding along. After a moment she caught his eye, frowning at him quizzically.

Head? he asked of the elf by pointing at the place of her injury on his own brow.

She nodded with a bit of a grimace, pointing at the firestone in his right hand, then making the gestures for "light" and "bad".

"It's too bright," Declan translated for himself. "Yeah, I know. I'm sorry." He gestured "apology"—one of the few extraneous signs he'd learned—before those of "seeing" and "walking".

Sorry, I have to see where we're going, he was trying for, and seemed to succeed because the elf shrugged without protest before looking away from him again.

Declan sighed in an unsatisfied kind of way. While it was certainly better than talking to Orsik—or no one, for that matter—the limit of their exchanges could be disheartening. He'd been kicking himself since the drey attack for not having made more of an effort to learn the language of the elves, something Bonner or Ester—or even Ryn, if the dragon could enunciate the tongue—might have tutored him in as they'd trekked north through Viridian. It seemed foolish, in retrospect. Sure, he'd been kept plenty busy training in magic and swordplay, but they'd known they would to delving into the world of the dark elves. It seemed, in hindsight, a rather large omission on all their parts.

Then again, focusing on his training hadn't been without its own fruit.

Declan glanced down at his left hand, resting on the hilt of ay'ahSel's borrowed sword while his right held the firestone aloft to guide their way. Focusing on the extremity, he sought the flow of power that Bonner had taught him to find, the current of magic rushing through his veins. Without the firestone acting as a conduit—drawing the energy to itself automatically and making the flow easy to find—the discernment was always trickier, always harder.

But not impossible.

After a few seconds Declan sensed the current, sensed the movement of the magic in his left hand. Focusing, he applied pressure to it, encouraging it to expand, to extend out of his veins and into his flesh and bone. The magic responded in a rush, causing his whole hand to seize up, but with a grunt of pain Declan focused on drawing it back again, on finding the middle ground.

When he did, when the magic was balanced, he was left with a tingling sensation similar to the one he'd achieved as they'd fled the tunneler.

Declan fought to hold onto the equilibrium as long as he could, keeping it steady for a good five or six seconds before it started to fluctuate, at which point he let it go. As the feeling of the magic faded from his hand, Declan allowed himself a strained grin. While he hadn't had the opportunity to test his theory—he could only manage the weave briefly and in the smallest section of his body, for the time being—he was rather convinced of the fact that he had deduced the secret to what he was fairly sure was imbuement, the only strengthening magic he knew of. It was what he had been working on in the hours of walking in which he and ay'ahSel held their silence, and he had to admit—as much as it pained him—that Bonner's drilling in of the fundamentals of arcanic law had been the base on which he had developed the concept. It felt odd to be teaching himself—he had barely a month's education in the craft, after all—but the fact remained that he was seeing progress regardless. So long as he was careful, so long as he maintained control, maintained focus, his abilities seemed almost to want to continue to expand faster and faster of their own volition, like the seed of the primordial's gifts within him desired to be let loose now that he'd *finally* tapped it. Despite the precariousness of their situation, it made Declan a little giddy to think about it. For the better part of several months, now, he had felt like the weakest link, like the runt of their group.

Now, though, he was starting to see a different future for himself...

Click-click.

Declan stopped so suddenly Orsik's snout hit him in the lower back when the warg failed to notice, nearly sending him stumbling forward. Ignoring the snuffling of the animal, though, Declan looked over his shoulder, instinctively dimming the light in his hand to the absolute minimum he needed to see by. It had been days since he'd heard that sound, the warning notice of the *er'endehn*, but he doubted he'd ever forget it.

Not after what followed the last time it had echoed through the dark...

Atop Orsik, ay'ahSel was sitting stock-still, bandaged head tilted slightly to one side, listening intently. At his hip, Declan's grip tightened about the hilt of his borrowed sword, but he thought better than to loosen the blade, not wanting to intrude on the elf's attention. After a few moments, the commander looked down at him, lifting one hand from Orsik's harness.

Wind. I hear wind.

With an altogether different kind of thrill, Declan whirled again, listening himself now. A second passed, then two, but he couldn't make out whatever it was that the elf had. That hardly made him doubt her, of course. He had known Ester to hear enemies from half a mile off and smell smoke on the air from many times that. If the senses of a *pure-blooded* elf were any better, it might still be a great ways before he, too, heard the wind.

The wind...

Wind meant an air current, and one far stronger than those they'd been following through these infernal passages. If anything, it very likely meant an exit, or at least the passage that led directly to one.

Close. They were getting close.

At once Declan started forward again, picking up the pace as best he could, ignoring the clatter of loose stone beneath his feet and the light splashing of water when his quick steps disturbed the pools he might otherwise have paused to drink from. For nearly ten minutes the three of them moved like that, Declan leading and Orsik following with ay'ahSel on his back. All the while Declan kept his ears open, listening as hard as he could for the telltale whistling of air that would confirm the elf's suspicions.

Before he made out the wind, though, another sound had his heart leaping first.

Crunch.

Declan stopped almost mid-step in surprise. Looking down, he was confused as something glimmered under his boot, and with a thought he expanded the light of the firestone again, letting it blaze in his hands. He blinked twice, not quiet believing his eyes.

Ice. At some point, the wetness of the walls and floor had turned to ice...

With wide eyes he looked back around at ay'ahSel, expecting the elf to have noted the same thing, but the commander was instead holding a hand up before her face, seeming to scrutinize it as she exhaled through an open mouth.

Even in the renewed brightness of the magic, Declan didn't miss the misting of her breath about the dark skin of her fingers.

"We're close," he said aloud this time, looking down the tunnel again and not even caring as his voice echoed up the narrow shaft. He could see, now, the glimmering sheen of the walls and floor, the light reflecting off of everything differently than it had when it had all been merely wet. The temperature was dropping. Enough for their breath to fog in the air and for the water to begin to freeze. For that to happen, they *had* to be approaching the exit.

Elation rocked through Declan, but he worked to temper it, unwilling to let himself fall into the trap of false hope. As he started forward again, he moved more carefully, not wanting to risk missing a cross-ways or a split that would have them lost among the tunnels again. The ice continued to crunch beneath his boots, and behind him he heard Orsik's steps doing much the same. Two minutes later, and the wind ay'ahSel had originally heard finally reached him, and Declan started looking in truth for the way out, the shaft that he believed more and more would render them their freedom.

Unfortunately, it turned out the mountain wouldn't be surrendering them without a fight.

It was as the sound of the gusting air got closer and closer that Declan's nerves started to rise. There was something odd about it, something…uneven. It was as though the wind were coming sometimes from nearby, sometimes from further away. After half a minute more, ay'ahSel confirmed his suspicions by catching his attention with another click of her tongue.

The moment he turned, she gestured the signs he had been afraid of.

Tunnel. Ahead. Big. Very big.

"Not good," Declan muttered to himself even as he nodded his agreement, pressing forward despite his reservations.

Sure enough, it wasn't long after that they stepped out of their narrow little shaft into open emptiness, and despite the healthy current of air he could now feel on his face, Declan's stomach dropped out.

They had been fortunate, over the last few days, to have been able to avoid most of the larger tunnels. They'd been few-and-far-between to begin with, and luckily the trio's guiding flame had never had them traveling along any of them for more than the steps it took to cross their width. That had been fine by Declan, because while the smaller shafts had sometimes drawn in around them until the stone felt uncomfortably close, they'd come with a measure of security, a sense of safety.

Narrow tunnels meant they couldn't be hunted.

Most unfortunately, the passage they stepped out into now was *anything* but narrow.

Declan held the firestone up as high as he could while he willed its light forth. It blazed white-hot in his hand, the glow of it blinding between his fingers after so many days spent in semi-darkness. Just the same, he let his eyes adjust rather than draw back the weave, wanting to see, to take in the space around them. He pressed the stone to glow brighter, brighter. Eventually his vision cleared enough to see by.

"Her Graces..." he cursed even as ay'ahSel muttered something that sounded much to the same effect behind him.

The passage they had come to stand in was by far the widest Declan could recall traveling along even before he and the others had met up with the *er'endehn*. An easy sixty feet across and just as high, the ceiling far above them glimmered with veins of ice where water had collected to run its course before freezing along the stone. From the right the wind blew, and glancing along the shaft southward Declan had to blink into the dark when the zephyrs drew tears from his eyes for the first time in nearly two weeks. The glow of his firestone did not penetrate this black, the cavernous extent of the opposite wall and ceiling fading quickly off into shadow.

It was not, however, the size of the tunnel that had drawn the curse from him.

Rather, it was the state of the passage, the scene it cut to either side and before them within the extent of his gentle sphere of light.

The space was, for lack of a better word, in ruins. The shafts they had been traveling along for the last weeks had typically been one of two things: smooth in the absence of moisture as whatever had carved them had torn through dry stone, or porous and pocked, hung with stalactites and carpeted with stalagmites formed over decades and centuries as water collected and seeped along the rock. This large tunnel, if Declan had to guess, had been the latter of these.

At least until not too long ago.

Newly broken stone layered the ground in a scattered mess, the dry, discolored edges along their surfaces betraying their recent fracturing. Beneath them, the floor of the space rose and dropped, evidence that pillars and spikes had once risen as thick as a forest along the passage. Above them, the same looked to be true, the ceiling an odd pattern of similar dips and ridges, while the walls looked roughened and newly torn. Declan knew what the place would have looked like not so long ago, had maneuvered on Orsik's back in Ryn's wake as the dragon had demolished a way for them through the pillars and lines of stalagmites that had blocked their way in the cavern where they had met the drey. On that occasion, Ryn had left a line of devastation as wide across as he was broad, his powerful forelegs and chest making relatively easy work of the obstructions.

And whatever had torn through *this* passage had been thrice the dragon's size…

"It was here."

Declan spoke aloud without meaning to, not so much as noticing ay'ahSel's wincing at his back when the words reverberated through the emptiness. He was too busy bending down, taking up a chunk of rock with his free hand and turning it over to examine. It looked to have been part of some larger formation, one side rippled but smooth, the others all dry, even dusty.

"It was here, and not long ago," he repeated, dropping the rock again to look around. He had to consciously force himself to peer into the dark south of them, deeper into the mountains.

All the same, he couldn't help but imagine the shape of a thousand scrambling teeth blooming out of the shadows, thundering along the tunnel towards him with terrifying speed.

Click.

Declan looked around as ay'ahSel sought his attention. The elf had—perhaps instinctively—donned the helmet they'd been keeping for her in the travel bags, forcing it over her bandages. If she was uncomfortable, it was masked by the concern printed clear even on the spare narrow lines of her face he could see through the metal. Her eyes were trailing along the ground, taking in the destruction, and Declan knew he would have no need to struggle through explaining his discovery.

Even if she hadn't seen the tunneler before passing out, ay'ahSel was very likely more acutely aware of the danger the creature represented than anyone.

After a second, she raised a hand to sign.

North? Or back?

It was a fair question, and Declan considered it carefully, looking around again to scrutinize the far side of the tunnel the light of his firestone thankfully reached. There was no continuing passage, this time, no "forward" that they could take as they sought a different way out of the mountain. There was only to the left—following the air they both knew would see them free of that hellish maze—or back the way they had come.

The fact that he had to think about it almost made Declan sick.

After a few seconds, he lifted his own hand.

North. Fast. You. Me. On Orsik.

The fact that the elf didn't hesitate before nodding only had Declan's trepidation deepening. Returning to them, he stowed the firestone before hauling himself onto the warg behind ay'ahSel, who tensed despite herself as he pressed his chest to her back in order to take hold of the harness straps between her knees.

"Run, boy," he said, digging his heels into Orsik's side, praying as the beast took off that the wind rushing from their backs didn't bear more than the hope of freedom.

As they barreled northward along the tunnel, the light of the firestone went with them, whisked away on Orsik's strong legs. As it fled, the space they had been standing before the mouth of the smaller shaft quickly descended once more into darkness, the lingering illumination of the magic fading until it was only a glimmer on the ice that still lined the ceiling. Soon enough, even that was gone, and black swallowed everything once again. It should have stayed like that. It should have stayed, still and quiet, silent but for the rushing of air as the centuries had their chance to pass once more, as the ruins of the space were allowed to build up again into a forest of rock within the mountains.

Instead, it wasn't more than fifteen minutes after the light of the firestone had winked off in the distance that the stones began to dance.

CHAPTER TEN

It was ay'ahSel, unsurprisingly, who first made out their coming end.

While the elf had been stiff initially—clearly uncomfortable as Declan's broad chest crowded against her shoulders while they road—it wasn't too long before she relaxed, resigned to their situation. Over the course of twenty minutes or so Declan felt the tension in her back ease slowly, her posture becoming less rigid. It comforted him, in some small way. Once they were out, once they were free of the mountains, he would leave her alone on Orsik's back again, showing once more that he could be trusted. They could survive, he knew, so long as they escaped the tunnels, and having the commander's esteem when they inevitably met up with Ryn, Bonner, and Ester to greet her superiors could only be a good thing.

Then, abruptly, ay'ahSel sat bolt upright again, and all thought of freedom fled Declan as the elf snapped her head about, one eye peering around his shoulder to look back, taking in the black at their rear.

"*Sey eh'lyn,*" the commander hissed.

Whatever the words might have meant—whether they were a curse or a prayer or just a statement of fact—Declan didn't know. His mind, however, leapt immediately to the worst possible conclusion, and though he himself couldn't make out any sign of it, he knew what had caught the elf's attention.

It was coming.

"HYAH!" Declan broke the quiet they'd been running in to yell over the crunch and scrape of Orsik's paws across the stone. Driving hard into the warg's side in the hopes of conveying his desperation, he leaned forward heavily, bringing ay'ahSel awkwardly down with him. The elf, though, made no complaint, doing her best to flatten herself over the animal's back on her own as she added her own voice to Declan's. Orsik—whether sensing his riders' need or understanding the danger already—required no other encouragement, because his loping gate immediately began to churn faster, heavy shoulders and flanks rolling beneath the pair. Before long, they were once again hurtling along the tunnel at break-neck speed, running with the same panicked abandon they had all been possessed by when they'd first fled the beast.

This time, though, there were no stone walls to slow their pursuer down.

Unwilling to let go of the harness straps, Declan could do no more than reach for the warmth of the firestone against his chest. The sword on his belt leapt and jolted uncomfortably against his thigh with every lunging lope, by he ignored the discomfort, pressing the magic for more light, *more light*! Just the same, no sign of escape greeted him in the bloom of orange warmth this produced from his pocket. He looked left and right, searching every inch of the tunnel as they careened over the broken stone for the telltale sign of an off-shooting tunnel. Under him, he felt ay'ahSel's twisting this way and that as she did the same.

The passage, though, had been torn clean, its roughened walls absent of any nook or cranny around which escape might hide.

By the time Declan began to feel the trembling in the air, he suspected they were well and truly caught.

"Take a deep breath!" he shouted over the rumbling of the earth just as dust and stone began to flake away from the ceiling above them, momentarily forgetting that the elf didn't speak the common tongue.

Then, releasing the firestone as a vessel, he called on his magic in truth.

Immediately the air about them rippled as the heat erupted outward from his body, and ay'ahSel started hacking and coughing almost at once. Declan focused, fighting with the power that always felt like it was battling to get out, hammering at his will whenever he tapped it. The heat condensed, once more forming a shield above them more than around them, but just the same the temperature did not abate, ticking up little by little. Overhead, fractures of rock and ice the size of his fingers were beginning to rain down, coming loose in the quaking of the earth to break on the barrier he had created.

Unfortunately, this was small comfort compared to what was happening *within* the spell.

"D-des! Des!"

The words came in a wheeze, and a hand was suddenly clutching at Declan forearm. Looking down, he realized that ay'ahSel was just short of convulsing, one eye bulging in her helmet from where she had turned to look up at him. Orsik, too, he saw, was already struggling, the warg's billowing breath suddenly coming in wrenching gasps as the churning in his legs became unsteady, uneven.

Stop! the commander had said. *Stop!*

Horrified, Declan released the power, and within half a second they had barreled out of the lingering heat and into cold, fresh air again. ay'ahSel choked and gulped in a lungful, and under them Orsik spasmed as he seemed to do the same.

Declan hadn't realized it, hadn't noticed. He'd never channeled his truer power around anyone long enough to see it. His King's blood—his primordial's gift—seemed to grant him some resistance to the effect of his own weave, the heat of it never reaching him nearly as fiercely. ay'ahSel and Orsik, on the other hand, had no such boon, and Declan wondered suddenly how close he had just come to inadvertently killing his companions in a most horrible of ways.

The thrill of that consideration, however, was interrupted as—along with the disappearance of the heat—the shield that had been formed above their heads failed.

Thunk!

The first stone to strike them glanced off Orsik's right shoulder, causing the animal to snarl and drive forward even faster. Declan threw an arm over his head to protect himself and ay'ahSel, cursing to the Mother and All Her Graces as the rain of rock fell around them like savage hail.

No good. It was no good. Declan knew from experience that the crumbling of the world was only likely to get worse as their hunter neared. He had to protect them, had to defend them from the falling debris, or soon enough it would be boulders and sections of the mountain itself that came tumbling down upon their heads. But if he drew on his magic, he was just as likely to boil ay'ahSel and Orsik in their own blood!

No good. It was all no good.

Declan's mind raced, trying to come up with a solution. He had nothing more than his tenuous hold on the basic concepts of pyromancy. His weak understanding of self-imbuement was worthless, and served no purpose in the moment even if he'd been a master of the art. He had to shield them, had to defend them, but without drawing on a power he had barely any control over.

Or…

"Or I have to stop it," Declan muttered through his teeth, realizing there was one small sliver of hope left to him.

Without a second to lose, Declan made peace with the idea. It wasn't like the potential of his own death was a foreign concept to him. He was a veteran of the famed mercenary guilds of Aletha, tattooed with the marks of the Iron Wind, the Seekers, and all the other greater companies in the kingdom of man. He'd lived his whole adult life by the sword, and had long suspected that his fall would eventually be on the battlefield. He would have preferred it to come at the end of a blade rather than rotten fangs, but he suspected that if his little plan failed, death would be swift regardless. This way, even if he managed only to slow the beast, there was a chance ay'ahSel and Orsik would make it.

Dropping his shielding arm, Declan rapped his knuckles once against the side of the elf's helmet. She turned to look up at him, eyes calm again despite the horror they both knew was roaring up at their backs.

The commander, like him, had made her peace.

As quickly as Declan could manage while still making sure he got it right, he signed out a single phrase.

Go. No stop. Go.

And then, before the elf had so much as a moment to stop him, Declan let go of Orsik's harness, ducked, and rolled off the back of the warg with his arms wrapped tight around his head.

He thought he heard ay'ahSel yell something over the thunderous shaking of the earth, but he didn't have the time to spare her a thought as he hit the ground in a painful tumble. Had the tunnel been smooth, he might have gotten away without a scratch, but between the ruin the creature's passage had left and the presently-falling rubble, Declan had to grit his teeth against the uneven impact of stone and ice across every inch of his body as he half-rolled, half-slid to stop in the middle of the rumbling mess. Need and adrenaline fueled his desperation, though, and so he barely felt the throbbing ache of numerous cuts and a few bruised ribs as he shoved himself to his feet, whirling to face south, back down the tunnel. He could taste blood from where he'd bitten the inside of his cheek on impact, and could feel more trickling down one side of his face, plastering his long hair against the skin. None of it mattered. He didn't have time for it to matter. He had one chance, one *slim* chance, and knew he needed to take it now or lose it.

Drawing a single, steadying breath as more rock and ice fell to the earth all around him, Declan did what he could to calm his mind.

Then, with a cry, he flung his hands forward and willed out whatever flame it was that had lain too long dormant within him.

Declan did the opposite of focus in that moment, did the opposite of everything Bonner had ever taught him. He knew the cost—or suspected it, at least—but he didn't—*couldn't*—care. What he needed was not the surgical precision of the mage's casting, the meticulous care and direction the old man sought to teach him. It was not the even, measured drawing of his magic, the careful weaving of power into a spell as intricate as it was potent. No. Declan needed none of that.

What he needed, rather, was hell on earth.

WHOOM!

It was in the seconds that followed that, for the first time, Declan truly thought he gained a breath of insight into his own potential. Bonner had been saying it for months now, as had Ryn, but their compliments and kind words had always struck Declan as a means by which to encourage him, to keep him driving forward. He had thought their excitement exaggerated, or at least exacerbated by the fact that it had been near seven hundred years since either of them had seen much of anyone capable of wielding magic aside from themselves. For a single frightening heartbeat, the power Declan called on seemed to hesitate, as though surprised to find itself drawn without inhibition, without caution. It rose steadily, welling inside him, like it was testing the limits of its sudden lack of confinement.

And then it erupted into being with a concussive blast.

It wasn't fire that Declan called on. No flame or light. Instead, what he focused on was the more basic element of pyromancy, applying all of his will into the principle weave of *heat*. Instantly the air before and around him began to boil, rising in temperature so abruptly that the chunks of ice scattered about Declan vaporized in a blink and the debris falling down upon him was thrown aside by the rush of rising pressure. Even then, though, he didn't stop, knowing this was far, *far* from what he needed to draw out of himself. Instead, Declan dug deeper, pulling on the power of Ryn's gifts, wrenching at it with his mind in a desperate bid to call on more, *more.*

Heeding his command, the temperature began to rise steadily further.

It was dizzying to experience, not to mention painful. Declan did his best not to breathe, but when he had to, it felt like his chest would burst into flame. All the same, though, he suspected this was a fate far better than any other would have suffered in his position, because as he watched, the trembling rubble along the ground about him began to shift in color, going from the dark wash of subterranean rock to the dim glow of heated stone.

More! More!

Unheard by him, a growling bellow rose from Declan's scorched lungs, his still-raised arms trembling as he pressed the power he hadn't even known was there a month past. Bonner would have been horrified, he knew, would have been screaming at him to stop, to end his foolishness. Declan had no choice though, and it was with the desperation of a man whose life hung in the balance that he pushed harder. He didn't know if it would work, couldn't know. The only truth he was sure of was that if he didn't try, they would all three of them die. They couldn't outrun what was coming. They would be caught. So he had to try.

Either by the Mother's grace or some other fortune of the world, though, Declan was rewarded as he continued to strain.

First it was the smaller stones that changed. They heated the fastest, their lesser mass giving way to the magic most quickly. Then the larger rocks started to smolder, brightening steadily to a dim orange, then a hot red, then a blazing white.

Thirty seconds of agony later, it was the shaking ground itself that started to glow.

It was as soon as he noticed this that Declan made the only change to the primitive design of his weave of heat. With a focused thought challenged by the searing air that boiled all around him, he told the magic to move.

Forward, he begged of it simply, needing nothing else. *Forward.*

And, to his surprise, the weave began to shift.

Declan's whole body trembled as the magic condensed, the heat shifting from all around him to narrow steadily inward. Second by second Declan forced it to obey, forced the raging power to bend to his command. Second by second it closed in, drawing forward like he'd told it to. As it did, the scene around him reacted. To his back and sides the stones began to darken once again, their surfaces cooling as the heat drew away from them. From above, the rubble began to rain down again, and Declan could only pray he wouldn't be crushed by some falling boulder as sizable chunks of rock started rolling and sliding down the walls on either side of him.

Before him, though, the world caught fire.

In the condensed focus of the weave, the stone began to heat faster. As the earth shook and jumped beneath Declan's feet, the space in a wide cone before him started to burn in truth, growing incandescent as flames began to flick upwards, consuming the "gases" in the air that Bonner had taught him fed natural flame. The temperature was practically unbearable, and Declan could only think the one reason his skin and clothes hadn't caught fire were the protections lent to him by his King's blood.

He was convinced of it a moment later when, with a *crunch* of sound, part of the ground nearby collapsed into itself.

The portion of the tunnel in question only gave as a boulder the size of Declan's body fell from the ceiling to strike the glowing earth with terrible force. Just the same, it was what he had been hoping for. Bonner had taught him that *all* solid things, without exception, could melt if applied with enough heat. He'd never given it much thought, of course—just as many of the mage's lessons slipped his mind after he'd proven he'd learned them—but he would have to thank the old man for this tidbit of knowledge if he survived long enough to see his friends again. As he watched, in fact, the stone before him began to crack, then fall into itself.

And then, just as Declan's vision started to swim from more than the heat, the mountain began to boil.

In slow, lolling bubbles, the ground in front of him fell inward, sloughing off of itself in a steadily expanding triangle. It dropped in layers, slabs and chunks and fractures of rock slipping into a shifting, rumbling pool of red and black that splashed up droplets of brilliant orange as more debris fell into it from the ceiling, feeding the molten stone.

Watching his desperate plan come to fruition, Declan fought harder than ever against the heat that was threatening to bring him to his knees.

More! he demanded of the power again, feeling the hairs on his scarred knuckles—closest to the boiling pool—finally start to shrivel and burn. *MORE!*

Ten feet. Twenty feet. Fifty. As he urged his power outward, as he let it erupt untethered into the air and earth, Declan watched the stone collapse and melt into the ever-broadening cone. As the wedge of melting tunnel reached some hundred feet, though, he felt his mind scrape against emptiness, felt his power beginning to slip. In a panic Declan drew it back ever so slightly, unable to stop his vision from darkening at the edges as he found this limit.

No. *No.* He couldn't pass out now. Not now. He had to hold the weave, had to keep up this single line of defense he could provide them. If he failed, if he fell…

He *had* to hold.

Gritting his teeth so hard it hurt, Declan fought back, struggling more mightily than he'd ever done in all his life to keep a firm grasp of the massive spell. His arms screamed in agony, his fingers feeling like they were breaking as every muscle in his body tensed against the onslaught of the magic's demand. For a while more, as the shaking beneath his feet and the rumbling collapse of the tunnel around him reached a new extreme, Declan held. He forgot to breath, forgot to think, but he held.

Right up until the black at the corner of his vision began to close in.

"No!" he rasped out loud, not even feeling the heat against his lungs now. "NO!"

It was no use, though. The toll had come, the cost of allowing his power free reign. As though from a distant place Declan saw his hands stop their shaking, then saw his arms fall in unison. He witnessed himself blink, finding himself falling sidelong, one moment standing upright, the next hitting the broiling stone with a *crunch.* Hell continued to boil before him, and the world didn't end its collapse. Stone and rock thundered to the ground all around him, sometimes slamming down feet away, sometime splashing into the molten pool of rock. Through the haze and heat and deadly rain Declan thought he saw a shadow, a massive, all-consuming shape hurtling out of the black at the far end of the tunnel.

Then, though, he was falling away, dropping down into nothingness, chased by the sound of a resounding *splash* and an un-earthly scream that made the air itself shiver and quake.

CHAPTER ELEVEN

I imagine that was when the tables turned. We suffered loss, after that—terrible loss, even—but in retrospect I think that was when the battles that were still yet to come became ones we could win, rather than merely ones we would only struggle mightily not to lose. Once Declan discovered that strength, discovered the true potency of his gift, there was no reeling him back. His growth—after Ryndean found him crawling out of those mountains with Lysiat and Orsik—was so extreme that I did my best to keep my mouth shut whenever mention of Amherst al'Dyor was ever brought up again. Privately, after all, I no longer compared Declan's potential to that of his forefather.

Privately, I expected much, much more of him…

—PRIVATE JOURNALS OF BONNER YR'ESSEL

AAH!"

For the first time in half a millennia, the Endless Queen moved in truth from her throne of black stone, wrenching upward to stagger to her feet, uncaring of the flaking skin and tearing, desiccated flesh of her body. It was an involuntary act, an instinct of survival that even nearing seven hundred years of near-total solitude could not drive from the mind. While there had been some satisfaction in witnessing the end of much of the group's *er'endehn* escorts under the terrifying rush of the beast who had played host to her spirit, the escape of the one of King's blood *yet again* irked her. Though the unnamed creature had no eyes by which to see, she'd weaved sight into her spell of hosting after that failure. She had wanted to watch, wanted to *see* the end of Amherst's line with her own two eyes.

Instead, she'd found herself hurtling out of the black into a hellish world of fire and melting stone.

She'd severed the link, but not before witnessing the disaster of the trap. She could still feel the cruel gnawing of heat that had started to tear into her host as it had careened into the inferno, could feel the sensation of the ground—made fragile by the magics that had woven the flames—collapsing under the tremendous bulk of the creature. The pool had not been deep—maybe five or six feet at most—but it had been long and broad enough to cover the majority of the base of the tunnel. Together host and possessor had hurtled into the magma, moving at a speed far too quick to even think to slow down, and together they had sunk into it. The beast's soft flesh, absent bones or any kind of armor, had begun to be devoured at once, and nearly as swiftly as they had thundered down the passage, they had splashed to a massive halt.

That was when the molten stone had begun to rip at them in truth, and when the Queen had severed ties with the beast even as its time-torn skin erupted into flame and its rotten organs began to boil.

Staggering as she found herself on her feet for the first time in some five hundred years, the Queen clutched with bony hands at the threadbare remains of what had once been her proud, regal vestments, clawing at the place beneath which her heart had once beaten. There was nothing now, of course. There had been nothing for almost as long as she'd been beneath these mountains. Just the same, though, it felt the natural thing to do, scraping at her bony chest as the lingering sensation of heat and pain bit at her.

Pain… It had been so, *so* long since she had felt *pain*…

For a moment, something tapped at the Endless Queen's mind, an odd sort of relief, like the knowledge that she could still feel—even if only through the senses of another—might mean she was not as far gone from her old self as she sometimes feared.

Then, though, the relief was gone, replaced by nothing but bitter, boiling anger.

That magic… That power… The ability to render the world into fire and ash. That was not the strength of man. When Amherst's whelp had entered the borders of her mountains, he had been nothing but an empty shell, a vessel in which burned the potential for so much more. It had made her ache to claim his corpse for her own use, she recalled, though she'd known better than to try.

But *this* power? *This* strength?

That empty shell, if only for a brief time, had somehow filled itself with nothing less than a dragon's fire.

A sound, low and keening, built up in the Endless Queen's throat then. It rose, then peaked, until a scream of fury echoed through the darkness of the chamber. In that lack of light it would have been impossible to see the tendrils of black that rose briefly to ripple and dance out of the Queen's bone-thin limbs and shoulders, but even the blind would have heard the sharp *crack* of breaking stone as her power leaked out ever so slightly, just enough to permeate the solid bedrock beneath her bare, skeletal feet.

Permeate it, and shatter it like it was nothing more than brittle glass.

"Run, little man," she croaked into the emptiness, her voice dry as bleached bone, holding in her mind's eye the image of the figure collapsed at the far end of the fiery trap that had claimed the most terrible of her subjects. "I have greater plans for where you're going anyway…"

CHAPTER TWELVE

"Call my beast a wolf again, sir, and I'll be feeding you my fist in short order. Warg are noble creatures with—I daresay—more brains about them than ten of you might have combined.

Wolves, on the other hand, are nasty beasts I'd not be upset to see rid from this world..."

—Declan Idrys, correcting a overly-brave noble, c. 1080p.f.

...*Eht! ... Ve....! ....eht!"*

The voice, a woman's voice, came to Declan as though calling to him through deep, dark water. He was floating, he thought, limp and unburdened. He was cold, but that was nothing new. He had been cold for a long time.

Wait... Had he, though? Actually, Declan thought it had been some time since he'd been cold. The firestone he kept ever on his person had almost always been enough to see him warm.

So then why did he feel like he had been cold for so long...?

"Ve...! ...eht! ... Veht!"

There was the voice again, closer now, and Declan frowned. As he did, he realized suddenly that his eyes were closed. Why was that? Had he been sleeping? Was he *still* sleeping?

And why was he so *cold*?

"*VEHT!*"

ay'ahSel's shout, almost furious in its need, tore through the haze and confusion, and Declan came to in a rush. He was upside down, he realized, and it took several blinks for him to understand that he was hanging—much like the elf had for some time—slung over Orsik's back. The world was strange around him, too, and the first thing Declan registered as he jerked and lifted his head was that he was, indeed, cold.

Incredibly cold.

"What the—?" he started to curse, lifting his head in an attempt to get his bearings.

Immediately, he froze.

It was the light that hit him first. Dim and grey as it was, it was foreign in the instant it took Declan to register what it was. It filtered down through a scattered ceiling of shifting black, green, and white, and it was another second before he could grasp that what he was looking up at were *branches*, a heavy canopy of snow-laden limbs that bowed and rose in a wind he couldn't feel.

Trees? Declan only had time to think, astonished and uncomprehending.

And then, from his left, there came a rumbling snarl, and instinct took over.

Declan shoved himself up and away just as something large and pale lunged into view, only barely missing having his face ripped off by whatever the thing was as yellowish teeth snapped at his head. He slid back off Orsik's back even as the warg twisted sharply under him, the result being Declan half-falling, half-flying off the animal, and it was only some ten years of riding and fighting that kept him from breaking a leg. He tucked as he landed, tumbling and rolling through what felt like loose snow to come up on his knees. Sure enough, as he struggled to get his bearings, Declan found himself kneeling in a half-foot of fresh powder.

That, though, was the least of his astonishments.

He was, he thought, in the outskirts of some dense forest. All around him titanic examples of various evergreens rose like giants over his head, their broad trunks—the narrowest as wide as Declan was tall—crowding in on him. The snow he'd landed in was nothing but a narrow trail of the stuff that had snuck its way through the broader branches of the two nearest trees, trailing the dim light that had so shocked him. They were outside, he knew. They were free of the tunnels, free of the mountains and the stone's oppressive weight.

And yet, as it transpired, hardly any further from danger.

Before him, spinning and snapping, Orsik had ripped a narrow circle of dirty snow, earth, and pine needles into the forest floor from all his turning and clawing. Atop him, ay'ahSel seemed to be doing all she could to hold onto the beast with one hand, the other wielding one of her glassy swords high. Her head, however, was still bandaged beneath her helmet, and she looked like she was having trouble managing to do both things at once, her weapon never descending despite the shapes that had crowded in around the two of them.

Wolves, Declan realized with a thrill, and the last of his confusion was cast aside in favor of a sudden need to act.

The wolves of Eserysh—for Declan couldn't imagine they had reached any other open skies than those of the lands beyond the Mother's Tears—looked to be larger than their Viridian cousins. While the beasts he had known and seen growing up had typically been some combination of mottled grey or black and might have reached his thigh at the shoulders, the examples skulking before him now were white—as white as the snow settling all about him—and stood nearly to his hip. Declan would have been terrified—*should* have been terrified—especially as several of the closest creatures turned, hungry eyes on him, attention drawn to the fallen of their prey.

But wolves—from no matter what kingdom, it turned out—*all* feared fire.

Whoosh!

The flames came alive the moment Declan's fingers touched the firestone still mercifully tucked in his breast pocket, engulfing the skin of his left hand. With his right he reached for his hip as he made to stand, but discovered two unfortunate facts in the same moment. The first: the sword he had expected to be there was gone, and as he squinted beyond the sudden light of the fire he saw it hanging from ay'ahSel other hip.

The second: though he'd managed to get one foot out from under him, that was the extent his legs seemed willing to take his weight.

Fortunately for him, ay'ahSel, and Orsik, magic wasn't so limited by weak knees as swordplay might have been.

Or by lack of a *sword*, for that matter...

"HAA!" Declan howled even as he tugged the firestone free and palmed it, slashing the hand horizontally before him. His shout was more to draw the animals' collective attention than it was an attempt to intimidate them, trusting instead in the spell to do that. He kept the power tethered this time, channeled through the firestone, and the weave manifested as he'd hoped. A geyser of liquid flame erupted from his closed fist, spewing the air and ground in a seven-foot half-circle before him. One unfortunate beast who had just started creeping towards him caught a face-full of the flames, and its screams as it reeled back seemed to have every one of its pack mates taking pause. Leaping on the advantage, Declan focused the magics on the dying animal so that the thrashing form of the wolf was soon consumed in a raging pool of fire. Its screams keened off as the heat ended its suffering in a few quick seconds.

It was the example he had needed to make.

With a mix of yelps, yowls, and growling barks, the rest of the pack turned tail and fled. Even those furthest from Declan on Orsik's other side vanished into the trees in retreat, none keen to face the flames. Declan watched them go from his knees, holding onto the fire that flickered and burned across the forest floor. He could hardly blame them, of course. The flames took to the relatively dry layer of pine needles and long-dead branches eagerly, spreading quickly as—

"Oh shit!" Declan cursed, realizing his mistake and dropping down to plunge both hands into the fire, heedless of the uncomfortable twinge of their heat. It took a moment of scrambled focus to recall Bonner's lessons, but he had a grasp of the weave soon enough, threading his own spellwork into the natural flames it had produced. With a force of thought he drew the magic back, snuffing the life from it as he did.

Within a few seconds, nothing of the fight he had awoken to remained but a patch of charred earth and the single, smoldering corpse of the wolf he'd felled.

"Bloody hell..." Declan groaned once it was done, shoving himself back up onto his knees again, his mind continuing to reel from its abrupt awakening. Smoke hung in the air, making everything taste of burnt wood and soot, but through the haze he made out ay'ahSel dismounting Orsik with a *crunch* of frozen ground. Funny enough, the elf gave the warg an almost fond pat before moving towards Declan, walking a little unsteadily with her sword still in hand.

However long he'd been out for, it looked like the commander was still a ways from recovering from her head wound.

At the edge of the black half-circle, ay'ahSel paused, frowning down at the charred earth. She seemed to consider the ground—even toeing at the edge of it with one booted foot—but eventually opted to go *around* the flame-scorched space.

"*Mytos...*" Declan heard her muttering, and not for the first time.

"You're going to have to get used to magic at *some* point, you know?" he said with a lopsided grin, still not trying to rise from his knees again. He had the impression, judging by the trembling in his feet and hips, that a second attempt would end with him facedown in the soot.

Just how long had he been unconscious for…?

If ay'ahSel understood a word of what he'd said, she certainly didn't make any such indication. On the contrary, it was towards him that she frowned at next, taking him in even as she stepped around the curve of the burned space. As she came to stand beside him, she raised her free hand.

You. Body. Good?

It took Declan longer than he would have expected to parse out the meaning of the gestures, and the irony of his head swimming as he answered was not lost to him.

"How do I feel?" he muttered, considering before answering with his own simple gesture.

Bad.

To his surprise, ay'ahSel nodded at this like she expected it, responding as she did. The sign for sleep, then a new one he didn't know. A pointed finger trailed across the sky, from horizon to horizon, east to west—or what he thought was likely east to west as best as he could tell. This was followed by a pair of fingers held up.

"Sleep? Two?" Declan muttered, not understanding. "Two what? You know, if we're going to have this conversation, you could at least help me stand. My legs feel like they're—"

And then, as he was pondering the odd weakness of his limbs, it hit him.

"*Two days*?!" he demanded, gaping first at ay'ahSel, then at Orsik, as though the warg—who had come trotting up to sniff at the edge of the charred ground—could confirm the story. "I've been asleep for *two days*?!"

The commander appeared to glean enough of his outburst to understand, because she nodded once, repeating the sign. This time, Declan was sure of it.

You. Sleep. Two days, ay'ahSel said.

Declan couldn't believe it. How was that possible? And if he'd been asleep for two days…?

"What happened?" he asked quietly, looking to the elf again.

At her, and beyond her.

Free. They were free. Above the commander—high, high above her—Declan saw that the sky was less grey and more blanketed by a dense wash of rolling clouds. Sunlight barely peeked out now and again, sneaking between the branches of the woods to set the snow alight in flashes of white and shadow. Nothing but the wind made a sound, but the winter stillness was broken up now and again as dark birds—crows, maybe—flit from tree to tree. Though they weren't far into the forest—judging by the denser darkness that looked to come together through the trunks north of them—Declan couldn't make out hint or hide of the Mother's Tears, which means they had to be some distance from the ranges at least.

Two days? Two days, he had been unconscious? And ended up here? What had happened?!

There was one question, at the very least, that Declan thought he could answer for himself:

Where it was they were.

"The Vyr'esh."

He hadn't meant to half-whisper the name, but as he knelt there among the trees—the towering figures looming over him—he couldn't help but be reminded of the times he had skirted the border of the sister forest of these very woods far, far to the south. Though the *er'enthyl* and their red bear patrols would never have let any man get more than a dozen paces into the Vyr'en without putting an arrow through their eye, one could still stand at the edge of the stone-marked boundary and peer into its midst. It was a more-vibrant forest than this one—more colorful and alive—but the two still shared a similar feel, an aura that was like a weight on Declan's shoulders as he found himself kneeling there among the pines, already well into the embrace of the woods.

Wonder, power, and a sense that time did not exist in this place in the same way it did other parts of the world…

"*Saev Vyr'esh, veht*?" ay'ahSel asked of Declan, sounding the faintest bit surprised. The question shook him from his momentary reverie, if only because he'd actually understood it.

You know the Vyr'esh, human?

Declan nodded slowly, still not taking his eyes from the trees, but now was not the time to struggle with explaining the minor detail that Bonner and Ryn had told him of the place. More pressing was Declan's need to know what had happened.

Finally pulling his eyes from the awesome presence of the trees, Declan dropped roughly down to sit, his legs shaking even as he struggled to cross them. With the firestone still in hand, he ignored the bite of snow and the potential soaking of his cloak and clothes, knowing he could dry himself later, and instead drew a finger through the ash nearby, carving a shape into it.

He was pretty sure, after all, that his meager grasp of the soldier's signage would hardly be enough to convey the story he wanted to know.

The simple shape of a mountain—with an arched hole at its base to indicate a tunnel—was where he started, making sure ay'ahSel was paying attention as he first pointed at it, then gestured to the woods around them in unstaged bewilderment. The commander must have been steadily regaining her wits, because she caught onto the question almost at once. Dropping to one knee, she tugged off a glove—one of Ester's she must have pilfered from their packs—and began tracing her own shapes. She had a quick, delicate hand—another hopeful sign of her recovery?—and between her drawing and a few gestures here and there, Declan began to understand.

Over the course of the several minutes that followed, the story came together for him, forming half there in the snow and ash, half in his mind's eye.

The creature that had been chasing them—the "tunneler", as he'd called it—had been a *worm*, though hardly any sort of worm he'd ever known. It had been a thing of tremendous size, its body long and rippled with what he had to imagine had been undulating flesh, and he hadn't been mistaken in remembering the circular rows of rotting teeth that had formed its maw. After the passage had ceased shaking, the commander had turned Orsik around at once, returning to the place where Declan had thrown himself off the warg. With her own eyes, she had taken in the creature, at least briefly, watching it sink into the molten rock even as the trap had started to cool and harden around its body. Declan, too, she had seen, lying prone not twenty feet from its still-twitching fangs, but the lingering heat of whatever magic he had woven had been so harsh that she and Orsik hadn't been able to get more than close enough to barely take him out through the rubble.

It was for the better, too, because if they'd been any nearer she didn't know if the pair of them would have survived the dark flames when they'd come.

Declan was tempted, then, to hold the woman up, to ask for more detail, but he restrained himself as she sketched out fire consuming the tunnel, enveloping everything as she signed the word "black" over and over again. He knew what it meant, of course, knew what that fire represented. He'd seen it twice before already, once during a ghoul attack before he'd known of the terrifying world of magic and the undead, then again when Sehranya had set nearly a score of wights to ambush him and his friends. Black flames meant the destruction of a Purpose, the fracturing of the cruel magics that gave the dead life once more, providing them with a meaning for which to linger on the wrong side of the veil.

However it might have seemed in the moment, the worm had

likely not been a living thing for some time…

After the flames had finally died away, the gargantuan creature—unsurprisingly—had vanished, all trace of it gone save for the scorched marks on the stone and rubble that Declan's own magic hadn't already charred. Unfortunately, it had been nearly a half hour or so more before the same could be said for the heat, at which point ay'ahSel and Orsik had *finally* managed to reach him without their hair and skin catching alight. If it was odd to the elf that Declan himself had been untouched by the black fire—a fact he hadn't missed—it clearly wasn't as much a concern as the fact that lugging him up and onto Orsik's back had been tedious and taxing on her body and head. With deliberate, almost-annoyed gestures, ay'ahSel made it clear just how hard she'd had to work to get him away from that flame-torn place, and Declan had to hide a grin.

It hadn't been long after that, at last, that they'd indeed found the exit from the mountains, and Declan could almost feel the freshness of the chill air on his own face as ay'ahSel's stoic expression shifted—if only for a blink—to one of relief as her retelling arrived at their escape. She painted for him ever so briefly a scene of their exiting from the mountains not far from the base of the slopes, barely above the tree line of the forest that seemed to hug the very foot of the crags themselves. Declan almost regretted not having seen the sight for himself—the sprawl of the Vyr'esh that must have extended as an endless blanket of black, green, and white from the base of the Tears—but ay'ahSel moved on too quickly as the tale turned frightening.

Two days. Two days they had spent traveling west along the edge of the woods, she injured, he unconscious. Orsik was the one who had seen them fed, and Declan thought he could understand the abrupt affection ay'ahSel seemed to have for the beast as she recounted the warg's delving into the trees every night to drag back deer or elk or some other downed prey. She'd built fires for them, as well as pilfered what clothes she could from the traveling packs, but that had meant barely any sleep for her as she'd kept them all from freezing to death. Eventually the elements had gotten so bad that ay'ahSel had made the decision to trek deeper into the forest, a choice she was clear had not been made lightly.

It seemed, unlike the home of the wood elves, that the Vyr'esh was not a place even the likes of the *er'endehn* could tread freely.

And for good reason, Declan concluded as ay'ahSel drew her finger from the soot and leaned back on her heels, indicating that her retelling was at an end with a wave of one hand about them to show that he knew the rest of the tale. As formidable as the commander was, it was hard to imagine a lone dark elf of any level of prowess managing to stand for long against a pack of wolves the size Declan had witnessed. It was doubtful, too, that such beasts were the only danger among the trees, especially if the woods got as dense and dark as he suspected. Peering beyond the elf, north of her, Declan shivered a little, taking in the black with a new respect and healthy apprehension.

Then he shivered again, and realized abruptly that—while the drawing of the flames to chase off the wolves had warmed him temporarily—he was once more so, *so* cold.

The firestone still in his hand, Declan summoned the now-familiar weave of warmth about himself with ease, feeling the pleasant heat of the magic settle into his clothes and over his skin. He barely contained a sigh of relief as the chill vanished at once, pleased, too, that the wind high above them seemed largely blocked by the denseness of the trees. At once the cold fled, his trembling subsiding, and he looked to ay'ahSel again with the intent of figuring out how to ask her what the plan was.

He *just* caught the look in her eye before the elf managed to quell it, a curiosity that was equally mixed with both doubt and envy.

It had him studying her more closely, and Declan indeed saw at once that—beneath her armor—at least one layer of Ester's extra shirts had been pulled on, as well as pants. Despite the added insulation, though, the dark elf was trembling ever so slightly. The base camp—the outpost they'd all been heading to together when the tunneler had caught them the first time—must have been close to the foot of the mountain, because ay'ahSel didn't remotely look like she'd dressed for a long trek through winter woodlands. It explained why they were holding to the southern lip of the forest as they moved west.

And made Declan curse himself as a selfish fool for not realizing sooner he wasn't the only one who would have suffered the cold these last two days.

With a press of his thoughts the warmth extended. Declan managed, to his surprise, to warp the shape of the weave a bit more easily than he was used to, conserving his energy by focusing the spell on enveloping ay'ahSel deliberately, rather than merely bubbling outward in all directions. He wasn't surprised when the *er'endehn* flinched and leapt to her feet the moment the magic touch her, but he ignored the alarm in her wide eyes and continued until the elf was well in the weave's embrace. The commander, for her part, stood stock-still in the snow, rigid as a board until she seemed to sense the spell was finished with its shifting.

Then, at last, she relaxed with a sigh, grumbling under her breath about "magic" again but not stepping away from Declan, like she feared she might move out of the warmth.

Which she would have, Declan knew, not for the first time understanding a little more why Bonner had pressed him so hard on mastering the basics of pyromancy as they'd trekked to, up, and then through the Tears.

There was a snort, and Declan looked forward again to find Orsik approaching him at a trot, nose sniffing at the air. As soon as his snout hit the bubble of magic the warg's ears perked up, and a sound more like the purr of an oversized cat rumbled from the animal's throat as he immediately circled Declan to press in around him.

"You too, huh, boy?" Declan answered the warg's enthusiasm with a laugh, immediately taking advantage of the proximity to grab hold of a harness strap with his free hand and start to haul himself up off his knees at last. As he did, ay'ahSel seemed to remember herself, because she at once slid her sword back into its scabbard as she stepped forward to take him under the arm and assist. Between the pair of them Declan found himself finally on his feet, and he breathed his thanks to the woman with a nod even as he expanded the warmth of the bubble once again, making sure to envelope Orsik now.

"What now?" he asked of the woman, pocketing the firestone to sign.

Direction?

Waiting a moment to make sure he could stand on his own before letting him go, ay'ahSel answered with a simple raised finger.

"West," Declan voiced for her, following the gesture. "Still west. All right."

He nodded his understanding, which the elf returned. Then—with the barest uncertain flick of her eyes to the breast pocket his firestone was now stowed in—she stepped by him and took hold of Orsik's straps herself. Though she didn't manage to hide the grunt of effort it took, ay'ahSel was atop the animal in short order, mounting him with a return of much of the grace that had been stolen in the days immediately following her injury. Once she was settled, she twisted in her seat and—without so much as a pause—offered her hand to help Declan up.

He almost smiled as he accepted it, half-climbing, half letting himself be hauled up to settle in behind the woman. With a tug of the straps, ay'ahSel had Orsik turning about, and then they were loping off through the trees, Declan's thoughts for once free to linger on something more than escaping the bowels of the earth. For the first time in what felt like years, he could ponder other, less pressing things.

Like whether or not it was possible to become friends with someone you could barely speak with.

CHAPTER THIRTEEN

"LEFT!" Declan bellowed, the elvish word rough on his tongue. A few paces in front of him, ay'ahSel snapped about at once, her black blade flashing in a clean, high arc through the air even as she did. The fox-headed creature that had slunk its way around to her flank didn't even have time to completely get its crude club up for a downswing when the sword severed both its arms above the elbow.

The limbs and weapon fell to the forest floor in three separate *thuds,* blood leaking into the scattered white of the snow as their prior owner staggered away from the elf with a screech.

It turned out that Declan had been more than a little right about wolves likely being the least of their worries in the Vyr'esh. In the two days since he'd woken up—their fourth free of the caverns of the Tears—they'd been accosted no less than seven times altogether by animals and beast alike, all of whom had made it obvious the potential meat of a man, elf, and warg had outweighed any potential risk to their persons. The wolves *had* been the most frequent—though Declan thought the three assaults came from different packs each time, which was frightening in its own fact—but a pair of bears had also ambushed them as they'd camped along a frozen stream one night, as had a single massive, feline creature that he might have called a cougar were it not for the fact that the animal had been half again as wide as any mountain cat he'd had the misfortune of stumbling upon.

In the end, however, all of those animals had either been felled by his and ay'ahSel's blades—she'd lent him her second sword again once he'd proven himself capable of using it aptly—savaged by Declan's pyromancy, or fled from the light and heat cast by the fire.

The biggest trouble, at the end of the day, was the one enemy who did not so readily fear the flames.

The wereyn.

"BEHIND!"

ay'ahSel's shout had Declan whirling in time to catch a left-come swing at his ribs, the crude club of wood and bone *thudding* awkwardly into the ever-keen blade of his borrowed sword. Unperturbed by the entanglement, Declan bent back and snapped a kick upwards, catching the short beast—who looked to be more boar than man—squarely in the neck. The very subtle tingling in Declan's leg jolted slightly with the impact, and the wereyn's hoglike squeal was cut off as his foot crushed its throat. Before it could stagger far, though, letting go of the stuck club to clutch at it neck, Declan's left hand slashed in its direction.

The poor thing couldn't even scream in pain as the liquid fire that sprayed across its face and torso ripped into it, burning skin and cracking the shallow surface of its skull as it boiled everything inside in an instant.

The fight, though, was hardly done.

Quickly Declan kicked the club free of his blade, then spun again as a roar and several heavy footsteps told him his next opponent was fast on approach. The sword came up with him, but he ended up cursing and diving out of the way as a massive specimen of the monstrous race drove by him with its stag's head bowed low. Its deliberately broken antlers, dirty and sharpened to deadly points, missed him by inches, and Declan rolled to his feet at the ready, gathering a weave of force and heat in preparation of meeting a second charge.

Instead, there was another roar—far louder this time—and before the wereyn could even straighten fully to start to turn it went down under a ripping mass of grey-white fur and yellowish teeth.

"Good boy," Declan snorted, turning from Orsik's savaging of the screaming thing to face the greater fight.

Though ay'ahSel was still less than the spirit of graceful destruction he'd known when she and her unit had first come pouring out of the shadows beneath the earth, more than enough of her strength and guile had returned to make her a terror to behold. Even with one sword absent from her ordinary pair the elf had carved a ring of bloody annihilation into the group that had assaulted them, and was in the process of extending that circle further. No less than six of the beastmen's bodies lay already dead at her feet, and a seventh dropped—absent the better part of its head—even as Declan watched in fascination. His mere three—and a *half* he supposed, if he counted himself a strategic distraction for Orsik's last kill—felt suddenly wanting, but he wasn't about to kick himself just yet.

Every time he saw ay'ahSel fight, he became more and more sure of the fact that trying to keep up with her would have been not unlike trying to outrace a charger.

"Urk!"

Abruptly Declan's right knee partially buckled under him, and he grunted and cursed, staggering sideways a step. His distraction had cost him his focus, and the faint weave he'd spun into his limbs—already fragile—had failed. Grimacing, Declan clenched the firestone in his left hand in concentration, willing the magic back into his body. It took a moment to find the balance again, to find the delicate push and pull of the magics that he'd discovered worked best, but he'd managed it, and the minute tingling returned to his arms and legs as he stood up straight again.

With another grunt, he looked around, found a pair of arriving wereyn slinking out of the trees to his left, and charged them with newfound strength.

It had been the lingering weakness after his two days unconscious that had provided the inadvertent key to the secret of the weaves of imbuement. Whether it was the time spent unmoving and not eating, or some effect of the magical exhaustion that had been its cause, his fortitude had not returned remotely as quickly as he was accustomed. He'd suffered bed rest before, as well as some extent of the fatigue that he'd infrequently witnessed both Ryn and Bonner plagued by after they expelled too much magic in any short time, but *this* weakness had proven an altogether different beast. It clung to him, hanging across his shoulders and weighing him down even these two days later. It had been almost crippling from the morning he'd woken up, and when he'd failed to feel any better by the time they'd made camp for his first night awake—warm for once in the narrow circle of channeling runes he'd burned into the hard ground for them—a thought had struck Declan. Before, beneath the mountains, he had been trying to repeat the instance of power he'd experienced oh-so-briefly when saving ay'ahSel from the tunneler. It had been an explosion of strength borne of desperation, of the need he'd had to see them both free and clear of the rotten maw of the undead creature, and it had proven impossible to replicate. All he'd managed was the bare empowering of one hand, and then only for a brief few seconds.

But maybe—instead of continuing to chase that burst of magic—he could seek to attain a lesser measure of the spell, some weaker, subtler form of the weave...

Like, say... just enough to grant his arms and legs their usual strength.

This revelation had preceded a sleepless night of testing and experimenting, but Declan had just spent the last two days unconscious. A little missed sleep wasn't about to wear at him. What was more, his trialing had started to bear fruit almost at once, the moment he turned his attention from that shock of power to a gentler, steadier weave. With a decrease in the amount of strength he was attempting to bind into his limbs, the magics were less complicated, less volatile, and by the time morning had come Declan's ability to maintain this lesser spell of imbuement had extended from that short time in a single hand to several minutes in both arms.

By the time the following day had ended—with plenty of empty hours to practice as he and ay'ahSel had ridden Orsik ever-westward through the trees—his legs had followed suite, until Declan could at least weave himself into fighting form whenever an attack came.

He reached the two wereyn at a full run, catching them unawares with a blast of heated energy. The first of the beasts caught the magic full in the side, the hair along its arm, thigh, and half its face smoldering at once even as it was launched laterally to tumble in a ragged pile to the ground. The second Declan engaged with his blade, frowning at the mannish face that bared mismatched fangs too big for its mouth at him. This wereyn wielded no weapon, but the curved claws it sported at the end of too-long fingers were plenty dangerous, and proven so when the thing slashed at him even as he closed the last few steps between them. Ducking under the blow, Declan wasted no time with theatrics, driving his black sword into the beastman's belly before sidestepping and tearing the keen blade free through its side. As it collapsed behind him, he was already moving to engage the first wereyn that had managed to climb to its feet, taking advantage of the dazed look in its eyes to relieve it first of one leg, then its head as it fell sideways with a scream.

"*ON ME*!"

The command, yelled in elvish, had Declan whirling, and with a thrill he found that ay'ahSel had—at long last—possibly found herself in a situation that was beyond her ability to handle alone. Three more of the creatures had appeared from between the trees to join the two the commander had already been tangled with, surrounding her. She was doing a fair job of keeping them at bay, whirling and kicking up snow and pine needles as she slashed at the air in front of any wereyn that dared so much as feign closer, but even she couldn't move fast enough to take on any one or two of them without opening herself up to assault from behind. Orsik, Declan noted, had vanished, likely chasing some opponent or another off into the trees, leaving him as the *er'endehn's* only backup.

Fine by me, he thought, barreling towards the group as fire led his way.

Unfortunately Declan couldn't cast his favored weave of splashing flames at the back of the closest of the wereyn—a ram-headed thing that was moving around on all fours—too worried was he that ay'ahSel might be caught in the spells arc. On the other hand, he was more confident in slashing at the beastman immediately to the left of that nearest one, a short, squat thing that might have been a naked, wild woman aside from the black and white hair that coated its back and shoulders and what might have been oversized badger's claws for hands. The cruel magics spewed from Declan's fist once more, and a scream of pain and fear told him the fires had struck true.

He didn't look to check. He was already cutting, cleaving the dark sword into the back of the ram-headed wereyn's legs, bringing it down heavily as the limbs collapsed abruptly beneath it with a shriek.

From there the fight ended in short order. ay'ahSel needed no other signal that help had arrived than the scream of the two felled beasts, and in a flash of sun and snow on glassy black a third of the group fell, then a fourth. Just in time Declan made sure his own pair were down for good, then turned with the elf on the last of the five, another fox-headed beast who held a crude spear capped with a rough stone tip in both hands. To its credit the wereyn bared its fangs defiantly as it backpedalled, threatening them with the longer weapon to keep them at bay while it tried to make its retreat. Declan, for his part, would have been happy enough to let it go, seeing no reason to risk either him or the commander getting skewered when they still didn't know how far they were from help.

But then, just as the wereyn's shoulders brushed the dark branches of a low-hung evergreen that might have been its salvation, yet another roar ripped through the forest, and Orsik's great bulk slammed into it from behind, bearing it to the ground as his massive jaws clamped about the thing's skull.

Even Declan winced when the warg strained, then ripped the fox head from the humanoid body with a sound like wet, tearing paper.

For a few seconds afterward, Declan and ay'ahSel stood still, scanning the edges of the bloodied trail the ambush had caught them on. Trusting the elf's hearing more than his—he wasn't about to make out anything over the sound of Orsik gorging himself on his last kill anyway—it was the trees Declan watched, tense and waiting. These wereyn had been of the wild kind, of the savage tribes and groups he and the others had seen some examples of when they'd been climbing the Tears weeks before. Like the first time the beastmen had ambushed him and ay'ahSel the previous day, this party had poured in as reinforcements came, not intelligent enough to form any true strategy, but in numbers that still made them dangerous as the shouts and growls and screams had summoned all near enough to hear to the fight.

Fortunately, though, after a tense half minute of nothing but the wind shifting the pines around them again, ay'ahSel relaxed at his side, and Declan, too, decided they were in the clear.

Body. Good? he signed at once after catching the commander's eye, managing the gestures even with the firestone held in his left hand.

She nodded in affirmation, then motioned the same question in return, gaze tracing him head to foot pointedly.

Good, he confirmed his own wellbeing before looking down at himself as well. His clothes—particularly his right side near where he'd torn the man-headed wereyn half-in-two—were drenched and bloody, but he didn't much care. With a little variation to his usual weave of warmth he could dry the fabric later, though both he and ay'ahSel—whose black metal-and-leather armor was similarly slick with gore—were in desperate need of fresh clothes.

After seven encounters—plus the wolves that he had woken up to—the dried blood had basically dyed everything an ugly red, and they weren't likely to escape the smell of iron without a long bath and thorough torching of their current outfits.

Apparently satisfied that he was unhurt, ay'ahSel turned and knelt at once to clean her blade on the rough fur of the closest of the bodies. Declan almost chuckled at the sparseness of their communication, but did the same with his own blade before sliding it back into its sheath at his hip. In addition to working on his weaves of strength, after the encounter with the wolves on first awakening he had made it a point to press ay'ahSel for several lessons in the language of the elves. His requests hadn't been complicated—they still got by mostly on the soldier's signals she'd continued to teach him—but hand gestures weren't much use in an active fight. He had already learned how to sign directions—such as "left" and "right" and "behind"—so it hadn't been hard to request the pronunciations of those words and a few others that would—and *had*—come in useful in the pitch of battle.

All in all, even if they still weren't any closer to finding signs of the promised base camp, it had been a productive—and *busy*—two days.

It wasn't long after that the three of them were on the move again, leaving behind the carnage as quickly as they could. They never bothered scavenging from the wereyn. The beastmen as a rule rarely carried anything of value on them, and reeked of filth and rot even when *not* dead. As a result, there was little to be gained from kicking their corpses about or collecting their weapons. Orsik was always allowed his fill as a reward for a well-fought skirmish, but in a forest as dense as the Vyr'esh, prey was hardly scarce, so the warg never took too long with his grisly meals. Neither Declan nor ay'ahSel had to say aloud that it was for the better, either, because with the predators of the forest clearly *already* too keen on the taste of man—or *elf*—flesh, lingering around fresh meat was the last thing they wanted to do.

For a little while they rode in relative silence, both of them more interested in their surroundings than anything else, concern that other enemies might be lingering in the area not easily dispelled. It was about a quarter hour—and two miles at Orsik's trotting speed—that the leftover tension in ay'ahSel's back subsided in front of Declan, and she turned in her seat to fix him with one appraising eye.

After a moment, a hand came up so he could see it,

You fight good.

Declan had to hold back a scoff, turning it into a cough that managed to breach the limits of the spell of warmth he'd once more weaved about them, misting a bit at the edges of the magic. He was surprised for one thing. The elf had hardly ever initiated conversation between them, and certainly never to *compliment* him.

"Where did that come from?" he asked of the woman, doing a poorer job of hiding a doubtful smirk as he answered with his own signs. *You fight more good. More, MORE good.*

There was doubtless a more eloquent way of saying what he meant, he was sure, but it was the best he could manage, and Declan was honestly pleased to get that much across. He was learning quickly and—though the lessons were hardly as arduous as the training he and Ester had suffered at the hands of Ryn and Bonner—the complexity of the sign language was often enough to make him miss the old mage's damn "arcanic laws" and "methodology of spellcraft."

Yes. I fight better. Much better.

Declan deduced the last signs of ay'ahSel's reply in context, and laughed dryly.

"Humble too, I see," he said as he continued in kind. *Where you learn fight?*

"Ysenden."

Declan blinked, a little surprised. The elf had answered in spoken word, but that alone wasn't all that strange. They'd been switching back and forth more and more whenever one or the other thought it was appropriate, or there was a learning opportunity. What had taken Declan aback, rather, was the tone of the elf's answer.

Proud, maybe? And… a little sad?

He frowned, but fortunately his limited language was enough to voice his curiosity aloud.

"*Ysenden bad*?"

The response was immediate and telling. ay'ahSel stiffened in her seat, and a hiss of anger escaped bared, white teeth that were suddenly visible through the open slats in her helm.

Clearly Declan's question had come close to blasphemy, if not stepped clean into it.

"Sorry, sorry," he said at once, holding up a hand in what he'd come to learn was a universal signal of apology. "Uh, so… *Ysenden not bad*?"

He'd forgotten the word for "good", but made do, and the question seemed enough to appease ay'ahSel's irritation. She nodded curtly, then looked forward again, still rigid. For a minute or so after this Declan was treated to silence, and he'd just started thinking he had accidentally ended the first real conversation the elf had ever tried to start with him when she spoke again.

"*Ysenden vy eht. Ysenden vy ul'sed.*"

He only caught one word aside from the name of the city, but it was enough to clue Declan in.

"Ysenden is beautiful," he translated for himself. "And Ysenden is… uh… *vy… ul'sed*?"

He tried to make his curiosity sound as genuine as it was, as eager to carry on the discussion as he was to learn more. He knew next to nothing of the great city-state of the *er'endehn*, of the last and only bastion to have withstood the onslaught of Sehranya's forces when she had declared herself to the world by descending upon her own people. He'd carried an image in his head since Bonner and the others had first told him of the place, but having experienced the Vyr'esh now he wasn't as certain his crafted picture of ten thousand great structures woven into and between the trees was likely to do the place justice. Ysenden had stood against the Endless Queen, and his recent experience with the dark elves of Eserysh spoke more to the ruling law of practicality and usefulness than any focus on real culture or beauty. If he'd had a thought to consider it in the last two days, he supposed he would have conjured up the image, rather, of some great black fortress rising out of the trees, a circular keep of hard, cold stone and rigid edges, unforgiving and simple in their make.

But here was ay'ahSel telling him it was beautiful…

In answer to his question, the dark elf appeared to consider how best to translate. After a moment she turned and—with an expression not without its doubt—held up thumb and forefinger barely a fraction of an inch apart.

"*Y'sed,*" she said with deliberate enunciation, then broadened the space between her finger tips to as wide as she could get them. "*N'sed.*" She lifted her other hand free of where it had been holding onto Orsik's harness for stability, apparently trusting in her balance and the warg's slow gate as she spread her arms out, palms inward and facing each other. "*Ul'sed.*"

Declan was rather pleased to have followed along, and he grinned. "Close. Far. Very far." He nodded to show his understanding.

"*Ysenden vy ul'sed.* Ysenden is very far away."

Whether she grasped that he'd comprehended or was merely gratified that he was trying, ay'ahSel did something then that he had never once witnessed before.

She smiled.

Then, as quickly as it had come, it was gone, and the elf was turning away again to look forward, taking up the straps once more.

I'm not the only one who is far from home, Declan thought suddenly, watching the black hairs of the elf's plume sway back and forth across the back of her helmet.

It struck him, then, that there was perhaps a reason his image of Ysenden was so cold and hard. In his experience the *er'endehn* had been little more than just that: icy and unbending, more interested in protocol and structure than anything else. Not once in the four days after they had left the drey behind had the dark elves interacted with any of their group but Ryn, and then only when absolutely necessary. Not once had they expressed any curiosity—much less *interest*—in their "prisoners" despite the fact that the four of them had included a human, a dragon, a mage, and a half-blooded wood elf. It had always given Declan the impression that the *er'endehn* were more automaton than living thing, like breathing puppets capable only of executing their actions in specific, inflexible sequence.

And yet now, more than a week separated from any of her kin and very possibly as far removed from anything she could call "home" as she had ever been, Lysiat ay'ahSel was starting to break from that mold little by little.

There was more, too. More that pointed to the dark elves being something greater than the emotionless black stone they might have been carved from when Declan and the others had first encountered them. There was the way they fought, for one thing, the way ay'ahSel—even injured—swept across a battlefield with all the fluid grace of wind over an open plain. There was the complexity of their language—language*s*, Declan had to correct for himself, emphasizing the plural in his head—and even the master of crafts beyond that of swinging a sword.

He'd had little light and opportunity to examine any of the *er'endehns'* armor in the tunnels, but the dim illumination of the sun through clouds had given Declan his chance over the last few days, and what he saw had amazed him. The gold-bound black of the metal-lined leather was not, as he'd thought before, without ornamentation, but was merely so subtly detailed it was next to impossible to make out the meticulous adornments that wound their way over and across the surfaces of the armor. Patterns had somehow been stained into the metal, distinct in the right light, depicting intertwined, stiff lines and knots like branches growing around, through, and into each other. The leather, too, was marked with similar symbols, but—though Declan had never braved running a finger across any portion of the armor for fear of losing his hand—he was almost certain the surfaces of the materials were unblemished, smooth and clean without additional ridges that might provide counter-productive purchase for an enemy's blade. The *sound* of the leather, too, astonished him, for no other reason than there *was* no sound, or at least hardly enough for any but the sharpest of ears to make out even in a deadly quiet room. He'd considered and cast aside the possibility of enchantment given the *er'endhens'* clear distrust of magic, and settled instead on the likelihood that every suit was custom-fit to an individual, with each inside layer of every plate and flap lined specifically for silence. Silk, likely? Or animal fur? Whatever the case, Declan knew men who would have given their left hand for armor of this quality, and the longer he spent with ay'ahSel, the closer he was to counting himself among them.

It only convinced him further that there was more to the dark elves than Ryn and Bonner had been able to tell him when they'd revealed the people's existence in the first place, and certainly more than Declan would have assumed at a glance.

Deciding he couldn't pass up the opportunity to know more, Declan brought up a hand, but hesitated. He had been intending to try to ask the commander to describe Ysenden for him, but he wasn't sure how to pose the question.

In the end, he decided to go for the long shot, sticking his hand over her shoulder to gesture as best he could.

Speak. More.

The elf looked around at him again, frowning and clearly not understanding.

"Tell me more about *Ysenden*," he told her, being careful to enunciate the name of the city as she pronounced it before repeating his gesture.

Speak. More.

The elf seemed to understand then, the eyebrow he could make out rising in surprise. She opened her mouth, looking all the world like she would have been happy to say more, but paused and frowned again, clearly considering herself how best to explain. After a few seconds she looked ready to try again, but before she could get so much as a word out they were interrupted by a voice tearing through their thoughts.

DEC… EC… LAN!

Declan started so hard he nearly sent himself sliding off of Orsik's back. In front of him ay'ahSel, too, jerked in surprise, and she twisted forward again at once, gaze snapping from tree to tree in alarm as her hand slid automatically to the handle of her sword. Beneath them, even the warg had jolted to a stop, snorting and sniffing at the air in confusion, clearly having heard the voice but not understanding it. Their reactions made sense, of course. The broken words—the scattered syllables of Declan's own name—had been soundless, coming from nowhere and everywhere. More than a week away might have shaken Orsik's familiarity with the mind magics, and Declan didn't think ay'ahSel could have heard that voice even a score of times before they'd gotten separated from the group.

They'd been deliberately practicing mind-speech privately at the time, after all.

"Ryn..." Declan hissed, not believing what he'd heard for a moment, eyes immediately lifting to the bare line of the sky they could make out through the branches above their west-leading trail. For a second there was nothing.

Then the voice came again, louder and clear.

DECLAN!

"RYN!" Declan answered, laughing as he tossed a leg off of Orsik to slide off the warg. He'd momentarily forgotten how weak he was still feeling, and his knees gave out the moment his boots hit the ground, but he didn't care. He shoved himself back up at once, just managing it even without the help of magic, and started limping up the trail as fast as he could, eyes still glued to the sky. He didn't hear ay'ahSel shouting after him in elvish, nor her urge to Orsik to start chasing after him when her confused questions went unanswered. He was too focused on the heavens, watching the clouds with an overwhelming sense of relief. He knew what to expect. For Ryn's mind-speech to have been so fragmented, then so clear, he had to be closing the near-mile distance between them quickly. His hawk's form would not have managed that sort of speed, which meant...

WOOSH!

With a downward blast of icy air that managed to briefly penetrate Declan's spell of warmth, a massive, familiar shadows swept overhead from the north, looking to be in the process of circling around to meet them as it set the treetops to swaying. Declan laughed with joy, seeing the great shape of the dragon's true form vanish, then appear again a few seconds later a ways ahead, great wings beating heavily as Ryn came to a stop in midair.

Then he dropped below the treeline, and the distant crack and snap of breaking branches was shortly followed by the heavy *BOOM* of the landing dragon, the impact of his descent so great that a fresh fall of snow, needles, and pinecones came loose from the evergreens all around them, showering Declan, ay'ahSel, and Orsik alike.

None of them cared.

Despite the protest of his weakened limbs, Declan ran as best he could. The deer trail had been partially covered by the shaking of the trees, but he didn't need a path anymore. With ay'ahSel atop Orsik loping steadily along behind him, he barreled through the woods in the direction he knew the dragon waited, unable to stop himself from shouting his friend's name as he did. The Vyr'esh was so dense that despite Ryn's proximity there wasn't so much as a hint of him for nearly half a minute, the trees swallowing all with their somber weight.

And then, ahead of him, Declan saw the brightness of rare clear air, and a few seconds later he was stumbling out into what had been a small clearing made wider by the dragon's arrival.

Ryn had shifted from his larger form, having taken the shape of his *rh'eem* as he waited for them. He stood anxiously not far from the edge the woods, all seven feet of his scaled form tense with anticipation, and the moment he saw Declan the dragon was bounding forward to meet him.

Declan! Thank your damned *Mother!*

They met in a rush, the dragon taking and embracing him so hard Declan's feet actually left the ground for a second. He wheezed as his friend's inhuman strength squeezed the air from his lungs, and had just started to fear he was going to break a rib when Ryn put him down and pushed him away to hold at arm's length.

Are you all right? Are you well? I've been searching for days*! What happened? How did you—?*

The dragon's rush of words only stopped when ay'ahSel made her appearance, stepping out into the clearing atop Orsik with a crunch of snow.

And you all *made it! Well that will certainly smooth things over back at the camp…*

"We're *fine,* Ryn," Declan assured the dragon, extracting himself from his friend's grasp to wave down at his clothes. "A little banged and in *desperate* need of a change of outfits, but fine, I promise."

Ryn nodded slowly, though his expression was dubious as he took the three of them in, white-gold eyes lingering on the red-stained fabric of Declan's shirt and pants, then the bandage about ay'ahSel's head that was still just visible under the lip of her helmet.

If you say so, though you both look much the worse for wear than when I saw you last… He paused, his gaze dropping to Orsik as the warg padded happily over, tongue lolling and fangs glinting in the sort of smile only a creature his size could manage. *All* three *of you, rather.* Ryn bent down slightly to scratch the animal under the chin, earning one of Orsik's rumbling purrs of enjoyment as the dragon eyed his neck and face. *Where did these wounds come from? They look like teeth marks.*

"Wolves," Declan answered simply, eyeing the warg himself. Orsik was as battered as he and ay'ahSel, and indeed had a scattering of new bite marks to show for his efforts in their fights. "You lot haven't encountered any?"

Hardly, Ryn snorted. *I've sensed the packs—and worse—in the woods, but they've stayed clear of the camp.*

For the first time, ay'ahSel spoke up. "*Vulf fehn a tres y'ehn.*"

Ryn made a face. *Yes, I supposed you three* would *have made more interesting targets, alone like you were. But this bad?* He fingered one of Orsik's new wounds with a claw carefully as he pet the warg between the ears with his other hand.

"This is nothing," Declan answered with a snort, rolling a sleeve up to show the dragon his forearm, the skin—long-scarred by an unfortunate encounter with drey blood some months prior—still largely bare and hairless from the inferno he'd been forced to summon in the mountains. "That thing—the tunneler, I called it—caught us just as we were nearing the exit. Nearly brought the ceiling down on me before I could kill it. The wolves haven't been much of a hassle, in comparison."

He didn't see Ryn freeze mid-pet, ay'ahSel having caught his attention from atop Orisk to his left. She must have caught his meaning—he'd been teaching her the common words for "wolf" and the like just in case—because she signed her additions sarcastically.

"Oh, well... There were the bears too, I guess," Declan translated. "And the cat. And the wereyn."

When he looked around at Ryn again, the dragon had turned to stare at him, slack-jawed and wide-eyed.

"What?" Declan feigned confusion, hiding a grin even though he knew what was coming.

It took his friend a moment to answer.

...That thing. The creature, in the tunnels... You killed *it?*

Before Declan could answer, though, ay'ahSel beat him to it. In fluid elvish—of which Declan only caught the words "fire" and "dead"—she seemed to summarize the events beneath the mountain in quick order, leaving Ryn looking only more stupefied when she finished.

You *did that?!* the dragon demanded of Declan almost the moment she finished her retelling. *Are you* insane*?!*

"Thought you'd say that," Declan answered, his laugh a little forced. Despite the days—and miles—of separation, he was a ways yet from shaking the feeling of fire and magic and trembling stone from his memories, much less the scream of the worm as it had been first consumed by the molten rock.

For good reason, Declan! Ryn's voice came through as a hiss. *What if you'd failed?! You've not even two months of training! Weaving something that big… What if you'd passed out sooner?!*

"Then we'd be dead," Declan said, shrugging. "All three of us. But no more dead than if I hadn't tried, Ryn. There was no outrunning it. You know that, and ay'ahSel will tell you there was no fighting it on even ground, either. She got a good look at it before it went up in flames. If we hadn't stopped it, we would have been flattened against the floor of the tunnel. At *best.*"

Ryn looked like he wanted to argue, his expression still alarmed, but after a second or so seemed to think better of it.

Fine, he finally allowed with an exasperated kind of sigh. *If you had no other choice, I suppose there's nothing else for it. Still, I'm surprised you're standing, even* if *you survived. Draining yourself like that… I know of more experienced mages who put themselves in a coma for doing much the same, Declan.*

In answer, Declan grimaced. "I almost did. I was out for two days apparently. It helped to have this one—" he indicated ay'ahSel with a tilt of his head "—yelling in my ear that we were basically done for if I didn't wake up. She brought me back in the middle of a fight with a wolf pack." He shivered dramatically at the memory. "Not the best way to come to, I assure you."

It was Ryn's turn to snort, and he looked to *er'endehn* again. *Your brothers worry for you, Commander. They will be pleased to have you back in one piece.*

The elf grunted dubiously, bringing a finger up to tap at the side of her helmet pointedly as she answered.

'Mostly' one piece? Ryn laughed. *Bonner can see to that, I assure you. I'm positive he'll want to get his hands on the both of you as soon as he can, if you'll allow it. And speaking of*—he turned back to Declan—*I recommend we get moving. We're about half a day's walk from the camp, though we can cut that down significantly if Orsik is still willing to keep carrying one of you.*

"ay'ahSel can stay with him," Declan said with a nod. "He's used to her, now. She spent a day out cold herself, and he's been her legs ever since."

Good. There was a whirl of movement—and a hiss of surprise from the dark elf—and a second later Ryn's dragonling form had been replaced by the warped, black charger that was so similar to the horse he had known growing up. *Then I'll carry you.*

"You sure?" Declan asked, uncertain. "Your true form is hard to take, isn't it? Aren't you tired from—?"

Declan, I've been in my true form for the better part of the last five days, ever since I was given leave to look for you by the camp commander. If it wasn't so cold above the trees I would carry you all and have you back in a half hour. I've paid my due in sleep, don't worry, so get on.

Satisfied, Declan shrugged and did as he was told. Taking hold of Ryn's mane, he started to pull himself up

Only then did he recall that—while Ryn's appearance had certainly chased a little bit of life back into his legs for a moment—he was still very, *very* weak.

The dragon's equine head turned to look around at him in concern, ay'ahSel and Orsik circling around his other side already in preparation to depart.

Everything alright?

"Fine," Declan answered quickly, not wanting to worry his friend. Instead he took a moment, centering himself, and called on his weave of strength once more. The magic slipped into place with ever-increasing ease, and the moment the tingling thrum of the magic had returned to his limbs, Declan slung himself up and over his friend with a jump and heave, settling

The dragon eyed him a moment longer, his concern clearly not alleviated as Declan settled into the long-familiar place on his back. Still waiting for them nearby, ay'ahSel seemed to sense that something was off as well, because she was frowning between the two of them.

Only when Declan had taken ahold of Ryn's mane in both hands and flashed him another smile did the dragon seem to shake off whatever worry he'd been carrying, turning forward to begin stepping carefully through the largely-flattened snow of the disturbed clearing. Ahead of them, the dense cover of the Vyr'esh loomed once more, abruptly no longer as threatening to Declan.

"Here's to the hope of fresh clothes and a hot meal by day's end," he breathed to the chill wind, his elation refusing to cool despite having to hold onto his spell of imbuement to stay seated upright.

Beneath him, Ryn, too, grinned then, picking up the pace a bit once Orsik and ay'ahSel had fallen in behind them.

Only if you tell me everything, starting from the moment you ran into that tunnel like a bloody idiot, he answered as the forest claimed them once more.

CHAPTER FOURTEEN

It turned out to be excellent fortune that Ryn had found them, because the *er'endehn* had—according to the dragon—drawn back from the foot of the slopes after the ay'ahSel brothers had returned not only absent their commander and the majority of their unit, but bearing reports of drey and a more fearsome monster beneath the peaks. Declan had wondered briefly if the elves' recounting would be taken seriously, but it seemed the slaying of their soldiers was more pressing than the possibility of misinformation. The *er'endehn* might be long-lived, but such longevity came at the price of their fertility.

To a people like the dark elves, the loss of more than a half dozen of their best—including the commanding officer, at least for a time—could not have in any way been taken lightly.

It was *into* the forest, therefore, that Ryn led them, still moving west, but angling north as well. They rode for four or five hours—Declan filling his friend in on the full story of the last week all the while—steadily slipping deeper and deeper into the trees. As they did, Declan had the impression that the Vyr'en was *rising* around them, the pines and spruces and winter oaks growing even thicker, with the space between the frozen ground and their lowest branches climbing proportionately to match. It was an awesome sight to experience, looking around as they followed icy streams and managed the ups and downs of the deeper woods, though day eventually gave the illusion of turning to evening beneath the ever-thickening canopy of the elven woods. Declan, in the end, pulled out his firestone to help see by, earning his closed hand not a few suspicious looks from ay'ahSel whenever Orsik came loping up to ride near them. He didn't mind. He knew the elf had warmed to the magics over the last few day—literally *and* figuratively—and he doubted she would say a word crosswise unless he accidentally set the underbrush on fire again.

And the view—the towering monolith-like titans looming out of the gloom all around him—was worth a sidelong glance or two.

Nearly there.

Ryn's announcement—coming at the end of Declan's retelling of the fight they'd had with the wereyn not long before he'd found them—had Declan and ay'ahSel both looking up expectantly. Ahead, a light could be made out, its brightness like shifting slashes through the trees as the dragon picked up the pace. Putting the firestone away at once, Declan waited with anticipation as the glow grew closer, broadening by the second. Within a minute the grey sunlight was reaching them again, and soon after they road out of the tree line and onto the narrow shore of what Declan had to assume was a wide, frozen lake, the heavier *thuds* of Ryn's hooves over the hard ground turning to the crunching of icy snow once more. A flat plain of white extended before them, untouched save for the occasional gust of the wind casting whirls and spirals of powder into the air now and again, and above them the clouds of the sky churned freely, silent but menacing.

It was across the lake, though, maybe a quarter mile away as the crow flew, that Declan's attention had fallen.

The camp was not an overly-impressive sight, at least not from the distance they stood now. As Ryn turned south to lead Orsik around the loop of the shore that would eventually take them to the other side, Declan studied it with a mixture of excitement and apprehension. There were perhaps a hundred small, black tents in clean rows nearest the trees, with a trio of larger pavilions erected closer to the water. There was no barricade or palisade to speak of, but such defenses were hardly to be expected from a small forward base such as this, if ay'ahSel and the others were to be believed. Truth be told, the only impressive thing about the place seemed to be a lack of smoke despite the numerous fires one could make out even from the other side of the lake, like the dark elves had gone through every effort to keep the sign of their presence in the Vyr'esh as small as possible. If that was the case, though, it seemed odd that they would set their encampment on an open shore, rather than deeper into the trees…

Unless…

"I guess I'd want to see my enemies coming, too, if they were dropping from the sky…" Declan muttered.

What was that? Ryn asked of him without turning around, steady gate churning through the snow beneath them as Orsik and ay'ahSel followed close behind.

"Nothing," Declan answered with a shrug. "It just seems like they took the warnings about the drey seriously, if they're more keen on keeping an open line of sight on the clouds than shielding themselves from the elements."

They hardly needed warning, Ryn told him. *The drey were the reason the ay'ahSels and their unit were in the mountains in the first place. Apparently one of them was sighted hunting over the woods, some weeks back. Unfortunately, the foul things* are *more living than dead…*

"Which means they need to eat," Declan finished the dragon's lingering suggestion with a shiver, imagining for a moment a drey beating its great, bat-like wings as it circled one of Viridian's valley towns.

It didn't make for a pleasant thought…

They were around the south end of the lake in five minutes, and it was another five before they were near enough for Declan to start making out the familiar sounds of soldiers at work. Even the *er'endehn*, it appeared, could not be silent when grouped in scores and hundreds, and he almost smiled at the nostalgia, recalling the countless times before that he and Ryn had ridden into the setting grounds of one mercenary company's mission or another. Even clear of smoke, the wind brought the smell of burning wood and cooking meat to them, and at his back Declan heard Orsik growl and bark in excitement, undoubtedly sniffing at the air with his ears up in anticipation as he ran.

Unfortunately for the warg's stomach, they didn't make it another twenty feet before there was a *thrum* of sound from their left—nearer the tree line—and a flash of black *thudded* into the snow only a few body lengths ahead, the bottom half of a narrow shaft, feathered in dark plumage, not even quivering as it stuck out of the white.

An arrow.

Ryn came up short, and from behind Declan heard ay'ahSel shouting in elvish for Orsik to stop as well. The warg just managed to do so, slipping to a halt at their side with a snarl of annoyance, but no one was paying attention to the animal's irritation at being held up from his next meal.

Declan, Ryn, and the commander had all turned to look up the steady slope of the shore, watching a pair of figures clad in familiar black-and-gold armor melt out of the woods as though they'd been a part of the shadows themselves.

The two dark elves were tall and slim, like the rest of their kind, but Declan only saw this because the heavy black cloaks hanging about their shoulders were opened and pushed back as the pair sighted along arrows drawn in their direction on the strings of matching, recurved bows. Though the ground was icy and broke beneath their booted feet, the soldiers never so much as glanced away from the four of them as they came sidelong down the way.

Fortunately, their proximity to the camp seemed to have brought back ay'ahSel's martial flame, because she was snapping at the sentries before the could take more than three steps in their direction.

"Syt! Est ay'ahSel-Hev! Veht yst dregun ys veros!"

Stop! Declan translated for himself privately, pleased to have caught most of the words. *I am Commander ay'ahSel! The human and dragon are friends!*

The sentries froze in their tracks, but did not lower their weapons, nor did they exchange so much as a sidelong glance. After a moment the one on the right shouted back what was clearly a question, too fast and too complicated to understand. The commander's answer, in turn, was lost to Declan, as was the following quick back and forth, though he did note ay'ahSel pointing at Ryn, and suspected she was explaining that he was indeed the dragon the sentries would doubtlessly have known had been in camp a few days prior. Another few tense moments passed in which the two soldiers spoke to each other quietly, still never looking away or releasing the tension on their bows.

Then, though, the arrows were lowered at last, and when one of them addressed ay'ahSel again—waving for them to ride by—it seemed to be with a good deal more respect.

"*That* was intense," Declan said aloud, turning as Ryn started moving again to sign in ay'ahSel's direction.

All right? he asked, hoping she would pick up what he meant.

The elf grimaced, and though her response was lost in the resuming beat of hooves and crunch of clawed paws, the single word was familiar enough to him that he was able to read it on her lips even as Ryn answered his question as well.

Sehranya, the dragon's voice filled the absence of the elf's. *This is a people with a very old memory, Declan. Just because you walk—or ride, as the case would be—doesn't mean you will be treated as a friend. Even if you bear the colors of the Ysenden.*

Declan shivered again, adding a troop of undead soldiers in the regalia of Aletha to his already-frightening imagining of a town under attack by the drey.

"Fair enough," he answered quietly.

It wasn't more than another minute before they were in clear sight of the camp, taking a small bend in the shore, and as they made their final approach, Declan realized that—while simple as it might be—the grounds were a good deal more impressive than he'd been able to tell from across the lake. The tents—even the common foot soldiers'—were crisp and clean aside from a scattering of snow, their black-dyed cloth accented in burnished gold just like the *er'endehns'* armor. The fires were aligned in surgical rows that allowed for easy movement along the shore, and closer to the frozen edge of the water the three greater pavilions formed a wide V to face the rest of the tents, two smaller ones at a slight angle on either side of the largest. Above this middle structure a single banner was raised, black-and-gold like the rest of the camp, depicting the outline of a curved sword bisecting a strung bow, though whether this was the emblem of this forward company or the coat of Ysenden itself Declan couldn't guess.

He didn't have a moment to ask, either, because they were stopped a second time as they closed in, this time just beyond the edge of its outermost tents. The trio of soldiers that held them up this time were less aggressive, standing on the cleared sand where the snow had been melted or shoveled away to find the drier ground, but gloved hands were still on the pommels of sheathed swords as Declan and the others were addressed.

Once again ay'ahSel took the lead on the exchange, and this time Ryn was kind enough to act as translator.

They've asked who we are, and where we're coming from, the dragon said without looking around at Declan as the threesome of guards took them all in carefully. *The commander has informed them who she is, and explained our presence.*

Declan nodded along, having caught most of this early back and forth. At that moment, though, the middle sentry's eyes fell on him, sliding from his face down his bloodied shirt and cloak, then finally settling on the sword hanging from his left hip.

"Ah *dammit*," he cursed their carelessness even as he saw the elf's mouth draw back in the barest hint of anger, his white-red eyes widening as the hand on his own sword tightened about its grip.

"*Veht ken sabres?!*" the sentry demanded of ay'ahSel, though he didn't look away from the borrowed blade. "*Sabres dys er'endehn?!*"

Declan didn't need a translator for this exclamation, but Ryn was already speaking.

He wants to know why you've got an elven blade, the dragon snorted. *And here I always found these people so observant.*

His annoyance, however, seemed nothing compared to ay'ahSel's, who swung a leg off of Orsik to slide down into the snow before making a line straight for the sentry who'd spoken. The elf in question went stiff, apparently realized he'd just made a demand of a superior officer, and his posture—along with those of his two comrades—only tightened further once the commander had reached him and brought her face so close to his their helmets might have been touching. Whether she explained the state of her injury or merely reminded the foot soldier of his position, Declan didn't know, but a few seconds later the trio all nodded together, shouted something that must have been the equivalent of "Yes, ma'am!", and stepped aside as one to allow them entry to the camp. Her job done, ay'ahSel looked over her shoulder at Declan and Ryn to give two quick signs before stepping into the line of the tents proper.

I don't underst— the dragon began to say, but Declan interrupted with a laugh as he threw a leg off his friend's back.

"Dismount. Follow," he explained. "She's not one for too many words, usually. I've gotten used to it."

Ryn grunted. *Apparently. Learning the language of soldiers. That's a rare honor. I don't imagine any man since Herst has had that privilege after Sehranya's fall.*

Declan, who'd moved to take one of the straps of Orsik's harness with the intent of leading the warg after ay'ahSel, frowned back around at the dragon.

"Herst? Why would Herst have learned soldiers' signs?"

Didn't I tell you? Ryn sounded genuinely surprised. *His sword master was a—*

Whatever the dragon said, though, was lost to Declan, because in that moment the sound of footsteps—quick and light despite the snow—reached him from behind. Instinctively he turned with a shout of alarm, hand going for the sword at his belt, but too late.

There was a blur of black-and-gold, a flash of silver, and something slammed into his chest to bear him heavily down to the ground with a *crunch* of sand and snow.

CHAPTER FIFTEEN

"They say love has no place in war, but I challenge you to find me a war that was not fought—in some part—for love. Love of a country. Love of a people. Even love of another.

If anything, it could be argued that love and war got hand-in-hand more often than not..."

—SKYLUS THORNE, FIRST GENERAL OF ALETHA, C. 450P.F.

Despite the—strangely—pleasant nature of her company, Ester was in no mood to smile. It had been some time, in fact, since she'd been of a mood to smile, which was rare for her. Even when her mother had been summoned back to the Vyr'en she'd managed to find some joy in her father's company. Even when her home had been sundered into nothing by the fight between Ryn and the drey that had set off their flight from Viridian, she had managed to laugh.

But, now—for *days*, now—her smile had failed her, and its absence had not gone unnoticed by even those most recent to take her company.

"You are a sad sort of character, are you not, yr'Essel?"

Ester flinched at the unexpected question, deliberately timed to match the moment she released the arrow that had been drawn to her cheek. Only muscle memory and years of constant practice allowed her to regain control at the very tips of her fingers, and the shot *thrummed* through the air in a blur of black. It struck true, *thudding* deep into the narrow red line painted in a jagged stripe between the scales of bark in a pine some fifty yards deeper into the forest, quivering to a standstill just under the elvish number "14" detailed in the same color above the marking.

Impractical as hauling proper targets into the field was, the dark elves had had to make due when it came to setting up a practice range for the length of their outing.

Without looking over her shoulder, Ester drew another arrow from the quiver slung below her low back, knocking it as she scanned the woods for number "15". "*What makes you say that*?" she asked aloud.

"*I think what my brother means to say—*" a different, steadier voice answered her now "*—is that you have seemed quite low of spirit, these last days.*"

Ester snorted. "And what would you know of my spirit?" she muttered in the common tongue of man as she found her mark, drew, and paused only a breath before releasing.

Though it had been nearly impossible to spot in the shadows of the woods, the arrow struck below the "15" as intended, the sound of its impact ringing briefly through the emptiness of the trees.

Satisfied with herself, Ester lowered the bow and looked over her shoulder at her companions. "*Would you have me act differently? I seem to recall Colonel Syr'esh made it clear we are no longer your prisoners to order around.*"

Aliek and Tesied ay'ahSel sat not far from one another among the great, gnarled roots of a pine whose girth might have matched that of a small house. Like every soldier of the *er'endehn* they were bedecked in the same armor and black cloak Ester herself now wore, gifted to her by the camp commander in place of her older, torn vestments. Their own bows in hand, too, the pair exchanged a brief glance of concern before Aliek—the more level-headed of the two, if any dark elf could be called "more level-headed" than another—answered carefully.

"*It is true we are no longer your captors, yr'Essel, but this is irrelevant.*

We do not ask as those who escorted you from the mountains, but as those who would be your friends."

Ester smirked, looking away to unstring her bow, not replying until she started moving for a different dry root a bit separated from the siblings.

"It is difficult to so quickly trust those who a ten-day before would have cut my head from my shoulders with hardly a blink if commanded to do so."

It wasn't entirely true, of course. If she was honest with herself, Ester rather enjoyed the company of the two brothers—twins, in fact, she had learned. They were warmer than the other *er'endehn* she'd come to know in the last few days, and were far quicker to smile and laugh, especially Tesied. Without intention on any of their parts, the three of them had bonded slowly in the time it had taken them to escape the tunnels after the attack that had claimed the lives of most of the dark elves' comrades. Once Kellek Syr'esh, the camp commander, had granted Ester, Ryn, and her father temporary asylum after they'd revealed their knowledge of Sehranya's actions on the other side of the Tears, that bond had grown firmer.

After all, the Queen's last assault within the mountains had stolen something precious from all three of them…

"Who said anything about trust?" Tesied's question halted Ester's thoughts from slipping off into a dark place, and she looked up to find him watching her with the hint of a grin. "*One does not* always *have to trust to be friends, do they? I imagine you do not trust that dragon of yours not to roll over in sleep and squash you one day, and yet you are still very clearly friends."*

Something pulled at the corner of Ester's lip, a strange tension, and she only recognized it when Tesied pointed at her face with an exclamation of victory.

"Ha! You see! That was very nearly a smile! One sees the light in you yet, wood elf. You cannot hide it forever!"

"Shut up," Ester muttered, automatically slipping into common again as she averted her eyes by pretending to check her bow for splintering. There was no need, of course. The brothers had seen her equipped with proper *er'endehn* weaponry in apology for the loss of her saber in the tunnels, and the curved black wood, detailed in gold, was flawless, as were the arrows in the quiver at her back and the slender, elven blade sheathed at her hip.

There seemed to exist as much imperfection in the *creations* of the dark elves as there did in their coordination and combat.

"*Cease your teasing, Tesied,*" Aliek said with a sigh, pushing himself up off the tree to move towards the cleared circle of ground Ester had just been standing in. "*If she does not wish to speak, we should not press her to.*"

"*Bah!*" Tesied waved his brother's words aside with a loose hand. "*She is interesting! How can I not desire to speak with her more? She has seen the world, Aliek! She has seen the lands of man, witnessed the grandness of their opulent cities and silver rivers and boats made of glass and—*"

"*What in the gods above are you talking about?*" Ester asked him with a snort.

Tesied turned to her with wide eyes. "*Have you* not *seen them? My, what a disappointment. And here I was hoping to hear tales of their capitol. I had heard it flies a mile above the world, floating on the power of old magics and—*"

"*Who told you* that*?*" Ester asked with dry amusement. "*I've not seen Aletha, but I can tell you it certainly doesn't fly.*"

"*Of course not.*" Aliek had strung his bow as he'd steadily spotted his targets from the darkness of the woods. "*It can hardly be anything so grand. Likely a primitive pile of rocks upon which their King sits holding his own flag.*"

"*It most certainly isn't,*" Ester retorted, almost annoyed by the suggestion. Even largely-separated from the realm as she and her father had been, Viridian *was* her own kingdom, which made her feel like she owed it at least a *little* loyalty. *"I'm told it's a sight to take one's breath away. Walls no man—or elf—could climb, with the turrets of the al'Dyor's great palace climbing above everything from its midst. So many people live there that every quarter of Aletha could be its own city, and it stands in the center of a great, empty plain so broad that one can see it rising from the horizon as they—"*

Ester stopped then, though, taking note of the half-smile Tesied was trying to hide beneath his helmet, as well as the glint of amusement in Aliek's eyes, turned towards her to listen even as he'd knocked an arrow to his bow. She realized, suddenly, how thoroughly she'd just been played, and with a groan she crossed her arms and legs and leaned back against the trunk of the pine to glower at the brothers.

"You are asses. The both of you."

The brothers laughed together at that.

And then Aliek whirled, drew, and released.

His hand was already pulling a second arrow from his quiver by the time the first struck the target labeled "1". With a level of speed and precision Ester had only ever seen surpassed by her mother, the elf planted a shaft in every line painted in a wide arc at varying distances before them. In not even seven seconds, the final arrow was quivering beneath the red number "10", the echo of its impact ringing briefly off into the trees.

Though she'd witnessed this very feat a dozen times before, it was no less impressive to her now than it had been days ago.

It was another reason she didn't find herself complaining about the twin's lingering about her. Their companionship was certainly a buffer from isolation—her father spent most of his time in the pavilions in discussion with Colonel Syr'esh and his officers, while Ryn had left not a few hours after they'd arrived to scour the slopes—but as intriguing as the ay'ahSels found Ester, she doubted it measured by half to the interest *she* had in *them.*

Aliek and Tesied, while perhaps not perfect examples of the stony countenance most of the dark elves held themselves with, had nonetheless proven more than once that their brighter natures did not come at the cost of discipline or ability. Though they both specialized in the spear, their skill with every manner of weapon the *er'endehn* had at their disposal was uncanny. Ester had learned more than a thing or two from them in the art of archery, and that mostly just from watching. In the blade, too, she had been schooled, though those lessons had come in more direct fashion when the brothers had asked her if she'd had any desire to spar. The offer had been taken up greedily—*anything* to keep her thoughts out of darker places—and Ester had discovered that even Declan, despite being the most fearsome opponent she'd ever had the privilege of crossing blades with, indeed had a great deal left to learn compared to the fluid lethality of the ay'ahSels.

Declan…

Ester shook her head firmly, refusing to be dragged back to that place. She still held onto hope, still held onto the sliver of possibility. Her father consistently spoke of the man—and Orsik, too—as being nothing more than momentarily separated form their party, and Ryn's immediate departure and lack of return addressed his own equal conviction. It helped, to be sure, but as hard as she fought it, Ester felt a little of that hope dimming with every passing day, and it was too easy to dwell on reliving and rethinking that moment of Declan's disappearance. Could they have outrun the creature that had attacked them? Could they have found their way out? Could they have survived the cold and grey of the forest?

No, Ester's firm answer was silent as she forced herself yet again to focus on the moment, on the present. *They're alive.* He's *alive.*

Crack.

The distant sound of a breaking branch helped pull Ester from her mind, and she, Aliek, and Tesied all looked around together to peer north, further into the forest.

"*Your beast approaches,*" Tesied said, giving away only the barest hint of tension in his voice. "*Perhaps* it *will prove a brighter companion.*"

"*Doubtful.*" Aliek, too, spoke in a tone of slightly-forced calm. "*I smell blood.*"

Ester would have liked to laugh at the pair's subtle unease, but her poor humor betrayed her. What was more, she couldn't blame the two of them for their nerves.

No matter how talented one was with a blade, it was a fool who did not fear a creature that could tear them in half.

Eyera made her appearance only a second later, pale form slipping from behind one tree to another, then out again as she made her way steadily through the woods in their direction. Sure enough, Ester, too, could soon taste iron on the air, and the dragging sounds that accompanied the warg's approach told her the female had had a successful hunt. Indeed, after a dip and climb in and out of a frozen stream bed and a quick jump over the thick body of a fallen branch, Eyera reached them. Without so much as a glance of acknowledgement at the two dark elves she crossed the cleared shooting space, passing so close to Aliek that the elf had to step back smartly to avoid getting struck about the legs by the limp limbs of the young buck the warg was dragging along by the neck.

"Good girl," Ester said as the female approached, reaching out a hand. "Looks like someone's eating well tonight."

Eyera made not a sound, though, even when Ester's fingers found the coarse hair atop her head. Her ears hung low, too, and it was unenthusiastically that she circled into the nook of the roots by Ester's elbow, settling down to gnaw halfheartedly at the neck of the deer. Ester frowned, feeling the knot of sadness tighten in her chest at the sight of the somber warg.

It hurt to see, but it hurt, too, to be reminded of their mutual loss.

"It still boggles the mind that you actually ride *that thing, yr'Essel,"* Tesied spoke up eventually, watching Ester stroke Eyera's head as the female chewed. *"I've no idea what magics you've enthralled it with, but I admit to fascination."*

"My father is the mage, ay'ahSel," Ester corrected him quietly, speaking gently out of habit now that Eyera was by her side again. *"This is not spellcraft.* This *is friendship."*

"I didn't know one could be friends with such a beast." Aliek this time, and Ester didn't miss the fact that—perhaps unconsciously—the *er'endehn* had knocked another arrow to his string despite having finished his display of marksmanship. *"We usually just kill them, along with their masters."*

Ester bit her lip, then nodded. *"Yes. I can understand that. I was of your mindset not so long ago, believe it or not. But these are animals, not monsters."* She managed just the hint of a smile as she echoed her father's past words. *"And I've learned that the wereyn certainly think themselves masters, right up until the moment they become just another meal."*

"How encouraging," Tesied muttered dryly.

Ester gave a bark of a laugh. *"Is it so strange? There are those among the* er'enthyl *who ride bears into battle. I had imagined the* er'endehn *might have a similar bond with the land and its creatures."*

"They what*?!"*

The question, echoed in the same moment by both brothers, was genuinely astonished this time, and Ester looked up to see the two staring at her with wide eyes. Their blatant surprise was an uncommon sight for dark elves—even from the likes of the ay'ahSels—and Ester couldn't stop herself from letting out a single laugh.

"Oh yes. Great red bears they use to patrol the borders of their lands."

"And you've seen this? In person?"

Ester shrugged and dodged the question. *"It's hardly the strangest thing out there. After a fortnight in Ryn's company, I would have thought you two would appreciate that more than most."*

The twins exchanged a glance, but did not comment on her suggestion. It was odd—had *always* been odd—how little concern they and the rest of the *er'endehn* had always seemed to bear in the dragon's presence. There had been a little commotion when Ryn had taken to his true form just outside the camp before leaping to the skies a few days prior, but even that had settled in short order and with a few shouts from the higher officers. Ester had been prying little by little, but either the elves were *so* oblivious to the oddity that was their lack of alarm that they took no notice of her attempts, or they were as wary of the subject as she was curious about it.

"What else is out there?" Tesied's enthusiastic question cut across Ester's thoughts, bringing her back to the conversation. *"Days now we've been your shadows, and we know no more of the world beyond the Line than we did as boys in academy. Is it true that men breed like mice? And that they live scattered across the land? And what are the wood elves guarding their borders against? Humanity? Are you at war?"*

Ester blinked at the eager influx of questions, taken aback.

"I open up the smallest bit, and suddenly this is an interrogation?" she asked of the dark elf, offering a mocking scowl. *"If I didn't know better, I'd say you were tasked with working me for information for your superiors."*

Tesied gave her a smile that was at once amused and a little frightening. *"Hardly. This is curiosity. If we had orders to extract information from you, there are* much *faster ways of doing so. The fact that you still have all your fingers is a testament to that, is it not?"*

"Well you certainly know how to encourage one to be forthcoming," Ester answered dryly even as Aliek rolled his eyes behind his brother's back. *"But fine, since you've been so kind* not *to threaten my person... No one calls your mountains 'Karn's Line' anymore. Not even the wood elves. I*

doubt there's many left alive today who even know why it was named that in the first place."

Aliek's face shifted at once from one of exasperation to interest. "*They don't? Why in the spirits not?*"

"*The war,*" Ester answered simply. "*The assault against the Reaches by the traitors of the court of man. So much blood was shed that the ranges are knows as 'the Mother's Tears', now.*"

"*The war...?*" Aliek's expression was as confused as Ester had ever seen on any dark elf. "*But... Those aren't even the right mountains...*"

"*Seven hundred years is a long time for humanity,*" Ester said with a sigh. "*Some stories seemed to have become... confused over time.*"

"*More importantly: 'the Mother's Tears'? As in the goddess of man?*" Tesied offered a bark of laughter. "*Well we can at least be sure of one thing: our instructors were on the mark when they spoke of humanity's hubris.*"

"*I doubt any lessons you could have partaken in could have come* near *impressing the degree of humanity's hubris,*" Ester agreed with a snort. "*It is painful to behold, sometimes.*"

"*All of man?*" Aliek asked.

"*Essentially,*" Ester answered with another shrug.

"*Even your companion?*"

Aliek's follow-up question was careful, like he had been waiting for the right moment to broach the subject, and Ester stiffened. Like a battering ram had been taken to the walls she'd been fighting to build for herself, she felt that barricade crack ever so slightly. She went quiet, not knowing how to respond, and her silence must have lingered just a moment too long, because Aliek seemed he needed to clarify.

"*The swordsman,*" he said, as though Ester might not have known exactly who he was speaking of. "*Idrys, I think his name wa—?*"

"*I know what his name was.*" Ester cut the elf off too-quickly, unable to meet his or his brother's eyes all of a sudden as she found herself instead looking down at her own hand, still stroking a morose Eyera.

The silence came again, but this time it held, neither of the ay'ahSels pressing her. Eventually Ester steadied herself, but even after a calming breath her answer came out in half a stammer.

"*N-no. Not Declan. He is different.* Many *of them are different, truth be told.*"

"But him especially?" Aliek pushed gently.

Ester opened her mouth, but couldn't find the words to answer as an uncomfortable tightness built in her cheeks.

"I'd rather not speak of it, if it's all the same to you," she forced herself to get out after a second.

"It's not all the same, yr'Essel." It was Tesied who answered, and for once the glimmer of amusement was gone from his dark features. He spoke calmly, carefully and without malice, like his brother, but just the same his words were as firm as cold iron. "*Your friend, Declan…I would remind you that he accompanies our sister, assuming the two of them are still alive.*"

"*They are,*" Ester said at once, almost snapping. *"And I am well aware."*

"If you're so convinced that they are, then why is it clearly difficult to speak of?" Tesied kept on, leaning forward on his root over his unstrung bow. "*You are not of our world, wood elf. That could not be plainer. Despite the journey we know you and your companions have taken to get here, you have not been braced for the loss of someone close to you. We—*" he gestured between himself and his brother "*—have. Since the day we were born. But we are not unfeeling. Our academies teach us to control our emotions, not strip them away. If Lysiat is dead, then her spirit is at peace, and we will see her again. But we hope it is otherwise.*"

"We hope it is otherwise," Aliek echoed quietly, still standing with knocked bow in one hand.

"*So… what?*" Ester wasn't sure she followed. "*You want to know about Declan because… because you hope your sister is alive?*"

"We wish to know of this 'Declan' because if *she is alive, then her back is being watched by a stranger to us, and someone of a race you say yourself is often victim of its own vanity."* Tesied grimaced slightly. *"We wish only to know enough to decide for ourselves if Lysiat has a partner in survival, or an anchor to weigh her down."*

Ester bristled at that, and Eyera must have sensed her sudden anger because the warg let off chewing to lift her great head and growl towards the brothers, teeth bared.

"Quiet, girl," Ester said more out of habit than any real intention to put the female at ease. Indeed, she didn't say anything else until Eyera quit showing her fangs, though even then the warg preferred to continue to watch the *er'endehn* rather than return to her unenthusiastic gnawing.

"I feel I have failed to get a proper measure of you, Tesied ay'ahSel," Ester finally got out, forcing herself to keep her voice steady as she stared down the dark elf. *"I would have thought you a better judge of character. Did you forget there were three of your unit in that tunnel, yourself included? And yet* Declan *was the one who rushed in to save your sister. Is that not enough to deduce from?"*

It was Tesied's turn to stiffen, his expression shifting briefly to pain before settling into the impassive features of a true *er'ehdehn* soldier's steadiness.

"I would have, and you know it," he said too-calmly. *"I tried, even, and was stopped."*

"You were stopped because rushing into that tunnel would have meant your life as well as Lysiat's," Aliek cut in, frowning at his brother, but Tesied shrugged his comment off without looking away from Ester.

"I do not blame you, Aliek. You always did keep a better head in such situations. I was merely correcting yr'Essel's accusation of cowardice."

At the words, Ester felt the flame of her anger sputter and die as quickly as it had come.

"*I didn't intend to imply any such thing,*" she said quietly, feeling her shoulders sag a little. "*I am more than aware of the bravery of the* er'endehn, *ay'ahSel. Even yours specifically. I did not witness the felling of the drey, but the aftermath spoke for itself.*" She shook her head slightly. "*I meant only to point out that Declan has already proven himself to you. We know they survived that initial attack. He and your sister both. My father assured us of that much. But they only did so because of Declan's actions.*"

Tesied watched her for a long moment more, posture still tense, eyes still dead.

Then, at last, he relaxed, offering her a wry smile as he reached up to scratch at the side of his neck uncomfortably.

"*You've nothing to be sorry for, yr'Essel. I am as much out of line as you are, I think. I did not mean to imply that your companion was anything less than he seems, and we—*" he gestured between himself and Aliek "*—owe him a debt in the best of circumstances, and gratitude to his memory in the worst. I just meant that the line between courage and folly is a narrow one, and we wish to know if this Declan is a man above our understanding of his peers.*" Tesied, too, seemed to go a little limp, then, gaze falling to the ground. "*I apologize. Again, we are not unfeeling. It seems my concern for Lysiat has me a little more on edge than I would like to admit…*"

Ester was about to acknowledge the apology when, abruptly, Aliek burst out laughing.

"*Spirits, woman!*" he half-shouted to the trees. "*Tesied must have taken a fancy to you! I've not seen him apologize to anyone in a hundred years or so!*"

"*Aliek…*" Tesied growled in warning, looking at his brother sidelong, but he was ignored as readily as the sound of the wind through the canopy above them.

"*You should let him down easy, I think,*" Aliek continued, grinning now at Ester. "*Tell him you are taken, so he can start mending his broken heart. Do not be so cruel as to string him along.*"

"*Aliek!*" Tesied said again, more firmly this time, all while Ester mouthed at the air in surprise.

"I-I am no man's!" she got out eventually, feeling blood creep into her cheeks as she heard the squeak in her own voice. *"None have claim on me, and I would appreciate it if—"*

"I do not believe you." Aliek cut her off with another laugh, winking outright this time. *"Do not forget that we spent more than half a week in the company of your party before it was broken in two. We saw the toll not being able to speak took on you, and you and that Declan were still inseparable, about as much as this warg and her mate."* He gestured at Eyera, who had finally returned to her meal once she knew all was well.

This particular comment was fortunate, because it brought Ester's control of the situation back at once. With a deadpan expression she stared at the chortling *er'endehn* for a full five seconds before speaking.

"You mean her brother, *I assume? As the beast Declan road into the tunnel is to her. I know not what you intend to imply by that, ay'ahSel, but I recommend you choose your next words* very *carefully lest I encourage Eyera to find out what dark elf meat tastes like."*

Aliek's face froze mid-grin, and he might have been a statue abandoned in the middle of the woods for a moment. It was long enough for Tesied to turn the tables on his brother, jumping to his feet.

"Ha! Serves you right, bastard!"

At the words, Aliek shook off the momentary shock, though it wasn't his brother he addressed.

"yr'Essel, I am sorry," the elf looked mortified as he took a step towards Ester and put a hand on his heart. *"I swear on my life it was not my intention to imply that—"*

"That I would be inclined to lay with my brother, had I one?" Ester asked him sweetly, cocking her head. *"No? Because that's certainly what you seemed to be saying."*

"No. No. Not at all. I was jesting, I swear it. Had I known, I wouldn't have—"

Aliek paused as, at long last, Ester could no longer contain herself. She grinned, and the expression felt strange on her face, but hardly unwelcome, as was the laughter—the *true* laughter—that followed. All the while Aliek stood dumbfounded as Tesied snickered from where he stood, basking in his brother's discomfort.

"*You are toying with me,*" Aliek groaned eventually, and his relief was palpable despite the obvious attempt he was making to look annoyed. "*You mock me.*"

"*Only a little,*" Ester told him through laughs. "*I'm sorry. I felt the mood needed a change.*"

"*Days of trying to cheer her up, and all I had to do was make a fool of myself to get her to smile.*" Aliek shook his head, then waved towards Eyera. "*I'll bet they aren't even siblings, are they? Your warg. They* are *mates, are they not?*"

"*Quit while you're behind, ay'ahSel,*" Ester answered with a snort. "*They* are *siblings, and you* are *still an ass. It's just that you're less of an ass than you might have—*"

She stopped then, mouth hanging open in mid-sentence.

Under normal circumstances the ay'ahSels might have found this abrupt pause alarming, but they too had straightened, ears still sharp under their helmets. All three of them stood together in silence, then listening, straining. Ester wasn't sure, but she didn't think her mind had been playing tricks on her. A sound had reached them through the trees, one that had stolen her breath away as soon as she heard it. From somewhere west of them, hoofbeats through snow had faintly echoed through the trees, the familiar, thudding beat of a passing horse. It might have been hardly worth considering, expect for one fact.

The *er'endehn* didn't *have* horses.

And then, at her feet, Eyera lifted her head from her prey again to sniff at the air, ears perked and listening for the first time in more than a week.

It was enough to convince Ester.

She was off the roots and vaulting over and through their gnarled fingers in a heartbeat, bow held at her side. The training area wasn't far from the camp for obvious reasons, and so it wasn't more than ten seconds of running before she felt the breeze of the open air again and then made out the flat white of the lake through the evergreens. She heard the others chasing quickly after her, Eyera barking in excitement while the ay'ahSels followed in silence, but the brothers were larger and a little slower than she, especially over the uneven terrain of the woods. She was out of the tree line and on the lakeshore a dozen yards ahead of any of them, even the warg, and as her new leather boots crunched into the fresh snow she looked around, left and right.

There, a ways north of them like they'd passed by only shortly before, two pairs of familiar figures were in the process of being held up just outside the camp proper.

Ryn was the first that Ester's quick eyes recognized, his ink-black form—now the twisted shape of the horse that had acted as their pack animal for much of the trek through the northern woods of Viridian—in sharp contrast to the snow all about him. Orsik was beside him, looking a fair bit thinner than when Ester had last seen the beast, while a feminine figure clad in black-and-gold that could only be Lysiat ay'ahSel rode confidently atop him.

And to the commander's right, straddling Ryn's back and taking in the impressive sight of the *er'endehn* camp, was a tall, broad man with long brown hair that fell to his shoulders, the skin of his ungloved hands scarred and splotched by familiar wounds.

"Declan," Ester breathed, not believing her eyes.

And then she was running again, taking off just before the twins and Eyera could catch up to her.

She practically *flew* over the clean snow, uncaring of the spray of powder, uncaring of the cold and wind that bit at her exposed face and ears. She ran, careening after the group, seeing ay'ahSel descend off of Orsik's back and approached the secondary sentries. The commander spoke briefly, and then was stepping by the parting guard line, turning to wave the others to follow.

Ester caught up just as Declan, too, dismounted.

She thought she heard a yell of alarm, but she didn't care. She didn't notice the burn in her cheeks or the tears in her eyes as she threw herself at his back, didn't notice him spinning in surprise or even her abandonment of her bow to the snow. She collided with the larger man at full speed, slamming into his chest with arms wide and bearing him down to the cold, sandy ground.

"*OOMPH!*" Declan exclaimed as the wind was knocked out of him, and Ester felt his strong hands grab her about the waist and arm as though ready to throw her off. "WHAT IN THE NAME OF—?!"

He stopped, though, his exclamation choking off as he must have recognized her. She didn't know of course, couldn't know.

She was too busy burying her face into his chest, squeezing herself against him through too-thin, bloodstained clothes, feeling the warmth of what had to have been his firestone against her cheek, stowed in its usual spot in the pocket of his coat.

"Ester…?" Declan asked softly.

Before Ester could answer, there was another cry of recognition, and she made out two sets of feet churning by through the sand on either side of her.

"*Lysiat!*" the ay'ahSel brothers shouted together, their sister's name carrying more emotion than every other word Ester had ever heard them speak combined. "*LYSIAT!*"

"*Aliek!*" came the excited answer. "*Tesied!*"

Then, though, all other sound was drowned out as—with a howl of joy that was almost wolf-like—Eyera and her brother must have found each other.

Even then, though, Ester didn't look up. Even when she heard the warg start to roughhouse and dance and bark in happiness. Even when the ay'ahSels started jabbering in such rapid elvish she doubted anyone—including themselves—could have understood what they were saying. Even when she heard the confused questions—shouted over the commotion—of the sentries.

All Ester did was shut her eyes tight, and hold onto the man beneath her even harder, refusing for a moment to let him go despite the cold, wet ground she had dragged them down into.

"Ester…?" Declan eventually asked again, even more gently this time. At some point his own hands had moved to encircle her, pulling her equally close. When had that happened? "It's all right. I'm all right."

"You made it…" she mumbled into his chest, still refusing to look up, like she were afraid she might open her eyes and find him gone again. "You actually made it…"

Declan chuckled lightly. "Did you think I wasn't going to?"

She laughed, the sound coming out as half a sob. "We had a bet running. The whole camp"

"Oh? And how did you make out?"

"I owe a lot of people money."

Declan laughed out loud at that, the sound booming through her ears like a drum through his chest. It made Ester inexplicably happy, and at last she started to extricate herself from around the man, pulling her arms free from beneath him and to press herself off and shake sand free of her sleeves.

"Are those tears for me?" Declan asked as he started to sit up. His eyes—the familiar dark blue of a deep ocean—were full of concern, which was ironic given the shape the man was in.

"The wind," Ester answered quickly, deciding it was at the very least a half truth. "I hardly think *I'm* the one you should be worried about, though. God's above, Declan… What happened to you?"

Aside from a ragged week's beard and bags under his eyes from what must have been less sleep than he would have liked, Declan was also a bloody mess. Almost every inch of him looked to have been stained red, with some of the splatters clearly older than others, even turning to brown. Ester was pleased, too, that she hadn't had the mind to notice the smell, because the stench of iron was mixed with days of sweat and dirty clothes.

"Unpleasant, isn't it?" Declan asked with a snort, looking down at himself even as he started to climb to his feet. "We apparently had a harder time than you lot making it through the woods, and there wasn't much opportunity to wash or bathe." He sniffed at a sleeve and grimaced, then offered her a hand. "Compared to you, I feel like I smell like a sewer."

"It's not that bad," Ester lied, accepting his assistance to stand. "A very nice sewer, I'd say."

The nicest of sewers, yes.

The two of them started and turned together to find Ryn eyeing them in an amused sort of way. Now that they'd arrived, he returned to his dragonling's form, and so had his arms crossed as he cocked his head.

I wasn't going to say anything, but a bath is certainly in order, yes. For you and ay'ahSel both, Declan. Orsik, too, if we can convince him. First, though, I imagine Bonner will want to know you're alive, and we should probably let the camp's higher ups know as well. They'll want to get moving as soon as possible.

"Moving?" Declan asked, sounding surprised. "Already?"

Ryn made a face. *Without a doubt. Colonel Syr'esh would have seen us gone days ago. Bonner and I were clear that that wasn't an option, of course, and I'm pretty sure Ester made such a racket about it that the officers were all afraid of being knifed in their sleep if they suggested departing before we found you again.*

"I wasn't *that* obnoxious," Ester grumbled, feeling her cheeks flush again and being glad for the excuse of the cold air. "And I certainly wasn't the one threatening people. I seem to recall Father promising to turn every elf in the Colonel's pavilion into *trees* if they made any move to leave before we had time to go looking."

"Well I can't blame them, after the time we've had in these damn woods," Declan grunted, patting sand off his pants as he looked around. The ay'ahSels were still huddled together as they clasped arms and shoulders, and Orsik and Eyera had bounded further down the shore to tussle. "I can't believe you're all untouched. It was like the Vyr'esh itself had put out a bounty on our heads."

The forest is plenty dangerous, but I don't think it's the threat of what lurks in the trees that have the er'endehn *on edge.* Ryn shook his head before he, too, peered up the slope of the bank into the shadows of the woods. *They weren't pleased with the ay'ahSels report…*

"Ah… So it's the mountains that frighten them." Declan nodded in understanding. "Or what's *in* them, at least. Between the drey and the tunneler, I certainly can't blame them. And if their like is hidden among those passages, you know their master is, too…"

Ester shivered. She had no desire, however, to let the unspoken name of the Endless Queen ruin Declan's return, so she guided the conversation elsewhere.

"The tunneler?" she asked.

Declan nodded again. "The worm. Or at least that's how ay'ahSel described it. It was Sehranya's beast. Nearly killed myself taking it down, and even then it was the Purpose that ended up burning it to ash."

Ester's mouth went dry.

"The… the 'worm'? You don't mean…"

The thing that attacked us in the tunnels on the day we got separated, yes. Ryn was almost smiling outright now. *It's quite a tale. You'll have to have him tell it to you later.*

Ester gaped at Declan, not seeing his sheepish grin, and it was several seconds before she found her voice.

"You KILLED that thing?!" she demanded, so loudly that the ay'ahSels nearby paused to look around as one. "YOU?! HOW?!"

"It's... complicated," Declan answered hesitantly, suddenly looking like he wasn't sure he wanted to say anything more. "I don't think you'll be very happy with me if I tell you how..."

Ester scoffed, seeing where the conversation was going. "You probably did something infuriating, didn't you? You probably charged the bloody thing all on your own, or set up some ambush that was just as likely to get *you* killed as it was to work out! Am I near the mark?"

Closer than you can know, Ryn answered with a laugh as Declan's expression started to hint at panic.

"Ester, I promise you, if there had been any other way—"

"Oh *bull*, Declan Idrys!" Ester seethed, stepping up to him so that they stood barely two inches from each other. "First you charge a drey like a madman, then you run into a collapsing tunnel, and now this? I don't know if I'm more relieved you're alive or pissed you didn't get yourself killed so you could finally learn your lesson!"

"Well personally I would hope it's more the former, but I—"

"What's next, hmm?" Ester cut him off as she continued. "Going to hunt down the rest of the drey on your own? Or maybe you'd like to go straight for the source, and just figure out where Sehranya is hiding so you can—"

"*WHAT IS GOING ON OUT HERE?!*"

The feminine voice, blazing with authority, rang out over Ester's tirade and the distant play of the warg with such severity that Ester found herself shutting up at once. All together the nine of them—including the three sentries—whirled about to find a tall, wiry elf stepping out of the camp line with a purpose, her sharp eyes narrowed in irritation as she took in the scattered groups. Ester recognized her at once as one of the higher officers of the camp, but unfortunately had never caught the *er'endehn's* name or rank to explain what was happening.

Fortunately, the ay'ahSels had her covered.

"*Lysiat has returned, Major*!" Tesied shouted eagerly, pulling his sister to the forefront of their trio to show her off. "*Look!*"

The officer turned her scathing gaze on them, stare only softening a little when she took note of Lysiat ay'ahSel. Clearly she was unimpressed with Tesied's explanation of the situation, but Aliek came to the rescue before his brother was put at risk of being given a tongue lashing.

"*Major y'Rehl.*" He stood to attention as he addressed the woman. "*Commander yr'ahSel has been recovered, as well as the human and second warg we informed the camp officers of in our report. Master Ryndean has seen them returned, as he promised.*"

The elf—y'Rehl apparently—glared between the two brothers for several seconds longer, clearly intent on making her displeasure known, and even when she finally started stepping towards the trio her scrutiny did not leave the twins until she was within a foot of them. Only then, at long last, did she turn her attention to Lysiat ay'ahSel, the fire finally waning from her gaze.

"*It is good to have you back, Commander,*" the major said with something that was almost a smile, extending an arm towards the shorter woman. "*You have been missed. Are you well?*"

"*For the most part, yes, ma'am.*" ay'ahSel grasped the offered arm firmly, nodding in confirmation. "*Took a blow to the head I'm yet recovering from. Loathe to admit it, but I wouldn't have made it without the human.*"

The commander dipped her head in Ester and Declan's direction, then, and y'Rehl turned to follow her eye, taking the man in with measured steadiness.

"*I see… Then it seems appreciations are in order. You!*" She called out to Declan. "*Attend, if you would.*"

There was a moment of awkward silence as Declan—who clearly knew only that he was being addressed, with no concept of the order itself—blinked blankly at the officer.

Lysiat ay'ahSel came to his rescue with a cough.

"*Apologies, Major, but he does not speak the language of the* er'endehn. *He is a quick learner, however. Here.*" She looked to Declan, and made a few quick gestures. Ester watched his face crease into a confused frown, but then he was stepping away from her, moving towards the group.

"Wait." Ester followed him at once, catching his arm to hold him up. "You understood that?"

"She wants me to join them," Declan told her with a nod. "Well, technically she said 'collapse on me', but I get the gist."

Ester thought her eyebrows might have been reaching for the sky, and Ryn chuckled from her left. *He's had a busy week, Ester.*

Declan made a face. "You've got no idea." He looked at Ester. "Not like I learned the tongue in a few days, though. Can you help me?"

Ester, realizing her mouth was hanging open, shut it with a *click* before nodding. As he stepped away again, it still took her a moment to gather herself, shaking her head a little even before she followed, delaying only long enough to retrieve her bow from the snow. The worm, the woods, and now finding out he'd been learning the silent language of the *er'endehn* soldiers?

Suddenly the improvements Ester had seen in her archery felt wanting compared to what she realized she *might* have asked the ay'ahSel brothers to teach her…

y'Rehl watched the approach carefully, almost like she was looking for any sudden movement, and though her arms were now crossed over her chest, Ester didn't miss her eyes slipping more than once to the dark elf sword still hanging from Declan's hip. By the time they reached the foursome, in fact, the major was frowning ever so slightly, though it appeared her priorities in the moment weren't to demand as to why a *human* bore the blade of the *er'endehn.*

"I assume you will act as translator, wood elf?" y'Rehl asked finally, not looking away from Declan.

"Yes, ma'am," Ester answered deliberately. Though she was no dark elf—much less a conscript of the army—she thought it better to be safe than sorry when addressing one of the camp's upper echelon.

The major nodded once. "*Good.*"

Then she spoke to Declan directly.

"I'm made to understand you do not speak the language, and yet it's apparent you've made due. You have the thanks of the er'endehn, *human. I would know your name."*

There was a pause as Ester turned the words for Declan, and he nodded as she finished.

"Declan Idrys, ma'am. And the commander certainly deserves no less credit than I. We're hardly masters at it, but we've learned to communicate as needed. Only reason we survived."

"Is it?" The major sounded dubious. *"For days in the dark, then more in the Vyr'esh? And with a borrowed blade? I may not be familiar with the tunnels beneath Karn's Line, Declan Idrys, but I am older than most in this camp and can say for certain that no two soldiers of the* er'endehn *could survive long in these woods on their own. What's more, I do not believe you to be of a caliber with the swordsmen of my kind..."*

Ester grit her teeth at this. "*That's hardly necces—*"

"Translate, wood elf," the major cut her off almost casually, still not looking at her. *"It is Idrys I address. Not you."*

All the same, Ester hesitated, hardly willing to be bullied into speaking.

Then a heavy, dark presence stepped up behind her shoulder.

Translate, Ryn echoed gently, and the tenor of his voice made Ester feel like he was speaking only to her. *I suspect she has a point to make.*

"Well maybe she can make it without being rude?" Ester asked him under her breath, but she did as she was told.

Declan smiled dryly once he understood. "It's true I'm hardly a match for any soldier of the *er'endehn.* The commander has proven that twice over, and that was *after* it had already been made clear by the rest of her unit as well." He acknowledged Aliek and Tesied with a dip of his head. "We were not, however, without advantages. Orsik was with us." He gestured back towards the two warg who were still happily bouncing and tumbling through the snow further down the lakeshore behind them.

y'Rehl looked mildly amused once Ester translated. "*You expect me to believe that the beast is the secret to your survival? I am not a fool, human. You had best not treat me as one.*"

Declan raised both hands apologetically. "That was certainly not what I was implying, and I am aware of what you are getting at, ma'am. However, if you want to see the other tricks I have up my sleeve—" he put a hand over the pocket Ester knew his firestone was hidden in "—it might be best to do that elsewhere." He glanced pointedly towards the trio of dark elf sentries who still stood to one side of the conversation, perfect statues despite very clearly listening to every word that was being said. "Perhaps somewhere more *private*?"

The major stared at Declan for a moment. She did not chew on her cheek or fidget in any other sense as one might notice, but Ester could tell just the same that she was turning his words over, considering them.

At last, she looked over her shoulder at Lysiat ay'ahSel.

"*You would vouch for him, Commander?*"

"*Yes, ma'am.*" The woman answered even before Ester could start to tell Declan what the major was saying. "*I may not have been clear: this man has saved my life three times that I can count without thinking about it. Likely more. I would gladly vouch for him.*"

"*Us as well, ma'am,*" Tesied offered up, earning himself a seething glare from both his siblings. For her part, though, y'Rehl ignored him, looking instead to Ryn.

"And you, Master Ryndean? Would you vouch for him as well, or—?"

I would swear on my own life that Declan is a man to be trusted and respected, Major, the dragon answered before the officer could get the question out completely. *I have known him longer than anyone in this world, without exception. You will not find a more stalwart example of mankind, whatever reservations you might have.*

The major nodded, but there was the very faintest hint of a smirk on the corner of her lips that told Ester y'Rehl very likely didn't think being the most "stalwart example of mankind" was anything to be impressed about. Just the same, she lifted two fingers and made a following gesture.

"All of you, with me. I will take you to the Colonel. He sits with the mage as we speak." The smirk turned into the faintest sign of distaste at the mention of Ester's father. *"He will likely have more questions."*

What of our beasts? Ryn asked evenly, clearly pretending not to have noticed anything amiss about the command.

"Unless they can speak for themselves, leave them be. I trust they won't get up to much trouble on their—"

Declan. Ester. Call them, would you? I imagine Bonner will want to communicate with Orsik at some point, at the very least.

Smiling to herself at the flash of surprise that snuck across the major's otherwise hard features, Ester did as she was told, calling Eyera back to her as Declan did the same for Orsik. The warg came bounding up the shore at once, still playing even as they ran. Once they were all together—every *er'endehn* eyeing the animals nervously except for Lysiat ay'ahSel—y'Rehl made a sound of resignation before turning and moving into the tents at a swift pace, obviously expecting them to follow her.

In a narrow line, they did, stepping after the officer into the heart of the dark elf encampment.

CHAPTER SIXTEEN

I find myself, on this day, having trouble understanding the trepidation harbored by so many of my officers, though I'm hardly surprised by it. I am young to carry the title of Colonel, privileged as I am to have inherited the strength and mind of my father and many other greats of the fallen city of Syr'hend. While I claim this with pride, it comes with the cost—or blessing, perhaps—of having been born centuries after the great war. I have been taught that magic is a terrible thing, yes, but I cannot bring myself to loathe it in the same way those that saw the Witch wield it against our people do. I have hope, I must admit. Hope that what we learn from these strangers to our land may open long-shut eyes. There was a time, after all, where magic was not only welcome among the dark elves, but fervently sought.

Then again… I suppose that's exactly what brought Sehranya's destruction down upon us in the first place…

—PRIVATE JOURNALS OF KELLEK SYR'ESH, C. 1076P.F.

While she didn't take hold of him again as they moved, Ester walked so close to Declan that they bumped shoulders almost every other step. Ordinarily he suspected he might have found this proximity distracting—his heart had nearly leapt into his throat for joy when he'd found himself wrapped in her arms, even if she *had* tackled him to the ground—but for once Declan's attention was on everything other than the beautiful half-elf he was thrilled to stand beside once more.

He imagined, in a way, that what he was feeling was not unlike the wonder Ester had experienced when they'd shown her the streets of Ranheln for the first time…

It wasn't that there was all that much going on in the tight quarters formed by the neat rows of gilded tents that formed the *er'endehn* camp. Truth be told, there couldn't have been more than two hundred soldiers moving around them in total, and Declan had seen enough campaigns in his time not to be wowed by such a minimal force. It was, rather, *how* things were going on in camp that awed him so, as well as the place itself.

While the tents had seemed unadorned and unimpressive from the other side of the lake, on closer inspection Declan found that they were—like the armor of the elves—in fact meticulously decorated, but only in a fashion someone with a human's eyes could see from proximity. While simple in design, the dark cloth of the footsoldiers' quarters were lined with gold threading that gleamed even in the dim light of the day. The bodies of them, too, were stitched with thin patterns and motifs in the same color, like faint paintings across stretched black canvas. After studying several such structures, Declan realized the symbol was the same on each of the tent walls, and he decided at last that the motif of the curved sword and bow was very likely the emblem of Ysenden itself.

There was more, too, though. Delicate iron torch stands—unlit in the daylight—were staggered here and there along the walking paths, and every fourth tent a brazier was aglow, each one three feet wide and constructed of what looked to be metal leaves arranged like a blooming flower. As they passed the fourth or fifth of these, Declan was astounded to see one soldier put a boot on the top of the arrangement and—with what seemed minimal pressure—collapse the entire thing in and onto itself, sealing off the dying embers within without so much as a spark.

That would explain the lack of smoke, Declan though to himself as they moved by, watching the soldier in question turn and start to berate another who—if he had to guess—had accidentally brought back wet wood from the forest.

This incident, however, was clearly the exception rather than the rule, because the camp otherwise seemed to work with the precision of the finely-crafted pocketwatches one could find in the high-end storefronts of the largest of Aletha's markets. Despite the small number of soldiers, everywhere he looked Declan saw movement, whether it was elves patrolling the lines in pairs, or groups looking to be coming and going from the Vyr'esh with supplies and foodstuff. There were, however, very few shouts and calls over the tents, as he would have expected from even this smaller camp. Rather, the bustle of activity flowed in and around itself, the soldiers going about even the most basic tasks with a deliberate focus, largely lacking in distraction or mistake or collision despite the tightness of the quarters. Only the nine of them crossing through at a good clip appeared a sufficient enough oddity to draw attention away from assignments, and even then the disturbance appeared brief. Funny enough, it was on *him* that Declan discovered most eyes fell, then shifting to Ryn, then Orsik and Eyera. Ester, it appeared, had been among them long enough to have lost her novelty with the soldiers of the *er'endehn,* who for some reason seemed to find the presence of a human among their mix more curious than a dragon's.

"Same as in the tunnels…" Declan mumbled to himself, frowning as a duo of patrolling soldiers watched him go by with narrowed eyes, gazes only sliding to Ryn briefly, then the warg as they passed.

"Hm?" Ester asked at his side, looking up at him.

"Ryn," Declan said, speaking quietly as he nodded to their friend's scaled back ahead of them, managing the packed sand in front of the warg. "I don't care *what* kind of training these soldiers are put through. You'd think a bloody *dragon* walking through the middle of their camp would cause a buzz, but they all seem more perplexed that *I'm* here."

Ester grunted in agreement. "I see. Same as the mountains," she echoed. "I've actually been digging at that very oddity with the ay'ahSel brothers, but they won't say a word about it. It's like they're used to him."

"Maybe they are?" Declan offered. "Ryn has one of his dragons in Ysenden, doesn't he?"

"Arrackes," Ester confirmed, but shook her head as they all took a turn down a wider mainway that cut through the center of the camp. "But that wouldn't explain *this,* would it? If he's the only dragon in Ysenden—even if he's living there openly—would *every* soldier have spent enough time in his presence not to make some kind of fuss about it?"

Declan shrugged. "Probably not, but I don't have any better ideas..."

"Maybe there's more than one? It's been a long time since Ryn's been back to the Reaches. Maybe some of them left the mountains and took up with the elves."

"Plausible," Declan agreed, though he had his doubts. "As plausible as anything else, at least."

Before Ester could continue to theorize, though, they reached the edge of the lake shore, their narrow line stepping out onto a marginally wider swath of open sand to spread out a little as ahead of them y'Rehl held up a hand to indicate that they halt. All eight of them stopped short—Orsik and Eyera sniffing at the corners of the nearest tents as they did—and Declan had to keep himself from whistling as the major vanished into the middle of the three pavilions staked at the frozen edge of the water before them.

In addition to being larger than the footsoldier's tents, this trio of quarters were also marginally more decorative, not to mention more sturdily built. A dozen wooden butts of narrow lats and ribs extended from the edges of the circular canvas roofs, each carved with handsome, subtle patterns. Above them all the banner twisted and fluttered, sometimes in the wind, sometime in the rising heat that looked to be coming from a hole at the apex of the center pavilion's canopy. The entrances were grander as well, the two smaller flanking tents accented with gold draping over their single-flap doors, while the larger one had a two-flap access that was itself woven with spiraling patterns. Unfortunately Declan had only just started trying to make out the shapes of the threading—a pair of shields, he thought—before one side of this entrance opened to reveal y'Rehl again, motioning for them to enter.

"The animals, too?" Declan joked with a snort as the three ay'ahSels made for the open flap at once.

Ryn, who had come to stand on Ester's other side as they waited, shook his head with a bit of a smile. *We can leave them. I only had them follow to make a point.*

"Good for you," Ester said with a dry laugh, stepping forward to lead the way as Declan turned to address the warg.

"Orsik. Eyera." The two turned their broad heads in his direction at the sound of their names. "Stay put. We won't be long."

While the female blinked at him blankly, the male gave a grunt that might have been understanding before returning to his sniffing. Smiling to himself, Declan hurried to catch up to Ryn, who had followed on Ester's heels and was already ducking to step into the pavilion.

Stepping in behind the dragon, Declan found himself looking around in pleasant surprise as he took in the interior of the large tent. While the space was more black and gold, just as he'd expected, it was also much more brightly lit than he would have thought, illuminated—unexpectedly—by several lines of moonwing lanterns that hung from the wooden lats over their heads. A comfortably thick carpet padded the sand under their boots, and another brazier—just like the others they'd seen outside—took up the center of the open space, the gentle flames of the smoldering pile of embers within casting off enough heat that he felt it through his own weave of warmth. To one side of the interior a single cot was strung up, while on the other several crates were stacked with wide, rolled-up lengths of parchment that looked to have been carefully organized. Declan only had to wonder briefly what the scrolls were, because before them—on the other side of the brazier—a few figures were standing around a broad folding table, bent over what could only have been several large maps weighed down at the corners by various stone, candles, and even a sheathed sword. About a half-dozen elves made up the majority of the congregation, and while Declan couldn't tell at a glance what rank this grouping of *er'endehn* held, he knew by the stiffness of the ay'ahSels' postures that they were likely in the presence of the camp's highest officers.

Them, and a squat, bald man dressed in unadorned robes patterned now in myriad shades of brown, white, and green to match the winter pallet of the world outside.

"Declan!" Bonner boomed the moment the two of them met eyes, a broad grin splitting his braided beard. Stepping away from the table, the old man practically jogged around the brazier, brushing past y'Rehl without so much as a glance to reach Declan and take him firmly by both arms. "Welcome *back*! And here I was beginning to think I'd have to start looking for another handsome suitor for Ester soon!"

"Hello, Bonner," Declan answered genially, smiling down at the mage even as Ester squawked in protest at his elbow. "Sadly you won't get rid of me that easily. You and Ryn have taught me too well, it would seem."

"Of course we have!" Bonner chuckled patting Declan's arms fondly once before looking to the dragon. "Where did you find him?

Or *them*, rather." He looked to have just noticed Lysiat ay'ahSel, his cheer dimming a little as his green eyes went to the bandages still visible under her helm. "I count two of the three..."

Orsik is outside, don't worry, Ryn assured him. *And they were about a half-day's ride east of us as the crow flies. Just within the Vyr'esh's borders.*

"So close?" Bonner looked surprised as he turned to Declan again. "I feared those passages would take you further away than that, lad."

"They did," Declan said with a bit of a pained expression. "ay'ahSel and I have been in the woods for four days, now. Five, actually, counting today. The tunneler caught us a little under a week after we split with you lot, just as we found an exit. After we dealt with that, it was just a matter of tracking west again, hoping we'd run into you or your trail eventually. That's how Ryn found us."

"The 'tunneler'?" Bonner echoed, looking perplexed. His confusion only lasted a moment, though, before his eyes went wide. "Oh! *Oh*! You saw it?! The beast? And you dealt with it?! How? What was it? An annelid?"

"A-a what?" Declan stammered, half-laughing at the abrupt barrage of eager questions.

"An annelid!" the old man said excitedly. "A tubular invertebrate! Like an earthworm! It certainly *seemed* like an annelid from the glimpse I caught of it, but the *size* of that thing! How on earth did you manage to—?"

Abruptly there came a sharp, poignant cough, and Bonner shut up at once, turning to look back across the pavilion with a guilty smile.

"Ah... uh... *Syel, Syr'esh-Hal,*" he said a little sheepishly, seeming to address one of the dark elf officers in particular who stood on the far side of the map table. "*Ul'ves vehen.*"

Luckily for Declan, Ester had clearly already been ready to act as his interpreter for the purposes of this meeting, because she quietly turned her father's words for him at once.

"Apologies, Colonel Syr'esh. My friends have returned."

The camp commander, it turned out, was a surprise to Declan. For some reason he'd expected to find himself opposite a grizzled war veteran, bearded and weighed down with time and experience, but the elf looked no older than y'Rehl or any of the ay'ahSels. He had a handsome, clean-shaven face, and his white hair—exposed absent the helmet resting on the table before him—was cropped short, no longer than his ears. Counter to most of his kind, he was broad in the shoulder—almost as broad as Declan, in fact—which likely suited him well for wielding the large, two-handed blade strapped across his back.

Most surprisingly of all, however, was the fact that—despite Bonner's somewhat-inappropriate jubilation interrupting what appeared to be a very serious meeting—the colonel was not taking them in with any measure of hostility, and in fact almost looked amused following the old mage's apology.

"*Lysiat*," this "Syr'esh" called out once he knew he had their attention, turning white-red eyes on Lysiat ay'ahSel. "*Tend as ul vaca?*"

There was a rumbling of laughter from nearly everyone in the room, even Ryn and Bonner, and Ester worked quickly to catch Declan up.

"Lysiat. How was your vacation?"

Declan chuckled, bending an ear closer to listen to the half-elf's translation as ay'ahSel responded.

"*Yes, sir.*" The answer came with a nod. "*I don't foresee needing another one like it anytime soon.*"

The colonel smiled and nodded. *"No. I would think not. It is good to have you back among us. I hope you have thanked Master Ryndean for forcing my hand on staying put. You'd be trekking a fair ways longer back to Ysenden, had I had my way."*

"Understandable, sir," the commander answered, not even fazed by the higher officer's casual acknowledgement that he would have left them to die had it been his choice. *"I will have to find a way to repay*

both Master Ryndean and Declan Idrys for their hand in my survival."

Syr'esh very clearly didn't miss the hint ay'ahSel dropped with this response, because one eyebrow rose even as he turned his steady gaze on Declan. The elves of both races were long-lived, Declan knew, but despite that he could tell that Colonel Syr'esh was of a younger generation, perhaps even younger than the majority of his subordinates. He lacked even a hint of lines on his face, and his eyes were bright with energy. If anything, it made him all the more intimidating, not to mention impressive.

Declan suspected the *er'endehn* were not ones to allow anyone into the upper ranks of their military without solidly proven cause…

"You owe this man?" the colonel repeated, not looking away from Declan despite obviously addressing ay'ahSel. *"That is a story I would very much like to hear, I think…"*

"Colonel, if I might interrupt," Bonner cut in suddenly, stepping forward and to the center of the group to motion at ay'ahSel and Declan both. *"Your commander appears to be injured, and these two are both in need of rest and change of clothes."*

Definitely the change of clothes, Ryn echoed, earning himself a scowl from y'Rehl and the shadow of a grin from Aliek behind the major.

"Is that true, Commander?" the colonel asked of ay'ahSel, finally looking from Declan to the woman again and the bandages under her helmet. *"Are you in need of rest?"*

"No, sir," she answered dutifully. *"I am ready and willing to report at your convenience, sir."*

Bonner, though, wasn't having any of it.

"Colonel, if you would allow me to tend to them, I will have ay'ahSel in fighting form within the hour, and you can debrief them then if you must."

"I would debrief them now, Master yr'Essel," Syr'esh said, a little more firmly this time. After a moment, however, his eyes strayed back to ay'ahSel's bandages, and he appeared to ponder his decision a little

more intently. *"That being said… I've had a mind to see these 'magics' of yours for myself, I must admit. Would the commander need to be incapacitated as you treat her?"*

"No, she would not," Bonner answered with a frown. *"But rest and relaxation will do these two as much good as any spell I could—"*

"They will have their reprieve just as soon as I have my report, Master yr'Essel." The colonel's smile, while still warm, gave absolutely no impression that he would bear any further argument. *"As much as I am grateful to the spirits for the commander's return, the information she might provide us with is of greater importance than her immediate comfort. Isn't that right, Commander?"* He glanced side long at ay'ahSel pointedly.

"Yes, sir!" came the answer, prompt as a whip.

Bonner chewed on the corner of his beard for a moment, clearly not pleased with the situation. Eventually, though, he seemed to give in, because with a sigh he put his hands on his hips and dipped his head towards the crates on the left side of the space.

"Very well, but I trust you'll allow me to sit her down *while I work? All you elves are tall as trees, and I've no intention of conjuring myself up a footstool just so I can treat my patient."*

◆

Despite ay'ahSel recounting with terse, militant efficiency, it still took her the better part of a half hour to get through the tale of what had happened since her, Declan's, and Orsik's separation from the main group. She started by presenting the colonel with her damaged helmet, taking advantage of the fact that Bonner had her doff it after he'd sat her down to examine her bandaged head. As Syr'esh thumbed the dent in the black metal and handed the armor off to the other higher officers to examine, the commander spoke as best she could about the attack by the tunneler, as well as her injury and rescue at Declan's hand. While she talked, not a single one among the *er'endehn* gave any indication of surprise or empathy or emotion of any kind.

At least not until after Bonner had finished with his work, stepping away from the commander, and she got to the second attack.

Here, Declan had to keep elbowing Ester to continue translating, because the woman's astonished pauses came as frequently as widening eyes and glances by the officers in his direction. ay'ahSel spoke in detail of detecting the worm's approach, then their flight and Declan's choice to stand and fight. She spoke of the spell he had woven, of the terrible heat and melting of the ice and stone alike, though she at points required some clarification from him since she hadn't actually seen the initial setting of the trap. As Declan explained the magic and his plans—keeping to the very basics for the sake of the *er'endehn*—Bonner, too, started to watch him more intently, brow furrowed in what was either disbelief or concern, or possibly a combination of both. Whatever the case, the mage didn't have a chance to voice his thoughts before ay'ahSel was speaking of how she and Orsik had dragged Declan out of the tunnel and spent the next two days fighting for survival at the edges of the Vyr'esh before he finally woke up.

From there, there appeared to be little explanation to give, because ay'ahSel didn't do much more than indicate her and Declan's filthy, blood-stained clothes and armor and make clear that his flames were likely the only reason Ryn had found them in one piece.

As her tale came to an end there was an elongated pause while the officers all took her in, to a one—even Syr'esh—looking like they couldn't quite believe their eyes.

Then, all at once, the questions began to come so thick and fast Ester didn't have a prayer to translate more than a few words before someone's voice rose higher and more insistent.

QUIET!

Ryn brought order back to the space with a rumbling word, glaring at each of the officers in turn as the dark elves all started and stopped talking. When they were silent again, the dragon looked to Syr'esh.

Colonel, you have the stage.

The broad-shouldered elf nodded his thanks briefly before looking to ay'ahSel again. He was standing a few feet from her, front and center in the crescent of higher officers, and Declan could tell where his eyes were largely lingering:

On her head, studying the now-unblemished skin just above her right eye.

"First, Commander: how are you feeling?"

ay'ahSel, for her part, looked surprised at this opening question, a sentiment clearly shared by some of the colonel's subordinates judging by the shared glances happening behind Syr'esh's back. Standing off to one side—with little to offer the conversation at that time—even Aliek and Tesied ay'ahSel, too, traded a glance.

"Erm… Good, sir." The commander blinked then, as though only just realizing what she was saying. She lifted a hand to her temple, feeling around her forehead a bit with widening eyes. *"Very good, sir."*

"Better than when you walked in here?"

"Much!" ay'ahSel confirmed emphatically, turning to Bonner without even dropping her hand from where it was now pressing about her hair. *"Thank you, Master yr'Essel. Idrys had made mention you would be able to see to me, but this is miraculous."*

There was outright muttering from the other officers at this—the commander's words had to have been bordering on blasphemy to the older generation in particular, after all—but the colonel, for his part, looked nothing short of delighted.

"Excellent!" Syr'esh said, clapping his hands together and looking at Bonner as well. *"We will have to speak more of your abilities, sir! The High Chancellor's council will not be keen to let you two into the city, but if I can assure them you mean only to assist us, it will go a long way to convincing them."*

"'You two'?" Declan muttered sidelong to Ester. "Does he mean me as well? Should I tell him I'm only good for setting things on fire, at the moment?"

"Probably not," Ester answered, suppressing a grin with obvious difficulty. "Best we leave that bit out, I think."

"And why do they keep calling your father and Ryn 'Master'? 'Master yr'Essel'? 'Master Ryndean'? What's that about?"

"A being with the ability to flatten your entire contingent of two hundred elite soldiers strolls into the middle of you camp." Ester gave him a sidelong look. "Would you not treat them with the highest difference? Especially when there are *two*?"

"Fair enough." It was Declan's turn to hide a smile. "Don't let them start that with me, though."

"Why would they? All you're good for is setting things on fire."

Declan just managed to choke back a laugh—earning himself a curious glance from Ryn in the process—but before he could retort, Ester was translating for him again. The conversation seemed to have moved on, because one of the other higher ups was pressing ay'ahSel about the tunnels, now.

"And the beast beneath the mountain?" the older elf woman asked. *"Were there more?"*

"I cannot rightly say." The commander looked as disappointed in her answer as the officer did. *"It's possible the first and second attack were perpetrated by two separate creatures, but I doubt it. Their size and weight seemed of a like kind, judging by the collapse of the tunnels."*

Leave it to her to know that, Declan thought to himself, shaking his head in disbelief. He doubted any number of years under Ester's tutelage in tracking and forestry could have supplied him with such knowledge.

"And the winged?" asked an older male officer with one missing eye hiding behind a black patch. *"What of the Witch's winged?"*

Declan, not following the question, glanced to Ester, but she looked as perplexed as he was.

We call them the 'drey', Ryn cut in briefly as ay'ahSel opened her mouth to answer. *By the time your forces arrived among the Reaches in the last great war, my kind had already seen their numbers largely eradicated. I do not know how many of them the* er'endehn *would have had to deal with…*

"Enough, Master Ryndean," the same officer answered, gesturing to his eye. *"I lost this to one such beast, these 'drey', as you call them. Even seven hundred years later, I am not likely to forget them."*

Ryn dipped his head in acknowledgement, then again more quickly to ay'ahSel, giving her leave to answer again.

"I recall no indication that there were more than the three encountered," she said at once.

"Nor we," Aliek offered in support from the side.

"Even after the separation?" another pressed, a shorter male with a cropped white beard.

The commander shook her head. She'd finally let her hand fall to her lap, though she remained seated on the crate. *"No, but it must be said that I was not in any state of mind to make such observation for several days. It is possible I simply missed the signs."*

"Or if there are *more, they are sequestered or spread out elsewhere among the mountains,"* Syr'esh offered, frowning slightly. *"In either case, it seems we cannot discount the possibility that our southern border is compromised."*

"It is not merely a 'possibility'," Bonner spoke up suddenly, crossing his arms and—for some reason—glaring at the group of officers. *"And those mountains hold worse than the drey and this 'tunneler'. Perhaps now that another one of your own has added her voice to our account, you will believe what I have been attempting to tell you for a week: Sehranya lives."*

The grumbling from the group of dark elves rose again, and several of them showed the first signs of clear anger Declan had yet seen from their kind.

"You will not bait us with such words!" the female who had asked about the worm said through gritted teeth. *"Many of us here were on those cliffs when the Witch was scattered to the winds as ash! You yourself were closest of all, if I recall!"*

"Which is why my words should be tallied as evidence, not folly," Bonner said evenly. *"These attacks were not the first signs, either, as I have said. Ghouls. Wights. The wereyn's assault on the kingdom of man. Ryndean and I sensed the Queen's eye outright on the southern slope of the Mother's Tears—your 'Karn's Line'. She* lives, *and if you need any other proof of this, your commander has provided it."* He looked to Lysiat ay'ahSel, who eyed him warily. *"Commander, tell us again how the worm died.* Exactly *how."*

"In flame," the woman answered slowly, clearly uncertain on where the question was going. *"After falling in the pit of Declan's making."*

"And what color *were those flames?"*

"Black."

The answer came easily, but while ay'ahSel obviously saw nothing amiss in her reply, it was clear many among the higher officers did. To a one the elders of the group went stiff, leaving only Syr'esh frowning at the Commander.

"Black…" he repeated carefully. *"You're* sure *of this, ay'ahSel? It was no trick of the light? Or more of Idrys' magic?"*

"No, sir," she answered, though the obvious reaction had clearly shaken her confidence. *"It was like some great shadow roaring to life. And it rose from the beast itself. Declan was already unconscious by the time it came…"* As though on instinct, she turned to Declan, who answered the question in her eyes as soon as Ester finished translating.

Bad, he signed quickly. *Bad fire.*

"Black flames," the colonel muttered, turning to look at his subordinates. *"That is the work of the Witch, is it not?"*

Not one of the other officers, though, seemed to want to answer him. Most of them were still staring at ay'ahSel in shock, and those that *were* willing to meet the colonel's eye were clearly loathe to voice their thoughts.

Fortunately, they weren't the only ones in the room with long memories.

It is, Colonel. And it means you had best start listening to what Bonner has been telling you.

Ryn stepped forward, closer to the officers.

I am aware what you have heard. The draugr. The drey. The attack on Viridian and the Queen's—your 'Witch's'—eye. There is more, though, that I do not know if Bonner has gotten around to. Like the fact that it's possible Sehranya already has allies who have helped set these traps. Or that she nearly killed us as we approached the peaks of your 'Line'. We acknowledge your reasons for hesitating to trust a human, and a mage at that—

"Do we?" Bonner muttered under his breath in the common tongue.

—but his words have now been echoed by one of your own, and I hope you will take my own just as much to heart. The fact that you are all here already—not to mention had sent a scouting party into the mountains—tells me you are aware that something, *at the very least, is amiss.* Ryn's expression grew pained. *Well… now you know what.*

Unlike what followed Bonner's proclamation, Ryn's words were met with nothing but silence. It wasn't a cold silence, either, but rather the still quiet of many clever minds stunned into speechlessness all at once.

"Spirits help us," one of the officers finally managed to get out, and the choked prayer was enough to shake at least Syr'esh from his apparent shock.

"We will certainly be in need of them, if this all turns out to be true," he muttered, though he hadn't looked away from Ryn. *"Master Ryndean, I do not know if you recall, but the Witch fell initially on the* er'endhen, *when she first rose to power. On her own people. If she intends to ascend again, then it is more pressing than ever that we get word back to the High*

Chancellor and his council."

I do recall, Ryn said with a nod, *and I also agree. I appreciate your delay on our behalf, Colonel, but we should indeed set forth at once.* He glanced over to the table at the back of the pavilion, eyeing the maps still spread upon it. *Do we make for Ysenden? Is the city still the seat of power in Eserysh?*

Declan might have been mistaken, but he thought he saw several faces among the officers darken ever so slightly at the question. They regained their composure so quickly, though, that he could not swear to it.

At least until Bonner followed up.

"It is." The mage spoke in common again. "But be careful saying that too loudly. Our arrival in Eserysh appears to have been poorly timed."

"Why is that?" Declan asked the old mage directly.

Bonner took in a breath, then blew it out again heavily.

"Because, boy… it seems we've stumbled into the beginnings of a civil war."

CHAPTER SEVENTEEN

At Bonner's words, Ryn groaned, which Declan was glad for. It meant he didn't have to.

Ever since the decision had been made to seek out the assistance of the *er'endehn*—and hopefully convince their High Chancellor to bring them into the Accord of Four—Declan had spent more time than he cared to think about dwelling on the unpleasant history of the dark elves he was familiar with. As far as he knew, they had always been a martial people, unparalleled in discipline and combat, but before the rise of the Endless Queen that temperament had also led to one steady presence in the lives of the race:

War.

Eserysh—according to Ryn and Bonner, at least—had originally been a realm divided into a multitude of city-states, nations onto themselves, each wielding its own might and power. Conflict had been a constant truth, and though neither the dragon nor the mage had gone into any great detail on the subject, Declan could only imagine the sort of bloodshed that such strained relations must have caused.

And then, over the course of two years—a blink in the life of an elf—nearly every one of those bastions had fallen to Sehranya, leaving only Ysenden as the last hope of the *er'endehn* fleeing the ruins of their homes.

All at once, it made sense to Declan.

"Now we know why, at the very least," he grumbled, bringing a hand up to rub at his eyes with thumb and forefinger.

Know what? Ryn asked him first.

It was Ester—apparently catching on as quickly as Declan had—who answered for him.

"Why the Queen has started her attack *now*."

"Precisely."

Declan looked up as Bonner agreed. The old man hadn't turned to them, and was watching the officers as they talked hurriedly among themselves, clearly debating a hundred different factors introduced by what they'd just heard. Even y'Rehl had joined them, while Aliek and Tesied had moved to stand behind their sister, frowning in the direction of their huddled superiors.

"I've been thinking the same thing since I first sat down with this lot," Bonner continued, nodding at the *er'endehn*. "It's not just what they say. It's how they act. There's tension, everywhere. Bottled up like a coiled snake."

"More than one snake," Declan added quietly. "I saw it the moment Ryn asked about Ysenden. Two or three of them didn't like hearing it called 'the seat of power'."

Ryn seemed to catch on, eyes widening, but he could say nothing more without alerting all in the room to the conversation, so he just nodded slowly.

"They're vulnerable." Ester was the one to voice it. "Weak."

"Weak*ened*, at the very least," Bonner agreed. "It's been seven hundred years since the catastrophe that brought them together was eradicated, and these are not a people with short lifespans. The dark elves have raised a generation in that time? Maybe two? And the oldest among them have neither faded away nor forgotten."

"But why attack *mankind*?" Declan had to ask. It was the one thing he didn't follow. "If the *er'endehn* are vulnerable, why didn't she attack *them*?"

Ester looked about to answer, but hesitated, clearly mulling over the question. Ryn, on the other hand, put a hand on Bonner's shoulder, and the mage tilted his head in the dragon's direction a moment before nodding and speaking what was obviously a passed-along answer.

"Because an outright assault would unite them." The mage gestured again at the still-gathered officers. "It would be the one thing that would solidify them once more." Another pause as Ryn spoke to him privately again. "Besides, Sehranya tried once to take Ysenden with force, and she broke on the city walls." Bonner shook his head. "She might never have been one for strategy, but it's likely she learned her lesson from *that* failure, given what it cost her in the end."

"Meaning what?" Declan asked.

"Meaning that there's more than one way to deal with the *er'endehn*," Ester said quietly, and when he looked around at her Declan was alarmed to find her watching the dark elves with narrowed eyes.

"Right again, Esteria," Bonner muttered in confirmation. "Why waste the time and energy of many, when only a few might suffice..."

"I'm not following," Declan admitted, brow furrowing as he, too, continued to watch the elves.

It was Ryn, privately, who enlightened him.

We assumed mankind was the sole race that the Endless Queen has declared war on, since Viridian is the only kingdom to have been attacked. The dragon shook his head as Declan turned to look at him. *But what if that's not true? Sehranya very likely has at least one apprentice, at least one helping hand that we know of who has already infiltrated the world of man.* Ryn's eyes gleamed in the light of the brazier as he took in the higher officers, his gaze sliding across one elf after another, then even to the ay'ahSels. *Is it so great a stretch to think she might have found herself such assistance among the* er'endehn *as well?*

◆

For the remainder of the meeting Declan couldn't stop himself from resting his left hand on the pommel of the dark elf blade on his hip, fidgeting with the silver signet around his middle finger there as he did. It was a vain comfort—he doubted he'd so much as be able to draw the sword completely before someone among the *er'endehn* liberated his hand from his arm—but it was a comfort nonetheless. Despite their unfamiliarity—despite the strangeness of their language, the rigidity of their cultures, and the novelty of their features—Declan realized now that he had felt *safe* for a few bare minutes, just that brief time it had taken y'Rehl to walk them through the camp and into the colonel's pavilion. It had all been strange to him, and perhaps a little cold, but there had been a steadiness to the surroundings, in that taste of civilization he hadn't had in the long weeks since he, Ryn, Bonner, and Ester had left the city of Ranheln behind and taken to the King's High Road.

Now—with the echo of Ryn's words interrupting other cohesive thoughts—Declan felt hardly safer standing in that tent than he might have lost on his own among the thickening pines of the Vyr'esh that towered not a minute's walk up the shore.

Is it so great a stretch to think she might have found herself such assistance among the er'endehn *as well?*

Declan had to struggle to focus, after that, had to work to hear Ester's translation after the higher officers had finished with their mutterings and returned to the interrogation at hand. Lysiat ay'ahSel was once again grilled by Syr'esh and the others—in particular about the tunneler and its defeat—and over the course of another half hour proved not only unrelenting in their questioning, but also more knowledgeable in the subjects they were pursuing than Declan expected. He hadn't wondered before why the elves hadn't thought the *drey* enough evidence to seriously consider the possibility of the Queen's revival, but Syr'esh's older subordinates were quick to advise the younger colonel on the stitched nature of "the winged". It turned out that the working theory had been that the drey the ay'ahSel twins had already reported on were remnants of the old war, granted longevity by the dragon flesh that made up a portion of their bodies, but this idea was cast aside as soon as the nature of the tunneler was revealed. It was impressive, truthfully, to watch the *er'endehn* discuss the worm's Purpose so matter-of-factly, collectively agreeing that the presence of the black magic was indisputable. Despite their aversion to spellcraft, the older elves seemed at least as familiar with the subject as Declan himself was. They concluded with not even a minute's debate that if the tunneler had been cursed with a Purpose during the war, the feral drive of the magic would have made it known eons ago. The worm, all agreed, was newly cursed.

Sehranya lived.

And her influence likely lingers closer than you might realize… Declan couldn't help but think again, unable to stop studying the officers even as they seemed to conclude their interrogation of Lysiat ay'ahSel. The revelation weighed on him, now that Ryn and the others had opened his eyes to it. Sehranya, weaving insurrection among the *er'endehn*. He knew, of course, that even if this were true it was unlikely the traitor—or traitor*s*—stood there in the tent with them. This was an outpost, a base camp, and despite the clear influence Syr'esh wielded, he was yet only a colonel.

Just the same, Declan couldn't stop his palms from sweating as he stood among his friends, nor his mind from reaching for the familiar weave of the firestone in his breast pocket, warm and steady against his chest.

When the last of the questions had finally been answered, there was a final discussion among the high officers—kept brief this time—before they all claimed satisfaction with the information they had gathered. Eventually, it was towards *him* that most eyes fell, and the trepidation Declan was working hard to wrangle slipped loose. As Colonel Syr'esh stepped towards him, Declan fought not to swallow nervously, and he deliberately dropped his hand from the sword at last in an attempt not to seem suspicious.

Syr'esh, of course, didn't miss the moment.

"*Veht, y ven nevyl,*" he said with a light laugh, coming to stand before Declan.

"Human, you seem nervous," Declan understood even before Ester translated quietly for him.

He worked up a smile. "Forgive me, Colonel. All I've been made to know of your people is your prowess for battle. Traveling these last days beside Commander ay'ahSel—and her unit before that—has only convinced me I *should* be nervous when within sword's reach of any of you."

As Ester turned the words, a glimmer of amusement seemed to shine in Syr'esh's firm gaze.

"And here I have been told my whole life that mankind is a rash and petulant race. I admit you have me questioning that a little, Declan Idrys."

"A low bar to beat, sir," Declan answered, keeping his smile.

The colonel almost grinned then, he was sure of it. *"Perhaps."* Ester continued translating for the dark elf. *"But if half of what ay'ahSel would have us believe is true, I would say you are raising that threshold rapidly."* Syr'esh's gaze dipped, then, taking in first Declan's ruined shirt and jacket, then his pants and boots. *"And judging by your state, I'm inclined to believe her…"*

The colonel raised a hand, and the closest of the officers—Major y'Rehl—stepped forward to attend him at once.

"*Hal*?" she asked formally, and Declan understood the addressing of the colonel even without Ester having the time to translate.

"See Idrys fit with clean clothes and armor. Tell the quartermaster she may use any of my own spares if needed, given he and I are nearly of a size."

Syr'esh shifted, then, but it wasn't at the major he looked. *"Commander—"* Lysiat ay'ahSel, who had been watching the proceedings with subtle interest, at last jumped up from her box to stand at attention, clearly feeling better following Bonner's ministrations *"—this sword you've lent him. May he keep it?"*

Declan's mouth fell open, but before he could say a word in surprise or protest, y'Rhel beat him to it.

"*Hal!*" the major hissed, clearly not believing her ears. "*Yl veht! Yl mytosyl!*"

Again, there was no need for Ester's translation even as it came. *"Colonel!"* the major had protested. *"He is a human! He is a mage!"*

There came a grumbling of likeminded assent from among the other officers—and Declan even thought Aliek ay'ahSel, over by his sister, looked momentarily torn—but the colonel didn't so much as deign the dissenters, including y'Rehl, with a glance.

"I am aware." Ester was quick in her turning of his answer, though she didn't manage to capture the coolness Declan detected in Syr'esh's own words. *"He is also, apparently, the sole reason we now find ourselves furnished with critical information, not to mention Commander ay'ahSel's return. I do not recall you having anything to say cross-wise when* yr'Essel *was provided with armor and a bow."* He indicated Ester with a loose hand as he spoke.

Well that explains that, Declan thought, looking sidelong at the half-elf. He'd been wondering how she'd come to be outfitted in dark elf leathers, not to mention the bow she still held in one hand and the quiver of arrows on her lower back that had probably lost a few shafts when she'd tackled him.

"She is cousin, Colonel," one of the officers, the one with the eye-patch, spoke up in y'Rehl's defense. *"Er'enthyl. She can be trusted."*

"As can he, according to our field agents." Syr'esh continued not to look around at his subordinates, though his tone was growing more

and more stern. *"And* that—" he cut off y'Rehl as the major looked about to speak again *"—will be the end of the discussion. Commander!"* Lysiat ay'ahSel brought herself up straight. *"I asked you a question. The sword. Can he keep it?"*

"Yes, sir," Ester translated the commander's quick answer. *"If I can supply myself with another from our cache?"*

"Add that to the list for the quartermaster," Syr'esh said over his shoulder to a stone-faced y'Rhel, turning towards Declan again. *"Do you require anything else?"*

It took Declan a few seconds to realize the colonel had been addressing *him.*

"Me?" he asked, stupefied. He had to admit he was more than a little pleased to hear he would be allowed to keep the blade ay'ahSel had lent him, but being asked directly by the camp commander if he had any personal requests was almost alarming.

Again, the hint of a smile from Syr'esh.

"Yes. You. I do not carry debt gracefully, Declan Idrys. You have returned to us one of our most promising junior officers, risking your life in the process, and the information this has subsequently provided us may well prove invaluable. The er'endehn *are indebted to you,* despite what my officers may say."

These last words were said with force, which—despite the colonel never looking around—had several of the elves in question closing mouths that had just opened as though ready to protest.

Declan, too, had been about to start answering, about to say he was already grateful for the blade and would be doubly so for a change of clothes, but he stopped himself short. Considering the colonel carefully, he looked then to the higher officers and the sour expressions they were hiding with varying levels of success. None of them were likely to be among Sehranya's turncoats if she had any, it was true, but there was always the risk.

In fact, in the entirety of the pavilion, there was only a single member of the *er'endehn* that Declan was *sure* could be no traitor. Sehranya, for some reason, wanted him dead, along with Ryn, Bonner, and Ester, and there was only one elf who'd had ample opportunity to see him cut down without drawing attention, but had failed to do so. If he allowed himself to be a little greedy in his request, Declan might just earn him and his friends at least one ally they could trust without question among the dark elves.

And maybe even inch a little closer to Herst's legend in the process...

"Training, sir," Declan said at last.

Syr'esh, after Ester had translated for him, didn't blink or move, but Declan could tell all the same he was surprised when the colonel repeated the request back to him.

"Training, you say...? And in what discipline?"

"The blade, if I could be so bold."

Ester made an 'oh' sound beside him before turning the words, and this time Syr'esh's brow rose.

"I would assume you a capable swordsman, if you made it this far through the Vyr'esh, Declan Idrys. Are you really in need of additional instruction?"

"I am capable, sir, and that is thanks to an excellent teacher." He felt Ryn shift ever so slightly beside him, but continued on. "But even he has admitted to coming up short when it comes to swordsmanship. I fear I cannot compare to the ability of the *er'endehn* I have seen in action."

The colonel was silent again a moment as he took in Ester's words, watching Declan a little more intently now. Nothing had changed in the dark elf's face or countenance, not a twitch or shift in his posture or bearing. Just the same, though, Declan could tell he was being scrutinized more carefully, like the officer were trying to take in his mettle in an attempt to measure his worth.

Then abruptly, Syr'esh relaxed, raised one hand to rub at his neck in thought, then finally nodded.

"So be it," he said, and—despite several spasms of anger from the other officers at his back—no one spoke up in objection this time. *"If I had to guess, I'd assume you already have a teacher in mind?"*

Declan, despite himself, grinned ever so slightly.

"Yes, sir." Lifting a hand, he pointed across the pavilion. "Someone who handles a blade better than anyone I've ever known."

Every head turned to follow his finger. Only one figure stood unmoving, looking as though she were struggling to hide what might have been a half-annoyed, half-amused expression.

In the end, Lysiat ay'ahSel cocked an eyebrow at Declan as he smiled at her, not seeing Aliek's stern frown or Tesied turn his face away to hide a laugh.

◆

"I've said it before, and I'll say it again: you're a clever boy, Declan. I'll give you that."

Declan nodded his appreciation up at Bonner, who was seated comfortably atop a content Orsik as they walked. The warg had been nearly as delighted to find the mage as he had Eyera, and would likely have knocked the old man flat on his ass the moment they'd been dismissed from the tent were it not for Bonner's deceptive strength.

"Two birds, one stone," Declan credited himself, looking back at Ryn walking side-by-side with Ester at their back, Eyera taking up their rear. "I'd assumed you were going to push to have me trained by someone among the *er'endehn* anyway, when you had the chance?"

I was, the dragon nodded, skirting the hot edge of a brazier they passed, ignoring the curious glances of the dark elf soldiers gathered around its other side for warmth. *Though I did have someone other than the commander in mind. For you and Ester both, in fact, but it seems you've each taken care of that on your own.*

Someone else? Declan thought, a little surprised by this, but for the moment he was more interested in the second part of Ryn's statement, and he looked around at Ester. "You're training?"

"I'd hardly call it that," the half-elf told him with a snort. "The ay'ahSel brothers, Aliek and Tesied. I've picked up a thing or two watching them, but I get the sense they were more interested in me than in *teaching* me."

"Interested in… you?" Declan repeated, feeling something itch uncomfortably at his chest.

Ester nodded, seeming somewhere between amused and annoyed. "And you. They'd just started pestering me about what kind of person you were when the four of you decided to show up. Apparently they'd been trying to drag information out of me for days, if politely."

"Ah." Declan hoped he didn't sound *too* relieved as he looked forward again, following Bonner as the mage guided Orsik around a quick right and left. "I suppose that makes sense. I would have wanted to know what kind of blundering oaf *my* sibling may have been dragged off by, if I'd been in their shoes."

Ester let slip a laugh at that, and Bonner and Ryn both grinned, leading Declan to do the same. It was a strange feeling, but not unwelcome. He had missed his companions, missed their presence and their warmth. While Lysiat hadn't been a *poor* comrade over the last week or so, the disparity in language had made things difficult, conversation absent as it was. It had felt almost bizarre, for just a second, when he'd explained his plan to his three friends as soon as they'd been out of earshot of the dark elves and watched them follow his logic at once. It was a breath of fresh air, especially when all of them had seen the soundness of his idea. If Lysiat ay'ahSel had wanted him dead, he would be dead, they all agreed.

It was both affirming and a little deflating to think about.

Still, they had an ally, now, or as close as they were going to get for the time being. *If* Sehranya had her claws in the *er'endehn*, they had direct access to at least one officer they knew they could trust, even if she was only a commander. In the meantime, they would just have to stick to the plan, and pray to the Mother above they would reach Ysenden and its High Chancellor before whatever traitors might be lingering among the ranks of the dark elves made their first move. For this reason, Declan was doubly grateful Syr'esh had acceded to his request for training. If they were about to plow headfirst into what sounded like a brewing conflict among the *er'endehn*, then he needed to improve his combat prowess, and fast.

Fortunately, it turned out Declan wasn't the only one to have his abilities on the mind.

As they reached the western edge of the camp and made for the trees of the Vyr'esh itself—Bonner had apparently denied the offer of a tent from the elves, opting for "better accommodations"—the mage shifted atop Orsik to look down at him.

"Declan… I have a question."

Declan blinked, then turned to meet the old man's eyes. "Yes?"

"The worm. Its death. Did it happen as the commander said?"

Declan frowned, then nodded, following a path made by foragers through the snow as Orsik plowed his own way towards the forest a little to his right.

"Meaning she was also correct in saying you were unconscious for two days?"

Declan nodded again. "That's right. I think I would have been out for longer, if the situation hadn't called on her screaming at me. I'm pretty sure ay'ahSel would have stabbed me in the thigh to try to wake me, if I hadn't come to when I did."

"The wolves, yes. I recall." Bonner was watching him carefully again, as he had when ay'ahSel had been telling her story.

"Did I… do something wrong?" Declan asked eventually. He knew the answer, of course, or thought he did. He'd cast aside every lesson the mage had taught him to weave the spell that had proven the end of the tunneler, and he'd suspected—even before he'd cast it—that Bonner would have his head if he survived. Apparently the time for punishment had come due.

As it turned out, however, he was a little off the mark.

The only thing wrong is that you're standing right now.

It was Ryn who answered, and Declan turned to see the dragon following his path while Ester and Eyera had chosen to tail Orsik along the male's new trail. He raised an eyebrow, and the dragon gestured towards him with a clawed hand.

I'm not exaggerating, Declan. You're—quite literally—a walking question, at the moment, if it all happened as you and the commander say.

"Why is that?" Ester had to call out from the other side of a heavy pine as they finally stepped into the trees, leaping the bank of snow that had gathered along the base of the trunks that lined the shore. "It's been days since he woke up."

"Days that are hardly enough time to recover from arcane fatigue, as you should know, Ester." Bonner frowned around at his daughter as they came about the other side of the massive evergreen. "I'm disappointed. Has it been so long since your lessons? Perhaps I should have you join Declan in his instruction, now that we can resume them. He's getting very near that point in his education."

Ester, for her part, smiled nervously and waved the one hand not holding her new bow in declination. "No thank you. I found the laws of magic boring enough the *first* time you taught them to me, and that was before we realized how little talent I have for it all. Just answer the question, Father: why is it strange that Declan is standing right now?"

Bonner continued to watch his daughter disapprovingly for a moment as they headed a little deeper into the shadows of the woods, but finally turned about again as the sound of the wind and camp faded a bit at their backs.

"As talented as you are—" he addressed Declan "—I hope you would agree that you are very new to the arts of magic. Correct?"

"Correct..." Declan concurred, not sure where this was going.

"And you would agree that I—and Ryn, for that matter—are *not* new to this?"

"... I would..."

"Good. Then tell me, Declan: what happens when either Ryn or I overextend ourselves? When we apply more to the weaves than we should?"

Declan frowned, following now. He had seen Bonner brought low by an over-expenditure twice that he could recall. Most recently it had been when he'd practically pieced Ester's body back together in the unyielding stone of the Mother's Tears, but more alarming was the first time.

The first drey attack.

The assault by the imbued creature had nearly cost the mage—and Ryn—their lives. The old man had strained himself to the point of keeling over as he'd helped the dragon first in fighting the beast, then in preventing him from plummeting to the ground after Ryn had fainted in mid-air. The toll of the weaves had been so great that Bonner hadn't been able to conjure up more than a protective barrier to shield the two of them when the drey had crawled out of the hole the dragon had put it in, and after *that* nightmare had come to an end, Bonner had been tired for days.

As for Ryn himself, Declan already knew the cost the dragon had to pay to take on his true form. He'd witnessed his friend sleep for a full night and day after that same fight with the drey, and it was longer still before Ryn had felt well enough to travel.

"You're... tired," Declan finally responded to the mage's question, internally wincing at the lameness of his answer. "*Very* tired."

At his side, Bonner brought Orsik up short.

"No, boy," the old man said, still looking down on him as Declan stopped beside the warg. "We are *expended.* We are *empty*, or as close to empty as we can be without being in danger. You've experienced a little of this, I know. Have our lessons left you bright? Has summoning your flames again and again left you cheery and full of life?"

"... No," Declan conceded. "I'm exhausted."

It was true. He'd complained to Ester about it more than once. Bonner's training had always been nearly as draining as Ryn's was, when Declan and the half-elf had spared against the dragon for hours on end. He'd always attributed it to mental fatigue, but something told him Bonner was about to correct him on that concept.

"Of course you are." Swinging a foot off the warg, Bonner slid from the animal's back to land with a light *thump* in the lighter dusting of snow beneath the trees. "Something cannot be made from nothing, Declan. Magic is not free." The mage stepped forward to stand in front of him, then, and despite the fact that the man was a good foot shorter, Declan found himself holding his breath. Given his usually jovial nature, it could be easy to forget who the man was.

Bonner yr'Essel—formerly Bonner Fehn—court magus of the last king to have ruled Viridian when magic still held sway over the realm of man.

"We haven't gotten so far into your lessons, Declan, so I will spare you the minutia for the moment. Rather, picture this: a common man, ignorant of his innate potential for the arcane, is like a peasant. He is poor, and he has little, but he is not absent that which gives a man meaning in life. He is capable of joy, capable of purpose. Do you follow?"

Declan nodded hesitantly, completely at a loss as to where this metaphor was going.

"Now, imagine the awakening of that man's magic as the peasant coming into wealth. Usually—like most mages as they learn—this happens slowly. Little by little. The peasant has the opportunity to adapt to his gold, to learn how best to spend it so he does not end up without again."

Bonner paused to make sure he was paying attention, and Declan nodded once more to show that he was.

"Eventually the hope is that the peasant is no longer a peasant, but a rich and affluent individual, granted access by his wealth to all the wonders and curiosities of the world. The equivalent of a mage of power and ability." Bonner brought a finger up to the side of his nose. "Now, imagine if you would, what would happen if an event occurred that required that man to expend all his wealth at once, to empty his coffers, leaving himself with nothing."

Declan was starting to follow, finally. "You mean as a mage might if they needed to cast a spell beyond their usual ability…?"

"Exactly like a mage might, yes. The man is left penniless. What happens to him?"

"He goes back to being poor."

"As the same man he was?"

Declan shook his head, seeing at last what Bonner was getting at. "No. He goes back to being poor, but now he knows what it is like to live a life of wealth."

"Yes." Bonner agreed like they had arrived at his point. "And this can have a variety of effects on a person, depending on who they are. Perhaps he picks himself out of the dust and strives to build his riches up again. Perhaps he turns his back on that path and seeks to find the simpler pleasures he once enjoyed." The old mage frowned, dropping his hand from his face. "Or perhaps he gives up, and takes his own life in the despair of having lost so much."

It's much the same for mages, Declan. Ryn picked up for the man. *Only more… physiological. It is called 'arcane fatigue'. The body adapts, you see, when one's magic is awakened. It begins to depend on it, like it might if you grew a second heart that alleviates the workload of your first. Usually this happens over time, little by little, as Bonner said. It gives learning mages the opportunity to adjust to their 'changing' bodies, to learn the limits, and how to overcome them safely. This means that if they do dig too deep—if they are foolish enough or are forced to draw on too much of their magic—the fatigue they suffer can be mitigated and lessoned.*

"This is what has happened to Ryn and I." Bonner started up again as the dragon finished, Orsik snorting and ambling off behind him to nuzzle his sister again. "We have suffered fatigue before—you have seen it—but *our* bodies have been tempered to our magic for centuries, boy. A good night's rest or two, and we are often in fighting form again." The mage shook his head sadly. "But this is not the case for many, and certainly not all. There are those who succumb to fatigue that do not wake for days, Declan, as you did."

"And others that do not wake at all..." Ester muttered from where she stood by the warg, and Declan saw that she had brought a hand up to rest on Eyera's shoulder, as though seeking comfort as she watched him. Clearly the old lesson had come back to her, with her father's lecture.

Declan, though, wasn't looking for worry, in that moment.

"Why didn't I know this?" he demanded of Bonner, more alarmed than angry. "Why didn't you tell me?"

The old mage opened his mouth to answer, but paused, closing it again and looking at Ryn. For a moment Declan thought the two of them were communicating once more, but when he turned to the dragon Ryn was watching *him*.

To be completely honest... his friend answered after a moment, sounding a little at a loss for words. *We didn't expect it to be any issue you would suffer, Declan. At least not so soon.*

Declan blinked at him. "You never thought I would expend more magic than was safe?" he asked, trying not to sound too sarcastic. "Ryn, we've been attacked by ghouls, wights, drey, wereyn, and now an underground *worm* the size of a market square. *How could you think it might not happen*?"

"Ryndean misspeaks, boy," Bonner cut in before the dragon could answer. "It is not that we never thought you *would.* It's that we never thought you *could.*"

Declan turned back to him, confused now. "How do you mean?"

"I mean that you're a bloody wunderkind!" It was the mage's turn to sound almost a little angry now. "I mean that in the *weeks* that you have been learning the arts, you've made the progress that others take twenty times as long to accomplish! Think of Ester!" He shot an apologetic look at his daughter before continuing. "Years of work, Declan. Years!"

"And all I'm good for is starting the camp fire," the half-elf added with acerbic cheer.

Declan knew this, too. Had seen it. He'd been impressed the one and only time Ester had summoned up a fistful of flame for them to make *exactly* this point, but that had included the assistance of a firestone as a channel and it was obvious that small flash of magic had been difficult and painful.

"Your magic is—*literally,* Declan—growing at an alarming rate," Bonner continued as Declan pondered. "We've been saying it for months: your King's blood means your body in a vessel of incredible potential. It has *always* been. But you are filling that vessel at a terrifying pace. Forget the peasant growing his wealth over the years. Your body is more like a beggar being made king overnight!"

Declan smirked at that, about to accuse the man of hyperbole, but Ryn cut him off.

There's not an ounce of exaggeration in what Bonner is telling you, Declan. You can't see it—not yet—but the reason he and I had no fear that you would overextend yourself is because we didn't think you had the capability. Your pool of arcanic energy has outpaced the magic you've been learning by magnitudes. It's why you no longer feel exhausted despite using your weaves so much more frequently.

Declan's smirk turned into a weak sort of grimace. Bonner he could accuse of overexcitement, even despite the situation.

Ryn, though, he could not.

"So… what?" he asked. "I should be dead? I should have died after taking down the worm?"

"Possibly," Bonner muttered, taking on that not-uncommon air of academic interest. "Unlikely, though, given your dragon's gifts. I'm less impressed by your survival than I am by your *condition.* Arcanic fatigue is not limited to your next rest. It lingers, in new mages. Keeping to the metaphor: if you were made a king overnight, that spell you and Commander ay'ahSel have described would not be unlike having your royal rear dragged off your throne and tossed into the gutters. You should be suffering, or at least exhausted."

"Maybe he's just recovered naturally?" Ester asked from the side where she stood on her own now, Orsik and Eyera having ducked off to play again among the trees.

"No, that's not it either." Bonner was peering at Declan's body as though it were some broken mechanism that needed fixing, as though there might be a joint or knob loose somewhere he could just replace. "Judging by your reserves, you haven't even recouped as much as I would have expected if you'd really awoken four days ago."

Declan, for once, thought he had the answer to this quandary, but the rest of what the man had said caught him by surprise. "You can *see* my reserves of magic?" he asked with wide eyes. When Bonner didn't answer him, he turned instead to Ryn, but the dragon held up both hands to stop him as he shook his head.

Don't look at me. That's a gift earned, *not born with. I can't see more than a dirty ex-mercenary in desperate need of new clothes.*

"And a bath," the mage muttered, proving he was still listening. Declan was about to comment—not for the first time—how not all of them had the benefits of self-cleaning robes, when Bonner's green eyes narrowed.

"That's strange…" the old man muttered, stepping closer and bringing his face so close to Declan's left arm that his nose almost touched the claw-torn remnants of his sleeve. "Declan… are you channeling a weave other than your spell of warmth?"

"Yes," Declan told him. "I was going to say as much a second ago. I figured something out while we were separated."

"Figured what out?" Ester asked curiously, looking him up and down like she might see whatever it was her father was scrutinizing.

Before Declan could tell her, though, the mage himself gave a *whoop* of excitement.

"Gods, boy!" Bonner exclaimed, taking Declan's arm in both hands suddenly, his grip like warm steel as he turned to lift the limb in presentation. "Ryndean! Look at this! *Look at this*!"

I just *said I've not got your eye,* the dragon grumbled, but he—and Ester with him—moved forward to gather around the two men just the same. *Just tell us what you can see!*

"Suffusion!" Bonner was practically squealing, and Declan actually winced at the pressure on his arm, muscle and bone protesting under the mage's unnatural strength. "Bloody *corpomancy*! He's figured suffusion out all on his own!"

Ryndean, for his part, gaped first at Bonner, then at Declan, then back again as Ester frowned in obvious loss beside him.

Then the dragon, too, was snatching at Declan, taking up his other arm in clawed hands.

What?! Not possible. Declan, pull against me.

"Wait," Declan tried to interrupt, at a loss for what was going on. "What's suffusion? I was trying to tell you, I think I figured out how to—"

Just pull! The dragon cut him off, staring at the arm he was holding like it had turned to gold.

Declan—feeling as baffled as Ester looked—decided it was best to do as he was told, and tugged against Ryn's grip even as he focused on his spell of strengthening to make sure the weakened limb wouldn't betray him.

The dragon—a moment ago looking as excited as Bonner—appeared immediately disappointed, and he released the arm to frown at the mage.

Are you sure? I don't notice any difference. If anything he—

"Declan." Bonner looked to him even as he waved off the dragon's words. "Release your suffusion."

"M-my what?" Declan stammered. "I'm telling you, I've figured out how to—!"

"Your suffusion, boy!" Bonner was almost shouting with impatient excitement. "Your weave of strength! The corpomancy that's been keeping you upright for days now, I would wager!"

"'Suffusion'?" Ester asked. "'Corpomancy'? Is that… 'body' magics? What kind of spell is—?"

Then, though, she gasped, because Declan was sagging in Bonner's grip.

He might now know what the man was talking about—had he been incorrect to believe he'd deduced imbuement?—but it was obvious he wasn't going to get answers until he did as he was told. With less than a thought he withdrew the spell, pulling it away from his body, and at once the fatigue returned. His legs nearly buckled as the support of the magic was taken away, and even his head felt suddenly heavier after all morning spent riding. If Bonner hadn't been holding him up, Declan was quite sure there was a real possibility he'd have ended up with his rear in the snow again.

"Oh!" Ester exclaimed, rushing forward to grab him by the other arm and help hoist him back up. "Declan!"

What is this? Ryn asked in alarm. *Bonner, what's wrong with him?*

"Nothing whatsoever is wrong with him," the mage said with a grin, looking up into Declan's face. "Good, that's good, boy. Call on it again. You're damned heavy, even for a lunk of bone and brawn."

Declan nodded numbly, and it took him a few seconds to gather the spellwork again. As the weave spread through his body once more, though, he stood up straight, realizing he could even *breathe* easier with the magic's assistance.

"*Now* will you tell me what you're talking about?" he demanded of Bonner, pulling his arm loose of the old man's grasp—though he didn't make a move to step away from Ester's as she hesitated to let go of him. "What 'body magics'? Is that what happened?"

Happened? Ryn asked, scrutinizing him more carefully now. *What do you mean?*

"I had a moment when I was dragging ay'ahSel out of the tunnel," Declan explained, though he didn't look away from the mage. "The magics acted on their own, giving me strength. It's the only thing that got both of us out of the way of that damn worm. I thought it was imbuement, like the drey. I've been working on figuring it out ever sense."

To his surprise, Bonner made a face at that.

"Oh no. Most certainly *not* imbuement, Declan, no. This—" he poked the scarred arm he'd just let go"—*this* is *suffusion*, or at least the beginning vestiges of it. A basic form of corpomancy: the art—as Ester has deduced—of bolstering one's own body and mind with magic. And as for that little show of you falling apart—" Bonner turned disapprovingly to Ryn "—that was the arcanic fatigue you've been holding at bay with sheer *will*."

The dragon, for his part, blinked.

Then, jaw slackening, he looked to understand.

He's been holding himself together, he muttered, sounding astounded. *By constantly channeling the weave, he's been keeping the exhaustion at bay.*

"Excuse me," Ester groaned as she let go of Declan at last, raising her free hand in the air like a school child as she glared between the dragon and her father. "For those of us *who have no idea what you two are talking about*, an explanation would be appreciated."

"Seconded," Declan said with a curt nod. "You're leaving us behind again. This *isn't* imbuement?" He flexed one arm and made a fist, feeling the faint tingling of the magic thrum as he did.

Ryn and Bonner exchanged another look, and seemed to decide silently that the dragon was the better choice to explain this time.

No. Not imbuement, Declan, he repeated. *That is a dark art, requiring the taking of another creature's or being's life force and infusing it permanently into another's bones and body as strength. It is cruel spellwork, with the victim dying slowly as their heart and lungs grow too weak to beat, or else left eternally depleted and crippled if the necromancer is feeling merciful.*

"Necromancer?" Ester repeated in a hiss.

Ryn nodded. *My understanding is it's* theoretically *possible to imbue a living thing, but it involves the carving of runes into the very bones of the receiver.*

"The pain would be intolerable," Bonner continued for the dragon. "Any breathing being would die of shock. So—" he waved a hand as though to say "obviously"—"the dead make the best candidates."

Declan could understand Ester's grimace of disgust at these words, but there was more there, too. Something that had sent a shiver up his spine.

Carved into bone?

"Wait… Like the bone charms?"

The way Bonner and Ryn looked at him—half-impressed and

half-resigned—told Declan he had thought right.

The bone charms. Sehranya's greatest tool of expansion. He had only ever seen one—hanging from a leather thong around the neck of a dead captain of Viridian's Vigil—but even that brief sight of the thing had left an impression he doubted he'd ever forget. A small loop of bone—like the cross section of a femur or the like—it had been notably marked with etched script that had, briefly, reminded him of the runes Bonner had only just begun to teach him about. *These* symbols, though, had been something other than the careful, flowing chirography of the mage's magic. They had been… crueler, somehow, colder, as though Declan—though unable to read them—could see a bloody and terrible story etched into the harsh edges of the emblems.

It didn't help that a minute later that dead captain had risen as a wight to ambush them all, along with every other member of the Vigil unit who'd originally lain slain around him.

"Despite my jesting, Declan, you *do* have an eye for all this, don't you?" Bonner was studying him proudly. "Yes. Sehranya's charms *are* a form of imbuement. Very likely the first form, in fact. The drey came after, and even then the strengthened among them were few and far between. It is alarming, in fact, that every one of the creatures we have thus far come across appears to have been pervaded with such weaves."

Sehranya has been busy, these seven hundred years… Ryn muttered from the old man's side.

Bonner nodded, looking—just for a moment—much older than his sixty- or seventy-year-old appearance. "Yes, she has indeed…"

There was a pause as all of them felt the weight of their flight—and fight—again, but Ester was fortunately in no apparent mood for wallowing.

"Then what is *Declan* doing, Father?" she pressed, crossing her arms. "You've not explained anything yet."

"Oh!" Bonner regained his enthusiasm immediately, bouncing back from the momentary soberness in a blink. "No, I suppose I haven't!" He looked to Declan. "I'm not surprised to find you have a talent for corpomancy, boy. You'll recall the stories of your forefather, I gather?"

"I do," Declan answered. "They're the reason I've been trying so hard to master this."

"As well you should." Bonner pointed at the center of Declan's chest, just inside of where the firestone lay in his breast pocket. "Suffusion is the *body* half of corpomancy. The drawing of power from one's own magic. The environment, too, at later levels. It is not a constant thing like imbuement—at least not initially—but the goal *is* to break one's physical limits, and ultimately so consistently that the end result is not so different."

"Like you do," Declan said, stating it as a fact rather than a question.

Bonner grinned. "Yes, like I do. What gave it away?"

Declan smirked. "What didn't? You tearing half a boulder out of the stalagmites in the caverns was a pretty blatant example."

Ryn and Ester both snorted at that, earning themselves a glare from the old man.

"Yes, well..." he slowly looked back to Declan. "*That* was certainly not an illustration of my regular ability. It required additional magic poured into my weaves. Still, it *is* an example of suffusion, to be sure."

Declan couldn't help himself, at these words.

"Meaning *that's* what I'll be able to do one day?"

Bonner scoffed. "Boy, you should know by now that I specialize in verdamancy and auramancy—earth and healing magics. I am *not* a battlemage, despite whatever you might think to the contrary. No..." He narrowed his eyes at Declan. "You... What *you* should be able to do one day will very likely make tossing a hunk of rock about pale in comparison."

It was Herst's one talent in magic, Ryn offered up as Declan stared at Bonner. *Not so great of one, even, but still enough to compliment his natural ability with the blade. After he'd accepted my gifts, his potential for corpomancy grew alongside his talent for pyromancy and natural physical prowess. You have the latter of those already, and it's obvious you're on the path of eventually mastering fire.* Ryn grinned. *At the speed you learn, I'd say it won't be too long before you'll be able to jump off my back mid-flight, like he once did.*

"*What*?" Declan and Ester demanded together, earning a laugh from the dragon.

Oh yes. Not from too far up, of course. There are limits to even magic, as I keep telling you. But he could always make an entrance when he really wanted to. Never did learn to fly, though… Ryn trailed off distractedly at that.

"I'm sorry," Declan said with a shake of his head. "Fly? Herst wanted to *fly*?"

"And he might have, if he'd had a knack for aeromancy!" Bonner said with his own chuckle. "That was more his sister's specialty, though, and she never had much of a taste for the skies. Wouldn't even take to dragon-back, from what I recall."

No she didn't… Ryn confirmed, his thoughts still obviously elsewhere.

Declan and Ester gaped at the pair of them, then at each other, then at the mage and dragon again.

"I'm sorry, let me be clearer," Declan eventually got out, bringing a fist up to feign a cough to clear his throat.

Then he looked right at Bonner and yelled loud enough for the words to echo eerily through the dim light of the trees all around them.

"Herst wanted to *FLY*?!"

"Yes! *Yes*!" Bonner shouted back, covering his ears reflexively as Ester laughed at Declan's side. "Is it so strange a desire?"

Declan had to admit that was a good question.

"I mean… I suppose not? It's just…" He shook his head. "How

is that even possible?"

Bonner squinted at him for a moment longer. Then—when he seemed sure he wasn't about to be bellowed at again—he dropped his hands with a sigh.

"There is an enormous amount of energy in living things, boy. There were theories by the court mathematicians of my day that the human body possessed enough energy to level a city—or more—if it could be harnessed and unleashed all at once. This, in fact, is the very principle behind corpomancy." Bonner waved a hand at Declan's chest again. "Harnessing every ounce of one's potential, then going beyond even that. Eventually, as I've said, this is to be done efficiently. At the beginning, though—*especially* if a study of the art is taken without proper supervision—" the old man raised an eyebrow at him "—it's a constant drain on one's system *despite* all that untapped energy."

Declan frowned at him. "Meaning what, exactly?"

In answer, Bonner smiled.

Then he reached out, put a single finger over Declan's heart, and pushed.

Declan gasped as what felt like restrained lighting coursed its way outward from the point the old man had touched. He staggered back, not even hearing Ester's shout of alarm as she made to follow him, only to be restrained by Ryn taking her gently by the arm. Declan would have yelled, would have cursed by the Mother and Her Graces, but the sensation was all-encompassing, all-consuming. It wasn't painful, per se, but it *was* the single most uncomfortable feeling he had ever experienced in his life. He was reminded in flashes of the wash of agony brought on by the drey blood that had left most of his upper body scarred, and for a second he wanted to retch, a combination of the alien distress and unpleasant memories making him nauseous as the lighting spread outward. In a few seconds it was out of his chest, and while he could breath again he still had to grit his teeth while it crawled down his legs and arms. The sensation reached his knees, and he collapsed, first onto all fours, then onto one side as his elbows, too, gave way. Finally he could yell, and he did so, rolling onto his back as it continued to spread outward.

Then it reached the tips of his fingers and toes, and vanished.

For a long moment Declan didn't move, breathing hard and staring up at the dim black and grey of the Vyr'esh's canopy high above his head. Eventually, when he was *sure* the horrid feeling was gone for good, he scrambled to roll over and shoved himself to his feet.

"What the *hell*, Bonner?!" he snarled at the mage, who hadn't lost his now infuriating smile. "What was that?!"

"You tell me." The man smiled, crossing his arms and cocking his bald head to one side. "How do you feel?"

Declan paused at that. He wasn't willing to stop glaring, but he took an account of himself in silence as Ryn, beside Bonner, let go of Ester again.

It was strange, he realized. He felt… good. *Very* good. Better certainly than he had since the slaying of the tunneler, but also more than that.

If he had to guess, Declan thought his body felt better than it ever had in his entire damn life.

"What did you do?" he breathed, finally looking away from Bonner as he lifted an arm to clench and unclench his fingers before his eyes. He could tell, even with that small movement. Long years with a hilt in hand told him his grip—already impressive even for his size—was stronger than before. *Everything* felt stronger than before.

"Nothing, really," the mage answered with a chuckle. "Are you still channeling your suffusion?"

Declan blinked at that, then focused inward. To his surprise he was indeed still holding onto his weave of strength, and having an easier time of it than ever before. If he'd lost hold of the spell during whatever episode Bonner had just put him through, he seemed to have instinctively grasped it again.

"What in Her Graces…?" he muttered, staring at the ground as he continued to inwardly study the flow of power along his arms and legs.

At least until Ester's growled demand brought him back again.

"Father. *Explain.*"

Declan looked up to find Bonner wincing under the seething stare his daughter was treating him to.

"Genuinely!" the mage insisted. "I hardly did anything! I just topped him off, that's all!"

Declan frowned, not following. "Topped me off?"

If I had to guess—Ryn sounded like he was trying not to laugh as Ester stalked towards her father, bow held up like she might beat the man with it—*what I think Bonner means to say is that he has replenished your reserves, Declan. The energy you'd depleted. He seems to have filled the magic you can draw on again.*

Declan's jaw dropped.

"You can *do that*?" he exclaimed, whirling on the mage so fast his boots nearly slipped in the snow beneath his feet. "You could do that this whole time? Then what have I been suffering for, after all our lessons? Why not just replenish me so I wouldn't be so spent?"

"Would you *liked* to have gone through that experience every evening, boy?" Bonner asked with a smirk, having backpedaled just enough to be out of his daughter's reach. "Having someone else's magic coursing through your veins? It doesn't get any easier, either. You *don't* acclimate to such a feeling."

"Ah," Declan stood up straight again, understanding. "No, I suppose I wouldn't."

Bonner snorted, and then his face softened a little.

"That's not the only reason, though," he said with a shrug, as though admitting something. "You *are* an exceptional pupil of the arts,

Declan, but that has almost as much to do with your own drive as it does Ryndean's gifts. You push yourself, push your body and mind, and it's that strain, over and over and over again, which has lent itself to the breadth of your growth. I *could* have 'topped you off' every night, yes, but that wouldn't be unlike healing you every time you finished sparring with Esteria and Ryndean. Using magic to do what the body should be allowed to has its consequences. Such spellwork might have eased your aches and lessened your fatigue, but it would also have largely robbed you of the improvements all that hard work resulted in." Bonner waved a hand at Declan's chest again. "Its the same for magic, for the 'vessel' that is your body. I know the stress our lessons have put on you, boy. Intimately so. And it is *for* that reason that I would not do what I just did except in the most extreme circumstances."

It clicked, then, and with a narrowing of his eyes Declan released his grasp on the 'suffusion' weave. It still slipped away easily enough—he had a long way to go before the spell was a natural part of his subconscious, he suspected—but its departure was different this time. Where before he'd sagged and needed help to stay upright, now the weight that descended on his head, limbs, and shoulders was lesser, lighter. Again he squeezed his hands—both of them, this time—and discovered a sensation of weakness that felt more comparative to his previous strength than true fatigue.

In 'topping him off', Bonner had banished the exhaustion of the previous days, and allowed him to briefly experience the *true* benefit of the suffusion, of the weave layered over his own natural strength.

"I see you've put it together," the mage said, and Declan looked up at him again in time to see the man give an approving nod. "Good. If that's the case, you should be able to tell me: why didn't you recover on your own?"

"Father, is *now* the time for a lesson in spellcraft?" Ester asked, still glaring at her father through narrowed eyes, but the old man ignored her. He was looking at Declan evenly, waiting for an answer.

An answer Declan actually thought he had.

"The weave was a constant drain," he said. "The suffusion was consistently drawing from me, from my reserves."

Bonner nodded curtly, and to the side Ryn gave a small sound of approval. "Exactly. Well that, and your spell of warmth. You may be prodigal, boy, but you are still a neophyte when it comes to magic."

Declan, at last, managed his own smile. "Not for much longer, I hope?"

Bonner smirked and rolled his eyes even as he turned away and started into the woods again, their lesson apparently at an end. "Don't start getting cocky on me now! Ask me that again in a hundred years or so!"

Declan laughed out loud, the sound feeling as foreign among the trees as might have the trumpeting of one of the elephants the Alethan circus sometimes brought over from the deserts of Sarahkan, across Borel's Sea. Still, it felt good, and seemed to have a relaxing effect on Ryn and Ester, left to stand with them as the mage pressed on.

Infuriating as he is, the man is *a genius, isn't he?* the dragon asked of them.

"That's the worst part about it all," Ester muttered. "Half a child, and yet..."

"And yet," Declan agreed, deciding to take the lead and stepping forward after Bonner. "Can't complain, though, can we? This must be the eleventh time at least he's saved my neck at this point."

No, we certainly can't, the dragon chuckled, moving to walk beside him as Ester hung back a little to call Orsik and Eyera to heel. *You couldn't have a better mentor, Declan. I hope you realize that.*

"Oh, I don't know about that," Declan muttered, not looking at his friend as they navigated the thick roots of a heavy pine Bonner had vanished around. "I had a pretty damn good one growing up."

And he's very proud of you, Ryn said with a smile. *But he also knows where his shortcomings are. Actually, he was pleased for that very reason, back in the pavilion.*

"Why is that?"

When you asked for instruction from the er'endehn. *You don't know it, but you're very nearly on the same path as your forefather was, in his training.*

Declan's brow rose at that. "Herst? How do you mean?"

Ryn looked at him sidelong. *You* do *recall he was a prince of Viridian, don't you? Maybe not the crowned heir, but a child of Igoric al'Dyor all the same.*

Declan rolled his eyes as the sound of Orsik and Eyera's thumping footsteps came up behind them. "Yes, I recall. What does that have to do with anything?"

I told you weeks ago. Ryn laughed dryly. *As a prince of Viridian, Herst was privy to the greatest masters the country had to offer. Them—*

"And others from beyond its borders," Declan finished for him, remembering suddenly.

It had seemed little more than a passing comment in the greater conversation in which Ryn and Bonner had revealed the truth of his lineage to him at last, and he'd certainly thought nothing more of it at the time. Now, though, after having witnessed the mastery the dark elves had over their chosen craft in person, it made sense to Declan.

Ester, however, beat him to voicing the realization.

"Amherst al'Dyor was taught by the *er'endehn*?"

She came loping up on Ryn's right, riding Eyera confidently as Orsik slid into step beside Declan, who automatically ruffled the massive animal's closest ear fondly to earn himself a rumble of pleasure that didn't pierce his attentiveness as Ryn continued.

By the best they had to offer, yes. The dragon was peering through the trees as he answered the question, likely looking to see where Bonner had gone. *Them, and the wood elves as well. It wasn't so strange a practice, at the time. You have to recall this was before the Accord, before Sehranya. Humanity harbored and educated the few children of the elven races who had a knack for magic, and scholars were traded all the time to educate one another on what our peoples had independently learned of the world. Soldiers, too, were exchanged, though most frequently this was to mankind's benefit. Martial masters from the* er'endehn, *trackers and archers from the* er'enthyl.

"Not sure what the wood elves could teach about archery that the *er'endehn* couldn't," Ester grumbled. "Aliek and Tesied make my mother look like an average marksman."

Your mother was a member of the Aveer al'En. The High Knights train to protect the ehn'Vyr'en family from assault and assassination. Ryn shrugged. *She was not among the master hunters of the wood elves, who could pin a falling leaf through thick woods from a quarter of a mile away.*

Ester looked a little prouder at that, but she started to deny all the same.

"Maybe, but you should see what those brothers are capable of before you say anything to the contrary. It's like they were *built* for war. Honestly, I've learned some things just by standing around and watching the pair of—"

Declan, what's wrong?

Declan heard Ryn's concerned voice from a long way off, having stopped at the top of an embankment that led down to a frozen river across which Bonner's footprints could be seen in the snow. He'd reached out to place one hand onto the trunk of the closest tree, leaning into it for support as his sense of balance was thrown into chaos.

For the first time in a while, the world before him had faded into layered images, Ryn, Ester, and the warg all nothing more than ghostly imprints beneath the flurry of memories that swam before him.

His mind had taken him to a brightly lit courtyard of sand and stone, the walls all about him distinctly of Viridian design. Above, the sky was clear save for a few scattered clouds, the sun reflecting brightly off the clean steel of the sword that flicked and thrummed before him in quick, polished patterns.

His target, however, might as well have been made of wind and smoke for all the opportunity Declan had of hitting him.

The figure was shirtless, a sheen of sweat making his black, scarred skin shine in the day. His long white hair—as long as Lysiat ay'ahSel's—was bound in a tight braid down the back of his neck, and his pale eyes shone with concentration. His hands were behind his back, and for a moment Declan thought they might have been lashed there until he saw the dark hilt and tip of a sheathed, black-and-gold sword protruding from either side of him, and he realized the stranger was holding onto the scabbard of the weapon as a handicap.

It made the dark elf's movements all the more incredible.

Despite the speed and fluidity of his patterns, Declan's blade—*Herst's*, rather, he knew—couldn't catch more than clear air as he tried again and again and again to score a single strike on the *er'endehn.* The elf dipped and weaved and stepped both in and out of range as needed, upper body bending and twisting more like the dance of the boxers that sometimes held matches in the Alethan markets than a swordsman. Declan kept trying to up his pace, kept trying to up his speed, but the elf only seemed to expand the gap between the two of them with every passing moment, almost like he saw where the blows would be coming from before Declan even knew how he would strike himself. For nearly fifteen seconds the sparring continued like that—Declan not hearing Ryn and Ester climb the bank to rejoin him—before it ended so suddenly he could have blinked and missed it.

A slashing, horizontal blow of his sword, a duck and twist by the elf, and the heavy pommel of that sheathed blade catching Declan square in the gut from where it was still held behind his opponent's back.

He only got a glimpse of the *er'endehn's* face—white teeth grinning from within a cropped black beard and strikingly square jaw—before he doubled over and felt himself falling towards the sandy ground.

It was snow, though, that puffed up around him as he collapsed, the memories vanishing in time to find himself just starting to tumble forward down the incline towards the riverbed.

Declan!

Ryn, with all his inhuman speed, reached him first, grabbing one arm before be really started to slip. Ester was right behind him, and had him by the collar of his filthy shirt an instant later. Together the pair of them hauled him back up over the lip of the slope, pulling him all the way onto his feet.

Declan! Ryn repeated, alarmed. *What was that? What happened?*

"Are you alright?" Ester, too, was half-shouting in concern. "Are you unwell? I *knew* that old fraud would do something stupid! 'Topping-off' my ass! You could have broken your—!"

"N-no!" Declan finally managed to stammer out, blinking away the last lingering images of the foreign recollections. "It's nothing. Nothing like that." He gathered himself as the two went silent, taking a breath before looking at Ryn. "It was Herst. More of him. More of his... his memories."

Despite the months now that he'd spent with this knowledge—not to mention the numbers of times before he'd been struck by just such flashbacks—it still felt strange to speak of the phenomenon aloud.

Ryn hissed something quietly in his native tongue, eyes going wide for a second before he, too, found his voice.

What did you see? he asked at last.

"Training, I think," Declan said, testing his legs and finding them sturdy as—with a crunch of scraping claws—Orsik and Eyera, too, rejoined them at the top of the bank. "Before the war, obviously. Before everything." He frowned, recalling what he'd seen. "There was a dark elf, there. I—Herst—was trying to hit him, but couldn't. Bastard didn't even draw his sword. Just kept it behind his back the entire time..."

Ryn stared at him a moment more.

Then the dragon laughed.

I've heard that story, he said, both he and Ester letting go of Declan now that he'd regained his balance. *The very first day of Herst's mentorship. He'd had teachers before, of course—the best the royal aids could find—but none of them could keep up with your forefather for long. Igoric sent a request to the High Chancellor of Ysenden of the day, and a few months later* Herst *was suddenly the one getting put down by his training partner, rather than the other way around.*

"It was impressive," Declan had to admit. "He made it look like the *ay'ahSels* could learn a thing or two from him."

Ryn grunted in assent. *Like I said: we were a more closely knit world, back then. According to Herst, the High Chancellor sent a rising star of their military. Likely a small price to pay for the ability to have the King of mankind owe the dark elves a favor, I think.*

Declan nodded, pondering this.

"Is *that* why he was so strong?" he asked, motioning as he did that they should continue moving. "Herst? I can see why you wanted to look for a better teacher for me in Aletha, if that was the case."

Ryn gave him a mocking glare as they took the descent together, Orsik and Eyera happily leading the way now that they were following Bonner's trail again. *Did you not* just *finish complimenting me on my excellent instruction?* The dragon feigned offense. *What need for a better teacher could there have been when you had a talking horse to yell instructions at you from a distance as you swung sticks at a tree?*

Ester, on Declan's other side, sniggered, earning herself a glare from him.

"You know what I mean," Declan grumbled at Ryn as they reached the icy edge of the river and began traversing it carefully, clawed feet and boots gaining purchase only in the layer of snow that covered it.

"An instructor like that… Pretty sure they could turn any common soldier into a sword fit for a royal guard at the very least…"

Ryn nodded. *Fair enough, but the quality of one's lessons only amounts to the potential of one's growth, Declan, as Bonner said. You might have the greatest mentor of the age when it comes to your magical training, but* you *are the one who taps into those teaching.* Your *drive.* Your *need.*

"*Your* big head, if you get any more compliments today," Ester chimed in, dipping around the pair nimbly as they reached the far edge and started ascending the steep embankment.

Declan laughed, but Ryn ignored her.

Herst was much the same. He, too, had Bonner's teachings, though his natural resonance with magic was far less than yours until he accepted my gifts. He had far greater mentors in the art of the blade, too—as you've just seen. But it was his own perseverance that brought him to the pinnacle, Declan. Nothing less than that. Declan saw the white-gold eyes take him in sidelong again. *And it will be yours that does much the same, I think.*

Declan would have chuckled then, would have told the dragon he had enough pressure to chase his ancestor's legend as it was without being compared directly to him, but the sound caught in his throat as they reached the top of the bank. There, not very far from where they stood on the frozen ground, Bonner had seated himself on the protruding root of a winter maple whose trunk was some twenty feet wide. He was kicking his feet and whistling a tune like a schoolboy at play, and the mischievous glint in his eye would have had Declan on edge had he not *immediately* seen what it was the old man was so happy about.

There, among the other gnarled fingers that made up the tree's base, the dark mouth of a modest cave was well hidden by the terrain and excavated dirt that had been mounded up around it, the layer of snow that helped to camouflage it all saying clearly that this was not a hole dug by Bonner himself.

Declan groaned, stopping short even as Ester jogged quickly to catch up to Orsik and Eyera, who were trotting towards the cave happily enough. At his side, Ryn smiled with a knowing nod, patting him consolingly on the back.

If it makes you feel better, this bear seems to be hibernating, so we're not likely to have to fish for it.

Declan sighed, moving forward again with the dragon. "Heart-warming. And here I was afraid I'd have to thaw the river to earn our keep again."

"No need, no need!" Bonner was grinning as they approached, apparently overhearing. "Carro didn't so much as budge when the three of us made ourselves at home." He gestured to Ester and Eyera, who were already vanishing down the hole without a second's hesitation. "And there's ample room for us. It's been dug out to accommodate his *substantial* weight and height. I don't foresee him causing any trouble for anyone."

"Of course you've named him." Declan had to stop himself rolling his eyes as he watched Orsik paw a little less surely at the lip of the cave's descent before deciding it was safe to brave. "And I'm assuming that all means I don't want to know just how big *this one* is, do I?"

Bonner shrugged before—still smiling—he shoved himself off his root to drop down after his daughter and the warg. "Come and see for yourself. Just don't be too loud when you do. Wouldn't want anyone getting crushed by a stray paw, would we?"

Declan only grumbled after the mage, earning another laugh from Ryn as the dragon made to follow Bonner underground.

Before he could take a step downward, though, Declan held him up with a hand on his scaled arm.

"Ryn..." he started hesitantly. "Just out of curiosity... Do you recall the name of the elf? The one who trained Amherst?"

Ryn treated him to a questioning look.

"It's just… It's on the tip of my tongue," Declan explained awkwardly. "Like Herst knew it. Like I should, too."

Ryn nodded at that, understanding. *The curse of two minds.* He snorted dryly. *Or part of it at least. Let me think…* The dragon frowned, concentrating, his serpentine head tilting up a little so that the steaming of his exhalation was distinct against the dark of the canopy high above. *Cirius?* he muttered, clearly unsure. *Cirian? No…* His frown deepened.

Then, all at once, his expression cleared, and he smiled down at Declan.

Ciriak, he stated with a pleased confidence. *Herst called him Ciriak.*

CHAPTER EIGHTEEN

To my friend Igoric,

As per your request in our last correspondence, I send this missive along with one of our best.

Though he is yet only a major of Ysenden's army, I can say with full confidence that this is a solidier who will rise high within our ranks, perhaps even to a seat on the Chancellor's council or beyond. Not only is he a master of the arts you seek to challenge the prince in, but he bears a keen mind and ever keener tongue. He speaks the language of man better than many of our own scholars, and might well prove more than an instructor in just the blade, if given the opportunity.

Put simply: I have lent you the sharpest and brightest of our swords.

I do hope it will not be forgotten.

All the best,
Ly'vena

—private letter to King Igoric al'Dyor of Viridian, from High Chancellor Ly'vena Fehr'en of Ysenden, c. 300p.f.

Liriak as'ahRen, Lord Commander of Ysenden, stood with arms crossed over his broad chest, back resting against the wall of the High Chancellor's study. The sword slung over one shoulder was uncomfortably pinned between him and the stone, but the weight of it was familiar and reassuring, just as was the heft of its twin hanging from his left hip. What was more, he didn't have much opportunity to move given his intentions for the evening, his choice of location deliberately just to the right of the chamber's double doors, wedged into the corner of the short, perpendicular wall that formed the lower north side of the depressed, arched entrance.

It was strange for him to be standing in that room. Ordinarily it was the High Chancelor's single place of privacy, the one room in the entirety of the city where he could be separate from the rumblings and filth of Ysenden politics. Of late in particular, the Chancellor had been retreating to the study every night he could as the sun set, seeking the refuge of the quiet space after his daily toil. Ciriak could understand why, of course. For one thing the ancient factions of the *er'endehn* had reared their ugly heads again, the unity of their race cracking and breaking despite long centuries of working together. The driving out of the old inhabitants of Erraven and their descendants a few months prior had been particularly ugly business, as had the gorilla assaults Ysenden had suffered ever since those exiled had settled once more behind the thick walls of the long-ruined keep.

For another, though, the study was as breathtaking as any other of Ysenden's miracles, and Ciriak could not complain about this rare opportunity to observe the space in earnest.

Like the arch he stood under, the north and south walls on either side of him started out perpendicular to the floor before curving upwards to meet in a perfect point. Near the far end of the chamber—some twenty or thirty feet from the doors—those walls ended, replaced by a score of flat, clear glass plates that formed a half dome which looked west to the very horizon, over the white and grey of the Vyr'esh far below them. It was a newer edition to the study, commissioned only a hundred years before, once half a millennia and then some had passed without sign of the Witch and her infernal winged beasts.

Bookshelves lined every flat surface—ordained with as many curios and artifacts as tomes and texts—and overhead the line of moonwing lanterns the servants changed every day hung in anticipation of a late night, illuminating the chancellor's ornate desk of polished wood and tempered obsidian. There should have been other furniture too—a scattering of decorative seats and chairs—but Ciriak had personally spent a good half-hour removing them from the chamber and hiding them about the great library connected to the study.

Too many were already aware of his plan. He'd seen no need to dodge awkward questions by involving others in setting the stage.

Admittedly, it was possible Ciriak's intentions had already been foiled, unfortunate as it was. The whispers that had encouraged him to form this plot had spoken of events that should have been carried out a quarter-hour before, as the sun's lowest tip reached the distant edge of the world. The light of dusk had filled the room in a breathtaking array of yellows and oranges, making even the books shine with dimming warmth, and Ciriak had tensed in preparation.

Then the sun had sunk lower, and that light had turned red as blood.

"*Damn*," Ciriak cursed under his breath, considering his options. If the guilty parties somehow knew they'd been found out, there was a good chance the four of them were already on their way out of the city, likely heading for Erraven to join the other rebels. He knew only one name—General Ryvus' spies hadn't been able to gather much more than that—but if he acted quickly then Ciriak might just be able to capture at least *one* perpetrator. It would likely leave the rest to escape, but there was a good chance their little group had been getting information from someone higher up, closer to the High Chancellor's inner circle. If he could snatch up Emmehk vy'Ur, then Ciriak would at least have the chance to find out if there was a traitor in the upper ranks of the city's officers, maybe even seated at the—

The faintest whisper of footsteps across the walkways outside jerked the Lord Commander from his thoughts, and he quickly stood up straight, careful not to make a sound.

One, two, three... four people, he counted silently, smiling grimly to himself. He wasn't displeased that these agents of rebellion had only been delayed in their planned attack, but he had to admit to a touch of disappointment. Even if they were the enemy, he or his seconds had very likely had a hand in training this little group.

Which meant that if they'd been *truly* prepared for what they came to do, there would have been no delay for Ciriak to stew in.

Their loss, the Lord Commander thought to himself with the faintest shake of his head as he heard the near-silent footsteps getting closer and closer. Fifteen seconds later they stopped directly outside the doors he stood beside, and in the pause that followed Ciriak heard the barest whisper steel sliding out of a half-dozen scabbards. He knew the signal to attack to come as a silent gesture, so he braced himself.

WHAM!

The doors burst open as boots planted heavy kicks just under both outside handles, breaking open the lock that was already largely decorative. Ciriak had tested the space himself thrice over, but all the same he felt his cheek twitch involuntarily as the thick wood swung inwards at him, only to jerk to a stop barely an inch from his face as the perpendicular wall to his right caught the edge of the door. His view now blocked, Ciriak listened as four pairs of feet sprinted into the study, and he could imagine blades raised and ready to swing. To their credit, not one among the traitors raised a voice that might have alerted any nearby sentry.

At least not until they realized the room was empty.

"*What is this*?!" a man's voice gasped.

Smirking, Ciriak uncrossed his arms, put a hand on the door, and shoved.

It swung away from him with a scrape of wood on stone as he

forced the edge to dislodge itself from the rough-hewn wall. That was, of course, more than enough to draw the attention of the four figures standing with their backs to him as the room revealed itself once more, and to a one they whirled in a flash of blades, spinning to face him with weapons—four swords and two knives between the lot—held high. Two of the would-be-assassins even started forward, instinctively looking to make a preemptive attack on the surprise presence that had appeared at their rear.

They faltered the moment the light of the sunset revealed Ciriak's bearded face to them.

"*Spirits save us,*" the one furthest to the right—another man—hissed. "*Lord Commander...*"

Ciriak didn't acknowledge his title, preferring instead to study the group one after the other as he took one step into the study, then another. As one the four of them backed away in equal measure, retreating further into the room until he had come to stand directly between them and the door, hands by his sides.

"*Well...*" Ciriak grumbled. "*This is a sorry sight, if I do say so myself. What shame must a soldier of the* er'endehn *suffer to convince them to cover their face, I wonder...?*"

Several hands twitched upward at his quiet barb, as though more than one of the group wanted—if just for a second—to tear away the dark cloths that covered every nose and mouth. Their garb, too, was similar, black-grey wool and cotton that was absent any hint of the gold filigree of Ysenden's mark.

"*Where is the High Chancellor, as'ahRen?*"

At the woman's voice, Ciriak turned his attention to the slender form of the figure second from his left.

"*Not here, it would seem,*" he answered after a moment. "*Though I have to wonder what made you think this was the place to look for him.*" He gestured lazily about the room. "*A leader should vet their information before acting on it, don't you think?"*

"*No,*" a distraught, masculine voice spoke up from the left of the woman. "*No. That can't be. He should be here. He's been here every night for months!"*

Ciriak locked eyes with this third member of the group. "*I suppose that would make you Emmehk vy'Ur?*" he asked slowly, smiling a little when the figure's dark features paled at the question. "*Oh yes. I know who you are, trainee. Cadet of the Chancellor's Guard, still doing your years cleaning the barracks. It's a pity. Another half decade and you and I might have met to see if you had the mettle for the job.*"

"*Spirits take the Chancellor!*" the woman to his left—apparently the leader of the group—spat, taking a step forward more out of anger than courage if Ciriak had to guess. Her obsidian sword and dagger flashed in the dusk light as she pointed the former right at his chest. "*This isn't the end. You will tell us where he is, and we will seek him out if it costs us our lives! It is time for our kind to be ruled by one of our—*"

"*Silence.*"

Ciriak's voice, still calm, dripped with frozen command. The elf stopped talking at once, faltering in her approach, and the Lord Commander finally reached for the hilts of his own weapons.

"*You are correct, if only partially so.*" He spoke steadily as he drew the black, curved swords together, slowly pulling them from their sheaths. "*This* will *cost you your life—it has already, in a way—but the same need not be true for your comrades. Tell them to drop their blades, and I will allow your head to be the only one that rolls in the next moments.*"

Beneath her mask, Ciriak saw the leader visibly swallow, her eyes darting left and right as his weapons came completely free. On either side of her, the rest of the group was backing away again, but that didn't stop the woman from snarling threats even as she started to do the same.

"*One more step and you will bear the cost of the humiliation you have caused us, as'ahRen!"*

"*Meaning you are indeed Erraven sympathizers,*" Ciriak said with a nod, not even hesitating as he continued his approach. "*That's one question answered, at the very least.*"

The leader looked momentarily stricken, realizing her slip of the tongue, but her anger was already overpowering her common sense.

"*We are the lifeblood of Erraven!*" she hissed, clearly deciding that if the cat was out of the bag she may as well dive deep. "*We are no* sympathizers! *Our sires were proud soldiers of—!*"

"*Your sires were the scattered leftovers of a broken city that Ysenden accepted despite a millennia of bloodshed between us,*" Ciriak cut across her coolly, still pressing the foursome back with steady, lazy steps. "*Do not lecture me on pride, child. I have likely lived longer than any three of you put together. Of everyone in this room, I am the only one who lost friends to the old wars, who lost family. I do not know where this newfound hatred of your people has climbed up from these last few years—this pride in a long-fallen banner—but it is a waste of time, and a waste of lives.*"

"*You mock the sacrifices of our people!*" the last of the group, to the right of the leader, snarled as the back of his legs found the edge of the High Chancellor's desk. "*You mock those who fell so that Ysenden could stand against the Witch!*"

For the first time all evening, Ciriak felt the bite of anger at the words.

"*I mock no one,* boy*!*" he rumbled, fixing the offender with a stare that made generals go rigid. "*I merely pity this vain cause you have all decided to throw your lives away for. No, that is* enough." He cut the leader short as she looked about to speak again "*None of us are here tonight to debate the merit of rebellion against a seat that has done nothing but vied for seven hundred years for the integrations of our old sects. You, you, and you—*" he lifted a sword to point at each of the masked elves in turn, forgoing only the woman "*—as Lord Commander of Ysenden, I hereby* *arrest you for treason and the attempted murder of the High Chancellor. As for you—*" he finally addressed the fourth "*—it is too late, but I will give you the choice of how you wish to—*"

He wasn't at all surprised when—even as he turned back to her—the leader lunged at him, seeking to take advantage of the brief moment of distraction as his eyes had gone to the others one by one. She made not a sound as her sword lead the attack, a clean, steady thrust at his chest that would have made even the most talented among Ysenden's soldiers proud. The strike was direct, without feint or fault, and Ciriak thought it likely most swordsmen might well have fallen to that speed and precision.

Even the attacker, though, didn't offer so much as a blink of surprise when his own sword swept up, dragging the offending blade away so that it cleaved through the air barely an inch from his right arm, his left weapon thrusting in and up in the same motion. The obsidian split through her flimsy garbs without so much as a catch, running her through at an angle as her own momentum carried her into the killing blow. Not done, however, Ciriak planted a foot and pivoted, twisting the impetus of her still-moving body so that she lunged past him even as her own weapons fell limply from her hands. With a hard flex of the wrist and a clean pull, he withdrew his sword from her side as she dropped away from him toward the broken doors, spraying the ground with an arc of blood as he finished the full turn.

In the end, Ciriak was left facing the three remaining figures as though he'd never even looked away, the only sign that anything had changed in the two seconds that had passed being the wet red that dripped from his left blade and the limp *thumps* of the corpse tumbling down to roll across the floor at his back.

"*She chose well,*" the Lord Commander said, eyeing the trembling swords and daggers of the others one at a time. "*But you need not. Drop your weapons and submit for questioning. Otherwise, I cannot promise your deaths will be anything so quick.*"

For a long, tense moment, no one moved.

Then—with heavy *thumps* and ringing *pings*—blades began to fall.

CHAPTER NINETEEN

"If that damn elf kills me, you get my ring..."

—Declan Idrys, to Ryndean, Primordial of the Dragons, post-training

"Left hand, Declan! Watch left hand!"

It was fortunate that, in the two weeks since they'd departed the frozen lake, Declan had gotten accustomed to Lysiat's simplified instruction. There had been a time when he would have questioned if the elf meant *his* hand or *his opponent's*, but with the passing days he'd improved not only in his understanding of the *er'endehn* tongue, but in his following of his trainer's rapid feedback. For this reason his blue eyes snapped immediately to the right, noticing the twist of his sparring partner's wrist just in time to see the blow coming.

Unfortunately, that didn't mean he'd gotten fast enough yet to *do* anything with such feedback.

Crack!

"Ah!" Declan shouted, unable to help himself as the heavy, smooth wood that made up the practice sword's blade caught him full in the shoulder, unyielding in its weight. His entire right arm spasmed in shock, and he very nearly lost his grip on his own weapon as he staggered sideways.

"Point!"

Gritting his teeth against the ache of the offended limb, Declan caught himself and looked around to find Tesied grinning at him, weapon still held where he'd landed the strike.

"Point," Declan acknowledged resignedly, straightening up with a grunt. The dark elf nodded, still smiling, before turning to jerk his head in summoning.

From the edge of the ring of dirt Lysiat had had them clear for their usual morning practice, Aliek pushed himself off the tree he'd been leaning against to trade places with his brother, rolling his wooden blade in broad circles to warm up his wrist.

"*Still think two enemies be unfair!*" Declan shouted past the twins in broken elvish as they crossed each other.

From the warmest spot she'd found among the rare shafts of light that marked a sunny day above the canopy overhead, Lysiat raised an eyebrow and muttered something while Ryn—standing at her left—looked to be trying to hide a laugh. Ester, on the other hand, seated on the cleaned-off body of a fallen trunk to the commander's right, shouted a translation back at him.

"'It's fair when you need twice the practice'!"

Declan shot the two women a sour look before walking a short circle about the ring, rubbing and shaking his shoulder out in an attempt to ward off the ache while Aliek waited patiently for him to be set.

"Maybe I'd complain less if I was actually allowed to use *everything I had*," he muttered to himself, finally coming to a stop and raising his wooden sword to indicate that he was ready.

As he'd hoped—and anticipated, truth be told—Declan was learning at an extraordinary rate, faster even then when Ryn had finally been able to work with him and Ester after they'd found a blade that suited the dragon. Ryn had since been outfitted with a similar weapon—a spare from Kellek Syr'esh's own arsenal to replace the one they'd lost to the tunneler—but he'd been content to remain an observer for these daily morning sessions.

Probably purely for the entertainment, Declan thought begrudgingly as Aliek flashed towards him in a blur of black and gold.

While he *was* indeed learning at an astronomical pace—he could actually survive an engagement with the brothers for more than handful of seconds now—the problem was that Bonner had completely forbade him from using suffusion when it came to his training. His reasoning had been logical, of course—reinforcement required a strong body as a base, and one could not improve one's physical abilities if they relied on magic too heavily—but in retrospect Declan wished he'd had an argument to protest the order.

The simple fact of the matter was that *without* his weaves of strength and speed—which he'd grown steadily more in control of with Bonner's help—he was still a long way from being a match for Tesied or Aliek, much less Lysiat when she chose to grace the ring herself.

Aliek's wooden blade cut at his head in a blur from below, forcing Declan to duck and lean sideways. He countered with his own strike at the elf's armored thighs, but the man just danced away before closing the distance again in a blink, thrusting at Declan's chest. Declan deflected and snapped the pommel of his sword at his opponent's face, but Aliek was already dropping himself to the ground as he spun to slash at Declan's right side. Twisting just in time to catch the blow on his own blade, Declan saw the elf reverse his turn to bring one leg around heavily at the back of Declan's ankles. This exact sweep had brought him down a dozen times over the last two weeks, and he was ready for it. Leaping up, Declan almost grinned as Aliek's leg passed by harmlessly beneath him.

He was less amused when the elf continued the twist, bringing the wooden sword around in a dervish to cut at his *left* side this time.

All while he was still in the air.

"*Ooph*," Declan grunted, getting his blade around just in time to block the blow awkwardly even as his new boots touched dirt again. He might have saved himself the point, but it meant he landed improperly and off balance, which Aliek *immediately* took advantage of. As Declan stumbled backwards the elf lunged, slashing again and again at his hasty defenses, his blocks and parries more desperate than calculated as momentum kept pulling his feet behind him.

In the end, the fight came to a close the moment his heel found the jutting root of one of the many trees that towered all about their little circle, and Declan was on his back in the dirty snow for what had to have been the thousandth time in a fraction as many days.

The sensation of something hard poking him in the chest even as he lay there didn't help his frustration.

"*Point*," Aliek said as he pressed the tip of his practice sword to the black cuirass of Declan's elven leathers, gloating less than his brother, but sounding the faintest bit amused all the same.

"*Point*," Declan granted him with a sigh.

The elf gave him a nod of approval and small smile, then let the blade fall in favor of offering Declan his free hand to help him up. Declan accepted it gratefully, and would have voiced his thanks as he was hauled to his feet had his attention not been immediately drawn away by a sudden pain in the side of his right shin.

Thwak!

"Ow!" Declan exclaimed, half-limping and half-hopping away just in time to avoid a second whack in the leg by Lysiat, who had appeared beside the pair of them like a demon summoned. "What was that for?!"

Though it was doubtful she'd understood the question—few of the elves had taken to Bonner's offer to teach them the common tongue of Viridian—the commander seemed to have been of a mind to give him just that answer already.

"*You jump*!" she growled in simplified answer, eyes narrow beneath the severe line of the white hair she'd pulled back in a swirling arc of tight braids. "*Why you jump*?!"

"To avoid the sweep!" Declan answered back, dodging another swipe at him by the wooden sword she carried. "To get clear of his legs and stabilize for a counter attack!"

Lysiat's gaze only sharpened further, but Ester and Ryn had by that point crossed the practice ring to help.

Declan, you're supposed to be practicing your elvish, the dragon reminded him, holding a clawed hand out to keep the commander from advancing further. Over one shoulder, the gold pommel of his new blade—only a foot or so shorter than his old steel one—flashed briefly in a ray of sunlight. *We're not far from Ysenden. The greater your mastery of the tongue, the less trouble you're likely to have in the city.*

Declan wanted to groan at that, but even Ester was watching him expectantly now as Tesied, too, joined them, so he gave it his best shot.

"*I leap to miss leg*," he said, turning to Lysiat and doing his best to mime the circular kick with his free hand. "*To miss Aliek's leg.*"

"*Sweep.*" Ester offered him the elvish word.

"*I leap to miss Aliek's sweep*," Declan corrected with a nod of thanks to her before looking to Lysiat again.

The commander looked a little mollified at his use of elvish, but she was still shaking her head. "*With me*," she ordered him, indicating the clearing even as she started for it herself. Declan followed dutifully, and a few seconds later they were facing one another in the very center of the space.

"*No jump*," the commander said with a sharp shake of her head, signing the same with her free hand and using her single practice sword to point at his legs. "*Never jump. Know why*?"

"Obviously not," Declan muttered in frustration, but a glance at Ryn and Ester's stern looks at the edge of the circle had him sighing and answering more deliberately. "*No. Do not know.*"

Lysiat seemed to have expected this, because she jerked her sword upward in obvious gesture. "*I show you. Jump.*"

Declan would have groaned at the bad feeling budding in his gut at the order, but he knew better than to argue. Making sure he had a firm hold of his blade, he squatted dutiful before shoving himself up and into the air.

The elf was on him like an arrow shot from a bow, her blade cutting at him straight on. Declan grimaced, blocking as his feet touched down again, but at once he found himself in the same position he'd been with Aliek, backpedaling against Lysiat's onslaught. Fortunately for him, the commander was clearly not intent on shoving him out of the ring, because after three or four steps she stopped.

"*Again,*" she ordered curtly, motioning to the center again.

This time when he jumped, she slashed at his side, as her brother had. The blow came even faster this time, catching his guard in midair, and as a result Declan landed even more awkwardly than the two previous times, nearly twisting his ankle before falling to one knee with hardly a prayer of defending himself from Lysiat's follow-up. The commander pulled the blow, halting her wooden blade an inch from his left temple, then drew the weapon back as she stepped away and motioned for him to stand.

"*Legs are foundation,*" she told him, signing along with the words and watching while Declan planted his sword into the frozen ground to leverage himself up. "*You know this. Sacrifice foundation, sacrifice life. Why sacrifice life?*"

Declan thought this was a *little* dramatic, but answered all the same, gesturing himself in the language of soldiers for practice even as he spoke roughly. "*No warriors like the* er'endehn, *in Viridian. No speed like the* er'endehn. *A human doing that… Doubtful.*"

Lysiat's gaze narrowed again, and she snapped an order.

"*I jump. You will strike.*"

"Wha—?" Declan started to ask in common, but she was already lunging at him.

She didn't fight at her usual speed, which was the only reason he managed to hold her off as well as she did. Her slashes and strikes were still quick, true, but in two weeks Declan had adapted well enough to keep up to *this* pace at least, if not easily. It offered him the opportunity to keep an eye on her body, watching her hips and knees in particular.

When the subtle crouch came, therefore, he was ready.

Lysiat leapt at him in a flying thrust, going for his upper chest. Declan sidestepped and swung in the same motion, aiming a heavy blow at her open side. The commander twisted and just managed to block, as he had, but as skilled as she was she remained slight of body and—therefor—weight. The impact hit a fraction of a breath before she landed, and as a result she was knocked completely sideways, visibly staggering for the first time Declan had ever seen. Nimble as always, of course, the woman managed to turn the momentum into a one-handed summersault and was back on her feet in a blink.

Still, her point had been made the moment the wooden sword had struck true.

"You *are human, Declan,*" she said steadily, signing that they were done as he remained tense. "You *have speed. Not many humans, perhaps, but if* you *have speed, others have speed, too.*"

A memory of a stocky woman with a scarred face and short grey hair flashed across Declan's mind, and he almost let out a nervous laugh. He wondered if Cassandra Sert had ever cleaved someone open midair, and decided it was entirely possible.

"*Jump is opening,*" Lysiat was still saying. "*Like any opening, when looking for it, will see it.*" She pointed with her sword at Declan's lower body again as she repeated herself. "*Legs are foundation.*"

"*Legs are foundation,*" Declan echoed, understanding. "*Jump is opening.*"

Lysiat offered him a small smile, not unlike Aliek's. "*You see. Good. Ready for again?*"

Declan sighed, reaching up to rub his sore shoulder once more, but nodded all the same. Lysiat started out of the circle at once, motioning for Tesied to replace her.

The moment her brother was in place and she'd found her patch of sunlight again, the commander slashed her sword through the air while Ryn and Ester looked on.

"*Again*!"

◆

"Ow-ow-ooowwww!" Declan grumbled an hour later, wincing as Bonner prodded at his bare back from behind. "If I wanted to get stabbed more I would have just asked to stay in the ring!"

"Instead of complaining, how about just working on holding still?" the mage grumbled in response, brow furrowed in concentration as he worked.

Declan, in answer, offered him a deadpan gaze over one shoulder. "And *how,* exactly, would you recommend I do that, in this moment?"

They were, like every morning after training, on the move again, which meant he and Bonner were on foot as Ester rode Eyera at their backs. Orsik was off in the woods since his usual passenger was busy being healed after the day's usual beating, and Ryn's tall form could be seen now and then ahead of them, having joined the higher officers at the front of the march to ask after their estimated arrival in the city. All around them the *er'endehn* soldiers moved in calculated disarray, optimizing their speed by forgoing an ordered file in favor of a wider spread of bodies across a dozen yards in either direction. Their dark figures slipped across the floor of the Vyr'esh like wraiths, traveling in near-silence despite their number. Only Declan and his party made any real noise, but it had been some days now since the lot of them had stopped receiving the irritated glances from the soldiers at every sound, their presence finally seeming to have been accepted within the ranks.

All of them suspected that Ryn had much to do with that—including the dragon himself—but not one among their four could ever seem to come up with a single valid reason as to *why* whenever they put their heads together about it.

It was also possible, of course, that their place among the soldiers had merely become accepted as the two weeks had passed. Bonner's magic—originally vilified in most every eye within the old encampment by the lake—had been steadily growing in esteem among the *er'endhen,* in particular after he'd managed to save the mangled limb of a sentry who'd been nearly dragged away by wolves in the night. Ester—who had always enjoyed at least *some* measure of acceptance by elves given her *er'enthyl* blood—had earned herself a reputation as an excellent student and steadily-improving marksman, and had even recently taken to joining the nightly hunting parties that pressed into the trees each evening as they made camp.

As for Declan…

Declan was still the odd man out, he knew, but he was equally aware that this was steadily changing. While a majority of the soldiers still watched him carefully whenever they had the chance, he had grown closer with the ay'ahSel siblings since starting his training, even slowly earning the right to address all three of them by their first names. Tesied had come around almost from the start, boisterous as he was for an elf, with Aliek following his twin with a little more reservation. Amusingly enough, Lysiat had opened up practically immediately after that, like the commander had only been looking for an excuse to be less formal with Declan and his companions. He didn't blame her delay. She was a middle officer of the *er'endehn* military, with a greater need for decorum then her sergeant-ranked brothers. After so long in solitude together, it had been a little saddening to see her initially shell up again once they'd reached the safety of the elven camp, but the promptness of her return to the more-casual air the two of them had started to share in the tunnels and outskirts of the forest told Declan she'd only been doing what was expected of her. The elf had made up for it, too, both in and out of the training circle. Beyond those morning sessions, the siblings also joined them for meals, and even in the march if any of them were ever at liberty to do so.

In the time since they'd left the southern rim of the Vyr'esh behind, Declan was almost ready to call Lysiat—as well as her brothers—friends, a fact that he suspected had lent itself to the reduction in narrowed stares thrown their way over the last half-month.

Though still not as much as this odd reverence the elves seemed to have for Ryn, he couldn't help but think to himself, catching another glimpse of the dragon through the trees ahead of them.

Then he winced as, with a pulse of tingling energy, whatever Bonner was doing to him made something *thunk* into place.

"Ow..." he hissed for the hundredth time, glancing back again. "What was that?"

"Dislocated rib," the old man answered simply, pulling his hands away from Declan and wiping them off on the front of his robes. "Not the last one you'll suffer before you catch up to those demons, I expect. All done now, though."

"Thanks," Declan grumbled, rolling his newly-healed shoulder experimentally as he pulled the black shirt that was part of the wardrobe Colonel Syr'esh had seen him fit with from the camp commander's spares. "And you're probably right. I'm surprised I haven't broken a bone yet."

"'Yet' being the operative word," Ester said, heeling Eyera up to them now that she saw her father was done with his work. "I'm glad Ryn still thinks I should be spending more time training with him before asking Lysiat to take me on, too. I think those damn brothers in particular like using you as a practice dummy." She watched Declan finish tightening the threads along the split neck of his shirt before continuing. "Want your leathers?"

"Please," he answered with a nod, holding up a hand expectantly as Ester reached into one of Eyera's traveling sacks. "And glad I'm not the only one. It would be a different story if I was allowed to suffuse myself." He glared around at Bonner even as Ester pulled out and handed him his folded cuirass. The elven armor was truly incredible—as compactible as it was sturdy—and he took a moment to admire the workmanship for the hundredth time in the last two weeks. He had learned—as he'd studied the elven language further with the ay'ahSels—that the patterning and adornments of the gold gilding were not random or without reason. They denoted, as it turned out, the *rank* of a soldier, as chest and shoulder markers did in the Vigil. Declan's, ironically, apparently labeled him as a "colonel" given that they had been Syr'esh's, but he doubted any among the sharp-eyed *er'endehn* would *actually* confuse him for an officer of the army.

Pulling the chest piece over his head, he listened as Bonner addressed his comment with a huff.

"I've told you a dozen times already. If you let yourself depend too much on your weaves then—"

"Then my body itself won't improve, and the base on which I build those weaves will be lacking, yes, yes." Declan's voice was loud in his own ears from inside the leathers as he struggled to pull them on. Despite Syr'esh apparently being about as broad as any elf came, the Colonel's dimensions had still proven wanting to Declan's own, making the armor tough to don and doff. He had a hope that he'd be able to find a craftsman in Ysenden who could outfit him with a more appropriately-sized set once they reached the city, but Declan couldn't help but expect their reception—particularly his and Bonner's—wasn't going to be so warm as to endear them to the local population within any reasonable frame of time.

"I'll tell you what," Bonner said with a sigh. "I will allow you to maintain a minimum weave of suffusion during training, but—"

"Wait, really?" Declan grinned at the man excitedly through a ruffled sheet of hair as he finally managed to tug the cuirass down over his chest, freeing his head. "That's fantas—!"

"*But*—" Bonner repeated pointedly "—only if you start your mind-speech training again."

Declan groaned, almost missing Ester handing him his shoulder pauldrons. "Bonner, we've been through this. Every time I tried in the tunnels, you and Ryn looked like you'd been hit in the head with a hammer. I can't control my magic enough to keep from—"

"If Ryndean and I can't handle a little ringing of the ears, we've not much business being a former court magus and a bloody *dragon* now, do we?" Bonner told him, dismissing his trepidation with a frown. "Truthfully, Declan—while your concern is appreciated—it is irresponsible. Imagine if you could have communicated to us after you'd fled that worm with ay'ahSel? How much easier would it have been for everyone to know you were alive?"

"Honestly Bonner, given that an undead beast the width of a large house was attempting to take a rather large chunk out of me, I'm not sure I would have had the thought to do so even if I'd been able to." With a dull *clunk* the shoulder armor set itself in place via the clever overlapping ridges in the metal details that lined the leather. With the second under his other arm, Declan worked to knot off the cords that would lock everything together as Ester stifled a laugh over head.

Ignoring his daughter, Bonner frowned. "But that's entirely my *point*, Declan. With enough training, calling out to us wouldn't have required 'the thought to do so'! Do you separately consider every action when you walk, when you swing a sword?"

"Of late, yes," Declan answered, pushing the other pauldron into place. "When it comes to the sword at least. The ay'ahSels make me feel like the ten-year-old boy I was when I first picked up a blade, and not in a good way."

Bonner rolled his eyes. "Regardless, what I mean is that with practice, it can become a natural thing, innate. And if you're going to argue with me that mind-speech would not have come in handy a thousand times already on this blasted journey of ours, then I will fuse that armor into one solid piece so that you can never get out of it again!"

Declan chuckled but didn't respond. The mage had a point, of course. Being able to communicate privately or across extended distances would *certainly* have been useful in more than one way, even before he'd know anything of magic or dragons or draugr. If he was honest with himself, Declan's hesitation came simply from the fact that he was *exhausted*, and almost always so. His training under Lysiat aside, no time had been wasted by Bonner in starting up Declan's magical instruction once again, focusing simultaneously now on pyro- *and* corpomancy. The resulting improvement in both arts had been as steady as ever, and equally as exciting, but it also left Declan more and more drained, which he had a greater appreciation for after his inadvertent bout of arcane fatigue. It was more a mental and physical exhaustion this time around, but the results were much the same, particularly given that he still channeled his weaves of warmth and strength at nearly all times other than training.

Speaking of which, Declan thought to himself, reaching inward. The spell of warmth he'd previously summoned—emanating from the firestone now looped about his neck from a heat-resistant thong of leather Bonner had enchanted for him—had waned with the distraction of Bonner's healing, as had his unbound suffusion. Now that his rib was back in place, though—he would *definitely* get his revenge on Aliek one day for deliberately driving him backwards into a tree—he called on the weaves once more, the now-familiar tingle of magical energy joining the heat to wash out of his chest into his arms and legs, then his fingers and toes. Over the last two weeks the spell of strength had become a much stronger sensation upon initiation—almost uncomfortably so—and Declan had to hold his breath a moment before the prickling subsided to a dull, quiet hum of power that he knew would fade within the hour to almost nothing.

It paid, after all, to have the greatest living mage mentoring you on how to manipulate and compress your spells so that they were stronger, steadier, and less obtrusive all at once.

Declan! Grab Ester and Bonner and get them up here! Quickly!

Declan blinked, surprised by the abrupt ring of Ryn's voice through his ears. He didn't miss the urgency in the dragon's words on the other hand, and so spoke up at once to cut off Bonner, who he hadn't realized had continued his tirade on the importance of learning to mind-speak.

"—because there was the time you almost got your head ripped off by a wight. And just the evening before that, you could have called for help directly when that warg pinned you down. Luck got you through both of those disasters. Luck and—"

"Ryn wants us to join him at the head," Declan told them quickly, looking from Bonner to Ester, who was already holding out his bracers for him to take next. "Now. It seems important."

The mage stuttered to a stop, but the yr'Essels exchanged only a quick glance of alarm before he found his tongue again.

"Esteria, lead the way."

Ester nodded, waiting only for Declan to accept the metal-lined bracers before clucking Eyera into a trot, her father right on the warg's heels. Declan trailed them as quickly as he could while donning the armor, ignoring the mixed glances of curiosity and subtle irritation cast their way by the marching elves they overtook.

He had one bracer on completely by the time they reached the head of the march, and was busy lacing up the other when he stopped short, taken aback by the sight that greeted him.

Ryn was standing still, one hand outstretched to hold back Colonel Syr'esh, whose steady features were in sharp contrast to the irritated expression of the higher officers who flanked him as they snarled questions at the dragon that even Declan could tell all amounted to "What the *hell* are you doing?" He would have bet Ryn's unexplained privilege in the eyes of the elves was the only thing that had kept blades in their sheaths until that moment, but then a glint of light caught his eye and he noticed—with no small measure of alarm—that Lysiat, Aliek, and Tesied were all standing nearby, swords and spears drawn respectively. For a second Declan feared that the ay'ahSels had readied their blades in answer to Ryn's hand on the Colonel's chest, but then two things caught his eye that spoke otherwise, though neither bode well. First, the dragon too had drawn the great four-foot sword Syr'esh had lent him, its black blade and gilded hilt steady in his left hand despite the weight.

Second, neither Ryn nor the ay'ahSels were looking at each other, but appeared instead to be scanning the trees before them even as the march came to a slow halt at their backs.

"Ryn, what's happening?"

Bonner was the first to speak up, pushing through the last line of officers without a care for the upturned lips more than one of them showed at his passing. Declan followed the mage, shouldering through when needed as he left Ester atop Eyera, the half-elf already instinctively scanning the forest herself for trouble.

Bonner. Declan. Ryn sounded almost relieved to have them in sight. *Something's off. Something's wrong.*

Declan tensed up at once, one hand going immediately to the blade at his hip as he felt Bonner pause beside him in much the same fashion, but the dragon had already turned from them again to address

Syr'esh and his company.

Colonel, he rumbled. *How many soldiers did we leave the lake with?*

Syr'esh frowned at him, but before he could answer Major y'Rehl—standing not far to his left—spoke up in anger. Declan didn't catch everything she said, but he was pleased to find he at least got the gist of the statement without needing Ester beside him to translate.

I will place my hand wherever I see fit if I believe it may save a life, Major, Ryn growled back, not even looking at the woman and repeating himself more urgently. *Colonel, I ask again. How many solider did we leave the lake with?*

This time, when more of the officers started to voice their protest, Syr'esh held them up with a raised hand. He was watching the dragon with a frown, his otherwise-even gaze making it impossible to tell if he was concerned or angered by Ryn's sudden trespass on his person.

In the end, he appeared to decide answering was in everyone's best interest.

"200 of our kind exactly," Declan thought he'd caught. *"Six ranking officers to offset the six dead in the mountains."*

Ryn gave a low snarl at that, the answer obviously not to his liking as his attention immediately returned to the woods. To his left the ay'ahSels' tension redoubled, and Declan had to appreciate that the siblings, at the very least, had spent enough time with them now to be clearly willing to trust the dragon at his word.

Then again, the last time Ryn had warned them all that something was wrong, the tunneler had crushed most of what had been left of their scouting unit…

"Ryn, what's going on?" Bonner repeated in a hiss, moving to step up between the dragon and the colonel, pushing Ryn's arm down and away from Syr'esh.

I came up to ask how much farther we had to go, Ryn explained, gold-white eyes not leaving the trees. *The Colonel said we'd have a day and a half more to walk once we reached some river called 'the Lyons', so I searched the woods to see if we might be approaching it.* He nodded in a northeasterly direction. *The river is there, barely half a mile off.*

"And?" Bonner asked, clearly doubting that that was the end of the story.

And not including our party, there are only 196 souls in these woods with us, Bonner.

The chill that swept across their gathered number then was so absolute it was palpable in the stiffening shoulders of several of the officers and soldiers standing around and before Declan. It convinced him, at long last, that there was more to the elves' respect for Ryn than the mere fact that he was—in most respects—a higher being than they. Esteem did not explain how every single *er'endehn* around them seemed to understand immediately what Ryn's words meant. They knew—intimately so, it seemed—of Ryn's senses, knew of his ability to extend his conscious into the world about him. Declan would have found it suspicious, he was sure, except that the immediate implication of Ryn's statements was far more disturbing.

"Four gone?" he asked, taking his own turn to push his way forward to stand on the dragon's other side, between him and Aliek. "You're sure?"

He asked more out of habit, knowing full well what the answer would be.

I'm sure, Ryn said with a slow nod, and his eyes—a moment ago so intent on the woods before them—seemed to focus on something else as he expanded his consciousness to recheck. *There are 196 dark elves with us in these—*

But then he froze, distant eyes going wide, entire body unmoving.

"Ryn?" Declan asked quietly, reaching up to put a hand on the dragon's shoulder. Even then, it was a few more seconds before he got an answer.

195, Ryn hissed. *Now it's a 195...*

The winter cold was nothing as compared to the chill that descended on them, in that moment. For two frozen seconds not a one among their number so much as breathed, taking in this implication. Four had been lost since the morning—roll call would have notified unit leaders earlier, otherwise—and a fifth had vanished even as they'd been standing there.

And what was more...

"You can't see what's taking them, can you?" Declan breathed, a cool calm starting to climb its way up his spine.

At his side, Ryn hesitated, lips tightening to bare his white teeth slightly as he obviously pressed his senses, willing them to go further, deeper.

Then, though, he shook his head slowly.

"Sehranya...!" Bonner hissed, and that single word was enough to finally get the dark elves acting in a flurry of commands.

"Arms!" Declan understood Syr'esh's bellowed order, but the other shouts and instructions that cascaded from this were lost to him in the furor. Before he knew it soldiers had spilled out in front of him with weapons drawn, and in seconds he, Ryn, and Bonner were facing the inside of a living wall of *er'endehn*, Lysiat, Aliek, and Tesied among those standing directly before them. Declan looked around, witnessing in amazement as all about them the scattered soldiers collapsed in- and outward to form a single wide ring, almost perfectly circular despite the trees and the unevenness of the terrain. Some strides behind him, Ester cursed as she, too, watched the precision of the elves in amazement, until suddenly they and the higher officers were the only ones left standing within the defensive formation.

The moment the last of the elves had settled into a ready stance, however, the world went silent again.

Declan listened, then, straining to make out any sounds that might reveal what it was they were facing. He had an inkling himself, but didn't want to voice the possibility aloud for fear that doing so might make it real. All around him, the others were just as still, just as silent. Even Eyera was unmoving, ears twitching this way and that as Ester leaned down to rest a hand atop her head.

Eyera...?

Declan had to stop himself from cursing as he realized their mistake. He looked up at Ester, who had stiffened as she touched the hair between the female's ears, like the feel of it had triggered the same realization. Her green eyes were wide, her mouth shaped into an "oh" of concern.

But before Declan could even think to turn to Ryn and Bonner to tell them of their ommitance, there came a snarling roar from the trees to the east, shivering with fury through the winter with such force that many of the elves to the north and south spun to face the direction of the call.

"Orsik!" Declan and Ester hissed together.

Just as neither of them was fool enough to cry out, however, nor were they stupid enough to try and break the elves' defensive formation. Instead, they were forced to listen as the sounds of an intense battle briefly echoed through the trees, punctuated by the unseen warg's snarls and barks and howls of pain before ending with the unmistakable ripping of flesh immediately followed by the distant *thud* of something falling to the frozen earth. With bated breath they all waited, every eye not disciplined to watch their north, south, and west flanks fixed on the direction the noises had come from. Declan heard Ester muttering a prayer to her gods above, and Eyera at last broke the quiet with a pitiful whine, clawed paws crunching over the ground as she turned east to sniff at the air.

For a good fifteen seconds or so, nothing happened. The forest was silent again, and Declan felt a heavy stone start to build in his gut.

"Oh no..." he breathed, struggling to fight off the beginnings of grief that had started to join the tendrils of fear already wrapping about his heart.

Then, however, there came a whistle from a little down the line, and his and every head around him capable of doing so whipped about in time to see a heavy, grey-white form come limping from around one of the great pines just south of where they'd been looking.

"Orsik!" Declan shouted, forgoing the silence after the chaos of the unseen battle. He was bolting along the line even before Eyera had been able to gain purchase to chase after him, and by the time he reached the point of the formation closest to the warg the elves had already parted to let the animal in as they recognized him. Declan was at his head in a blink, nearly sliding across the dirty snow on his knees, and immediately started looking the male over in concern.

"By the Mother..." he growled as he accepted a whining nuzzle, Orsik burying his great head into the crook of his arm as he keened in pain.

The warg had been in worse shape, to be certain. After their fight with the drey in the tunnels, Orsik had very likely been at death's door, and would have crossed the threshold had Bonner not been there to see him back to fighting form. In comparison, the injuries he presented with now were hardly anything to be concerned with, but it wasn't the dripping blood that seeped from the wounds that alarmed Declan so, nor the animal's favoring of his front left leg.

Rather, it was the nature of the damage itself, presenting as long, narrow lacerations in parallel groupings of threes and fours, cutting deep into the warg's flesh despite his heavy, matted fur.

Claws, Declan knew. Only claws could inflict this sort of wound.

It was Ester, however, who beat him to the name, having slid down from Eyera to kneel at Orsik's right side, running a hand in line with some of the more severe gashes.

CHAPTER TWENTY

SYR'ESH! Ryn's voice was a roar of urgency. *SECURE OUR PERIMETER! NOW!*

Declan looked around to find that the dragon and Bonner had both hurried to join him and Ester, along with the Colonel and the rest of his higher officers. Syr'esh himself was studying Orsik's lacerated sides, brow furrowed, and he didn't immediately respond to Ryn's demand.

It wasn't until several of his subordinates—the elders of his circle—approached him to speak in low hisses in the elf's ear that he looked suddenly concerned.

Of course, Declan thought, watching the Colonel look sharply at the older officers as though requesting silent confirmation. *They would know, too. They would know what this means.*

Just then, however, any further encouragement to act was made meaningless, because there was a shout of shock from the east line of soldiers, alarming in and of itself given the usual austerity of the elves.

Declan knew, however, as he and Ester both shoved themselves to their feet to look to the trees once more, that what he would find would likely draw alarm from even the *er'endehn*.

A figure had appeared, tall and thin, lurching out from behind the very tree Orsik had only just come around. It paused on seeing the defensive line, standing in familiar, gilded black leathers to take in the formation. It would have been easy from a distance, perhaps, to mistake the thing for one of the very soldiers it was studying now, except that it seemed to have lost its helmet in the fight with the warg, revealing pale, colorless eyes set above a leering grin framed by loose, lank white hair.

That, and the fact that—while the stump of a missing left arm, severed at the shoulder, didn't bleed—the cruel, bony tips protruding from the fingers of its one good hand dripped red into the snow at its feet.

SPEARS DOWN! Ryn roared, rushing by Declan and Ester as he moved in preparation of supporting the line. *SPEARS D—!*

Too late.

With a screech that was both joyous and horrible, the wight launched itself forward, heedless of the bristling weaponry set against it. Already gifted with the speed and guile of the dark elf it had been in life, its reinforced agility—supplemented by dark magic—allowed it to slip between the hafts of the spear-wielders as they tried to adjust to meet it. In a blink it was at the line, running itself onto a sword even as it slashed with terrible claws at the throat of the weapon's owner, ripping the soldier's neck open just beneath the lip of her helm. The elf crumpled, falling to her knees with a gurgle as the comrade to her right stuck the wight with another blade, skewering the thing completely despite its armor.

Unsurprisingly, this blow had as little effect as the first, and a moment later the *er'endehn* was staggering backwards with a scream, clutching at the face of his helmet where the thing seemed to have caught his eyes with a slash of its hand.

NO! Ryn was bellowing, struggling to find an opening with which to use the great blade still drawn at his side without risking cutting down the elves themselves as the soldiers collapsed inward on the wight. *ITS HEAD! STRIKE AT ITS—!*

Fortunately for them all, Declan had started moving the moment the creature had first struck the line.

He was behind Ryn in two strides, drawing his sword as he reached upward. Catching hold of the dragon's shoulder, Declan pulled up even as he leapt, willing power into his weave of strength as he did. Two weeks of hard study paid off when he managed to launch himself into the air, arching up some eight or nine feet to clear the line of elves, landing on the other side of it into a roll. He was on his feet in a heartbeat, already turning as he took hold of the leather thong about his neck and ripped it loose, drawing out the firestone from under his breastplate. With a snap of the cord he had the vessel in hand, launching himself at the wight's back. The creature was fast, though, faster than the similar beasts he'd faced who'd been crafted from the fallen Vigil troops, and with a jerk of its body it wrenched itself away from the elves to whirl on him, pale teeth bared under dead eyes, the two swords that had pierced it still sticking gruesomely out of its chest and side. Ordinarily Declan suspected he would have been dead inside of a second. *This* wight bore the body of an *er'endehn*, bore the speed and skill of the soldier whose flesh it wore. He had yet to go toe to toe with any of the ay'ahSels in the training ring, and they were opponents not even infused with the power of a necromantic master.

On the other hand, with a real blade in the hand of a true enemy intent on killing him launching itself at his throat, Declan was no longer limited by Bonner's instruction of restraint.

There was a low *whoom* of expanding heat as he met the creature fist-first, flames erupting from his knuckles and fingers as his spellwork blasted outward from the firestone clutched in his palm. The weave was muted, Declan not wanting to catch any of the soldiers at the wight's rear in collateral fire, and served little purpose other than to slam the creature backwards again, cutting off its lunging momentum to send it staggering and screeched as the skin of its face bubbled and blistered.

Declan, however, wasn't done.

With a speed and strength only possible under the effects of his corpomancy, he closed the distance between them in a breath, coming into range before the creature had a chance to find its footing again. The thing actually seemed to blink at him in surprise, like he'd caught it unawares, as his new black sword flashed in a screaming arc through the air, catching it cleanly in the side of the head. The heavy blade cleaved through skin and bone with a *crunch*, cutting off the top of the wight's skull in a blow that sprayed blood and gore across the forest floor. The rest of its body collapsed at once, but Declan threw a hand out to stop the elves surging forward to run the corpse through and make sure it was properly dead.

"NO! BACK! GET BACK!"

Though he hadn't had the time to work out how to say as much in elvish, the urgency of his shout alone was enough to make the *er'endehn* take pause, and just in time. With an unearthly, keening wail, black flames erupted from the fallen wight's wound, spreading downward to rip and tear at the body until every inch of it—including the chunk of head that had landed several feet away—was being consumed by dark fire. Forcing himself to look away, Declan scanned the trees once more to make sure he wouldn't be ambushed from behind, leaving the elves to watch in horror.

Only when the horrible scream of the broken Purpose faded did Declan turn to the defensive line again.

"*At head!*" he shouted in the best elvish he could muster this time, doing his best to sign the symbol for "sword" then "head" with the firestone still in hand. "*Strike at head!*"

He didn't have time to make sure the point had gotten across when there came another scream, from the south of the circled elves this time, then another from the west.

Declan, you and Ester support the east! Ryn called to him from the other side of the line, his towering form already turning towards the rising sound of fighting. *Bonner and I will see to the other flanks!*

Declan was about to shout back his understanding when the wall of soldiers before him tensed, and he whirled, throwing himself back just in time to keep from having his face torn off by a blur of bony claws slashing at his eyes. This second wight had been a female elf, but unlike the first she sported no livery of Ysenden, no black leather or gold plating. On the contrary, she looked to be wearing plain clothes that might once have been colored, like one might expect from a well-born commoner, and her long white hair might have been braided at some point, though it was now ragged and riddled with dirt and snow.

Not of the army, was all Declan had time to register, ducking under a second blow as he continued to backpedal towards the support of the elven line. *Not one of the missing soldiers.*

Thunk.

As it leapt at him again, an arrow ripped by Declan's right ear to lodge into the wight's neck, knocking it nearly flat. It recovered quickly, though, and grinned even as it launched itself forward again, attempting to screech around the haft buried in its throat. Declan had gathered up a more substantial spell of flames in his right hand, ready to blast the creature into ash if he could manage it, but just as he began to bring his arm up to cast the weave he faltered when two shapes whipped by either side of him, darting out from the line at his back. In a blink two spears had buried themselves across each other in the wight's chest, bringing it to such a sharp stop that its feet partially flew out from under it. At once it started scrabbling at the weapon's hafts, gurgling in anger as it glared with pale eyes, but before it could get a good purchase on the black wood to try and break it, a third figure arrived in a blur from the north, twin blades flashing in arcs of black. The first blow relieved the wight of a raised arm, but the second followed before the creature likely noticed it, biting into its neck just above what had to have been Ester's arrow.

This time the entire head fell to the ground, and the wail came in a ghostly shriek as the spears were wrenched from flesh already erupting into flame.

"At the head, he said?" Tesied asked aloud from beside Declan, giving him a grim smile as he and Aliek flicked their blades clean at their sides.

"At the head!" Lysiat called out in confirmation over the inferno, stepping around the black fire with both blades still and ready at her sides.

"*Glad you listen,*" Declan answered their taunting roughly, looking around just as the line at their back split to let Ester, Eyera, and Orsik through. The male was still bleeding, but he was no longer limping, and Ester answered Declan's curious look at the warg as they came up beside the group.

"Father did what he could with what time he had!" she said hurriedly, drawing another arrow to nock on her *er'endehn* bow. "Orsik can move again, but he'll need more attention later! More importantly—" she dipped her head towards the dark stain that was all that remained of the second wight "—that wasn't one of the missing soldiers, Declan! She wasn't wearing armor!"

"I noticed the same thing!" he agreed darkly, looking to the grey-black ash as the sounds of battle started to mount around them.

"*In elvish! In elvish, Declan!*"

With a step Lysiat had moved to stand beside the pair, looking frustrated. As the shrieks of the wights were being joined by the screams of dying elves, Declan supposed he could understand the sentiment.

"*More than gone soldiers*!" he did his best to elucidate as he indicated the stain with his sword. "*That one, not soldier! We fight more than gone soldiers!*"

As though to make his point for him, in the corner of his eye

Declan saw a shadowy flash, and he turned just in time to see not one, not two, but *three* squealing figures sprint out of the trees to strike the elven line just to the south of them, not a one among their number in the armor of Ysenden.

They didn't have time to be standing around.

"*AT HEAD!*" Declan bellowed once again, already bolting out of their little group to aim for the trio of wights that were in the process of tearing a hole in the formation. "*STRIKE AT HEAD!*"

And then the world was all blood and flames.

Despite the fact that they seemed to outnumber their enemy for the time being, the younger generation of *er'endehn*'s inexperience with dealing with the draugr took an immediate toll. Though he, Ester, Eyera, Orsik, and the ay'ahSels darted up and down the eastern flank to support the battle wherever they could, every time they turned around they saw another soldier fall, another of the creatures come flying out of the woods with a scream. For every one of the wights they felled it seemed like they lost at least one of their own, and no number of spells or arrows or blades could stop the deadly rush of the undead that seemed to be coming faster and faster. Before long the seven of them were forced to split up as a full-fledged wave of six wights came spilling out of the trees, Declan yelling for Ester to support Lysiat and her brothers before shouting for Orsik.

As it turned out, his weeks of magical and physical training, along with the warg's natural size and savagery, proved a devastating combination when backed up by the stoicism and skill of the soldiers of Ysenden.

Slashing out with his left hand, Declan didn't have time to concern himself with the sanctity of the forest as he sprayed the ground before one of the undead with a line of liquid fire, catching it about the legs so that it crumbled to the burning ground. Leaving the crippled creature to the elves—the draugr still viciously clawing at the frozen earth as it attempted draw itself forward—he and Orsik engaged another each, the warg slamming one wight in weather-worn rags to the ground to tear at its face as Declan took on the other with his sword leading the way. Even with his improving corpomancy he was hardly a match for the thing's speed, but he could move well enough now to at least keep from dying as he gathered up another spell. When the wight slashed at him wildly, he just managed to dodge under the blow and come up behind it with some clever footwork. The creature spun in the same breath, and Declan got his blade up in time to sever the claws of one hand that might otherwise have caught him in the face. As the draugr screamed in frustration, though, he punched at it, willing more magic out of the stone this time. With a small explosion of controlled fire the thing was sent catapulting backward, old clothes alight and burning. With a gruesome series of *shlunks* it was impaled on the waiting spears of the *er'endehn,* ready in support now, and in frightening cohesion the soldiers stepped away from each other even as they brought their polearms inward, bearing the thrashing thing to the ground kicking and screeching.

Declan was already turning away when the black blades of swords flashed, and the screaming was replaced by the wail of the shattered Purpose.

They do learn quick, he admitted to himself, running forward to meet another wight as it came sprinting out of the trees.

With Orsik's assistance, Declan soon lost count of the creatures they felled. Seven, perhaps? Or eight? It felt strange, to forget himself as he fought, to give in to his body and his instincts. It had been months since he'd felt such confidence in himself, since he'd felt at least on even footing with his enemy. He had almost lost the feeling, truth be told, almost buried it. For most of his life Declan had almost always been the strongest, almost always been the fastest and the best. For most of his life he had been able to fight calmly, collectedly, without losing himself to fear and disbelief. It had only taken him a few short months to lose touch with that assuredness, he saw now. The ghouls. The wereyn. The wights. The drey and tunneler especially. They had stolen that from him.

But now, as he thrust his blade into the mouth of one undead even as his flames consumed the chest and head of another, Declan realized that he was finding it again.

Another fell to the magics, collapsing into the roiling pools of broiling fire that had steadily grown around Declan as he fought. Orsik had gotten smart to the weaves, too, and didn't hesitate to slam his own opponent sideways into the heat with his massive head. Declan's sword flashed, and a third screamed in fury as it found itself missing an arm, then was silenced as some soldier or another deftly thrust their spear past his shoulder to take it through the eye. All the while Declan stayed calm, stayed focused, his confidence building with every passing second.

With those same ticking moments, though, he knew also that the elves were dying.

It was a slow, methodical butchery, but the slaughter was happening all the same. Three or four minutes into the fight now, and the wights were still coming faster and faster. Like the sounds of battle were drawing the creatures for a mile all around them, their unending press was a constant, crushing force. Declan suspected the only reason Ryn hadn't turned yet was for fear of setting the Vyr'esh ablaze, but if things kept going the way they were, he knew the dragon would be forced to take his true form before too long, forest be damned. With every step back he and Orsik were pushed, with every fallen body of a soldier he had to step over, Declan's suspicion that they were going to be overrun grew. He didn't have time to turn and judge, but if he had to guess he suspected their total losses would amount to half their number soon enough, the killing happening quicker and quicker as they were pushed closer together.

"Shit..." he muttered under his breath, sweeping another arcing torrent of flame over the ground, forcing a new trio of wights to scatter and split around the magic.

Then, from somewhere behind him, there came a single, ringing shout he recognized.

"*AVRETE!*" Colonel Syr'esh was yelling at the top of his lungs. "*AVRETE NORS! AVRETE!*"

Only the single word for "north" was not lost on Declan, the other not among those he'd learned so far. As the wights came around the edges of his burning magic to collapse in on him, he could only hope he'd be able to follow the lead of the soldiers at his back as he crouched low, blade ready and a powerful weave of force already gathered in his left hand, ready to send at least one or two of the creatures staggering back into the fires.

In the end, he needn't have bothered.

There was a *thrum*, and the wight furthest to his left was slammed sideways, dark flames already growing from the shaft the of the arrow buried in its temple. The other two died equally as quickly, the one at his right as one spear severed a leg above the knee and another cleaved through its neck as it collapsed towards the ground, the left in a single flash of glossy black as Lysiat lanced once again into view, sword slashing through enough of its skull to drop it. Declan was left feeling rather disappointed as he called back his weave, standing straight with the intention of shouting his thanks to the ay'ahSels for their timely arrival over the triple shriek of three destroyed Purposes.

Before he could get a word out, however, the twins were on him, grabbing him by the arms and starting to haul at him, shouting as they did.

"*NORTH!*" they were saying. "*NORTH!*"

Declan, bewildered, only had time to see Lysiat calling for Orsik, the warg bounding to the elf's side, before his view was blocked by another large, grey-white form.

"Declan!" Ester shouted from atop Eyera, her bow still in hand. "They've called the retreat! Run! RUN!"

Declan didn't have to be told twice.

Pulling himself free of Aliek and Tesied's grips, he stumbled only briefly before he was sprinting northward right along with the elves, keeping up only by pouring every ounce of focus he could into his corpomancy. Over more bodies than he cared to count did he hurdle as they fled, not daring to look back even after Lysiat caught up to them, riding on Orsik's back. Ordinarily he might have found the sight of the elf clutching the warg's fur for handholds rather amusing, but he had no space to feel anything other than the slick *crunch* of the cold ground under his boots as he ran. All around him the soldiers were retreating, sharing the call to make north as they did. Where there had been two hundred not five minutes before, there were now indeed hardly more than half that many, and Declan felt his focus shaken by nausea at the sight of so few thundering along beside them. The shrieks of their pursuers, growing in fervor and volume with every step he took, didn't help that sickening feeling, and he at last couldn't stop himself from glancing back.

"*Shit!*" he said again, louder this time, as he saw why the higher officers had called for a withdrawal.

Pouring out of the western and southern woods, at least four-score white-haired figures in various states of dress were hounding them with all speed, mouths almost unnaturally-agape as they screamed with their horrible glee. The east line, he realized suddenly, hadn't taken a fraction of the attack the rest of the formation must have, and with a sudden drop of his stomach Declan feared abruptly that there was perhaps a different reason Ryn hadn't shown his true form yet, nor Bonner cast any spells to slow the enemy.

Cursing again, he tried to scan the fleeing backs of the soldiers ahead of him, but distinguishing black and gold from black and gold was difficult at a full sprint. Through the trees and scattered underbrush, he doubted even Ryn's *rh'eem* would have been obvious to him among the running figures.

Ironically, Bonner's comments about mind-speech sprang to mind, and Declan found himself swearing he would take the mage up on his offer if they made it through this mess.

First things first, though…

"Ester!" Declan shouted as they half-ran, half-slid down a sudden slope in the forest floor, sending snow and dirt spraying everywhere. "Where's Ryn? Where's your father?"

Before the half-elf could start to answer, however, a familiar voice rang through his head.

Here, Declan! On you left!

Declan looked west, and indeed found the dragon bounding in their direction through the woods. He had taken to his wolf's form for speed, and despite what appeared to have been some delay in retreating was catching up to them fast, his new sword sheathed in his jaws.

"Ryn!" It was Ester's turn to call out. "Where is Father?!"

Safe! the dragon answered them, leaping clear over the better part of a fallen tree to land beside Lysiat and Orsik, matching pace with them. *He's gone ahead to prepare the way!*

"The way?" Declan repeated in a shout, vaulting over a small boulder as the thunder of their feet and the continued screeching of the wights nearly drowned out his voice.

Ryn nodded. *The river.*

Apparently even the ay'ahSels had spent enough time around them to have a sense of what that meant, because not a one of them said anything to this.

"Where did they come from?!" Ester demanded instead, ducked

low over Eyera as the warg continued to churn the ground beneath them. "The wights?! You couldn't see them?!"

The faint clink of metal had Declan suspecting the dragon was shaking his wide head. *No. I could not, though that's hardly surprising. I doubt I could feel them* now *even if I tried, and there must be nearly a hundred in that pack.*

"Comforting," Declan grunted.

As for where they came from, I haven't the faintest clue, Ryn continued. *I am not familiar with the Vyr'esh. For all I know they might have been scattered about us the entirety of the last two weeks and simply chose now to attack.*

Declan was doubtful of this theory, however. That the draugr had been hidden from the dragon's sight was indeed no surprise—the Endless Queen had been using the same trick for months now—but Ryn had caught the first presence of a drey in the tunnels after learning to look for what *wasn't* there as much as what was. Doubtless the smaller size of a single wight would have made such a distinction harder to sense, but more than the *hundred* they'd fought and were now fleeing from? It didn't align.

No. It was more likely the drey had been lying in wait for them, had been dispatched for the exact purpose of ambushing them. The way they'd come pouring out of the woods little by little also led Declan to imagine that whoever—or *what*ever—had woven the creature's Purposes into such a task had spread them through the forest in preparation, like they'd only had a general sense of what path the forward unit would be taking back to Ysenden. It was too much of a coincidence, otherwise. What was more, if Declan understood the essentials of necromancy as explained to him, then keeping the wights scattered throughout the Vyr'esh for longer than was necessary was likely ill-advised. Exposing corpses—even magically-preserved corpses—to the winter elements was a good way to lose flesh, to lose limbs and bodies to the cold and wind. Beyond that, while the wights might be able to fend for themselves, Declan knew first-hand that there were beasts among these woods that would be a challenge even to any single or pair of undead, and were likely hungry enough to offer that challenge. Declan grit his teeth as he came to the grim conclusion that Sehranya had indeed very likely beaten them to Eserysh.

In fact, it seemed like she might already have somehow established herself more permanently than any of them would have liked.

Declan's consideration of this cold thought was interrupted by an exclamation of anticipation from Ester. A few seconds later, even he could see the light through the trees that had clearly caught her attention, the sign that they were reaching a break in the dense sprawl of the woods.

East! Ryn barked at them as they approached the open air. *Half a hundred yards east!*

Wordlessly they followed his command together, shifting course slightly to the right. Most of the fleeing elves around them adjusted in the same fashion upon hearing the dragon's voice, and within twenty seconds or so they were bolting out of the trees and onto a shallow, snowy bank beneath the rare sun that had held throughout the morning's march. Before them, the river—the 'Lyons', Declan recalled—extended in a flat, frozen expanse some forty yards across, the grey-white of the ice beneath the wind-blown snow reflecting the blue of the sky and the light of the day in a mix of azure brilliance that might have been pretty any other time.

For the moment, however, Declan saw nothing more than a means of escape.

To Bonner! Ryn shouted, already bounding across the frozen flow, claws offering him good purchase despite the sheer sheen of it. *Cross to Bonner!*

Looking to the far bank, Declan indeed saw that the old man had long-since beaten them to the other side. What was more, he was not standing idle at the edge of the ice, but instead his hands flung out before him, red-orange light building ominously about his fingers and palms as he appeared to mutter with eyes fixed on the river.

Though he might still be in the earliest stages of his magical training, Declan knew the gathering signs of a powerful weave, particularly one as destructive as what Bonner clearly had planned.

"CROSS!" he bellowed after Ryn, immediately setting out to follow the dragon as quickly as he could. "CROSS NOW!"

Ester translated his words with equal fervor behind him, and the few elves who'd been lingering uncertainly at the edges of the Lyons began hurrying after Declan. Moving carefully, he did his best not to slip as he struggled across, trusting the ay'ahSels, too, to follow with Ester and the warg.

He was just over half way to the far side when there rose a scream, piercing in the brilliance of the open air, and he looked over his shoulder in alarm.

Whereas the scattered elves who had been trailing behind him were fighting not to fall as they crossed, the wights had no such reservations. Though many of them slipped and dropped within a few yards of setting off across the ice, the ones that did started crawling across the river with frightening speed using their claws for purchase, and those that did not caught several of the more cautious stragglers within seconds. Declan saw one elf go down as an undead in the same armor as the soldier leapt on his back in a spray of blood, then another as two more caught up to them together, ripping and tearing even as they fell. Declan forced himself to look away, forced himself to focus on Bonner getting closer and closer, noticing as he did that the spell in the mage's hands had bloomed into something of terrifying proportions. The red light had expanded, solidifying and linking into arcs of crimson lighting, and even as he continued to struggle forward Declan saw those flickering lines dip and rise away from each other, growing steadier and stronger with every passing second. By the time he was less than ten yards from the shore, the spell had formed itself into a magic circle that expanded as it swirled, runes of power shaping themselves out of the air in the same red lines.

"Hurry!" Bonner was shouting now, and Declan could have sworn the mage's eyes had started to glow with bloody brilliance through the sheen of the spell. "HURRY!"

A handful of heartbeats later, Declan was off the ice and onto the northern bank, turning and gathering his own weave as Ester and the others clambered into the snow not far behind them.

Taking careful aim, Declan solidified his flames as best he could into his fist. It was his first attempt at casting any focused projectile outside of his controlled training with Bonner, but now was not the time to fear failure. A dozen elves were still scrambling across the river, faces tense and focused even as the screams of their dying comrades shivered over the glimmering ice at their backs. The wights behind them who'd caught no prey had not stopped, of course, and it was through the broadest gap between the soldiers before him that Declan launched his first spell as Bonner's weave crackled and continued to build beside him. With another *whoosh* of expanding air, a ball of flames erupted from the four fingers he'd raised to help align his aim, rocketing away in a blazing trail. Fearing missing altogether, he'd targeted not the undead themselves, but rather the ice directly before the largest group of three he could safely see. There was a small explosion as the weave struck the frozen river, echoed by squeals of fury as two of the wights were blasted backwards. The third—while not having been caught in the lingering flames of the fireball directly—staggered sideways two steps before black flames bloomed from its head, licking out first from around the heavy sliver of broken ice that had taken it through the jaw.

Encouraged by his success, Declan gathered a second projectile and launched it to similar results, then summoned up a third.

Before he could fire off the fireball, however, Bonner was shouting out from beside him.

"BACK, DECLAN! GET BACK!"

As the size of the magical circle had expanded to some six feet in diameter, Declan only needed to be told once. Reaching out, he took the hand of one soldier who'd very nearly reached the edge of the ice, hauling him onto the shore without ceremony and half dragging him back nearly to the tree line. Once they were at what he hoped was a safe range, Declan watched, open-mouthed, as Bonner waited only for the last of the elves who had survived to step clear of the ice.

Then, with a roar like some violent god of fire and death, the old man set loose his gathered spell.

In a flash of crimson, all sound vanished momentarily from the world. The day seemed to darken, the light of the sun above shifting and dimming until it was as though night had fallen twelve hours early. Then everything brightened again, but no longer in the colors of sunlit morning. Red. Everything was red, illuminated by a brilliant sphere of compressed, crimson energy that boiled and swam between Bonner's hands. Declan had to cover his eyes at the sight of the thing, seeing as he did how the darkness of the shadows cast by the spell cut vertically from his shielding fingers to his face.

And then, with a ringing return of sound, the first bolt of lighting struck.

CRASH!

The red arc fell not from the sky, but leapt instead from the roiling sphere of magic in Bonner's hands to cut up then down again, like the magic had been reaching for the heavens only to be pulled earthward by gravity before it could climb too high. It thundered not into any of the still-approaching wights in particular, but bolted down instead into the frozen river, cracking it with a brief flash of fire like a burning boulder dropped on glass. Several massive slabs of ice came loose of the rest, rising and bobbing briefly as smaller shards blasted through the air.

That, though, was only the first bolt.

CRASH! BOOM! CRASH!

Again and again and again the red lightning leapt from Bonner's hands to slam down into the thick ice, shattering it section by section in an arc growing outward from where the mage stood. More portions tilted or even flipped outright, dumping and dragging the screaming wights into the dark flow of water waiting under the frozen surface. Within five seconds, a twenty-yard radius of the Lyons was a fractured spider web of broken ice, and in ten the lighting was nearing the far bank of the river and extending for fifty yards to the east and west. When the spell struck the south shore, the mage let out a bellow of concentration, and the weave suddenly stopped extending forward, the arcs dipping only further up and down the river.

Then, at long last, the spell seemed to run its course, because with a final "*BOOM!*" one last bolt of energy tore lose a ten-foot section of the ice upstream from them, and then the red faded to let the light of the day return once more.

Even as the sounds of wind and rushing water reached Declan and the others again, however, not a word was spoken, each and every onlooker too awestruck by the sight before them.

The steady, heavy ice they had all escaped across was no more, the once-solid sheet more open river now than frozen surface. From the west, a distant crushing sound was steadily growing louder as the sections and chunks of ice blasted loose of the larger body began crunching and crashing into each other and the still-solid Lyons downstream of them.

Of the wights that had been pursuing them across the river, not a hint remained.

"Mother's *bloody* mercy..." Declan finally managed to breath, hardly remembering to blink as he gaped at the utter destruction disguised as a steadily flowing river.

There was a *crunch* of snow at his back, but he didn't have the will to turn around and see who was approaching him as he continued to stare. After a second or two, Ryn came to stand beside him, still in his wolf's form, white-gold eyes on the water as well.

I did say you had the greatest mentor of the age, didn't I? the dragon said, actually managing to sound just the littlest bit amused.

CHAPTER TWENTY-ONE

"Fail me again, and suffer the consequences. I would remind you not to forget that death need be no release from punishment, in my presence…"

—The Endless Queen

Gonin Whist smiled wryly as Bonner Fehn's chaotic spell came to an end. He watched the mage drop his arms and stagger, one foot actually splashing into the icy flow of the river before the one of King's blood darted from his place by the shifted dragon to catch the old man by the elbow, drawing him back. Satisfied, Gonin dismissed his scrying weave with a sweep of one hand, obliterating the cycling runes of sight and transportation scrawled into the ground he knelt on, giving himself a second or two to allow a return of his awareness to his own body.

When he'd regained his presence of mind, Gonin rose to his feet, his lank, grey hair and the fur lining of his robes shifting slightly in the chill winter breeze as he tilted his head to the heavens above.

He stood in the broad patch of light he'd made for himself by felling one of the giant titans of the Vyr'esh. The base of its trunk eaten away by searing flames, the great evergreen had come down with a *crash* that had sent snow and ice showering from the canopy above to the ground, but Gonin had estimated himself more than far away enough from his intended prey that he could get away with it. He'd needed a clean line of sight to the sky, after all, as well as a cleared patch of ground in which to etch the runes, and in the end it had been well worth the trouble.

He'd found them again.

The loss of the wights was a negligible thing. Gonin and his Queen had long since made sure there were more where they'd come from, and the draugr had felled far more of the elven soldiers than their own permanent casualties. What was more, the undead currently being swept down the river would likely get tangled up in the rapids and frozen waterfall a mile or so upstream, allowing for their general retrieval. Even had that *not* been the case, the sacrifice of the wights would have been worth it.

He had found them.

The Queen's fury had been a terrible thing when the one of King's blood had felled her "wurm", as she'd called it. They hadn't even been in communication when Gonin had felt the rage through the crystal speaker's charm still hanging from his neck. Worse, the bitch elf who had been accompanying the man had apparently dragged him out of the mountains before reinforcements could be sent to finish off the job, removing them from the Queen's realm and the eye she'd been able to keep upon them. Gonin suspected the earth itself must have shook when *that* escape had happened, as he'd felt his master's seething ire even in the simple command she'd given him, which had drawn him back from Viridian and into the icy forests of Eserysh.

And now, he had succeeded.

They would be heading to Ysenden, he knew. The livery of the soldiers who'd been escorting the four companions and their beasts had promised as much, as well as the presence of the twin spear-wielders and their elder sibling the Queen had described as having been among the elves who'd escaped the Mother's Tears alive. Gonin smiled again as he considered the possibilities this offered him and his master. The one of King's blood likely expected to find security in the city of the *er'endehn*, safety. He likely expected a haven within which he'd be able to grow stronger, he, the dragon, the half-elf, and that thrice-damned Bonner Fehn together. There might have been some truth to that, at one time.

"No longer, though, you foolish little man," Gonin said with a satisfied grin up at the sun.

Then, with a thought, he called to his mount, summoning it to him from the skies as he began to plan.

CHAPTER TWENTY-TWO

Grief is a thing mankind might assume lacking among the elves, particularly the stoic brethren of the er'endehn. Humanity—in suffering loss—tends to break, if even only temporarily. We weep. We scream. We fall asleep clutching at ourselves, wishing only for a way to fill the void that has suddenly appeared within us at the loss of our loved one. By comparison, the most emotion one will sometimes see from an elf in similar circumstances is a stillness, a silence of voice of body alike. They may seem as cold as stone, unwilling to even shed a tear for the gone.

Do not be fooled. Consider—instead—that when one lives for a thousand years as man might live for fifty, loss forms such a great part of ones life that it becomes imperative to shield one's self from its claws, lest one be lost to the depths of mounting grief as the centuries wear on…

—Disparities of Race in Modern Society, by Seckle Gelt, c. 290p.f.

"*Erraven,*" Syr'esh was saying darkly, ignoring the sergeant who was in the process of bandaging the shallow lacerations that bled down the colonel's left shoulder where a wight's claws had torn through the leathers of his armor. Instead, he merely pointed at a spot on the map being held up for him by two of his surviving higher officers as he repeated himself. "*Erraven.*"

Declan, following the colonel's finger, could only agree.

It was a miracle the map had survived. Most of the soldiers tasked with carrying the tents and gear had either abandoned the weight at the call for retreat, or died before they'd had a chance to. After the morning they'd all had, though, Declan thought they were owed a little good fortune.

Erraven. The ruins of the ancient city—as explained by the elders of the Colonel's remaining inner circle and translated by Ester—had apparently been no more than ten miles west of them when they'd been attacked. They had all—Declan, Ryn, Ester, and even the ay'ahSels—been pulled into this emergency meeting the moment they'd absconded deep enough back into the woods for the dragon to announce them free of pursuers. For half an hour now they'd been debating what had happened, how it was they had come to be ambushed. Declan had been pleased to discover that Ryn and Ester both had made the same realization he had over the course of the fight, as had one or two of the older officers. A horde of undead—like that which had been used by Sehranya seven hundred years ago to attack first Eserysh, then the Reaches—was one thing to expose to the elements and dangers of the frozen woodlands. The scattered wights had been another.

Sehranya had a foothold, it had been agreed, and as soon as this had been decided the map had been called for, and the likeliest sight of such a bastion identified almost immediately.

Are we sure the city still stands? Ryn asked of the elves, the reptilian features of his *rh'eem* looking up from the meticulous emblem that was Erraven on the map. *It would have been abandoned for centuries now, would it not?*

"It stands," was all Declan understood of the Colonel's response before having to bend down so Ester could translate into his ear. *"Our kind approach nothing without seeking perfection. That includes our homes. The ancient cities—Erraven, Syr'hend, ys'Vaal, and the rest—may be empty,*

but they are not absent."

"We use them, on occasion." Major r'Rehl offered in addition, wincing slightly as speaking obviously strained the wound along the side of her neck that was bleeding through its bandages. *"As outposts on patrol. They may be far gone from the metropolises they once were, but their walls are sturdy and a far cry better than the trees at blocking the wind and snow in winter."*

Ryn nodded in understanding. *Then I agree with the Colonel. Erraven has been claimed by the Endless Queen, or more likely whatever subordinate it is she's sent to establish a stronghold in your lands. It is very possible the city is being used as a garrison.*

"Then what do we do?" Declan asked as the elves around him all exchanged grim looks. "Is dealing with it an option as we are now?"

Not on our own, no, Ryn said with a shake of his head as Ester turned Declan's question for the benefit of the *er'endehn. I might be able to torch it from the sky, but there's no telling what could be waiting for me approaching the city. There might be drey, or worse.*

"Worse than the winged?" Major y'Rehl sounded like she were attempting to come off with her usual dubiousness, but her doubtful expression no longer held the same fervor it might have even earlier that morning.

Ryn nodded. *Liche, perhaps. Or a true necromancer, like the one we crossed paths with in Viridian. Some higher intelligence of Sehranya's ilk has a hand in this. We know that much.* Something *had to weave the Purpose into those wights, and regardless of what they are I would be hesitant to engage them on my own. Perhaps if Bonner wasn't out of commission...*

Collectively, every head in the meeting turned together. While they had secluded themselves from the rest of the recovering soldiers that had survived the assault, Bonner had immediately excused himself from the gathering in favor of settling into the nook of a nearby tree before pulling his hood up and searing a rune of warmth into the wood at his back. He was asleep now, they could all tell, Orsik and Eyera curled up protectively on either side of him, and no one—not even the elves with their minimal understanding of magic—spoke a word of protest at the sight. Between the combat and his weave of destruction which had freed them of the pursuit of the wights, the mage had been largely spent already, but he'd passed their march further into the Vyr'esh hurrying from one injury to another, stopping bleeding, sealing wounds, and getting soldiers being dragged along by their comrades back on their own feet. By the time Ryn had called the halt, Bonner's complexion had been pallid, and Declan doubted the man would wake until the next morning at the earliest if no one roused him.

"*Colonel... I would ask that you bring Master Ryndean and his companions into your confidence.*"

Declan almost missed Ester's translation of the words, taken aback as he was by the fact that is was *Lysiat* who had spoken. For the most part, the ay'ahSels had stayed silent throughout the meeting, voicing their thoughts only when asked for by Syr'esh or one of the other higher ups, apparently all too aware of the fact that they had been included more due to their growing bond with Declan and the others than any merit of status or rank. It was strange, therefore, for the elf to speak so out of turn, and y'Rehl was only one of several faces to tense in disapproval at her words.

The Colonel himself, however, was not among them.

Syr'esh was instead looking at Lysiat ponderously while he pulled his shirt back up over his now-bandaged shoulder as the attending sergeant stepped away. The man looked to be considering something, and Declan, Ryn, and Ester all had the sense to wait for him to speak before voicing their curiosity.

Bring them into his confidence about what?

"*Master Ryndean...*" Syr'esh finally looked away from Lysiat to Ryn, seeming—for once—just the slightest bit hesitant. "*The situation regarding Erraven is… erm… further complicated by other factors, I'm afraid."*

Oh? Ryn raised an eyebrow. *More complicated than the possibility of an army of draugr, drey, and necromancers within two day's march of Ysenden?*

"Indeed," Syr'esh admitted with a dry smile, waving off the frowns of his officers as he continued. *"You are aware by now, I assume, of the… trouble our city has been facing of late? I had informed Master yr'Essel of it before your return to us."*

"More like he dragged it out of us," y'Rehl rasped, earning herself a sharp look from the Colonel, as well as more subtly from each of the ay'ahSel siblings.

We are aware of the insurrection, yes. Ryn nodded, ignoring the Major. *The timing of it all is suspicious, to be sure, but what does that have to do with Erraven specifically?*

"Much and more, most unfortunately. These rebellions have a distinctive identifier, you see: they are driven by bloodline. Both old and new."

"The bloodline of the old cities?" It was Ester who asked the question, voicing Declan's own suspicion, though he'd only barely understood her.

"*Indeed.*" It was the Colonel's turn to nod at the half-elf before looking to Ryn again. "*You have lived long enough I believe, Master Ryndean. I assume you know the tumultuous history of the* er'endehn*?"*

I and all of us here, Ryn confirmed, crossing his arms and narrowing his white-gold eyes impatiently. *Is there a point to this, Colonel? I'd not have taken you for a man who dances around a subject…*

Syr'esh took the calling-out to heart, clearing his throat before his own gaze sharpened. *"Ahem… Indeed. You are correct. My apologies. I am not typically in the habit of sharing information outside my officers, let alone outside my own race."* He gathered himself for a moment, frowning between Ryn, Declan, and Ester briefly, but when he continued it was in a surer tone. "*Of the old states, Erraven and Ys'vaal held the greatest power outside of Ysenden, along with Syr'hend, where my own parents fled from. Unsurprisingly, it is some of the old residents of those cities and their descendants who have been making the greatest trouble for our High Chancellor and his council, these last months. Of those three, however, the blood of Erraven had been the greatest threat, even making some direct assaults on the Chancellor himself, or at least attempting to. As close as it is to Ysenden, a much larger portion of the city's population managed to make it to safety compared to the others, whose ruins are further south of us, closer to the mountains Sehranya descended from. As a result, even only the portion of Erraven's blood who count themselves among the dissenters had not been of insignificant number."*

"'Had' been the greatest threat?" Declan repeated, not having missed the tense. "'Had not' been of insignificant number? You speak in the past tense, Colonel. What happened?"

Syr'esh grimaced slightly once Ester finished translating for him. *"It was an ugly business. Said bluntly: the High Chancellor and our Lord Commander had them and their families largely corralled several months ago… and exiled."*

Declan felt a shiver he didn't like crawl up his spine at these words, and it took him a moment to place where the fear had come from. As Ester's mouth dropped open beside him and Ryn dragged a palm across his face with a groan, however, he figured it out. The dark elves could be cold, yes, but he'd not judged them to be cruel. Winter might not have been in full bloom a few months ago, but it would have been coming, and he couldn't imagine the Ysenden military driving whole families—including at least *some* children, he had to assume—from the city if they thought it meant death at the hands of the elements, or worse.

No… If they had been exiled from the safety of the walls, it would have been because they had a place to go.

The blood of Erraven, Declan repeated to himself with a chill, realizing what this meant.

They would have made for the city, Ryn spoke for them all, sounding grim. *They would have made for the ruins of Erraven.*

Syr'esh nodded slowly. "*And they did. It was confirmed, long before we—*" he gestured to himself and the other dark elves "*—set out from the city on the word of our scouts that a winged—a 'drey', as you say—had been sighted circling the southern edge of the Vyr'esh.*"

They would have settled in the ruins. Likely with the intent of starting over. Ryn's expression was darkening by the second. *Few weapons between them, I assume, and fewer intact defenses.*

"They would have been sitting ducks," Ester breathed, she too having clearly kept up with the dragon's train of thought.

"The clothes."

All of them, even the elves, turned to look at Declan as he spoke through grinding teeth.

What was that? Ryn asked him.

"The clothes," Declan repeated, feeling something like an angry nausea welling up inside him. "The rags and the like some—*most*—of the wights were wearing. The only armor was on the few soldiers we'd already lost before we realized what was happening." He stared straight ahead, feeling like he could have lit the bark of the tree he was glaring at aflame if he could weave rage into fire. "That's where the rest of them came from. The rest of the draugr."

"The rebels…" Ester groaned, looking suddenly a little sick. "They were the rebels…"

Despite his own fury, Declan managed to lift a hand to the half-elf's upper back to comfort her as she bent forward slightly, clearly feeling ill. Ryn translated for them, and by the lack of surprise on Syr'esh's face—though some of the other officers looked distinctly more alarmed—it was clear the Colonel, at the very least, had already come to the same conclusion.

"*A thousand souls,*" he said quietly. "*More since, I've no doubt, assuming any other rebels faced the same punishment…*"

"We've been feeding them to the horde?" It was Aliek's turn to speak out of place, though no one looked disapproving this time, too busy were they trying to control their own emotions. *"Spirits save us..."*

There was a long, tense moment of silence after that, the only sounds coming from the wind above them and the groans and movement of soldiers through the trees just south of them.

"So what do we do?" Declan asked at last, feeling now was *not* the moment to reflect. "If we can't make an assault ourselves, we ask for assistance, right? Assuming there will be an assault?"

Syr'esh nodded slowly after Ester translated. *"Indeed. The Chancellor will not abide this news. He'll want Erraven cleansed, and as quickly as possible."*

"We need to stop the exiling as well," Lysiat said quietly. *"Every soul cast from the city is one more for Sehranya to claim, clearly."*

Another nod, this time from every head that formed the circle.

"So... What do we do?" Declan asked again.

This time, Syr'esh's eyes were hard when he answered.

"We continue on to Ysenden. We continue on to Ysenden with all haste."

◆

If Declan had any lingering doubts regarding the fortitude of the dark elves, they were dispelled in the following hours. Despite their pains, despite their wounds and their fatigue and the fresh memories of seeing their kin so brutally slain, when the Colonel's command to march was announced, not a voice rose up in protest. Ninety-three. That was how many had survived the ambush, according to Ryn. Ninety-three opportunities to lash out in anger or fear or exhaustion.

And not one said so much as a word.

The going was slower than any of them would have liked, but steady. It had been made clear they would be marching with little rest, so they pushed only as fast as was prudent. The plodding pace lent itself—not for the first time—to Declan's appreciation of Orsik and Eyera among their company. The warg stayed closer at hand as they resumed the trek north, ears flat and noses always dipping this way and that as they sniffed at the air. Orsik had only barely been further patched up by Bonner before the mage had collapsed, but the male made no complaint as they walked, the blood that matted his sides having congealed and frozen into his fur to seal his wounds enough to move. The old man himself rode Eyera with Ester, having barely been roused, and had promptly fallen asleep again as soon as he'd settled in behind his daughter to wrap his arms about her waist and rest a bearded cheek on her upper back. Declan knew his worries were baseless—Bonner yr'Essel was about as unbreakable as Ryn was—but seeing the old man brought low like this dragged up feelings of concern, and not *just* for his health.

With Bonner incapacitated, Declan was suddenly the only "mage"—if he could yet call himself that—left to defend their sorry group in case of another attack...

Then again... Where that realization would once have been a stressful pressure, Declan had held onto his newfound confidence. He knew, now, what he was capable of, or at least what he was limited to being capable of in the moment. No longer did he feel defenseless, vulnerable. No longer did he question his value among their little party. For too long had he felt like the weak link among his comrades, felt surpassed even by Orsik and Eyera, who could at least down prey large enough to feed them all if needed. No. After weeks—*months*, actually—of training, Declan had finally had his eyes opened to the possibilities of the future.

For the time being, though, those eyes were fixed on the woods around them as what was left of the once-proud elven unit moved, and he limited any further training to silently working on his corpomancy, drawing and retracting the weaves of strength into and out of his body with deliberate, practiced care.

The sun of the morning, occasionally sweeping across them through the rare break in the canopy above, eventually gave way to a dimmer afternoon, and before too long the limited light by which they traveled was fading. The elves pressed on into the closing dark, and Declan knew they would keep going long after his own human vision failed him. Still, there would be a limit to how far they could go before it became dangerous. As the shadows deepened around them, he had a thought, and he started to scour the ground, hoping to find what he was looking for in time.

As though the Mother herself had blessed him with luck, it wasn't more than a minute before his searching was rewarded.

Falling back from the others for a moment, Declan crouched down at the foot of a fairly young spruce, grateful for the spell of warmth that emanated from the firestone hanging once again from around his neck. After a moment's study, he took hold of the cold, rough surface of one of the two head-sized chunks of what was likely granite half-embedded into the ground among the tree's roots. He cursed as he discovered that the stone wouldn't move even when he suffused himself with as much magic as he could put into his limbs, and he was about pour heat into the frozen earth to soften it when a shadow came up to lean over him from behind.

What are you doing? Ryn asked curiously.

"Perfect timing," Declan answered with a grin, pointing at the rocks. "Haul these out for me and you'll see."

Ryn's inhuman strength proved a greater enemy to the frigid ground than it could resist, because the granite came out with a few hearty tugs of the dragon's clawed hands. Once loose, Declan took one of rocks, leaving the other in his friend's arms for the time being, and focused on it even as the two of them hurried to catch back up to the rest of the march.

By the time they'd rejoined the others—Ester, the ay'ahSels, and even Orsik and Eyera having turned to watch their jogging return curiously—Declan had poured enough magic into the granite to have it blazing with heat and light.

"Here," he told Ryn, trading him the newly-formed firestone for the other still-dim rock. "There's not so many of us scattered about any more. If you and I take these to the front of the line, we might be able to keep on for a while."

Ryn raised an eyebrow at the sizable hunk of glowing granite he'd taken hold of without so much as wincing, his progenitor's blood having resonated with the pyromancy immediately. *That's a good thought, Declan, but you know I can't maintain your human weaves for too long before they—*

"I know," Declan said with a nod, already focusing on his own stone. "We can trade off whenever yours starts to dim."

Ryn, seeming satisfied with this suggestion, nodded as Ester sighed with a resigned sort of envy above them and Lysiat, Aliek, and Tesied all looked on in awe, along with every soldier in the nearby vicinity. A few minutes later, Declan was atop Orsik and pressing towards the front of the march, Ryn on foot right behind him. The warmth and light of the large firestones they held high—Declan's resting on one shoulder—drew a mix of murmurs and mutterings as they passed, but none of the soldiers raised any real question or alarm. Even once they reached Syr'esh and his officers they were greeted with nothing more than a few glares here and there, but with the Colonel's almost grateful permission, Declan and Ryn took their places a few body-lengths away from each other to lead the way.

With the firestones offering just enough illumination to guide their path, it was well after midnight before Syr'esh finally called for a rest, and even then only out of concern for the state of his soldiers. Everyone—Declan and Ryn included—was more than happy with the respite, and within a few minutes the majority of the *er'endehn* had huddled up into groups of fours and five to share warmth as they slept. Ryn offered to watch till dawn if someone would be willing to tolerate his hawk's form on their shoulder the next day, and after Declan had agreed, even y'Rhel thanked the dragon before turning in.

The next morning, Declan awoke to the ugly sound of something heavier than snow striking the canopy above them. Blinking away a fatigue that had only been mildly lifted by a half-night of rest, he pushed himself unsteadily up from where he'd settled down between Orsik and Eyera with Ester and the still-largely-unconscious Bonner. A couple runes had kept them all warm enough, but the minimal heat of the channeling scripts was of little comfort when something hard bounced off Declan's leather-clad thigh to skitter off across the ground.

"Well that's just great," he muttered, eyeing the thumbnail-sized ball of hail as several other similar examples managed to make it through the branches and leaves above them to pelt ground and bodies alike.

The only advantage to the weather was that no one had too much trouble rousing themselves when the officers started shouting that it was time to break camp. Even Bonner finally stirred from his fatigue, giving Declan and Ester a weak smile before gratefully accepting to sleep more on Eyera's back behind his daughter. By the time they were up and ready to move, Ryn had returned to them looking haggard, and, as promised, quickly took to his own rest on Declan's shoulder after strapping his sword to Orsik's harness and shifting to his—mercifully *much* lighter—hawk's form.

After a cold meal that consisted mostly of dried military rations, it was in a frozen, uncomfortable silence that the group started to move again, making their way ever northward as the barely-visible dawn slowly brightened the sky through the trees. Not even the ay'ahSels talked among themselves as they plodded along under the cruel pelting of the hail, and Declan and Ester only exchanged a few bare words to alternately check on Bonner and Ryn respectively, preferring instead to keep their eyes on the forest around them or the often treacherous ground. Too many times in the last fortnight had Declan caught the toe of a boot on a stone or root hidden beneath the shallow snow, and—though he thought his companions might have welcomed a laugh at his expense given the dismal atmosphere—he had *no* desire whatsoever to suffer soaked pants and fur, even if he *had* gotten plenty of practice at drying his own clothes of late.

Fortunately for everyone's spirits, however, it was little before noon when Bonner finally woke up in truth.

"Well… If this isn't the most miserable lot of long faces I've ever seen in my life."

With a warming leap of his heart Declan turned just in time to find the old man swing a leg off Eyera to slide to the forest floor even as the warg kept on moving. Bonner didn't miss so much as a step as he landed, and was walking in line with Declan and the ay'ahSels at once, stretching and looking around with a curious sort of air.

"How are you feeling?" Declan asked him. "That spell at the Lyons was… something else."

"*In elvish. In* elvish, *Declan.*"

Declan started and turned to see Lysiat, Aliek, and Tesied all staring between him and Bonner with wide eyes, the commander having been the one to berate him. Apparently the three of them were about as eager to speak to the mage as he was, though the awe in their eyes spoke to a different sort of interest.

The river, after all, would have been the first time they had seen Bonner in something closer to his element.

Wait until they realize fire magic isn't his forte, Declan thought, smiling to himself.

"*Yes, in elvish, Declan!*" Bonner joined in teasingly, speaking slowly and simply so he could follow. "*I feel fine. Sore. But fine.*"

"That magic, Master yr'Essel!" Tesied hissed like he'd been holding back for a day now to ask. *"What was…?"*

The rest of the elf's words were lost to Declan, sadly, but fortunately Bonner had his back.

"Slowly, Sergeant," the mage said, holding up a flat palm to tell Tesied to ease up. *"Declan does not speak well. Slowly."*

Tesied looked torn, like his desire to shower Bonner with questions was battling the man's request to be more considerate, but Lysiat beat him to the punch.

"The magic, Master yr'Essel," she repeated evenly in her brother's place, raising her hands to sign in the soldier's tongue in an effort to help Declan follow along. *"Was it dark magic?"*

Declan was so proud of the translation he'd managed for himself—using the signals he and the commander had never stopped practicing—that he almost missed how random a question this seemed.

Bonner, though, sighed almost like he had been expecting it.

"No, Commander." He answered with a shake of his head. *"Not dark magic."*

Lysiat frowned. *"But…dangerous. It was dangerous magic."*

This seemed to be more of a statement than anything, which had Declan confused until Bonner groaned in exasperation.

"What I'm going to have to do to scrub these poor souls of their misconceptions," he muttered in common before switching to elvish to address Lysiat again. *"Dangerous, yes. All magic is dangerous. But most magic is also…*not *dangerous."* Bonner frowned at his poor attempt to explain, giving Declan a disgruntled look and speaking to him directly. "This is your fault, you know. If you'd learned elvish growing up, we wouldn't be stuck communicating like dullards."

Declan snorted, pleased to see the man's fire returning. "Blame Ryn, then. Of anyone that was a part of my life back then, he's the only one who might have managed it."

"Fair point," Bonner grumbled in answer, green eyes shifting from Declan to the great black bird perched on his shoulder, beak and head tucked under one wing. For a second he looked to consider the sleeping dragon.

Then, with a wicked grin, he brought up a finger, clearly ready to deliver an aggressive poke.

"Father, I would remind you that if I put an arrow through your hand, it will heal inside of a minute, leaving me with very little to feel bad about. Leave Ryn alone, if you please."

Ester brought Eyera in close enough to prod her father in the side with the toe of her boot as he froze, caught red-handed.

"Ouch." He rubbed at his ribs, grumbling as he turned to his daughter. "Don't blame *me*. *He's* the one still passed out."

"He stayed up through the night to keep watch, probably with his senses engaged the entire time looking for little more than shadows," Ester said with deadly steadiness. "Unlike *some* people, he has not slept since yesterday morning. Therefore—" she shoved her boot into her father's chest repeatedly this time, a prod making every word poignant "—you will *leave. Him. Alone.*"

"Ouch!" Bonner exclaimed again, batting Ester's foot away before stepping around to the relative safety of Declan's other side. "Very well! Very *well!* I'll let the blasted lizard sleep, I swear!" However, once Ester looked satisfied, he decided to push his luck. "As for your not-so-subtle accusations of sloth on my part, I would have you know that forming a lightning helix is *no small feat*, particularly for one who lacks any real affinity for fire!"

Ester's glare had the man squeaking and cowering again in an instant, but Declan was too intent on Bonner's words to play into the pair's game.

"A 'lightning helix?" he repeated questioningly, looking around Ryn's small form to Bonner. "Is *that* what that spell was?"

"*Declaaan.*" It was almost alarming to hear something very much like pleading in Lysiat ay'ahSel's voice, and he turned to find her and her brothers watching him imploringly as she signed *and* spoke with emphasis. "*In. Elvish. Please.*"

"Ah…" Declan stuttered, a little at a loss as to how to even *begin* discussing what was obviously *very* complicated pyromancy in elvish, given he doubted he'd be able to wrap his head around it in common as it was.

Apologies, Commander. I'm afraid Declan is hardly the only one unable to elucidate on the intricacy of magics of a nature as Bonner has so recently chosen to demonstrate.

As one, every head among them turned to Declan's shoulder. Ryn was in the process of untucking his head from his wing—carefully, given the slim horns that curved from over each vertically-split, white-gold eye.

"Ah! You're awake!" Bonner exclaimed, bending around Declan's back to stick his tongue out at his daughter. "You see? There was no need for that savage beating."

Ester rolled her eyes as Ryn stretched his neck and wings out.

Yes, I am *awake,* the dragon said steadily, and his tone made it clear he was hardly pleased with that fact while he looked around as the occasional *thud* of hail striking heads and trees and frozen earth continued to echo around them. *I imagine it would be hard for a* boulder *to catch any amount of significant rest when you are close at hand, Bonner.*

The old mage looked a bit more sheepish at this. "Ah… Sorry about that. One tends to be a bit… err… excitable after one sleeps for the better part of twenty-four hours."

I wouldn't know, would I now? Ryn said coolly, glaring at the mage.

Bonner only grinned back apologetically.

With Ryn's—somewhat disgruntled—assistance, the conversation became a lot smoother, and Declan found his mood brightening significantly as Bonner happily dove into the intricacies of the spellwork he'd used to send the wights into the churning waters of the Lyons. The "lightning helix" turned out to be as complicated a weave as it had appeared, soon leaving Ester losing interest and Ryn sounding like he would have preferred to be translating any other topic. Declan, on the other hand was riveted—not the least bit because he was pleasantly surprise to find he actually *understood* a modest part of Bonner's explanation—as were Lysiat, Aliek, and Tesied, the siblings all listening with mouths agape in a rare show of awe despite the fact they couldn't have comprehended one word out of two even with Ryn's assistance. It seemed—for *er'endehn* who had been raised to fear magic as an enemy—the concept of spellwork that could do the kind of thing Bonner had shown them at the edge of the river was enrapturing.

As the march continued onward, Bonner managed to cleverly morph the conversation into a training session. Apparently seeing an opportunity to "scrub" some of those misconceptions he had been complaining about, he encouraged the ay'ahSels to observe Declan's practice. Ryn saw this as his cue to leave, muttering about "singed feathers" as he leapt off Declan's shoulder to flap up to Ester's, apparently starting a private conversation with the half-elf as she began talking about her estimation of how much distance they'd covered since the dragon had been asleep. In their own world, Declan, Bonner, and the dark elf trio were soon jabbering as quickly as Declan's limited elvish and signaling would allow, in particular once the old mage had him alternating between his suffusion spell and pyromancy. Showing off Declan's steadily-improving grasp of the different arts, Bonner had him challenging the elves in a variety of strength competitions between working more acutely on his ability to summon flames without the help of the firestone.

The rest of the morning and part of the afternoon passed in such a manner, conversation and demonstration allowing them to ignore the pelting of the hail—which had gotten worse, Declan thought—expect for on the rare occasion the filtered ice struck any of them. At some point Orsik came over to nuzzle at Bonner's hand hopefully, and the mage tended to the rest of the warg's minor wounds even as he kept one eye on Declan's training. After that, he'd taken to the animal's back, and continued offering instruction and encouragement as the elves looked on.

Declan was *just* starting to feel the build of fatigue behind his eyes—likely two hours into the session—when Ester brought Eyera in close beside them again.

"*We're slowing down*," she said in elvish. Ryn, still on her shoulder, nodded as Declan and the others turned to look up at her.

We are, the dragon agreed, the pale clouding of his faint pupils looking to relax as he extended himself. *I'm assuming that means—Oh…!*

Whatever the dragon had sensed brought him up short, his hawkish body even straightening in surprise.

"What is it?" Bonner was the first to ask him.

Before Ryn could answer, there came a shout from the head of the march—Syr'esh's voice, Declan thought—immediately echoed several times through the remaining force. At once the elves who had been scattered through the woods on either side of them began to fall in, and with a sharp word from Lysiat the ay'ahSels too, started to take their leave.

"*What happens?*" Declan asked after them coarsely, starting to feel a little excited. The fact that no one was yelling or running seemed to say they at least weren't being attacked again. "*We arrive?*"

If Lysiat and Aliek heard him, they were still too straight-laced to answer. Tesied, on the other hand, looked back to shoot him a sly grin, then nodded very briefly before falling in behind his siblings. In a blink they were gone, likely headed back towards the front of the march as the foot soldiers continued to form in around and in front of Declan and the others.

Yes. We've arrived.

Ryn changed as he dropped from Ester's shoulder, his form mostly humanoid again before he even hit the ground with a *thump*. By the time he stood up, his *rh'eem* had replaced his hawk's form completely.

The city is less than a half-mile ahead of us, the dragon continued before anyone could ask, moving to Orsik to take up his sword from where it was still strapped to the now-healed warg's harness. *Looks like the Colonel wants the unit to form up for presentation.*

"So close?" Ester asked quietly, sounding a little disbelieving. Declan could sympathize. It had now been nearly two months since they'd decided to seek out the hospitality—and help—of the *er'endehn,* not a week having gone by without exhaustion, complication, or battle. For them to be so near the goal of their journey now was… well… difficult to process.

"What's it like?" Declan decided to ask instead, the anticipation still building as he looked to Ryn. "Ysenden? What's it like?"

The dragon was still strapping the great black-and-gold blade to his back, but he shook his head at the question. *I think you're better off seeing it for yourself. It won't be long now.*

Despite the disappointing answer, Declan held his tongue, supposing Ryn had his reasons. Over the last months he had seen some truly incredible things, however, so if his friend was expecting him to be dumbfounded by whatever it was that awaited them beyond the edge of the forest, he suspected the dragon would be disappointed. He'd seen too much, now. Ryn's true form, memories of a long-lost era that weren't his own, the draugr, Bonner's powers. As a cloud passed across the sun above them, casting a slowly growing shadow over the canopy to the north, Declan had to shake his head as he considered just how different the world he now knew was to the one he—

But then he blinked, lifting his head with a frown.

A shadow? No. That couldn't be right. It had been storming all day. There would be no sun to speak of above the trees to form such a thing.

But... there *was* darkness. It was subtle, visible more in the absence of the few spots of cleaner light that made it through the snow- and ice-caked branches of the Vyr'esh than anything else, but it was there. Like night falling inch by inch with every step they took, blocking out a sky they couldn't see.

"What the...?" Ester muttered quietly beside him, and when Declan glanced at her he was relieved to see she, too, had her eyes lifted. Bonner looked up at his daughter's words as well, frowning at the growing darkness ahead of them, while Ryn kept on with his gaze set forward. Declan considered asking the dragon again what sort of "city" it was they were approaching, but thought better of it, doubting he would get any answer different from the first.

When they finally stepped out of the woods again, he was glad for his decision.

The Vyr'esh ended so abruptly, only Ester's sidelong warning let them know they were approaching the edge. Ordinarily daylight—even on a dismal afternoon like this one—would have foretold the approach of the edge of the woods, but something seemed to be blocking the sun, tricking the eyes into seeing only more shadow before them. The forest ended, however, spilling the march in an ordered line into the storm, but despite the harsher pelting of the hail as they abandoned the shielding canopy, Declan could only stare.

"What in that is good and holy...?!"

A mountain. They had stepped out of the forest onto the cleared foot of a lone, single mountain rising up, dark and ominous, from the trees.

But... No. That wasn't quite right. If this was a mountain, there was something distinctly odd about it. Even as close to the base of the black-and-grey slopes as they stood, Declan could tell that—rather than a jutting peak—the top of the great rise before them was… flat. Like some god had taken his sword to the furthest heights of the roughened shelves and crags that made up the slopes, relieving it of perhaps a quarter of its total height. Despite his earlier assumptions, Declan had never in his life seen anything like it, and he could only gape at the sight until more shouted orders brought his gaze down again, to the base that rose up before them.

The base, and the massive, jagged crevice that cut into the slopes, its depths hidden by a heavy stone wall and a single massive, iron-bound door, flanked on either side by half a dozen *er'endehn* whose clean armor marked them as soldiers not of Colonel Syr'esh's command.

"Oh. My. Word." Bonner's voice was tinged with wonder, and when Declan tore his eyes from the entrance guard he found the mage looking not at the grand gate, but rather still upward, at the top of the great rise before them. "Unbelievable… It's a bloody volcano…"

CHAPTER TWENTY-THREE

It turned out—to Declan's complete dismay—that the mountain was in fact *not* flat, but rather *hollow*. Had anyone insisted on this before he saw it with his own two eyes he would certainly have questioned their lucidity, but when the gate was lifted for the officers at the front of the line—drawing upward into the stone itself—Declan was made a believer when he saw the well-lit wall of a rough-hewn tunnel within.

A "volcano". A rupture in the great earthen "plates" that made up the world, deeper even than the leylines. Bonner could only give them a quick lesson, but his words were both mesmerizing and terrifying. He spoke of molten stone layers that were theorized to exist far, far below their feet, and how occasionally that magma rose to produce exactly what they saw before them. This volcano was clearly "inactive" he assured them after Ester and Declan had stared at him in horror following this description, but there would have been a time—millennia earlier, likely—when the land all around them had been flattened by an explosion that had likely blown the highest parts of the heights above them into the atmosphere. These details made *no one* feel any better, of course, nor did Bonner's description of running rivers of boiling earth that would have spilled across the very land they now stood on, razing everything in their burning path.

Fortunately—or unfortunately, rather—they were distracted soon enough by raised voices from the front of the line of elves.

"What's that?" Declan asked with a frown, cutting Bonner off as the old man started to delve into an explanation of how an eruption of such magnitude might have blotted out the sun.

"Not sure," Ester answered, leaning forward atop Eyera to peer towards the front. "If I had to guess, though, I'd say the Ysenden guard probably doesn't have to deal too often with a returning patrol saying they've brought strays home."

Ysenden.

Declan nearly choked on the thought. *This* was Ysenden, the great city of the dark elves. In his awe—in his disbelief—he had nearly forgotten that fact, but as he looked up again he indeed noticed some abnormalities among the crags. Here and there what looked like flat panes of glass caught the dim light of the day, often shielded under an outcropping or the like. To the west, almost around the edge of the "volcano", he thought he could make out a protrusion of some sort, extending out of the stone high, high above them, like a dome made up of more panes framed together to form the semi-spherical structure.

Ysenden...

"Master Ryndean. Master yr'Essel. Come with us, please. Declan and Ester, you and the warg as well."

Declan's attention was brought back as he barely caught the request. Dragging his eyes from the hidden city, he found that Lysiat and her brothers had returned, she leading as Aliek and Tesied flanked her dutifully, clearly coming back on the orders of the colonel or one of his remaining officers. Lysiat's face was stony—even more so than her usual resting expression—and Declan felt a twinge of unease as he observed the commander.

At his left, Ryn sighed.

Can't say this was unexpected, of course. The dragon looked around at Declan and Bonner. *You two stay behind Ester and me. Hold onto Orsik and Eyera. Ester*—he turned to look up at the half-elf—*dismount, if you please. I don't think it will do us good to give anyone the impression we might be looking down on them.*

With a nod, Ester did as she was told. Declan and Bonner, too, fell in as instructed, requiring no explanation. If they assumed that Syr'esh and the others had reported their presence accurately, than there was a decent possibility that Ryn and Ester would be treated as honored guests first and foremost.

It might offer a buffer to the fact that they—the first specimens of their respective races to visit Ysenden in more than seven hundred years—had arrived in the company of two human mages and a pair of wild animals…

Without another word they followed the ay'ahSels up the line of the halted march, the elven soldiers parting for them in a practiced fashion. As he led Orsik through the *er'endhen*—holding onto a strap of the warg's halter as though to falsely imply he had any control of the beast—Declan couldn't help but be amused by the range of emotions he saw hinted at in the faces of the stoic soldiers. There still, despite everything that had happened, was a healthy dose of dislike and contempt in the lines of some of the dark elves' features, visible through the spaces of their helmets. It could hardly be called a surprise. Mistrust ran deep in this place, of humankind and magic alike, though most of these soldiers couldn't have known of either from more than stories. What *did* surprise Declan, on the other hand, were the other emotions he saw signs of here and there. A brief nod of encouragement. A slight bowing of a head in respect. Even one elf—who was missing an arm that looked to have been tended to as only Bonner could have—offering the barest smile as they passed. It made Declan feel a little bit better despite the situation, and by the time they reached the very front of the line he was holding his chin high, ready to meet whatever resistance they were about to face.

He nearly lost his composure, though, when he saw that this

particular battle was already being waged for them, and with surprising determination.

"*Veht?*" one of the twelve guarding what had to have been the gates to the city demanded furiously, and Declan was just able to see that the patterns in his armor likely denoted him as the watch leader. "*Veht?! Ysenden yn?! Ny!*"

"*Sed,*" Colonel Syr'esh answered calmly. "*Nom yst hal? Ny. Ny yst hal.*"

Declan frowned, muttering sidelong to Bonner. "Is it just me, or did the colonel just pull rank on a gate guard?"

The old mage was looking just as displeased. "Yes, he did..." he answered slowly, sounding like he couldn't quite believe it. "That doesn't bode well."

Declan nodded in agreement, coming to a halt behind Ryn and Ester, who had stopped several paces behind Syr'esh and the watch commander.

Forcing a superior officer to pull rank would have been bad enough among the King's Vigil, but within the army of the *er'endehn*? Declan would have thought it a shocking event even if the dark elves standing around them hadn't been baring their teeth in outrage almost to a one. He could understand the surprise by the sentries, of course—the garrison had been little more than a scouting party, without the means by which to send word ahead to prepare the city for their arrival—but the gate was already opened, which meant their path had likely been halted only *after* the colonel had reported that the dark elves weren't returning alone. Sure enough, Declan noted that the rest of the watch had closed in to block the way into the torch-lit tunnel beyond them, cutting off their entry while their commander and Syr'esh argued.

Was his and Bonner's presence *that* big of a concern that a minor officer would disregard a superior's word so fervently?

"Now he's yelling about his 'duty to the city' being greater than anything else," Bonner muttered in annoyance as the elves' words grew too heated for Declan to follow. "Blast… At this rate we'll be lucky if the guard don't try to skewer us where we stand."

As though his words had tempted fate, it was in that moment that the watch commander looked beyond Syr'esh's shoulder to catch sight of their gathered party. The first thing he seemed to notice—not unexpectedly—was Ryn, but despite his eyes growing momentarily wide it wasn't more than a second or two before they slid from the dragon to Ester, then finally between those two to Declan and Bonner.

Declan didn't miss the shift in the elf's expression, and clenched his jaw as he saw what would happen next.

"You just had to say something, didn't you?" he growled to Bonner.

Before the old man could ask him what he meant, the order came. The watch commander went for his weapon—a single sword sheathed on his belt—even as he shouted for his subordinates to do the same. In a flash the glossy black of elven blades were drawn or bared as spears and more swords bristled from the other sentries. Amazingly, however, they weren't the only weapons brought out into the light, because Syr'esh's shout echoed the inferior officer's, and a heartbeat later Declan, Ryn, Bonner, Ester, and the warg were walled off from the threat as every member of the colonel's inner circle and the nearest foot soldiers closed in to protect them. At any other point in time Declan might have laughed when he realized that the blade closest to him was held in none other than the skeptical Major y'Rehl's firm grip, but the tension of the situation did not allow for such lighthearted irony.

For several seconds the two groups of elves stood gauging each other. Syr'esh was the only one in the vicinity who'd not drawn his blade, standing stone-still before the watch commander's bared sword, but despite this it was apparent that the lesser officer was—at last—nervous. He and the rest of his minor retinue looked suddenly less confident in their position, as though they hadn't expected anyone to seriously try and stop them as they drew blades on Declan and the others. Finding themselves instead facing down their own kind, their confidence was clearly waning, though the unit leader seemed yet unwilling to back down.

"*WHAT IN THE SPIRITS IS THIS*?!"

The only reason Declan understood the bellowed phrase was because Lysiat had treated him to a hundred variations of similar cursing during their morning training sessions. Every head in the vicinity—including the sentries and their commander—shifted to look to the tunnel entrance, where a surprisingly-broad, aged elf was thundering out from under the raised gate with what looked like another twenty soldiers at his back. Despite Declan not being able to see the patterns on the figure's armor, he could tell *at once* that this was an officer of import by nothing more than the response to his arrival. As soon as the elf stepped out into the grey and hail, every blade dipped downward as each man and woman in the vicinity snapped to attention, Syr'esh included.

If the colonel was showing deference, then that meant…

"*Halus!*" the watch commander was the first to speak. *"Syr'esh-Hal revs ys veht y mytosyl!"*

Halus… "General", Declan guessed, catching the rest of the insubordinate elf's words as well.

Colonel Syr'esh returns with humans and mages.

It would have been understandable, given the anger in the watch commander's tone, for this new ranking officer to have responded with a certain level of alarm. Indeed, as the twenty *er'endehn* who had accompanied the general spilled out of the tunnel to face them, Declan suddenly wondered at what point Syr'esh would order his own soldiers to stand down if only to avoid ending up facing off with whatever portion of the elven military was garrisoned in the city. At the very least Declan suspected he and the others were about to be surrounded and detained, doubly so when the general's eyes swept to him and his companions, lingering on each of them in turn, Ryn in particular.

Declan, therefore, had to cock an eyebrow in surprise as the aging general—rather than shout for their seizure—eventually looked back to Syr'esh, his initially stern expression breaking into a wide smile before he brought his arms up as he approached the colonel swiftly.

"*Enfa*!" the old elf said as he reached Syr'esh, embracing him firmly. "*Yst revs! Yst revs!*"

"Huh..." Bonner snorted from beside Declan, looking on as the colonel raised his own arms to return the general's solid welcome. "Well that's a stroke of luck, I hope..."

"What is?" Declan had to ask, finding himself at a loss as the watch commander—still standing beyond the two higher officers—looked on furiously.

"His father, Declan." Ester was the one to answer, glancing back at him over her shoulder and pointing. "That's Syr'esh's father."

"Oh," was all Declan could answer with, feeling the knot of worry in his gut lessen.

This was, fortunately, the point at which Bonner decided to start translating for him in earnest, which made everything come together much faster. It appeared that General Syr'esh—who Declan thought he should have *guessed* was the colonel's parent given the pair's matching breadth of chest and shoulders—was the commanding officer of Ysenden's standing defense, and one of the highest ranking members of the military in the entirety of the city. The old elf listened intently as his son filled him in on the events of the last month, ignoring the wind and elements in favor of sharing their story. The colonel spoke quickly and to the point, explaining how Ryn, Bonner, and Ester had arrived first with Aliek and Tesied, and how Declan had saved Lysiat and been guided to the camp some time later. He told the general of the tunneler, of their trek northward, and when he got to the previous day's attack by the wights, the older elf looked over the gathered soldiers again heavily, taking in their reduced number with a frown. He put a hand over his heart at this point, as though in respect for the dead, but still answered his child.

"We're being allowed within," Bonner said with a sigh of relief. "He's going to summon the Lord Commander—his superior—before we're presented to the—"

But then, even as Colonel Syr'esh turned and motioned for the remainder of the garrison to head into the now-cleared tunnel, the mage froze. He wasn't the only one, either. Before them, Declan noticed Ryn and Ester stiffening as well, going rigid at something the general seemed to have said.

"What?" he demanded, suddenly worried. "What is it?"

As the soldiers began to move out—the ay'ahSels stepping towards their group again as though ready to guide the way once more—Ryn was the one to answer, though his words weren't directed at Declan in particular.

Does anyone know what the general meant, that 'the Chancellor has been expecting us'?

CHAPTER TWENTY-FOUR

"He is our greatest ally, and therefore our greatest hope. Any of you who do not see that are either fools, or so blinded by your prejudice that you have allowed your ego to outweigh your duty to this city..."

—Ciriak as'ahRen, Lord Commander of Ysended, to the High Chancellor's council, c. 800p.f.

Ciriak as'ahRen was in the middle of overseeing the afternoon drills for the Chancellor's Guard when the runner arrived, darting through the pairs and groups of sparing soldiers with the guile bred and trained into the armed messengers of the *er'endehn*. The elf's footsteps made hardly a sound over the polished floor of the training chamber, and he reached Ciriak so quickly that his shadow barely had time to flicker in the torchlight of the room before he was whispering in the Lord Commander's ear.

Ciriak listened intently, then nodded and dismissed the runner again with a word. The messenger was gone in a flash, exiting the chamber again before the Lord Commander had even located his second in the throng.

"*Mysat. Our guests have arrived. Take over. Work them hard.*"

The petite elf he'd been addressing—dressed in the white-and-gold armor of the elite guard like the rest of the fighting soldiers all around them—disengaged from her own bout against two opponents at once to give him a brief bow of acknowledgment. The chain of command settled, Ciriak swept from the room after the runner as Mysat began shouting orders at once. Ordinarily the Lord Commander might well have chuckled to himself at the image of the diminutive Major berating the proud soldiers of the High Chancellor's personal retinue, but now was not the time for amusement.

Despite what he'd been told, despite his absolute trust in the information he'd been imparted with not a quarter hour before by the Chancellor directly, Ciriak had to see for himself if his master had spoken true.

With quick, firm steps he strode down the dark halls of Ysenden's upper levels, ignoring the subservient bows of the elves he crossed paths with. Even the few children he saw as he moved dipped their heads and stepped out of his way, and with a cleared path the Lord Commander was out of the tunnels inside of a minute, stepping into the light of the city proper with a sullen breath of relief as he paused just long enough to look up.

Despite the miserable weather of the day, he'd spent too long within the heavy walls of the city to be satisfied with anything less than the cleaner air of the middle sanctum.

Still a great ways above him, encircled by the pinnacle portions of the mountain that had long since been deemed to dangerous to dig into, the mouth of Ysenden opened up to a grey, somber sky. From the distance he stood below, Ciriak might have thought it was raining, except he knew that the temperature beyond the slopes of the city would have allowed for nothing short of snow, sleet, and hail at this time of year.

Not that it mattered inside the walls, of course…

Turning right, Ciriak didn't have to walk more than a dozen yards before reaching the closest of the hundred ornately-decorated gondolas that lined the sloping surface of the inner cavern, the grinding sound of their chains and pulleys a constant thrum in the background of the bustle of city noise. Approaching the enclosed platform, he nodded to the gondola attendant, who politely cleared the few others waiting to descend with a word, not a one among them complaining when they saw who it was that was claiming the elevator. Stepping aboard, Ciriak didn't have to wait long for the attendant to pull a bright white-and-gold banner from the breast pocket of his black jacket, holding it over the side to indicate priority of descent to the directors who would be standing far, far below them. Sure enough, not a handful of seconds later they were dropping, the two otherwise alone on the platform, gaining speed as the pulley laborers undoubtedly strained at double-pace while other workers from the gondolas closest to Ciriak's rushed over to assist.

Despite the hurried descent, it was nearly two minutes before the Lord Commander reached the bottom of the city, during which time he took in Ysenden with a sort of tired fondness while his mind worked in a blur. The walls of the inner sanctum looked like they'd been carved into a hundred circular floors atop one another—tunnels leading from there into the markets, residential areas, and military quarters of the city like a maze further within the stone—but in reality it was all a single, spiraling floor that ascended at such a slow angle one could hardly notice the incline without dropping something perfectly round on the ground. The gondolas were staggered every fifty feet or so, the great beams that supported them colored alternating patterns of red, green, yellow, and blue to indicate if they stopped every single, fifth, tenth, or twenty-fifth floor. As a result, the city was constantly in motion, even in the depths of any night, with the angled rise and fall of the elevators only adding to the churning through of the one hundred and fifty thousand residents of Ysenden.

The air warmed, too, as they descended. The heights of the city within the mountain would have been enough for a variation in temperature regardless, Ciriak was sure, but the scholars of the *er'endehn* spoke too of the ancient heat that rose from the bottom of the sanctum, a subdued power that was the dormant remnants of a much more fearsome force a long, long time ago. Regardless, the warmth was enough that whatever precipitation managed to enter through the mouth of the mountain above them very rarely reached the floor of the middle cavern, offering a mesmerizing experience of attempting to track hail trails before they vanished into nothing three-fourths of the way to the bottom. Again, however, Ciriak had no mind to take in the sight, his focus still on his disbelief.

Was it possible? Was it *really* possible?

"*We've arrived, Lord Commander*," the attendant said quietly, offering Ciriak yet another bow in the second before the gondola touched down in the carefully excavated pocket carved out of the stone floor that allowed the platform to rest flush with the ground. Stepping off with a brief thanks, the Lord Commander nodded his appreciation to the dozen bare-armed elves breathing heavily around the massive circular wench only partially hidden in the alcove behind the elevator. The moment he was clear of it, there was a shout, and the platform immediately began to rise once more. He paid it no mind.

He paid none of it any mind.

The brilliance of the great floor of Ysenden's middle sanctum held no fascination for him in that moment. Not the smoothed stone he walked across—polished naturally over millennia by more footsteps than one could comprehend—nor the trees of the carefully crafted *yr'es*—the indoor woodland that was both a park for the city residents and a training area for the elven soldiers—that took up the near quarter-mile diameter in its very center. The steam of the hot springs rising from the great mouths of the eastern wall of the cavern failed to catch his eye, too, as did the brightness of the "bottom market", the bazaar lit by a hundred torches so that visitors could browse the bright wares and foodstuffs on display there at any hour of the day.

No. All Ciriak cared about was the southern face of the sanctum and the great rend through the otherwise-solid breadth of the stone that was Ysenden's one and only entrance.

Was it *really* possible…?

◆

The jagged tunnel through the base of the small mountain was longer than Declan had anticipated, and it was more than a minute's walk along the rough-hewn passage that he started to feel an unwelcome weight in his stomach. Despite the light of the torches carefully ensconced every dozen feet or so in a staggered pattern on either jagged wall, the ceiling above them was high enough to be hidden in shadow, and the smooth stone under their feet was damp with condensation. Before long, Declan found himself back in the tunnels beneath the Mother's Tears, and his left hand went to his sword automatically as he listened to the thrumming of more than a hundred booted feet echoing back at him.

He wasn't the only one to be suffering from bad memories, either.

There was a light pressure at his elbow, and he glanced down to find that Ester had dropped back to walk beside him, her eyes partially hidden behind a short sheet of her sliver-gold hair that had come loose of her usual plaiting. She didn't look at him as they moved, nor spoke a word, but the tightness with which she held onto his arm with one hand was enough to tell him she, too, was not a fan of the dim space. Her touch was comforting, as always, and Declan felt a little better as he looked around, taking in his other friends.

If Ryn and Bonner were in any sort of discomfort, neither of them showed any signs of it. The dragon was looking ahead and walking like being surrounded by a hundred dark elves while entering their mountain home was the most normal of circumstances in the world, while Bonner was muttering to himself and stroking his beard with one hand while he looked up into the darkness, peering at the walls and stone in obvious study. Orsik and Eyera, on the other hand, were less pleased with their situation, and Declan couldn't bring himself to hush the warg as they growled in displeasure at the damp air. Further ahead, the ay'ahSels, too, were actually displaying a similar measure of unease, their usual guile and confidence replaced unanimously by tense shoulders while all three stared rigidly ahead, like they didn't want to look around and be reminded of a place they would rather forget.

Fortunately, forgetting became easy not long after a brighter light indicated they were nearing the end of the tunnel, some three or four minutes after they'd entered the mountain.

"Gods above..." Ester hissed, her grip tightening on Declan's arm as her awe was echoed by her father's similar words when they finally stepped out onto dry, polished stone.

Declan, for his part, had no words to express his own astonishment.

They had emerged into what might technically have been called a "cavern", except the term could hardy constitute the vast, open space of the place. It felt like the massive chamber could have held the entirety of Aletha, if the city's quarters were stacked one on top of the other. Almost as impressive, though, was the expansive floor of the place, a grey-black ring of solid, well-trodden stone perhaps two hundred feet in width, which encircled nothing less than a small, bright forest of verdant moss and evergreens not much smaller than those of the Vyr'esh. Declan could make out people coming and going from beneath these trees, some looking like they were returning from a casual stroll, others in a hurry like they'd cut through the forest to make for some place or another on the far side of the ring.

"Declan." Ester tugged at his arm to pull his attention from the inexplicable "indoor" woodlands, pointing when he tore his eyes from the greenery. Not far to their immediate right, a slight incline in the great floor before them had been carved into a subtle upward angle, forming a wide ramp on and off of which dozens more people were coming and going every few seconds. Many among these unarmored dark elves gaped, often looking back to stare even as they climbed, but Declan hardly noticed them and their—for once—colorful clothes as his eyes instead followed the trailing line of the ramp as it looped around the massive wall of the chamber, forming what he realized was a single spiraling floor that wrapped an innumerable times around the cavern as it climbed upwards. What was more, these rising rings were hardly the only way to ascend the interior of the mountain, it seemed, because what had to have been no less than a hundred narrow structures of carved, bound timber and chains claimed the sides of the narrowing floors, colored in a pattern and completed by moving platforms that were rising and dropping at various speeds everywhere Declan looked. These apparatuses reminded Declan of the man-powered "elevators" he'd heard the al'Dyors had had built in the tallest reaches of their palace, except those of Ysenden reached almost to the very top of the volcano rather than a measly dozen-story tower. The stone of the cavern continued to rise beyond for a ways more, unblemished by whatever tools had been used to carve into the lower parts of the wall, and at the very top of the space a vast, roughly-circular opening allowed for a not-insignificant view of a boiling grey sky high, high above.

For some reason, in that moment, all Declan could think about was how beautiful the place must have looked in the full sun of a bright spring day.

"Unbelievable," he finally managed to get out, so quietly he was pretty sure only Ester heard, because the woman gripped his arm just a little tighter as though to silently state her agreement.

"Well… I suppose we know now why Sehranya failed to take the city…"

Bonner's words had Declan and Ester both finally looking down from the incredible sight. The mage, for his part, was looking around with wide eyes while Ryn nodded on his left.

Agreed. Erraven sounds like it was a walled city. If we assume the rest of the elven strongholds were the same, it becomes understandable why they were so easily overrun while Ysenden held firm.

"She didn't have the drey until her attack on the Reaches, right?" Declan decided joining the conversation was the only way he was likely to keep himself from staring around with his mouth hanging up. Even as he talked, he couldn't stop from lifting his eyes to take in the heights of the city again. "There would have been no flying down *into* this place, when she attacked."

"Small wonder she ended up making for the Vigil's war," Ester added, gazing around again herself. "What sort of fool would be willing to break their forces against a stronghold like this?"

"One who can raise those forces again with little more than a wave of her hand, Esteria," Bonner said, though he sounded less like a lecturing father and more like a worn old man as he spoke. "Don't forget that it took the Queen two years to get fed up with trying to break these walls. Had she had the patience, her eventual victory was not an impossibility."

"*HALYEN, YS!*"

The sudden shout had all of them except Ryn jumping in surprise, with even Orsik and Eyera's ears coming up as they lifted their broad heads to see what was going on. General Syr'esh, it seemed, had been the one to make the announcement, and Declan only had to wonder as to what was going on for a moment as every elf around them—from the freshly-polished city guard to the exhausted and injured soldiers of the advance brigade to the general and colonel themselves—stood at rigid attention.

"What's going on?" Ester asked, brow furrowed as she frowned and stood on her tiptoes, trying to see around Ryn and her father's backs.

Declan, though, reached around and took her by the arms, pressing her down gently. He, unlike her, was tall enough to see over the heads of everyone but Ryn, and he knew what had drawn the attention of the *er'endehn*. Even at a glance, too, he understood why the soldiers had all snapped to, and—for the first time since encountering the dark elves of Yseresh—he feared what might happen if they broke that decorum.

Though the city was bustling with life around them, only a single figure among the scattered crowds was moving towards their retinue with any deliberate intent. What was more, the way the throng parted around this elf would have been enough to tell Declan he was important, but the way he carried himself—the way he *moved*—was vastly more intimidating. He was a tall, broad figure, if not as broad as the Syr'eshs, and his black armor—not even hinting at any lining of gold or other color—was a bit heavier than most of the plating Declan had thus far seen from the elves. Despite this, he might have been wearing silks given the ease at which he carried himself, head up and shoulders back, the paired swords—one over his shoulder and the other at his hip—sitting more like extensions of his person than common weaponry. Declan wasn't sure why, but even having seen Lysiat ay'ahSel in her prime, even having seen the twins with their fearsome skill and even the common soldiers stand against the terror of the wights, he got the distinct impression that *this* person could have faced off against any three of the finest blades that stood around him and come out on top.

Declan. If I'm not mistaken, that is the Lord Commander of the elves. The highest-ranking officer in the er'endehn *military. Tread lightly.*

Declan didn't even blink as Ryn's low words reached him, and was unsurprised to feel Ester flinch slightly as the dragon spoke to her privately, too. There was no doubt Bonner had been informed as well, because after a second the mage stood a little straighter and cleared his throat quietly, clearly readying himself for an important exchange.

The Lord Commander—who Declan saw sported a cropped beard streaked with white as he neared—reached them in no time as the residents of the city continued to part around him like fish giving deference to a shark. His white-red eyes—sharp despite his obvious age even for an elf—flicked over all of them in his final steps, for once pausing only as long on Ryn as they did on any of the others. Declan was among the last to be scrutinized, and when their gazes met an odd sensation clenched at his chest. It took him a moment to place the feeling—particularly after the Lord Commander looked away to address Colonel Syr'esh and his father—but when he did he couldn't help his face from twisting in confusion.

What he had felt was… recognition?

"I… think I know him…" Declan said quietly, not believing the words even as they came out of his mouth.

From in front of him, Ryn looked briefly over his shoulder to fix him with a curious eye, Ester doing the same from his side. She'd let go of his arm at some point, and was standing as tall as she could in an obvious attempt to show the same respect as the soldiers around them.

"What are you talking about?" she asked him sidelong, and he could imagine her trying to speak without moving her lips.

"I don't know," Declan answered under his breath. "I just… I recognize him."

Before Ester could voice any further disbelief, Bonner spoke up.

"I'm not surprised." He sounded—if not shaken—at least a little taken aback. For a man of the mage's ability and stoicism, it was disconcerting. "*I* know him as well. It's not you that recognizes him, boy. It's Herst."

Declan understood in a flash, feeling his mouth form an "oh" of comprehension as the flash of memory came back to him. A palace courtyard. The glint the steel. A scarred elf moving like wind around Declan's flailing sword.

He remembered, then, the name Ryn had given him.

"Ciriak…"

He must have spoken louder than intended—or the old elf had hearing surpassing even Ester's—because the Lord Commander paused in the solemn conversation he had been having with the Syr'eshes to look up with a dark eyebrow raised in surprise.

"You know me, human?"

Ester gave the smallest gasp at the question, which Declan almost mirrored. Being addressed directly by what sounded like the second-most powerful dark elf in the entirety of Eserysh was alarming enough, but that was hardly what had him mouthing at the air.

Rather, his surprise came much more greatly from the fact that the Lord Commander had spoken to him not in elvish, but in the common tongue of Viridian.

Taking in the dangerous figure before him, Declan hesitated. On the one hand, the entire reason they had made for the stronghold of the *er'endehn* was to beg for the race's approval of the Accord of Four. That meant—undoubtedly—that some conveyance of Declan's lineage would be in order, but he wasn't sure that then and there was the place to awkwardly explain how it was that he had known the Lord Commander's name.

Fortunately, Bonner's silver tongue came to the rescue.

"He does, as'ahRen. And he's not the only one."

The elf looked from Declan to the old mage, then, frowning slightly. For a moment he seemed not to understand, but then his eyes widened and he stepped by the Syr'eshs at once, the officers and soldiers standing in his way parting in a blink.

"Fehn?" the Lord Commander asked, not believing his eyes. "Spirits take me. Bonner *Fehn*?"

"The one and the same, Lord Commander." Bonner offered the elf a brief bow of respect before looking up again. "Though you were but a major when last we crossed paths, I believe, and I have since wed. I am Bonner 'yr'Essel' now."

The Lord Commander—Ciriak "as'ahRen", Declan now knew—halted before the old mage to take him in in disbelief. Looking the old mage up and down, he shook his head slowly. "But… How? It's been centuries, ever since the cliffs…" His eyes, though, shifted briefly from Bonner to Ester, likely observing the green eyes she shared with her father, and understanding seemed to come quickly. "Ah… 'yr'Essel'. You wed into the *er'enthyl*, Magus?"

"I did." Bonner offered the elf a smile, then seemed to think it was best to change the subject away from himself. "You've kept up with your common, sir. I admit myself impressed."

"Yes, well…" as'ahRen's eyes drifted to Declan, then. "Old habits die hard, as they say in your land. And I have to admit I thought it only a matter of time before our people encountered each other again one way or another. Though I must say I hadn't quite imagined it would be under these… circumstances…"

Circumstances that will require extensive explanation, Lord Commander. I'm afraid Colonel Syr'esh and the others can only convey a fraction of the world's troubles to you.

Ryn's statement had everyone in the vicinity turning to him, including not a few residents of the city passing nearby. Their response—surprised but immediate—had Declan thinking again that there was something going on among the elves that he couldn't quite place.

How had they—even the common passerbys—known to look to *Ryn* in that moment?

"Oh…!" Esters' sharp inhale had him turning around again, though, and he cocked his head in confusion at the sight before him.

as'ahRen—the *Lord Commander* of the great race of the *er'endehn*—was bowing to Ryn, and not just in the same manner of respect Bonner had treated him to shortly before. The elf had bent at the hips, one hand in a fist over his heart, his head dipping so low it was nearly past his waist. It was clear, too, that Declan's astonishment at this was hardly unique. Bonner was blinking in surprise before him, and Ryn himself took a half step away from the officer, clearly taken aback. The elves all around them, too, began murmuring in confusion. There was a flinch of motion, and Declan looked up just in time to see General Syr'esh, standing behind his son, composing his face, which for just an instant looked to have twisted into something like outrage. The aging elf caught Declan's eye, and a welcoming smile replaced the forced deadpan, making him wonder if he hadn't imagined the anger.

"Master Ryndean, I beg you to excuse my rudeness." Ciriak as'ahRen's voice was even, but he did not lift his head. "I would have introduced myself at once, but Magus F—Magus yr'Essel's presence caught me off guard. As you have no doubt deduced, I am Ciriak as'ahRen, Lord Commander of Ysenden's military and second to the city's High Chancellor."

Declan's eyes narrowed, and he was relieved when Ester and Bonner both seemed to have the same response. Ryn, too, had obviously not missed the oddity in the elf's statement, because he frowned and moved to stand tall again, looking down on the elf with a frown.

There was no discourtesy to apologize for, Lord Commander, he said calculatingly to the back of as'ahRen's bowed head. *Given the circumstances, your surprise is understandable. I have to wonder, however, why you have deemed* me*—of all of my companions—worthy of this deference. More importantly, however*—the dragon's own white-gold eyes narrowed as he studied the still-bowing man—*I would like you to explain how it is that you know my name…*

The muttering among the elves redoubled at this, which was to be expected. Thus far the entire conversation had been held largely in common, meaning that Ryn's words were the first of any significance the surrounding soldiers had heard. Some of the passerbys, too, were starting to linger as a result, and Declan suspected it wouldn't be long before they began drawing a crowd.

"I wish I had accepted the offer of lessons in your language, now."

Declan and Ester both looked around. Somehow Lysiat, Aliek, and Tesied had snuck around to stand behind them as the soldiers had started shuffling nervously, with the commander leaning in slightly so they could hear her. She'd spoken slowly enough for Declan to understand, but before either he or Ester could say anything in response, the Lord Commander was lifting his head, drawing all eyes again.

"I was notified of your presence some twenty minutes ago," as'ahRen answered as he stood straight before Ryn again. "By the High Chancellor."

The dragon's gaze only grew more suspicious at this, and he spoke again as Ester started translating the Lord Commander's words for the ay'ahSels over her shoulder in a whisper. *It would seem your master is well-informed. I wonder how he can be so knowledgeable of our coming and yet fail to be aware of a nest of wights festering not two days from this city...?*

If the dragon's words were alarming to as'ahRen, the elf showed no signs of it. "Such questions are best posed to him. I will say that you may understand better, once you meet."

And when will that be?

"Immediately. At the Chancellor's request. He knows you likely have your own agenda, but he is also aware that you have a... uh... 'friend' in the city. He is eager to see you reacquainted."

"Ah."

Declan, Ester, and Bonner all made the sound together as the pieces started to click. The elves' deference to Ryn. Their comfort around him, and their lack of fear. If Arrackes was already known to the *er'endehn*—as the Lord Commander was implying—then it all suddenly made much more sense.

And yet... If the sight of a dragon was already common for the dark elves, then why had no one made mention of it...?

You are aware of Arrackes' presence? Ryn sounded like he was trying to hide his relief behind a veil of iron. *I must admit I'm surprised. Is he well? Why am I not able to sense him?*

"Huh." Declan frowned at these words. Ryn had indeed detected the city from some distance away, but had made no mention of the guardian dragon he had tasked to watch over the elves so many centuries ago. Was it the nature of Ysneden? He'd had trouble extending himself within the Tears. Was it possible the heavy stone of the volcano they stood within was blocking Arrackes from being—?

"He has masked himself from you, for the time being, Master Ryndean. He apologizes, but feels it is best that you meet again on his terms, so as to avoid a... scene."

'Avoid a scene'...? Ryn repeated, sounding like he was starting to get impatient as he crossed his arms.

It was at this moment that Bonner—wisely, Declan thought—decided to keep the conversation from risking derailment.

"as'ahRen," the mage said, stepping forward, "we have with us nearly one hundred soldiers in various states of exhaustion and injury, many of whom require additional aid and *all* of whom have lost half their comrades in the last day. I would politely request that we adjourn this discussion and that you take us to your High Chancellor as promised. We—as well as Colonel Syr'esh—" he gestured toward the younger of the Syr'eshs still standing nearby "—have much information to impart, all of it only varying levels of critical. I am sure your master will explain things to our satisfaction upon meeting." At this point, Bonner looked pointedly at Ryn, trying to get the dragon to reel back his irritation. Ryn obliged, relaxing marginally, and the Lord Commander answered with enthusiasm.

"Agreed. On the subject of my soldiers, please excuse me for a moment." as'ahRen turned back to the Syr'eshs at this, addressing the general in elvish. Declan only caught the words "injured" and "health", which were enough to deduce that the higher officer was being ordered to see the wounded and haggard soldiers treated. As soon as the general nodded in understanding, the Lord Commander looked to Declan and the others again as he indicated that they should get moving.

"*Colonel Syr'esh, you as well,*" as'ahRen said over his shoulder as Ryn started walking in the direction he'd indicated, northwest into the great chamber of the central city.

The colonel nodded, but hesitated. The pause obviously was not missed by the Lord Commander, who stopped as he'd made to lead them when Declan, Bonner, and Ester all started following behind the dragon with Orsik and Eyera dutifully in tow. as'ahRen offered the younger elf a questioning word which Declan missed, as he did Syr'esh's response, but Ester was already speaking before he could ask her to translate.

"He wanted to know if something was wrong," she said quietly. "The colonel has asked if he is expected to report to the Chancellor." She frowned as Declan listened. "The Lord Commander has said he is—he doesn't look pleased—and Syr'ehs is—Oh."

The abrupt end to the translation was no issue, because the colonel's intensions became clear as he motioned for the attendance of someone behind Declan and Ester. In two steps Lysiat, Aliek, and Tesied were all at their superior's side, standing at attention with their gazes dutifully raised over the Lord Commander's head. After a quick exchange of words, as'ahRen gave a nod, then spun away from the lot of them to take lead of the group. As Declan and Ester stepped in behind the man—Ryn and Bonner walking ahead of them again—they were joined by the ay'ahSels *and* the colonel, though none of the elves looked intent on talking while in the presence of their commanding officer.

Smart man, Declan thought, eyeing Syr'esh sidelong. If they were about to have to explain the tale of how it was the *er'endehn* had turned a hunting mission into an escort party, then Lysiat and her brothers would be invaluable in completing the story.

Traversing the city was more or less what Declan had expected. Crossing the great ring of stone at an angle—skirting the incredible patch of woodlands at its center—the Lord Commander cut a swath for them through a crowd that seemed much thicker than it had only five minutes before. Had their party been absent as'ahRen's escort, Declan rather suspected they would have garnered an impressive assembly of onlookers, but as it was no one seemed to want to linger too long around them. Despite the oddity of their presence, despite the dragon, two humans, and half-elf, the Lord Commander's presence was enough to counter the astonishment and intrigue of the masses. Even Orsik and Eyera, padding along loyally at the end of the line, got nothing more than scattered, wide-eyed looks and a few whispered words that might have been curses among the dark elf onlookers.

It only made as'ahRen's aura more imposing, and Declan couldn't help but watch the old elf as they walked, thinking he knew, now, how it was Amherst al'Dyor had become the most renowned swordsman of his time…

The Lord Commander led them without delay along the ring in a loop about the city, no one speaking a word while they moved. It gave Declan—and the others around him—the opportunity to take in Ysenden's heart in a bit more detail. Aside from the forest, a market of some sort took up a large swath of the cavern floor, extending from the trees to butt up against the rough-hewn walls of the space. More of the elves' moonwing lanterns hung over this bazaar, the combined illumination of the moths casting shadows over the lowest of the rising floors. In the light, Declan saw a hundred tunnels and doors leading away from the spiraling fairway, the flow of foot traffic stronger here and there, while in other sections only a few people moved about, making him think the labor, commercial, and residential districts of

Ysenden were likely separated.

Of the people themselves, Declan saw a range of ages, though he wasn't familiar enough yet with the lifespan of the *er'endehn* to guess at the actual years most of the residents might have been carrying. Additionally, he saw few children moving about, and no adolescents whatsoever. He chalked the latter absence up to the rigorous training the dark elves put their young through from an early age, but the former was more likely due to the low fertility of the race. Indeed, had they been walking through Aletha there would have been as many street urchins and orphans scurrying about as children under the supervision of their parents, with the yells and shouts of the little ones at play—or work—almost as prevalent as the calls of the adults.

It made Declan a little sad, if he was being frank with himself. The city around him was a marvel, as were the capabilities of the *er'endehn* soldiers.

What could the dark elves have achieved, he wondered, if the Mother had granted them the same bounties as man…?

It wasn't too long before the Lord Commander led them to the edge of the cavern ring, where he commandeered one of the blue, finely-crafted gondola platforms with a dip of his head to an attendant dressed in black. The elf leapt to at once, pulling some kind of small, white-and-gold banner from his jacket to hold over the side of the elevator, and almost as soon as Declan and Ester coaxed Orsik and Eyera aboard they were rising steadily upward.

"Oh, well that's a sight…"

Bonner was the first the break the silence as they ascended, and everyone but the warg turned to find the old man looking out over the floor of the cavern while it sped away from them below. He certainly wasn't wrong, and Declan found himself compelled to step up beside the mage to take in the view himself, basking in the colors of the milling crowds, the rise and fall of the other platforms, and the lights of the market that surrounded the trees.

"Incredible..." he muttered.

"Glad you think so."

The Lord Commander's voice, coming from Declan's other side, almost made him start in surprise. He glanced around to find the elf looking down on Ysenden as well with a fond eye, having gotten there without making so much as a sound despite his armor and the fairly-crowded platform.

"Then again, I thought much the same of your cities, during my years spent in Viridian," as'ahRen continued, white-red eyes drifting up as they moved side to side, obviously following the passing floors of the cavern opposite them. "Your walls and turrets and towers."

"I was told the *er'endehn* were masters of such crafts, Lord Commander." Declan was pleased that he managed to keep his voice steady as he replied. "Erraven was a walled city, was it not? Whose ruins still stand, I hear."

as'ahRen offered him a sidelong look, then. "The *er'endehn* are masters of every craft, sir, but we have the time to make such things, the time to devote to grasping the intricacies and expertise in our professions. Man, though..." He chuckled darkly. "It amazes me to this day, thinking back, the things man is capable of, despite your oldest living not a tenth of the lifespan we elves can reasonably expect."

"Ha..." Declan matched the *er'endehn*'s somber laugh. "Would you believe me if I said I was thinking something very much to that extent?" He gestured out over the open cavern, where before them what looked like sleet had started to shimmer downward through the air, and he realized with further wonder that the outside hail hadn't been able to reach the bottom of the volcano despite the great opening still high above their heads. "Mankind grows quickly, and we spread quickly. In seven hundred years the *er'endehn* do not seem to have expanded enough to extend themselves out of Ysenden again. Despite that, you thrive in your own way, and manage to create... well, all *this.*" Declan couldn't help but let his awe seep into his voice a bit, but he didn't mind.

Ysenden was worthy of that awe.

Beside him, the Lord Commander turned to him with a puzzled expression. "You're well-informed, for a human." The elf's voice was even, but carried a note of interest as he looked Declan up and down, gaze pausing on the hilt of the elven sword on his opposite hip. "I had assumed you were the magus' apprentice, but you're more warrior than mage, I think. Who are you, if I might ask?"

Declan opened his mouth, about to answer, but before he could get a word out Ryn's voice cut him off.

To call Declan Bonner's apprentice is appropriate enough for the time being, Lord Commander, the dragon said, stepping up to stand just behind them, his height allowing him to see over their heads without issue.

The Lord Commander gave no reaction to this cutting off other than another slight arching of one brow.

"Might I at least ask for your family name, Declan...?" he trailed off expectantly.

"*His name is Declan Idrys, sir. Please do not judge. Very talented, for a human.*"

Lysiat ay'ahSel had apparently deduced the trend of their conversation from Ryn's words, because she'd spoken up from where she, her brothers, and Colonel Syr'esh were standing, still at attention along one side of the platform. Though the colonel's mouth twisted in the slightest hint of disapproval, the Lord Commander appeared unbothered by the woman's insertion into the conversation.

"'*Idrys*'?" he repeated, a small frown creasing his beard. Then he asked the commander a question Declan didn't catch.

Fortunately, Lysiat's answer caught him up.

"*I speak simply. For Declan. As he learns.*"

"Ah." The Lord Commander turned back to Declan then, more

interested now as they continued to ascend. "You're learning the language, are you?"

Declan hesitated, not sure of what he should be saying, but a bare nod from Ryn in the corner of his eye told him it was all right.

"Yes, sir," he answered. "Attempting to, at least. Many have been teaching me, including Bonner—er, Magus yr'Essel—and Esteria." Declan motioned to Ester, who bobbed her head in greeting as the Lord Commander turned briefly to size her up and down.

"The wood elf dialect is not so different from our own," as'ahRel said after a moment, nodding in approval. "It would seem you are blessed by the spirits, Declan Idrys. To have such mentors as yr'Essel and his blood, not to mention the praise of our own Commander ay'ahSel…" The elf's gaze dropped to the sword again. "I knew a youth once, about your age. A human like you. He had a knack for the sword and some small skill with magic. He is… long passed, now, unfortunately." There was a brief hint of sadness in the creases of the officer's wrinkles, but it was gone before he continued. "Has humanity forgone its banning of the arcane? I was under the impression your royal family had decreed it illegal some centuries ago."

Declan smiled slightly, but thought it better not to let slip that he suspected he knew very well to whom the old elf was referring. Instead, he gave the Lord Commander a small bow of acknowledgement. "It would seem I am not the only one who is well informed. I am indeed fortunate that the magus has taken me under his wing, and to keep in such great company as Master Ryndean and Esteria. Commander ay'ahSel, too, has been a tutor of immense ability, as have her brothers."

He chose his words carefully, dodging any specific answer, and he thought he saw Ryn hide a smirk at being called "Master Ryndean".

"Oh? So the ay'ahSels have been mentoring you…" The Lord Commander spoke slowly as Declan straightened, turning away again as he did to study the hail falling in a trailing pillar far before them.

"A dragon, a court mage, a wood elf, and our own officers… One must wonder what you have done to earn such instructors, Declan Idrys…"

It wasn't phrased as a question, but Declan suspected the elf intended to get an answer regardless soon enough. For the time being, however, they lapsed into silence again as they reached what had to have been the midway point in their climb, the people far below starting to become indistinct patches of color moving around each other as they went about their day.

Another two minutes or so and the elevator started to slow. They'd climbed high, high enough for the temperature to drop noticeably, and Declan was glad he'd kept the heavy layers of his borrowed armor despite the warmth of the cavern floor far beneath them now. His breath misted before him as the platform finally came to a complete halt, and the moment it stopped moving the Lord Commander was stepping forward to take the lead once more.

"Keep close to your beasts, if you would," he said over his shoulder before moving off the platform to cut through the line of surprised elves who'd been waiting for the elevator. "The highest levels of the city are devoted to the High Chancellor and his council. If the guards here perceive any threat, they will not hesitate to take action."

Declan and Ester glanced at each other at this, then separated without a word to stand outside of Orsik and Eyera respectively. While Ryn and Bonner walked ahead of them, the ay'ahSels and Syr'esh split silently to join them as though reading their sudden concern, Aliek and Tesied walking with Ester, Declan joined by Lysiat and the colonel.

The floor they had climbed to was less crowded than the bottom of the cavern, but the elves they encountered—most wearing a similar black-and-gold uniform that could only have been soldiers' regulars—still moved out of the way just as promptly when as'ahRen approached. They walked only a short way along the curving path before the Lord Commander turned left, west into the mountain, and the moment they stepped into the arched ceiling of the tunnel the temperature rose again, like the heat of so many bodies had been trapped within the stone. Despite the narrower path the space was brighter than the entrance tunnel of Ysenden, and though the walls still pressed in and around him, Declan felt less anxious here, the gentler glow of the lanterns hanging every few yards from the apex of the arched ceiling offering a lighter feel to the air.

"*Lysiat.*" Declan's curiosity got the better of him as they took a turn in the tunnel, the ground sloping down suddenly. "*You know where we go?*"

The commander, he was surprised to note, was tense. A month past he might not have been able to tell, but the iron-blooded elf blinked at his question, and there was the barest hint of tightness in the parts of her cheeks he could see through her still-donned helmet. What was more, she didn't answer until she'd looked to Colonel Syr'esh for a nod of approval. Sadly, her response was not one Declan knew,

"*Ys livrerus.*"

His frown of incomprehension, fortunately, had her trying again in simpler terms.

"*The great place of study.*"

Though he'd understood this time, it made no more sense to him than her first answer, so Declan left it alone after giving her a word of thanks. Instead, he returned to taking in his surroundings, marveling once more at Ysenden's incredible conception.

Despite the fact that they were going deeper into the rock, the air was still clean, and the bare hint of a faint breeze he could detect on his face and through his hair spoke of some system of ventilation, either by design or construction. It gave these higher tunnels a lighter, breathable feel that did not match the general darkness of the walls, but the elves had broken even this somberness up as well with motifs and lines of color painted every few dozen feet or so. The spaces that they passed, too, were not left to blank stone and rock. Though many of the passages and rooms were obstructed by ornate doors of carved timber, the offshoots and chambers Declan *did* get a chance to peer into briefly were all decorated in some form or fashion, often with pennants and tapestries of various makes, as well as bright whites and reds painted over the earthen walls. For the first time, too, he started seeing once again the curved sword and bow that formed the emblem of Ysenden, most often on the banners, but sometimes carved into the rock and painted blue or green to stand out.

Adding to what seemed to be a growing brightness, as they pressed further into the mountain the soldiers they came across also changed. Declan couldn't have missed the first of the *er'endehn* they passed dressed in white-and-gold, the tall woman's armor in sharp contrast to the darker hues of Lysiat's and Kellek Syr'esh's beside him. Declan couldn't help but turn and watch her go by as they crossed paths, noting as he did how the other elves in the passage seemed to give her priority in a similar—if lesser—fashion as they did the Lord Commander. Not long after this encounter, however, the *only* soldiers they were running into were all bedecked in a similar fashion, and Declan didn't actually have to speak to get an answer from his *er'endehn* companions as he glanced around at them.

"*Guards.*" The colonel was the one to address his curious look, speaking simply in consideration. "*Of the Chancellor.*"

Declan felt his brow rise at this. "*More dangerous than other soldiers?*"

Syr'esh gave him a small smile. "*More dangerous than some. Not more dangerous than all.*" As he spoke he dipped his head sidelong at Lysiat, who turned away from her superior deliberately as though to hide her face.

Declan almost snorted at this. Lysiat ay'ahSel, embarrassed? The colonel had to have just paid her a compliment of some magnitude to get such a response out of the elf woman, he knew. There had never been any question that the commander was an exceptional talent even among her own kind—who else would have been entrusted with leading a lone hunting party after the drey?—but if the colonel was praising her as more capable than the High Chancellor's own shields…

Declan would have liked to press further, and was busy mulling over how to do so with his limited vocabulary when the Lord Commander turned down yet another passage. Taking the corner, Declan and the others stopped short as they found themselves not in another tunnel, in fact, but rather standing in a deep, ten-foot alcove leading to a set of twin doors that reached the very heights of the ceiling above them. Whereas the wood of the other entrances they'd passed had been ornate and carefully carved, however, *these* doors were plain, adorned only with the emblem of the city and a pair of matching, heavy iron loops for handles. Just the same, Declan had no doubt whatever lay beyond them was likely a great deal more important than anything that might have been hidden among the other chambers in the hollow mountain, because no fewer than three guards in white-and-gold stood on either side of the recess, looking like they'd been stiff and at attention even before the Lord Commander had arrived accompanied by their strange party. Indeed, the sentries didn't so much as blink until as'ahRen gave a quiet order, at which point the pair closest to the doors moved at once to take firm hold of the handles and heave.

To stand so steady when suddenly faced with a dragon, not even to mention the rest of us… Declan considered, having to stop himself from shaking his head in amazement. He was already aware that the common soldiers of the *er'endehn* went through hellish training, and often for longer than the typical man lived, so he couldn't *begin* to imagine what sort of regime these white-clad elves must have gone through on the daily in order to achieve this level of—

But then Declan had to stop thinking, because all he could do was stare.

Despite the blandness of the doors, despite whatever it was he might have been expecting, he was not prepared for the sight that lay beyond the entrance opened for them by the Chancellor's Guard. Rather than a tunnel, the alcove swept out onto a spacious platform of polished wood flooring, which itself seemed to be only the largest part of a raised walkway that circled a chamber so massive Declan doubted it would have fit within the largest ballrooms of the al'Dyors' palace in Aletha. It seemed to be equally as broad as it was long, but was twice as tall as it could be measured cross-wise. The main floor was below them, accessible via a handsome staircase leading downward directly in front of their group, but the walkway they stood upon was only the first of several that Declan could make out. He suspected the existence of a glass ceiling, too, because the place was bathed in grey light, and he could distinctly make out the dull *plinking* of ice against something hard high above them.

What was more fascinating than all that, however, were the books—the thousands on *thousands* of books—that lined every wall and surface he could make out.

The "great place of study" Lysiat had told him they were headed to suddenly made a lot more sense. The chamber was a library, but unlike any library he had ever seen. He couldn't imagine how many lifetimes it had taken to gather such a collection, and as the Lord Commander led them inward Declan could do nothing more than stare in all directions as more and more came into view from beyond the edges of the inner alcove. Sure enough, before long a wide, slanted ceiling of paned glass showed itself, offering enough light despite the stormy day to illuminate the entirety of the chamber. With a clear line of sight of the whole room, other curiosities came into view as well, because Declan was soon not only studying the tomes that lined the innumerable shelves of the place, but also a variety of what looked like artifacts, curios, and treasures that took up deliberate spaces here and there within the cases and on the occasional display tables that had been carefully arranged not to block access to the books. There were swords of every kind, as well as several skulls Declan mostly recognized, with a few exceptions. Gemstones and other bright, glistening rocks added some color here and there, as did the assorted paintings hanging off the walkways so as not to take up wall space. Even more texts, too, were on display, most closed on their pedestals, but a few opened and loose, as though someone had been reading and only recently walked away.

All in all, it was without a doubt the most incredible room Declan had ever had the pleasure of standing in.

"Ryndean? What's wrong?"

The worry in Bonner's question was perhaps the only thing that could have made Declan tear his eyes from the wonders of the chamber. Looking around, though, he realized with his own measure of concern that Ryn—unlike the rest of them—had not moved from his place on the other side of the doors as as'ahRen had led the way into the library. Instead, he had stayed put, and by the look of his clenched fists and tight jaw, had no intention of entering just yet.

Before Declan, Ester, or any of the others could say anything else, however, the dragon spoke.

Lord Commander. Is the Chancellor here already?

as'ahRen, who'd turned with the rest of them, didn't hesitate before nodding.

"He is." The elf gestured towards the other side of the library, where Declan noticed for the first time another plain, much smaller door half-hidden hidden among the shelves. "He awaits you in his st—"

In his study, yes, Ryn finished for the Lord Commander, cutting him off. He, too, was looking at the door on the opposite side of the room, his eyes distant, and Declan realized the dragon had likely engaged his senses when they'd paused outside the entrance. Even as they all watched, though, he seemed to come back to himself, standing straighter and muttering to himself in his own language before he at last stepped into the library. To the surprise of most—except as'ahRel, by the look of his steady expression—Ryn swept right by all of them to start moving with purpose around the walkway, his clawed feet clacking with every step over the wooden floor.

"Ryndean!" Bonner hissed, chasing after the dragon as Declan tugged on Orsik's harness so he, Ester, and Eyera could hurriedly do the same. "Wait! What's wrong? What's happening?"

Nothing is wrong, Ryn answered, his words in direct contrast to the irritation blatant in his tone. *Nothing whatsoever is wrong. Between the Queen and the wights and the withholding of truths, I am simply tired of all the deception.*

"'Withholding of truths'?" Ester echoed from behind Declan as they hurried the warg along after Bonner and the dragon. "What 'truths'? Who's withholding truths?"

All of them, Ryn answered, waving an impatient hand back to where as'ahRen, Syr'esh, and Lysiat and her brothers had stopped walking, the latter foursome held back at a raised hand by the Lord Commander. *This whole time. Our esteemed escorts, and our courteous 'host'. We have been misled, it would seem.*

"Misled *how*, Ryn?" Declan demanded. "You're not making any sense!"

The dragon, though, didn't answer until they were all the way around the room, having taken the final corner in the walkway to come to a halt before the door that apparently led to the High Chancellor's study. Even then, he only spoke as he reached for the plain iron handle, identical to the ones outside the library.

Misled by omission. By the elves and—he heaved at the handle—*by my own damn kind.*

The door was wrenched outward with a creak of wood, banging against the shelves beside it before coming to rest wide open for them. Declan—and Bonner and Ester on either side of him—tried to peer around Ryn as he stepped inside, but caught only a glimpse of more shelves lining a narrow room that seemed to end in open sky through glass.

I can't sense anyone in this room, he continued. *Not a soul. And yet the grand leader of the* er'endehn *is supposed to be waiting for us here.*

With these words, Ryn stepped aside, revealing the rest of the chamber to them.

The space was a handsome study, the books and baubles lining the walls complimented by the scattering of comfortable furniture apparently set about for guests of the room's owner. At the far end of it, an ornate desk of carved wood and glossy black stone sat, beyond which the wall was largely comprised of a partial dome made of triangular glass panels that looked out over Eserysh's western expanse, still dim and stormy. Hail *plinked* and *thunked* off this grand window, but it was not the rolling clouds of the far distant horizon that Declan took in. Rather, it was the lone individual standing with their back to them on the other side of the desk, silhouetted against the day's grey light.

The lone, *horned* individual.

As Declan understood—Ester and Bonner both hissing out curses on either side of him at the same time—the figure turned towards them, clasping his hands behind himself as he did. His black robes, accented in white and gold, drifted gracefully about him as he moved, and Declan found himself transfixed by a gaze that was both well-known and utterly unfamiliar. Red eyes, as red as blood save for the pale hint of white, vertical pupils, took them all in one at a time before settling on Ryn, at which point the figure dipped his head low in greeting.

Good afternoon, Ryndean, the dragon said, his disembodied voice a deeper timbre than the one Declan was used to hearing echo through his head. *It has been too long.*

That it has, Arrackes, Ryn responded dryly, crossing his arms over his bare chest. *Or would you prefer I just call you 'High Chancellor'?*

CHAPTER TWENTY-FIVE

Declan was, for once, the one to keep his head on straightest in the following moments. He suspected, in hindsight, that his more-recent exposure to the flood of wonders and terrors that had been hidden from man's eyes had finally hardened him to astonishment, because both Ester and Bonner might as well have lost their tongues for all the words they managed to get out as he led them one after the other to two of the chairs set about the first half of the study. After that, it had been to Orsik and Eyera that he'd looked, but the warg had padded in happily enough once it was clear there was no danger beyond the entrance, and were now moving about the room sniffing at corners and every shelf their noses could reach, which was most of them.

Deciding to leave the door open in case as'ahRen and the others were planning to join them, Declan finally turned to take in the two dragons, who had been facing off without another word after Ryn had spoken.

"Alright. Obviously there's some explaining to be done." He looked to Arrackes, hesitating only briefly. "Erm... I would think it might be best if you'd start, uh... Chancellor?"

The dragon at last looked away from his primordial to cast Declan with an amused expression. Aside from his red eyes, he stood in contrast to Ryn in several ways, including coloration. Instead of jet-black scales, Arrackes' were more grey, and striped with burgundy slashes along his face and neck that suggested his body as a whole was likely so marked. What was more, his horns were smaller, and he stood nearly half-a-foot shorter than Ryn—only barely taller than Declan himself, in fact—and the realization struck Declan suddenly that he had a comparison for the first time in his life. Though it might partially have been his relative youth—Arrackes had an air about him that spoke of an age more likely measured in millennia than centuries or decades—it was obvious even at a glance that Ryn was not only bigger, but very likely faster and stronger than the smaller dragon, even in the form of their *rh'eems.*

Was this *the difference?* Declan had to wonder as he took Arrackes in. *Was this what it meant to be a 'lesser' dragon? To lack the blood of the primordials?*

That would indeed be fair, I suppose, the older dragon answered at last, turning back to Ryn. *I should first apologize, I imagine. If I had been able to send word to you of the developments of these last centuries, I would have.*

So it's true? Ryn asked, speaking more in a growl than anything. *You admit it?*

That I am High Chancellor of the er'endehn*? Yes. It has been so for the last three hundred years, in fact.*

300 y—? Ryn started to snarl before catching himself. *Why? Or rather:* how*? This was not your task, Arrackes. This was not your duty.*

Not initially, Ryndean, no. Arrackes shook his horned head, starting to move around the desk as he continued. *But things changed, and I would argue this is exactly what your order entailed.*

Explain, Ryn growled.

The older dragon dipped his head respectfully as he came to stand before his sovereign. *You tasked me with overseeing the* er'endehn. *With observing and protecting them.*

Precisely. Not to rule *them.*

That was not my decision. Arrackes' tone grew a little sharper. *Believe me, that was not my decision. Not at any point has it so been for the last three centuries, in fact.*

Oh? Then whose decision was it, then?

"That would be mine."

Together every head in the room—except the High Chancellor's—turned towards the study door, where as'ahRen, Syr'esh, and the ay'ahSel siblings looked to have finally caught up to them. The Lord Commander strode in confident and tall, and again Declan was struck by the man's presence. By comparison, the colonel, Lysiat, Aliek, and Tesied looked almost-shy as they followed their superior, white-red eyes darting about briefly before settling on Arrackes, then looking away again quickly.

If as'ahRen could command the power to split crowds with nothing but a step, Declan supposed it made sense that the High Chancellor—the only office higher than the old elf's, if he understood correctly—could only wield even great authority.

"It was mine," the Lord Commander said again, looking to Ryn as he came to stand between the chairs Bonner and Ester were still seated in. "Mine, and the Chancellor's council."

The council? Ryn hissed in disbelief. *How? How would they allow this? Arrackes was sent to be a guardian, Lord Commander. Not a* ruler.

"Oh, it was hardly unanimous," as'ahRen admitted with a shrug. "There were certainly some who kicked and screamed until the very end, but the High Chancellor's mantel is one granted by the people, Master Ryndean, and the people had spoken. Some will still mutter and gripe behind closed doors to this day, even among those who have held their seats on the council all these centuries—General Syr'esh, who you have already met, is one such longstanding critic—but there's nothing to be done once the votes are cast." At the Lord Commander's back, *Colonel* Syr'esh blinked at this, but gave no other indication of reaction.

Well that explains the anger, Declan thought, recalling the brief expression he had caught from the guard commander when as'ahRen had bowed to Ryn.

Meanwhile, the Lord Commander had kept on, gesturing to Arrackes. "You say you'd intended to send us a guardian, Master Ryndean? You did more than that. You sent us one of the few beings in the world who had seen more years than our elders, who had gathered more knowledge and wisdom than the oldest of our people. More than that, though, you had sent us someone who possessed something none among the dark elves had."

And what was that? Ryn asked, sounding hardly like his mood had improved. *Does the ability to breathe fire have some merit to sitting on a throne of which I am not aware?*

Impartiality, Ryndean, Arrackes said softly, clearly trying to appease his primordial.

This answer was not one Declan had expected, nor had Ryn from the look on his face. Taking advantage of the momentary pause, Arrackes gestured towards the remainder of the unoccupied chairs.

Let us sit, and I will explain. Colonel—the High Chancellor turned his red gaze to Syr'esh and the siblings—*I am afraid I lack sufficient seating for us all. Will you and the ay'ahSels be comfortable standing, for the time being? This should not take too long.*

"*Yes, sir!*" the colonel answered at once, his voice steady despite the fact that he, Lysiat, and the twins were still more rigid than usual, standing near where Orsik was snorting at a particularly massive book that looked like it might have weighed some twenty pounds.

Excellent. Then if one of you would be so kind as to close the door, I will get started.

As Aliek stepped immediately towards the still-open entrance of the study, Arrackes and the Lord Commander both moved towards chairs. Declan followed their lead, looking pointedly at Ryn as he sat, wishing again that he'd been more diligent in practicing his mind-speech. Still, the urging jerk of his head towards the last—and largest—seat seemed to do the trick, because with a grumble of resignation the dragon followed suite.

There, Ryn said once they were all comfortable, narrowing his white-gold eyes at Arrackes. *Now that we've circled the wagons, will you* explain yourself*?*

Declan almost sighed, wondering if this was really for the best, but the older dragon only nodded as he began to talk.

Your presence alone speaks to the fact that we have much more important things to discuss, so I will be as brief as I can. When you sent us—Shaldora, Tylvenar, and myself—on our respective assignments, I think we can all agree that the southern realms were in chaos. We dragons were decimated. Humanity had lost most of its army and Elysia al'Dyor had razed Aletha of its greatest noble houses. The er'enthyl, too, *were reeling, grieving the loss of the heir of their ruling family.*

Arrackes paused briefly, here, waiting until everyone had nodded in assent.

What you may not *realize, however, is the fact that the troubles of the Reaches, Viridian, and the Vyr'esh were as nothing to the turmoil happening in Eserysh, Ysenden in particular.*

As Declan, Ryn, Bonner, and Ester all frowned at this, as'ahRen took over the explanation.

"While I will not discount the terrible losses suffered by the other races—your kind in particular, Master Ryndean, according to the Chancellor—your fight had come to an end. For the *er'endehn,* however, it was another matter." The bearded elf leaned back in his chair, crossing his arms and grimacing slightly, as though recalling an unpleasant memory. "On our ascent up here, Magus yr'Essel's apprentice—" he gestured to Declan briefly "—made an observation that even in seven hundred years, we dark elves have not propagated enough children to require our migration out of Ysenden. That is accurate, but not solely because of Sehranya. We were massacred by the Endless Queen, it is true—we lost seventy percent of our population as a whole to her armies before the remnants of the other cities made it here—but we slowed our own expansion after that."

A mage's apprentice? Is that what you've been told, Ciriak?

Despite the gravity of the story, there was a note of amusement in Arrackes' voice as he interrupted the Lord Commander's retelling, his red eyes moving between the elf and Declan, who couldn't help but swallow nervously.

as'ahRen, for his part, shrugged again.

"I'm aware that there is undoubtedly more to the boy, but Master Ryndean made it clear that was a conversation best had elsewhere."

Fair enough, Arrackes acknowledged, his gaze now lingering on Declan, motioning for the Lord Commander to continue.

"As I was saying," as'ahRen picked up at once, "the Witch—the 'Endless Queen'—had played her hand, but our fight was far from over. Ysenden had, very abruptly, become the home of not only its own people, but also the sole surviving haven of cities that had—for centuries before Sehranya's rise—never been less than passively sour towards it, and not-infrequently openly hostile. The dark elves are an often-militant people. Born to the sword and bred on war. For millennia Ysenden butted heads with the other greater factions of Eserysh. Erraven, Ys'vaal, and Syr'hend, where the family of our own colonel hails from." The Lord Commander motioned towards Syr'esh, who did not move despite very likely not understanding a word that was being said about him. "Even as we'd worked to hold at bay the Queen there had been tension, but once our march into the Reaches saw her destroyed, things only got worse."

Much worse, Arrackes agreed somberly.

Declan could imagine it, and he knew his companions were undoubtedly thinking the same thing. Life-long enemies—*generational* enemies—suddenly enclosed in the same walls, forced to cohabitate and collaborate. Even with a common goal as important as ensuring the survival of their race, he knew that such circumstance would have been bound to escalate, and likely eventually erupt.

"The relative peace that followed the war hardly last more than a few years," as'ahRen said, confirming Declan's deduction. "Within a decade, things had degenerated back into violence, very often even murder. It was a dark time, and one that lasted more than a century. Eventually, the *unspeakable* began to occur, most often in a bid by the other factions to keep Ysenden from staying the dominate presence in our own walls."

"What was that?" Ester was the one to ask, her green eyes wide as she listened. "What happened?"

The children, Arrackes answered quietly. *The violence began targeting what few children were being born to the* er'endehn, *all in an attempt by those loyal to the different cities to raise their own banner a little higher than the others.*

Declan felt his stomach clench, and a flinch of movement in the corner of his vision told him he wasn't the only one to react with such discomfort to this news. Aliek had gripped his spear so tightly the blade had briefly glinted in the light, and Declan thought it must have been hard for the ay'ahSels and Syr'esh to be left out of most of the conversation only to be privy to the worst parts.

"Gods..." Bonner was the one to speak up, now, his muttered curse almost a hiss. "How terrible..."

You cannot imagine, Arrackes agreed with a dip of his head towards the mage. *Nor, I think*—he shifted his gaze to Ryn, now—*will you be surprised when I tell you that* this *was the moment I chose to make myself known to the* er'endehn.

Ryn's posture had steadily loosened as he listened, and though he still sat with his scaled arms crossed over his chest, he only sighed as the lesser dragon addressed him.

No. I cannot. It seems I may owe you an apology, Arrackes. He closed his white-gold eyes as though suddenly too tired to keep them open. *Several, in fact. I had not thought I would put you in such a position, when I sent you here.*

Arrackes, though, shook his head. *You owe me no apology. I should have sought an opportunity to reach you and inform you of the developments, even if it meant leaving Ysenden myself for a time. I simply had no idea of where you might be, given the last I knew of you, you'd tasked yourself with guarding the younger of the al'Dyor siblings…*

At this point, the older dragon glanced once more in Declan's direction, eyes shining with that same hint of amusement.

No. You did well. Ryn shook his own head as he opened his eyes again. *Aside from the fact that I was hardly in the same place for more than a few years at a time, it transpires that any attempt you might have made to get to Viridian might well have been your demise, old friend.*

Oh? Arrackes frowned, but Ryn only held a hand up to stave off any further question.

We will get to that, especially since Colonel Syr'esh—he gestured behind him to the standing elves—*had the good sense to bring the ay'ahSels along to fill in any holes in the story. For now, let's just say that crossing the Mother's Tears—Karn's Line, if you prefer—would likely have proven a much more difficult endeavor than even a dragon could have managed, especially on one's own.*

Ah. The High Chancellor nodded grimly. *I feared as much when we received word that what could only have been a drey had been spotted near the foot of the mountains. Yes…* He seemed to ponder this all for a moment, then let out his own sigh. *So long as we get to it eventually, I suppose. Now… Where was I?*

"You were speaking of the murder of the children, Chancellor," the Lord Commander offered in assistance. "In the century after

Sehranya's fall."

Ah yes. Arrackes' face hardened. *So I was. That, and my choice to make myself known.* He looked to gather himself for a moment, taking a breath before continuing. *Fortunately for the sake of this tale, the matter is not so complicated. I had been tasked by the sovereign of my kind*—he gestured to Ryn—*as a protector of the* er'endehn *as much as an observer. Until that point, the only blood shed had been among soldiers and assassins, and I'd not seen it as my place to intrude on the affairs of the elves. When the actions of the extreme aspects of the factions began threatening the survival of the race by targeting the young, however, it was time to step in.*

"I still recall the day," as'ahRen said with a snort, leaning back in his chair and looking up to the ceiling in reminiscence. "The lot of us—the first 'council' we'd cobbled together from the four strongest factions in an attempt to keep the peace—bickering like children over the table as we each sought to place the blame on another. Then the doors are being flung open like they'd been hit by a battering ram, and there is Arrackes, standing in the entrance while the guards we'd set for us outside were still in the process of reaching for their weapons."

Things had been escalating for decades, so I'd taught myself the form of one of the Vyr'esh's eagles so that I might hide out in the yr'es *for the previous decade or so,* Arrackes confirmed. *That bit of forest in the middle sanctum you doubtless passed on your way up here. I was considered a curiosity of nature to be fond of—what sort of eagle was grey-and-red with crimson eyes?—so I was left alone when I occasionally flew through the tunnels to get to know the city. I had the advantage of shock and awe on my side when I took to my* rh'eem *in front of the guards.*

"Even the best soldier is vulnerable to surprise when a damn *dragon* manifests into being not three feet from where they're standing," the Lord Commander admitted in a grumble. "He'd appeared and shoved open the doors before anyone had a chance to so much as shout."

Bonner seemed unable to stop himself from chuckling darkly

at all this. "I have to imagine things deescalated quickly, after that?"

They did, Arrackes confirmed. *To this day I do not take my assignment lightly.* He dipped his head again towards Ryndean. *The primordial of my kind had spoken, and so I told the elves of the council in no uncertain terms that I would not allow the destruction of their race.*

"Meaning…?" Ester asked like she wasn't sure she wanted to know the answer, and she sank in her chair a little bit when the dragon's red eyes fell on her.

Meaning that I promised the absolute destruction of any city faction that sought to continue their senseless war, as well as the violent death of the leaders of said group if any more children were harmed as a peace agreement was established. As I said: I do not take my assignment lightly.

The silence that followed this statement was keen, but kept brief by Ryn, who was frowning again.

That was extreme, Arrackes.

It was, the lesser dragon admitted at once, and the sudden tension brought on by his dark words dissipated slightly as his shoulders sagged a little beneath his black robes. *In hindsight, there may have indeed been a better method of approach, but with the bloodshed growing by the day…*

The Lord Commander, however, came to the Chancellor's defense immediately.

"There was not." as'ahRen was looking at Ryn as he spoke. "Believe me, Master Ryndean, there was not. We had been at an impasse for years. Decades, truth be told. Ysenden's individual strength was substantially greater than any of the other cities, but the combined numbers of Erraven, Ys'vaal, and Syr'hend were more than a match. We needed an outside force—an *impartial* force." He stressed the word pointedly as a reminder. "We needed someone who had both the strength to press the factions into line, and the ability to do so without being accused of favoring one city or the other."

It made sense, Declan had to admit.

"The *er'endehn* don't possess any magic," he thought aloud, considering it all. "No matter how strong they are as a martial force, what use would blades be against a dragon's scales?"

"Exactly." The old elf gestured his agreement. "At the time, we were limited to steel and iron weapons, just like man and our *er'enthyl* cousins. Perhaps we could have overwhelmed Arrackes if we'd thrown everything we'd had at him, but most of us on the council of the time had been on the cliffs in the last fight against Sehranya. We knew what dragonfire was capable of, and had no intention of crossing it if it could be helped."

"'Limited to steel and iron'?" Bonner repeated curiously. "As I recall, you carried black weapons into the Reaches… Are your blades now not the same?"

"Not remotely." The Lord Commander reached up and unsheathed the weapon strapped over his shoulder, showing it off. The glass-like blade was narrower that the one at Declan's hip, but shone even in the faded light of the day just the same. "What you saw on the dragons' cliffs was nothing more than blackened steel, Magus. This, though…" He lifted the weapon before him. "Obsidian, man calls it, I think. Volcanic glass."

So it was *glass?* Declan thought, astounded.

"Not possible," Bonner answered at once with a frown. "I know of obsidian, sir. It was used by the forefathers of both elves and man for tool making. It can carry an edge unlike any other material, but it is brittle. It would not be able to sustain the sort of impact—"

Regular obsidian, perhaps not, Arrackes interrupted with a weary smile. *I am not surprised by your knowledge, Magus… did Ciriak say it was 'yr'Essel' now? Yes, it is true that regular obsidian could hardly hold its form—much less its edge—as a weapon, but the blades you have seen are* not *crafted from regular obsidian.*

"Well then what are they—?"

But Bonner froze mid-question, his eyes moving from the dragon to the blade still bare in the Lord Commander's hands, then back again. Something seemed to click, and his mouth dropped open.

"Now *that's* interesting…" he muttered at last, not looking away from the weapon now.

"What are you talking about?" Declan asked, the swordsman in him allowing curiosity to get the best of his willpower. He'd wondered, of course, at the nature of the incredible blades, but hadn't yet grasped elvish strongly enough to ask Lysiat or the brothers as to their origin.

Bonner pointed at the Lord Commander's sword as as'ahRen slid it back into his sheath with a smile. "That blasted glass is tempered. Not unlike steel. Obsidian typically forms when magma—like you might find in or around a slumbering volcano, funny enough—is rapidly cooled. It stands to reason that applying a *greater* heat to molten stone before quenching it might produce a harder variation of the glass."

"A greater heat." Ester's laugh was low as she shook her head in disbelief, clearly catching on first. "Like say—theoretically—dragonfire?"

Arrackes and the Lord Commander both offered her a small smile.

Exactly like dragonfire, the High Chancellor said. *But we digress.*

"I don't think we do," as'ahRen disagreed, looking to Ryn again. "We have explained how Arrackes came to be known by us, Master Ryndean, but your original question was how he came to become the High Chancellor of Ysenden, was it not?"

It was, Ryn answered, an edge returning to his voice again. *And in that, I have yet to receive a satisfying answer.*

"But you have." The Lord Commander reached over his shoulder to tap the handle of the sword he'd just stowed. "Our blades are only an example of our reason. And you've already seen others. The gondolas. Our armor. Even aspects of our military techniques and lifestyle. When you sent Arrackes here, you offered us a mind which had lived longer than almost any being in the world, and certainly seen more of it than any elf within Ysenden's walls."

The obsidian was my idea, Arrackes picked up the explanation. *An experiment related to a curiosity regarding the magma pools that still heat the city. There are caves that make them accessible to those willing to try. Much of the rest, however, came from the world as a whole.* He gestured towards Bonner and Declan. *Pulley systems and elevators I'd once seen in the Virisian city of Ranheln, when men and dragons were on better terms. The improvements to armor*—his hand drifted to indicate Ester—*came from the attire of the elite hunters of Vyr'en, who we would sometimes cross paths with in the southern ridges of the Reaches. There is more, too, much more, from medicine and foodstuff to the practice of thinning parts of the forest, like the woodcutters of man used to do along the western edges of our mountains.*

"It took centuries of work and steady development," the Lord Commander started again, still watching Ryn, "but what you have seen of Ysenden's majesty could not have been possible *without* the advice and concepts Arrackes has provided. Eventually, the idea was put forward that the individual who had the greatest ability to effect change in the city should be the one governing it, and the council—the majority of them, at least—agreed. Eserysh as a whole has always been the land of the *er'endehn,* so we have never had a law requiring the discrimination of another race's participation in society. As a result—"

As a result, there were no true barriers to putting forth a dragon's name in Ysenden's elections. Ryn sounded almost tired as he finished for the elf, nodding and bringing a clawed hand up to rub at one temple. *And they accepted this? The council? The people?*

"Again, there was certainly protest," as'ahRen admitted with a shrug. "Particularly from those officers of the council who'd held loftier positions in the cities of their birth and wished to see a return of that power. May'lek ed'Vyn had been the actual High Councilor of Ys'vaal before its fall. General Syr'esh—" he glanced apologetically at the colonel by the wall despite the language barrier that barred the younger elf from understanding him "—had been a member of the ruling family of Syr'hend, and held my position as Lord Commander there. A far cry from the overseer of the city guard he has been for four hundred years now. The old sisters Ylva and Elva Ke'reen had shared a similar position beneath the Chancellor of Erraven, though they've both long-since passed." as'ahRen's brow furrowed. "Regardless, the remainder of the council largely saw the value in the proposition."

And the people? Ryn asked again. *Given where we are sitting, I must assume they, too, were eventually swayed?*

"Not eventually," the Lord Commander answered with a laugh. "Immediately. There was additional dissent, yes—from the parts of the other cities who hated being governed by Ysenden, much less a being who wasn't even *of their own race*—but this was some four centuries after the Witch's fall. Most of the old guard—the ones who truly remembered their former homes—had either died away or grown too old to raise any protest, leaving the younger generation to make their own choice. And in the end—having seen Arrackes achieve what he had in the span of their lifetime—they made it." He waved to the room around them as though to say "and so here we are".

"And have continued to make it since, apparently," Bonner added, looking around the study dutifully. "I was made to understand that the *er'endehn* elect their council every ten years, and their High Chancellor every fifty?"

I see now why your… ah… 'apprentice' is so well-informed, Magus. Arrackes didn't look at Declan this time, but there was the definite hint of a smile in the corner of his mouth as he spoke. *Yes. The people of the city have been so gracious as to elevate me every half-century since, to my great honor.*

"Like they have a better option," the Lord Commander snorted. "Who do you expect they would want to take your place, after everything you've done? Me? Syr'esh? The rest of us are warmongers. Unfit to wear the mantle."

As always, you fail to acknowledge your own abilities beyond the sword, Ciriak, Arrackes answered with a sigh. Then, though, his red eyes were on Ryn again, then moving from him to Bonner and Ester in turn before settling on Declan. *Now, however, is not the time to rehash that particular argument. I know this is all much to take in, but if we have even satisfied you for the* time being *with this explanation, then perhaps we can address the more pressing matter?*

Despite the fact that the old dragon was looking at Declan like he was trying to see *through* him, it was obvious who Arrackes had been addressing. Sure enough, Ryn shifted in his seat, leaning back to place his elbows on the arms of the chair before interlocking his clawed fingers.

I have more questions on the subject, but they can wait, he consented after a moment, nodding himself towards Declan. *By the way you are staring at Declan, am I to assume you've figured out who he is?*

At these words, as'ahRen frowned and turned to take Declan in for himself, looking him up and down again with even greater interest than he had on the gondola.

I have my suspicions, given his ring, Arrackes answered, and Declan saw the dragon's crimson eyes dip to the signet on his left hand before he thought they lost focus as the High Chancellor extended his senses. *I can only faintly make it out, though.*

"And what is it we're supposed to be 'making out'?" as'ahRen asked sidelong of his master.

Arrackes smirked slightly. *For you to experience it would require a seed of magic you unfortunately lack, old friend. I doubt even Ryndean can feel the energy, young as he is.*

I am not so young as I once was, Arrackes, Ryndean said in half-a-growl, but the lesser dragon waved the comment aside with a lazy hand.

Of course. I imagine you are as much changed as any of us in the time since the war, if not more. Still, you yet count your life in centuries, not millennia. Are you going to claim you can sense it?

Ryn hesitated, glaring at the High Chancellor before answering curtly.

No, I suppose I won't.

Arrackes nodded, obviously having expected the answer. *It is unsurprising. Your primordial's blood strengthens your ability, but it does not hone your* skill. *That is something only time can wet, I'm afraid.*

"I ask again, then, as naught but a humble elf uninitiated in the grandest arts of the secrets of the dragons," as'ahRen interrupted before Ryn could speak again, sarcasm dripping from every word. "What is it I am *not* supposed to be making out, then?"

"A blood of Kings." It was Bonner who answered the Lord Commander, clearly as intent as the elf on keeping the conversation from deteriorating. "A particular set of gifts handed down through the generations of Declan's family."

'Handed down' might not be accurate, Magus, Arrackes said, turning to look between the mage and Declan again. *As far as I am aware, Tyrennus intended this power to be lent to a single man and his sister, not meant to be passed along. It does not happen with the hatchlings of the primordials themselves, for example.*

Were he still here, Tyrennus would say that it appears mankind's tether to the magic of their sires is less finicky, Ryn cut in.

Probably. The High Chancellor chuckled, and looked squarely at Declan. *You are fortunate to have such a guardian, apprentice. The majority of our kind might well have slaughtered the first child of Amherst al'Dyor in the crib to keep our magics our own.*

Declan opened his mouth, about to cut Ryn off as the dragon bared his teeth in anger by stating very clearly that he *did* appreciate his fortune, when as'ahRen took to his feet with a jolt.

There was a ringing silence as the Lord Commander stood there without saying a word, his carved features suddenly hard, staring down at Declan. After a moment the elf's white-red eyes started searching his face, then his shoulders, arms, and hands. as'ahRen frowned, clearly not finding what he was looking for, before finally speaking.

"You said your family name was 'Idrys', boy..."

Declan thought it best, in that moment, to get to his own feet, though he stood a great deal more slowly than the Lord Commander.

"It is, sir. And if you're searching for signs of Amherst al'Dyor in my features, I doubt you will find any. Seven hundred years may not be more than a handful of generations among the *er'endehn*, but it is ten lifetimes of a blessed man and four times that many births for us. I am a long, *long* way separated from your former student, Lord Commander, and I certainly claim nothing more."

For the first time since they'd walked into the room, Arrackes looked the slightest bit surprised, one scaled brow rising in interest.

'Student'? Did you mentor the crown prince, Ciriak?

"He wasn't the crown prince," the Lord Commander said over his shoulder, still not looking away from the Declan. "His sister, Elysia, was the heir. But yes, I did, and to this day I've yet to find a pupil with the same combination of drive and talent, even among the *er'endehn*. What he lacked in our natural ability he made up for twice over with hunger and a little bit of magic." He addressed Declan again, his gaze hardening. "You tread in dangerous waters if you profess to be the descended of Amherst al'Dyor, boy."

There is nothing to profess, *Lord Commander.* Ryn's voice was chilly as he spoke from his chair. *It is simply a fact. Declan is the only living progeny of Herst's—Amherst's, if you would prefer—eldest line. He is the son of a man who was the eldest of the oldest daughter of the eldest son of his own family, etcetera, etcetera. Seven hundred years I have been watching over this line. Declan*—the dragon didn't look away from as'ahRen as he spoke—*show him the ring.*

Dutifully, Declan lifted his left hand, displaying the ornate silver band about his middle finger, the black stone set within etched with the crowned stag and shield of the al'Dyors. The Lord Commander looked at it, frowning for a moment, then winced as—Declan assumed—Ryn lifted the cognitive magics that had likely hidden the truth of the signet's shape from the elf's eyes until that moment. Apparently as'ahRen was not unaccustomed to such weaves, because he made no comment on the sensation. Instead, he froze, the hardness of his features softening once more to interest as he took in the ring.

The *exact* ring that would have rested about Amherst al'Dyor's finger, even when the *er'endehn* had been the prince's instructor so many centuries before…

"I would know myself, then," he said eventually, bobbing his head at the sword on Declan's hip. "You and I will cross blades, Declan Idrys, and we will see if you are truly your forefather's heir."

Declan felt his hands tingle at this, though he had trouble deducing if this was more due to terror at the proposition or thrill at the opportunity. From behind the Lord Commander, Ryn straightened as though about to say something more, but Declan stopped him with a hand.

"I would take you up on that honor gladly, Lord Commander, and soon." He had to work to mask his enthusiasm as he offered the man a brief bow. "Now, however, is not the time, unfortunate as that is. For whatever reason, my 'King's blood' has proven more of a curse than a blessing in this last half year. It's why Commander ay'ahSel and her brothers stumbled across us crossing the threshold into your lands, in fact." He gestured to the still-waiting elves at this, who continued to stand motionless despite the fact that Orsik and Eyera both looked to have grown tired of exploring the study and had settled down to sleep on either side of the line of the four silent *er'endehn.*

"Oh? And what do you mean by that, boy?"

"He means we are being hunted, sir," Ester said plainly before anyone could speak up. "He means Sehranya has been hounding us since the day Declan saved me from being a meal for one of your 'winged'. The drey."

The Lord Commander's stiffened, and he turned to the half-elf.

"I assume this is the part where you tell me what happened to the other hundred soldiers who should have returned with you today?" he asked quietly.

"Wights," she answered bluntly. "Probably more than ten-score."

And eight times that many more at least lying in wait not two-day's march from here, Ryn added as the Lord Commander blinked in surprise at this news.

"What?!" the elf demanded, whirling on the dragon this time. Before he or Arrackes could say another word, though, it was Bonner's turn to speak up.

"Oh, it gets worse, as'ahRen. Much worse." The old mage grimaced. "We also have good reason to believe there are those among the *er'endehn* who are already aware of this, and likely have been for some time…"

A heavy silence followed this, in which even Arrackes finally began to look alarmed.

A traitor? The High Chancellor finally asked, watching Bonner intently. *Among the* er'endehn*? We are aware that there might be at least one turncoat on the council, but we assumed the betrayal was to the benefit of one of the other city factions. What elf would betray their kind to the Queen?*

"To that, I cannot answer yet," the mage said with a shake of his head. "But we equally cannot discount the likelihood. However it is that Sehranya has dragged herself out of the grave again, she has proven more cunning and level-headed this time around then when last she sought to take hold of the world. Even seven hundred years ago she attempted to take advantage of the war between man and the dragons. We cannot say she isn't doing the same thing now."

Arrackes and as'ahRen glanced at each other at this, both suddenly very tense.

"A spy for the Witch..." the Lord Commander eventually said, not looking away from the High Chancellor. "Within our own ranks... How did it come to this?"

It came to this because, those seven hundred years ago, man allowed his ego to supersede the needs of our combined peoples. It was Ryn who answered. *In doing so, he not only nearly allowed Sehranya to take hold of the world, but placed the wedges between our kinds that have only driven deeper with time. The tension between humanity and the* er'enthyl. *The absence of the dragons. The self-exile of the* er'endehn. *We cannot allow this to continue. Above all else—above whatever it costs—this time we* must *come together, or risk the Endless Queen succeeding where she once failed.*

as'ahRen, who had turned to listen as Ryn spoke, nodded slowly at this, clearly seeing reason in the dragon's words. Beyond him, however, Declan couldn't help but notice the frown that had creased Arrackes' scaled face, the first sign of the displeasure the High Chancellor had shown since their arrival.

That doesn't bode well, he thought, eyeing the lesser dragon in concern.

It was, fortunately, the Lord Commander who spoke first.

"And how would you suggest we accomplish that, Master Ryndean? The *er'endehn* are not what we once were, and it has been more than half-a-millennia since we had contact with humanity. I wouldn't be surprised if they've forgotten we exist."

"They have," Declan found himself answering, looking away from Arrackes to the elf. "I can attest to that myself."

The Lord Commander nodded like he had expected this. "Then that complicates matters."

"It doesn't, and it does not." Bonner spoke up again, leaning back on his chair to thrum thoughtfully at the wooden arms by his side.

"Oh?" The elf looked to him expectantly.

"I won't pretend that humanity's lack of awareness won't make things difficult, but the fact of the matter is that one can hardly deny for too long the existence of something they can see with their own eyes. If it comes to it, the presence of the dark elves on the battlefield will smooth out that confusion quickly enough. More importantly, however—" Bonner glanced briefly at Ryn, as though seeking his assistance in what he said next "—the pieces for the alliance of our kinds—of *all* our kinds—are already in place, and have been for a very long time."

Declan saw it again, then. The deepening of Arrackes' frown was so obvious that even Ester glanced at the older dragon in concern.

Once more, however, it was as'ahRen who took the lead.

"Explain," he told Bonner slowly. "How am I not aware of this, if it involves the *er'endehn*?"

Because seven centuries ago you and your soldiers wanted so little to do with the other races that you left the Reaches the moment the war was done. Ryn's voice was firm but gentle, neither placing blame nor forgiving. *You denied us the opportunity to beg your involvement in our plan—in Igoric al'Dyor's plan, rather, though he'd already been slain by the time Sehranya fell. I am a little disappointed, however—"* the dragon looked to Arrackes questioningly *"—why you have apparently not been informed of it since."*

The High Chancellor, for his part, stayed quiet, his jaw clenched in what Declan would almost have called disapproval. It was clear Arrackes knew what was coming, but whether due to his primordial's presence or an obligation to let as'ahRen hear it all for himself, he said nothing.

Bonner was quick to take advantage.

"Lord Commander," he asked of the elf, "have you ever heard of 'the Accord of Four'...?"

CHAPTER TWENTY-SIX

"Do not let yourself be fooled by their grace and their haughty air. Elves are just as capable of spite and bitterness as man, if not more."

—Zyl'eht Yrhst, High Chancellor of Erraven, date unknown

"U*nforgivable*!" General Sen'Hev, commander of Ysenden's forward scouts, snarled as she slammed an angry fist down on the long council table before her. "*First you trespass into* our *lands, violating our blatant desire to be left* alone, *and then accuse us of betraying our own people to the Witch?! Unforgivable!*"

Lessan, Arrackes said in warning. *Calm yourself. I have already stated that Ryndean and his companions are welcomed guests of the city, so there has been no trespass. By* any *of them.*

His pointed last words were clearly necessary, because from around the table there came more than one scathing glance or frown of disapproval scattered among the twenty generals of Ysenden that made up the city's council.

"Chancellor," Sen'Hev hissed insistently. "*You have said yourself that two of them are* mages! *And one a former court magus of the realm of man! Surely you understand how this city will feel at being forced to host such corruption within our—!*"

"Enough, General." It was the Lord Commander this time who spoke, his tone less forgiving than Arrackes'. "*This council's fear of magic is not without reason, but we are* er'endehn. *Since when do we allow* fear

to guide our thoughts and decisions?"

There was, for the first time in several minutes, a tense pause in the conversation, and Ester took the opportunity to draw in an unsteady breath from where she stood behind the High Chancellor's chair at Declan's right, between him and her father, with Ryn looming over all at his left. It had been well over an hour, now, since the meeting had commenced, and she was starting to think that if the dark elves debated every decision with this amount of fervor, it was unlikely they could have functioned for long as a society.

After Arrackes and Lord Commander as'ahRen had explained how it was the dragon had come to be the leader of the *er'endehn,* it had been Ester, Declan, Ryn, and her father's turn to tell their own tale. They'd started from the very beginning, when Declan and Ryn had saved her from the gruesome scene that had turned out to be a drey's feeding ground, and the full retelling had taken no small part of the day's grey afternoon. At Ryn's encouragement they'd skipped no details, hiding nothing from the lesser dragon and his second. They told them of the attack by the ghouls, then the drey, of their flight through Ranheln, and the ambush by the wights that had them deciding north, beyond the Mother's Tears, was the only viable option left to them. They told them of the horde of wereyn that were likely currently waiting out the winter in the husk of Sevylle, the mining town due north of Aletha, after a fall spent razing the northern valley towns of Viridian. They told of the butchery and burning ruins that were all that had remained of Elghen, of their ascent into the mountains, then their fall and journey into the dark. From there, it was the ay'ahSels who had taken over, all three of them explaining their assault on the drey that had arguably saved the lives of Ester and her party, as well as the choice to take the lot of them 'prisoner' until a decision could be made as to what to do with the group. They spoke of the tunneler's attack, and from there the story had split where Aliek and Tesied had led Ryn, Ester and her father, and Eyera from the mountains, while Lysiat told of her journey with Declan deeper into the bowels of the earth.

When they reached Declan's costly defeat of the undead worm, as'ahRen let out an impressed whistle, but otherwise he and the High Chancellor had stayed quiet throughout the story.

Only after the ay'ahSels—and Colonel Syr'esh, now—had gotten to the end of their recounting, telling the pair of the ambush by the wights that had decimated the forward unit—and their subsequent realization that the draugr could only have come from Eraven—did either the Lord Commander or dragon speak.

"*Spirits take us...*" as'ahRen had hissed as he'd heard this, slipping into elvish before catching himself and shifting to common again for Declan. "All of them? You're sure? Every exile we've cast out?"

We have to assume so, Ryn had answered. *As we have to assume this was very possibly part of a larger plan.*

Whose? Arrackes had asked. *Whose plan?*

"Whoever it is who has been stirring the pot of rebellion in Ysenden these last years," Declan had told them, then. "Is the timing of such an escalation after so many centuries, all while Sehranya *also* invades Viridian, not too convenient to be coincidence...?"

It hadn't taken much to convince the pair after that, especially when Syr'esh and all three ay'ahSel siblings swore on the banner of the city that the wights could only have come from Erraven, dressed as most of them had been. From there, Arrackes hadn't delayed in calling the Chancellor's council to order, summoning every general in Ysenden to a chamber the dragon and the Lord Commander had guided Ester and the others to themselves, on the same level as the study. Orsik and Eyera had been told to stay in the library—under the wary eye of the ay'ahSels—and so it was that Ester, Declan, Ryn, and her father found themselves keeping their own company again for the first time in what felt like years.

Or at least they would have been, had half of the council not been watching them in dubious concern while the other half lashed out with open hostility.

"*With all due respect, Lord Commander,*" an aged elf with a narrow white beard whose name Ester didn't know yet spoke up from the far end of the table, "*I do not think it 'fear' that feeds these concerns of ours. I would rather call it 'experience'.*" Despite the general's steady tone, his eyes were narrowed as he turned his attention to Declan and Ester's father. "*The last time we had any dealings with the magics of man, we paid the price in hundreds of thousands of lives lost. Would we not be wise to hesitate carrying on with such interactions again?*"

At Ester's right, her father grumbled something inaudible under his breath, though she thought she caught the words "waste of a good chair" among the mutterings.

Closer to their end of the table, Arrackes gave a sigh and leaned back. *Believe me, Beh'lys, that few in the world can appreciate the horror of Sehranya's power as much as a dragon. Ryndean and I*—he gestured over his shoulder to where Ryn stood motionless as he translated everything for Declan privately—*saw our kind unmade, then stitched back together into monsters* specifically *crafted to be our bane. I am not unsympathetic to your mistrust. I am merely frustrated in the fact that it is misguided and misplaced. This man*—he gestured this time with his other hand to Bonner—*is not your enemy. Far from.*

"*But how can you* know *that, sir?*" a younger elf, perhaps half the age of most of the others seated about the table, was glaring through the open slots of the black helmet he had chosen not to take off when he'd sat. "*In truth? How do we know that this tale they have spun for you is not some fallacy dredged up to trick us?*"

"*Oh, for god's sake.*" Ester's father had finally had enough, his gaze knife-like as it settled on the younger general. "*Get your head out of your arse, boy. We have trudged through blood and fire alike to bring you these tidings, and it is tiresome to hear your doubts weigh your swords."*

"*Boy'?*" the general repeated in a snarl, shoving himself to his feet before anyone could stop him. "*You prove yourself as much a fool as a charlatan, human. I have lived for four hundred years and have likely seen more death on my blade than the entirety or your company combined."*

Oh, well played, Father, Ester thought as she saw the man's expression abruptly shift into a cunning smile in the corner of her vision. On her left, Declan suddenly raised a hand as though to cough into, hiding his own grin as Ryn turned the words for him.

"*Four hundred years would put you at half my age,* boy." Ester could tell her father was barely containing his enjoyment as he emphasized the repeated word. "*Your assumptions at the abilities of mankind prove* you *the fool, I'm afraid.*" As the younger general's face slacked in disbelief, however, the mage turned his attention to the rest of the table. "*As for whether or not I am some agent of the Endless Queen—your 'Witch'—I have to call myself insulted."*

"*Because you think so highly of your position that you believe yourself more than her tool?*" General Sen'Hev asked mockingly.

Because he was one of the two mages who personally saw Sehranya's ashes cast off the cliffs of my homeland.

Arrackes' words came like the warning rumble of distant thunderclouds, low and absolute. Glancing at him, Ester saw that the dragon seemed indeed to be at last running out of patience, his red eyes intent on the scout commander.

Bonner yr'Essel and I met for the first time today, true, but we have crossed paths before, he continued, and the weight of his voice seemed to lay like lead over the entirety of the room. *He and Elysia al'Dyor finished the war that claimed those hundreds of thousands of lives the* er'endehn *still pine for. Those of you who stood on those cliffs should recall the fight, and the firestorm that brought it to an end. That was Magus yr'Essel and his pupil's doing, and I will swear so to every individual ear within the walls of this city if need be.*

Another pause, and Ester didn't miss many of the expressions shifting around the table, some slipping away from fury to grudging respect, while a few older faces briefly showed true interest before settling into the typical emotionless mask of the elves.

Arrackes let the silence hang a moment, this time, before speaking again.

Good. It seems that finally knocked some self-awareness into the lot of you. Every moment we waste going in circles here is a moment this reborn Queen has to solidify her position in Eserysh. With that in mind—and if we are done delaying—there are two matters that need be addressed.

When no one spoke out against him again, the dragon nodded to the Lord Commander at his right.

"*First and foremost—*" as'ahRen started up at once, speaking loud and clear "*—there is the matter of the potential traitor in our midst. If Viridian is under assault, it casts a different light on the uprisings we have been suffering these last years.*"

Ester caught the barest hint of annoyance at the word "uprisings" on a few faces, but no one said a word cross-wise as the Lord Commander continued.

"*It pains me to say it, but* no one *can be beyond suspicion for the time being, which is why I am instituting a temporary two-handed policy for the members of this council. You will each be assigned a pairing, with* both *parties' approval being required on any and all major decisions made in the immediate future.*"

No one so much as blinked at this, which told Ester the council was—at the very least—taking the matter seriously.

"*It is, of course, unlikely that the traitorous element is limited to this room, if it is even present here at all.*" The Lord Commander continued. "*For that reason, a full-scale investigation of every tier of our standing force will be initiated, which I will be personally overseeing, barring some necessary delegation. General Syr'esh.*" as'ahRel leaned forward to look down the table. "*As commander of the city guard, I am charging you with investigating your own house, as well as the residents of the city not a part of the standing army. Is this agreeable?*"

From his place closer to the middle of the council, the general who had greeted them at the gates of Ysenden—*undoubtedly* Kellek Syr'esh's father, now that Ester had a chance to get a good look at the broad-shouldered elf—nodded as he spoke.

"*It is. If I may make a request, however, regarding your 'two-handed' policy: I would ask that I be paired with General Ryvus.*" He gestured across the table to a thin woman in plain black-and-orange robes who had one hand on the table, index finger toying with a large gold ring that encircled her thumb as she listened. She, Ester had noted, was among those who'd expressed no true reaction to their presence, which was immediately explained as Syr'esh continued. "*If I am to investigate the populace, it would be best if I worked closely with the spymaster. She is of Ysenden's line, and is therefore extremely unlikely to have betrayed us. Our partnership would be of great assistance in the work I will need to undergo, and would at the same time address any potential concern of an improper investigation if* I *were suspected of treachery.*"

The Lord Commander pondered this for a moment, then looked to Arrackes. The dragon nodded his assent, and as'ahRen turned back to the guard commander.

"*A good thought. Yl'ah.*" He addressed the silent spymaster. "*Do you harbor any concerns?*"

"*None, sir.*" The elf's voice was surprisingly deep given her slender appearance, and she drew her hand into her lap as she dipped her head respectfully towards the head of the table. "*I have worked with General Syr'esh before on similar matters, and he is correct: I* am *among the least likely to be the betrayer, given that I was born within these walls. If anything, I think it speaks to his capability that he has already thought the value of our pairing through.*"

"Done, then," the Lord Commander said, rapping the knuckles of one hand against the table to mark the end of the conversation before looking around. *"The rest of you will be assigned your pairings before the end of the day. Now, onto the other matter: this council needs to decide what is to be done about Erraven."*

Ester thought she could have guessed, by the minute shifting of bodies in chairs, then, which of the present officers carried Erraven blood in their veins. There weren't more than three or four—the bearded "Beh'lys" among them—but faces darkened in general around the table at as'ahRen's word.

It was General Syr'esh who broke the tension first as he spoke again.

"I can start with a positive update: there are currently no prisoners set for exile, so that need not be a concern."

"Good," as'ahRen said with a nod, and Ester thought the elf might have looked relieved. *"We should pray to the spirits it stays that way."*

"Personally, I would recommend a dissemination of the... suspected *situation in Erraven to the general populace."* Another younger general, his white hair shorn nearly to his scalp, spoke up. By his hesitation stating the facts it was clear the elf still had his doubts about the verity of the information, but his skepticism was not enough to go against Arrackes' and the Lord Commander's sworn words. *"We have been lenient with the dissenters for long enough as is. An exile from Ysenden was of little deterrent when they knew they would be hailed as heroes upon reaching the ruins of the old city. If we spread word that Erraven is not the haven they thought it to be, we may see a hesitation in their willingness to act, at least in the immediate short-term."*

"Two birds with one stone," General Syr'esh spoke up yet again, nodding thoughtfully before looking up the table. *"I would second this. Kases is correct. There's no need to concern ourselves with where prisoners are going to go if we can make it that we have no prisoners, at least for a time. If*

we can achieve a lull in the rebels' actions by announcing the situation to the masses, it would also reduce the burden my men have been carrying, which will be important if we end up deploying the army to deal with Erraven."

"Is that the intention?" Beh'lys asked, looking around the table despite clearly addressing the question to Arrackes and as'ahRen. *"To raze the city again? There is still a history there, I would remind you, and bad blood lingers. If we were to trample across the graves of those lost to Sehranya in the last war, we risk—"*

A wizened elf with a scar cutting almost horizontally across her forehead interrupted the general from the end of the council. *"If we do not see the wights eradicated—not to mention what* other *spirit-forsaken corruption might hide within those walls—then we may well have many more graves to dig before the winter is out. History has merit, but we number too few to place its value above the good of Ysenden."*

"Particularly after having lost more than a hundred souls already to the creatures," a tall elf with a soft face added from the other side of the table.

Beh'lys, though, wasn't willing to be cowed.

"That is an easy thing for the blood of Ysenden *to say,"* he growled. *"It is not so simple for those of us whose families are buried beneath the rubble of Erraven."*

Ester watched then—with a mixture of exasperation and irritation—as the confrontation erupted from there. Other officers spoke up to support or scorn Beh'lys, while a few who she thought to be of Ysenden's line even stood up from their chairs in anger. The meeting devolved into a shouting match in seconds, and Arrackes started to stand, clearly intent on diffusing the situation.

A clawed hand on his robed shoulder kept him in his seat.

ENOUGH!

While the older dragon's early impatience had rung with a threatening weight, Ryn's snarled word bore an entirely different—almost physical—pressure. Had she not been accustomed to hearing his voice inside her head, Ester thought her knees might have buckled, and the council members who'd gotten to their feet or were in the process of doing so indeed slumped to a one. The former were suddenly forced to put hands on the table for support, while the latter dropped heavily back into their chairs.

Is this *the proud council of the elves?* Ryn's rumbled growl seemed to vibrate in Ester's skull as he took a step forward to stand beside the High Chancellor's chair. *Is* this *what the greatest of the* er'endehn *have to offer in a time of approaching war? Bickering and argument? Had I known to expect as much, I would not have bothered with the journey here.*

If there were any in the room who wished to protest at this statement, they were smart enough to keep their resentment to themselves. This was the very council that had once been cowed by the likes of Arrackes, after all.

Ester couldn't have known what the elves must think of the presence of a true primordial in their chamber.

Those of you of the line of Erraven, you may consider me disappointed. Ryn continued without letting up on the pressure in his words, white-gold eyes falling on Beh'lys in particular. *Seven hundred years—generations of separation, even among the elves—and you* still *have not been able to set aside your own wounds for the greater good. As for those of you of Ysenden's blood*—his gaze moved to the end of the table, where the two older elves were just starting to smirk in victory—*you hold the greatest power in your own city, and yet you still find it necessary to taunt those who have lost their homes and their history. They may be selfish, but I call* you *cowardly.*

A few flinches of anger at this, but still no one spoke.

If you would all cease to bicker like children, perhaps the more clever among this council will take note of the fact that no *decision has been made regarding the ruins of Erraven. We are in agreement, I imagine, that the draugr need to be disposed of, and with prejudice. We should not assume the thousand exiles you have cast from these walls are all Sehranya would have built up, in the time she has had. However, at the end of the day, our enemy is not a complicated one. Ghouls would be hardly more than fodder to the likes of your soldiers, and even wights cannot bear too complicated a Purpose. The drey and wereyn are more clever, and possessing of their own will, but they are still instinctive beasts. Most importantly: for whatever reason, we've also yet seen no sign of the liche that once stood by the Queen's side.*

"Meaning what?" the young general who had first crossed words with Ester's father asked, clearly trying to save some face as he met Ryn's eye stoically.

Meaning that if whatever horde lies in wait in Erraven has no commanding presence, it is entirely possible that this battle need not happen within the ruins at all, Arrackes answered in Ryn's stead, taking control of the conversation again now that the council had settled. *The wights encountered by Colonel Syr'esh and our guests in the Vyr'esh were obviously driven to kill, not to hide or lie low. If we make enough noise, it is entirely possible we can draw the undead to us.*

"That would be ideal," as'ahRen offered with a nod, jumping back in as well. *"Attempting to take the fight into the old city would only put us at a disadvantage, given the rubble and ruins. In the forest itself, we would be able to hold an established line."*

"A much stronger defense against the undead..." To the Lord Commander's side, an elf whose lined face made him look positively ancient wheezed in agreement, his clouded eyes half-lidded as he spoke. *"It has been some centuries since I took to the field myself, but I recall this much, at the very least. If we give the wights in particular any means to get at our backs..."*

Ester herself swallowed nervously as the shrunken general let the suggestion hang. In the forest she'd had the advantage of fighting atop Eyera, whose bulk and speed had helped to keep the draugr at bay long enough for Ester to put an arrow in each of their skulls. Even in a line, however, the dark elf soldiers—inexperienced in fighting such an enemy—had been broken. She didn't even want to think what could happen among the old ruins, where there were undoubtedly a thousand places from which to skulk and strike...

"So we lay seige?" Byr'esh asked, obviously being careful not to look at Ryn as he spoke again. *"We encircle the city? How much of our army would that take?"*

"I cannot recommend we deploy the entirety of the standing military," General Syr'esh cut in quickly. *"Not if it can be helped. My guards do not number enough to hold Ysenden if this is some sort of ploy..."*

"A valid concern." It was Sen'Hev's turn to speak, the scout commander avoiding Ryn's eye as well. *"It will not take us less than a day to gather the provisions and armaments necessary for any sort of sizable action, regardless. If you would grant me some additional time, I can have my eyes to and back from Erraven, which should allow us to gather much needed information."*

as'ahRen looked pensive at this, but eventually nodded. *"I think we can give you three days. That shouldn't break the odds in either direction..."* He eyed Sen'Hev carefully. *"I expect you to send your best, of course."*

"I will accompany them myself, Lord Commander," the general answered by way of promise.

"Then see to it. You have my leave."

There was a short silence as the scout commander stood at once, bowing to the head of the table before turning and striding briskly down the chamber. Reaching the double doors, she knocked once upon them, and they opened for her immediately, revealing several soldiers in the white-and-gold livery of the Chancellor's Guard. The moment the general was gone the entrance was closed again, shutting with a faint *boom* that echoed once across the stone of the windowless room.

As the conversation resumed, Ester thought she had at last caught a glimpse of the terrifying efficiency the *er'endehn* war machine was capable of.

"*While we await Sen'Hev's return, we will need to take stock of our ranks,*" as'ahRen kept on without hesitation, gesturing down the table. "*I agree with Sureht. While we should not assume to face* only *a thousand wights, nor can we ignore the possibility that this is a plot to make Ysenden vulnerable.*"

Ester wasn't sure who the Lord Commander was referring to until Syr'esh nodded his thanks at the support.

Ysenden cannot be left undefended, obviously, Ryn agreed from where he'd stepped back to resume translating for Declan again. *But aside from the numbers needed to satisfyingly defend the walls, I would recommend the deployment of as many as the* er'endehn *will allow. I would prefer we stand on the field and face a thousand twenty-to-one than regret hesitancy in the vice versa.*

Agreed, Arrackes gave his assent grimly. *Should rousting the Queen's foothold prove simple, it means only that the soldiers can return quickly. There is little harm in being overly cautious in this scenario.*

"*Then what can we spare?*" the Lord Commander followed up with, looking down along the remaining council members. "*How many would we need to safely hold the walls in the event of a trap?*"

"*With the alterations the High Chancellor has—in his wisdom—allowed in the last century, the number will not be insignificant.*" A narrow elf with a pinched face and a black goatee streaked with grey spoke up dryly, leaving no doubt what he thought of the "High Chancellor's wisdom". "*I feel the need to remind this council that I raised my concerns when the suggestion of glass windows and the like was brought up, and I would point out that—*"

"*Yes, General ed'Vyn,*" as'ahRen cut the elf off with what looked like a deliberate effort not to roll his eyes. "*We have all heard your concerns before, several times. Fortunately, you are charged with city develop-*

ment, not security, and the additions you are referring to were not deemed a substantial enough risk to counter their benefits." He looked around the table. *"Anyone else?"*

"Ten thousand would satisfy, sir," General Syr'esh answered at once, though he looked hesitant. *"I would prefer more, but ten thousand—in addition to my five—will be able to hold at bay a siege of any reasonable size until the main army returned."*

"Leaving us with thirty thousand?" the Lord Commander asked, and Ester recalled suddenly that Ryn had once told them the dark elves had flanked Sehranya with forty thousand blades in the Queen's final battle.

It hurt her heart to hear that those numbers had not significantly increased even all these centuries later, and she couldn't help but wonder just how many must have died in the rebellions that followed the war…

"Very nearly," an elf of middling years—at least for his kind—spoke up from further down the table. He wore white robes, and had the sword and bow of Ysenden stitched in blue thread across his chest. *"I regret to remind this council that we have already lost more than a hundred souls to the Witch's ilk, and I* cannot *recommend the rest of that command be deployed, including their officers."* He offered General Syr'esh an apologetic look even as he continued. *"They require rest and psychological care, and many among them are being treated for physical wounds, some permanently crippling. Given the death toll, I am honestly surprised more didn't come back in pieces."*

"Oh, so not *all* magic is deplorable, is it?" Ester's father muttered in quiet common from her side, forcing her to swallow a smile.

"Yes…" The Lord Commander looked suddenly grim as he answered the white-robed elf, eyes dipping to the table. *"Yes… Forgive me, General Vets. It has been so long since we've lost such a number at once that I hadn't thought to discount them… Are they doing well?"*

The general—who Ester assumed could only be the medical commander—nodded. "*I only had the opportunity to inspect the more gravely wounded before the council was summoned, but I gather from my seconds that all will survive.*"

"*And thank the spirits for that,*" General Syr'esh said, closing his eyes and tilting his head back to the ceiling. "*My son is a capable officer, but to be ambushed by an enemy we all thought long-struck from this world...*" After a second, the guard commander opened his eyes again and looked down the table. "*With your permission, Vets, I would celebrate their return. It might do the bedridden good to see their comrades up and about.*"

"*It very well might,*" General Vets agreed. "*Give them a few days of rest, and then feel free.*"

"*Good,*" Syr'esh answered distractedly, looking—like the Lord Commander before him—to the table again. "*That's damn good...*"

"*So a little less than thirty thousand,*" as'ahRen himself summarized, glancing back to Ester and the others. "*I would deem that a satisfactory force to lay siege to Erraven, wouldn't you, Master Ryndean?*"

I will have to defer that opinion to you and the High Chancellor, Lord Commander, Ryn said with a short bow. *My companions and I are unfortunately not familiar with the old city, nor the surrounding lands.*

"*That's one way to put it...*" Ester heard someone mutter from down the table, but she didn't look around fast enough to catch the naysayer. What was more, neither Ryn, Declan, nor her father looked to have made out the quip, and—though she saw a brief tick of annoyance in the elf's face—the Lord Commander seemed willing to ignore it in the interest of keeping the tenuous peace they had managed to cobble together.

"*Then I* do *deem it enough,*" he said before looking to Arrackes. "*Chancellor?*"

The older dragon looked to consider the choice, one clawed finger scratching absently at the table as he thought. After a few seconds he finally nodded, sitting up straight before speaking firmly to the room as a whole.

So be it. You know your duties, all of you. In three days time we march with thirty thousand, including those of us here who are not essential to Ysenden's daily functions. Dismissed.

The discharging of the generals to their responsibilities was so abrupt, Ester wasn't the only one taken aback. Several of the generals blinked, and from her right her father tried to speak.

"Wait, we've yet to discuss—!"

His exclamation, unfortunately, was drowned out by the scrapping of some twenty chairs and the thudding of boots as the council departed the chamber, many in conversation while they moved. Ester saw the medical commander Vets speaking with the two generals of Ysenden's line that had drawn Ryn's earlier ire, and Syr'esh had caught up to the spymaster Yl'ah Ryvus, undoubtedly coordinating their partnership. Ester's father tried again to speak, but it was no use, and only after the council had completely departed and the doors had been shut once more behind them was his voice able to be heard once again.

"High Chancellor Arrackes…" the mage began, clearly working to keep the anger from his voice as he turned to the older dragon, who had kept his seat. "Might I enquire as to why you failed to bring up the *most* important part of the conversation we presented you with?"

Arrackes, for his part, said nothing for a long moment. Eventually, however, the silence lingered too long as Ester, Declan, and Ryn continued to stare at his back as well, all while as'ahRen sat quietly by, watching the exchange warily.

Magus, I regret to admit that you and I have different opinions as to the benefits of your 'Accord of Four'. Very *different opinions.*

"Oh?" the mage responded. "Is that a fact? You failed to say as much when we spoke of it earlier, I believe."

I failed to say anything *on the subject, in fact, and quite deliberately.* Arrackes at last took to his feet, standing up and stepping away from his seat to face Ester and the others. *Truthfully, I find it a little alarming that you would assume me receptive to the concept, given what happened last time my people were subject to the weaves of the Accord.*

Arrackes… Ryn said in warning, but the lesser dragon only shook his head at his primordial.

With all due respect, Ryndean, this is not something you can command I change my opinion on. I never *thought it wise that Tyrennus allowed us to be included in those magics, before or after the war with Aletha.*

"Aletha's *nobles*," Declan corrected coolly. "I am living proof that the Accord was crafted with a mind to *preserve* the relations of the races, not eradicate them. Igoric al'Dyor was murdered for attempting to weave a lasting peace, High Chancellor."

Your kind lost a king, Declan Idrys, the dragon answered evenly. *Mine lost more than ninety percent of our entire population. What say you to that?*

"We say that the Accord is not a perfect magic." Ester's father saved Declan from having to respond. "But it *is* the greatest chance we have to rid the world of Sehranya and her like once and for all. A binding of our four races would give us no choice but to collaborate against her."

Is that so? Arrackes asked, looking to the mage. *Then why have the wood elves of the Vyr'en not already joined mankind on the battlefield against the wereyn? Or the dragons?*

"The Accord is not enforced regarding conflict that can be won without assistance," Ester's father answered. "Otherwise it would require the ruling parties of each race to deploy for every minor tussle or skirmish. If Ryndean has not felt the pull to intervene, then the weaves have calculated that the wereyn are not a great enough threat to extinguish mankind on their own."

So that's why… Ester had pondered the same question herself for some time, though—knowing her father—she'd figured there had to be a good reason. By the brief look of understanding on Declan's face, he too must have been pleased to have an answer to that particular mystery.

It is possible that this is why Sehranya has deployed nothing more than the wereyn into Viridian, Ryn picked up for the mage. *It is* also *possible that it's the reason the dark elves are now being targeted by the draugr. If she knows that you are the last holdout of the pact, she would be aware too that your people are the most vulnerable.*

'Holdout' is hardly a fair term, Ryndean, Arrackes said, a spasm of irritation in his jaw. *As I recall, the* er'endehn *were already in the middle of a war against Sehranya when Igoric al'Dyor called the other races to council. Even then it took a* year *for the negotiations to conclude and the Accord to be enacted, time in which man, the* er'enthyl, *and—yes—even the dragons could have aided the dark elves even* without *the assistance of magic.*

"We hardly knew what we were facing!" Ester's father growled in answer to this. "Igoric was the one who foresaw the danger, who tried to—!"

"There is another concern, if I might interject."

Lord Commander as'ahRen stood up from his chair at last, having only listened to the argument silently until that point.

"You know now of our history, of the events that followed the old war." The aging elf spoke calmly, but his gaze was unyielding. "Humanity has rebounded, as it is wont to do, and the *er'enthyl* lost only a handful of soldiers and their crown prince to Sehranya's efforts. Of the four races, the *er'endhen* and the dragons alone are still suffering from our losses. Should we bind ourselves to this 'Accord of Four'—should we allow ourselves woven into its magics—we would be at a great disadvantage."

Ester frowned at this. "Would it not be the opposite, Lord Commander? Should you accept the Accord, and be targeted by Sehranya's full strength, then the other races—"

"Would do what, yr'Essel?" the elf gently cut her off with a sad look. "Come to our aid? Assist us? Perhaps the attempt would be made, but it is not so simple. Karn's Line—your 'Mother's Tears'—is a brutal ascent, and we know it now also to be the realm of the Witch. Even if the al'Dyors you say still hold power ordered their armies into the mountains, how would that be received? To the common officers and soldiers, how would that be any different than ordering the mass suicide of the ranks, particularly if the greater part of mankind has forgotten the *er'endehn* even exist? And the wood elves? And the dragons? The *er'enthyl* would have to cross through Viridian, which it sounds like would be a declaration of war with the populace of your realm even if the al'Dyors and the family ehn'Vyr'en know better. And the dragons? How would they even know to come?" The Lord Commander gestured at Ryn. "Their primordial is standing right here."

And even if he should return to the Reaches in time to assemble help, there is no guarantee they would agree to gather, Arrackes added darkly, looking suddenly very tired.

Ester felt a stone sink into her gut at these words, and she turned to see Ryn—the ever-towering, strong Ryn—wince ever so slightly. It was true, after all. From what the dragon and her father had told them—long before they'd even made for Ysenden—what had been left of the dragon race had largely blamed their young primordial for bringing the destruction down on their heads when he'd saved Amherst and Elysia al'Dyor from the blades of the Kant, al'Behn, and Vostyk houses. It was madness, of course—the nobles had been looking for a reason to expand mankind's influence regardless—but the fact remained.

Ryn was—despite being the last primordial of the dragons—an outcast among his own kind, those few who had stayed loyal to him largely scattered across the realms.

"As I said, the Accord is not a perfect magic," Ester's father spoke up, his voice growing stronger where Ryn had been dealt a lowering blow. "But even with its imperfections, it remains our greatest shield against Sehranya's plans. Should she manage to form a wedge between any of our four races—should she break Aletha, or Ysenden, or eradicate the remaining dragons—then those lost lives would be as nothing compared to the risk of our collective kinds being wiped from the map."

I do not claim that the magics are entirely without merit, Magus. I merely am not of the same opinion as you that the advantages they provide outweigh the risk to my people—to both *my peoples.* Arrackes' fatigue was increasingly apparent, and Ester couldn't blame the dragon. His age aside, the High Chancellor had very suddenly been saddled with the news of Sehranya's return, the death of more than a hundred of his soldiers, and the responsibility of dealing with the Queen's already-established foothold in his lands.

And that wasn't even counting the subservience he was clearly working to show Ryn, which—even as she thought of it—Ester's father decided to turn to.

"Ryndean," the mage hissed, looking to the black dragon. "You cannot allow this. If we fail to establish the Accord…"

He let his concerns hang, trusting that Ester, Declan, and Ryn were aware of the possible repercussions. The dragon, however, said nothing for several seconds as he watched Arrackes with a frown on his face.

Unfortunately, I'm afraid there's not much for me to do here…

"But—!" Ester's father began, but it was Declan who cut him short with a shake of his head.

"Bonner, if I'm not mistaken, Ryn doesn't mean to imply he *won't* do anything. He means he *can't*." The younger man gestured to the council table standing empty behind the High Chancellor. "Even if he were to command Arrackes to tell the elves to join the Accord, it would mean nothing. The society is a republic, not an autocracy."

"The boy has the right of it, yr'Essel." as'ahRen spoke up again, moving to stand with crossed arms on the other side of the Chancellor's empty chair. "What's more—and I admit I'm hardly the most knowledgeable when it comes to your 'weaves'—at the end of the day the High Chancellor is not of the *er'endehn*. Would his assent to submit to the Accord even hold? Would you not need the agreement and binding of the council, rather?"

Bonner bit his cheek at this, considering.

"I'm not sure..." he admitted after a moment. "I would have to study the magics a bit more. I have to admit that when we crafted the spell, it never occurred to any of us that the High Chancellor of the *er'endhen* would ever in fact *not be* an *er'endehn*..."

Then it seems that settles the matter for the moment, at the very least. Arrackes promptly seized the opportunity to end the conversation, standing a little straighter. *I will not prohibit you from bringing up the Accord with the council, Magus. Should they deem it the correct course of action, I will bend to their will. I merely ask that you refrain from doing so until* after *we have dealt with the current situation in Erraven.*

Declan frowned at that. "All due respect, High Chancellor, but without your support—or at least that of the Lord Commander's—" he nodded pointedly to as'ahRen "—the council is unlikely to so much as consider binding themselves to the weave. It took us weeks for *some* of Colonel Syr'esh's command to not see our magics as anything more than foul, and that was with the support of the ay'ahSels and the colonel himself."

Then I suppose you have your work cut out for you, Declan Idrys, Arrackes said with a nod. *If the Accord of Four is indeed as pertinent to the survival of our world as you all deem it to be, I genuinely hope you find the means by which to convince the council.*

"And what if we managed to convince you...?" Declan asked tentatively.

Arrackes gave him a weary smile.

Then everything I know and love will have already burned to the ground, and there will be nothing left for me to lose regardless.

CHAPTER TWENTY-SEVEN

Loyalty is a complicated thing. It is—as are all aspects of intelligent psychology—a layered concept. Take a soldier—a common soldier—for example. Loyalty seems a simple enough concept to apply to this person. Loyalty to the crown. Loyalty to the country. Loyalty to military. In those terms, conflict is unlikely. What happens, however, when one adds other things to the mix? Loyalty to one's brothers in arms, or one's home, or one's family, even. What occurs, suddenly, when an order from the crown to which that common soldier is supposed to bend the knee challenges a sense of allegiance to something outside the common prevue?

After all, at the end of the day, what a person must be most loyal to is nothing less than their own conscience...

—*The Curse of Ego,* by author unknown, c. 450p.f.

ou play your part well," General Sureht Syr'esh said as he opened the door to his private offices, stepping inside before motioning for the figure following him to enter.

"I hardly think my own acting worthy of praise by comparison, General," the husky voice of Yl'ah Ryvus, the council's spymaster, answered in fluid elvish. *"As I understand it,* you've *been maintaining your masquerade for centuries now, after all..."*

Sureht grunted nondescriptly, closing the door again the moment the figure had stepped into the office. They looked around, the feminine features of their face twisting into a smile at the modest accoutrements that decorated the plain stone walls of the chamber, as though amused by the space.

It was a smile that made Sureht—former Lord Commander of Syr'hend before its fall—shiver in discomfort.

They had detoured for only a single stop after departing the council chambers, pausing at Yl'ah Ryvus' personal rooms momentarily to pick up a large package, a cloth bundle wrapped about something roughly the length and width of a man's thigh, now being held reverently in the figure's arms. Catching sight of the desk, however, they moved towards it without pause, depositing the hidden object so carefully upon the lacquered wood it might have been a newborn child.

"I admit I feared us discovered, when as'ahRen spoke to you directly," Sureht said, watching the form of Yl'ah Ryvus stand up straight to examine the room again. *"I hadn't realized you would be able to imitate her* voice *as well as her form."*

The figure dropped their gaze to smile at him directly, that same amusement lingering unpleasantly in eyes that were not theirs.

Then, with a wave of one hand over the heavy gold ring about the thumb of the other, everything about them changed.

Yl'ah Ryvus' tall, slender form shortened and broadened, becoming slightly hunched. The white hair cropped to her ears lengthened and darkened, becoming lank and greasy, and the sharp features of the dark elves paled and wrinkled. Within a few seconds, the spymaster was no more, replaced completely by an old, human man with long, limp grey hair.

Unfortunately, aside from the black-and-orange robes Sureht had pilfered for him days ago, Gonin Whist's insufferable smile was all that remained of the previous graceful form.

"You selected Ryvus for me specifically because she hardly ever saw fit to speak at such meetings." The old mage's natural voice was weaker and

crueler than the spymaster's. *"In that, you chose well. But my master is vigilant. Of late she has been experimenting with a variety of... uh... 'borrowed' magics. When physically changing one's entire appearance, it is only a small leap to adapting the inner workings of the body as well, vocal cords included."*

"As you say..." Sureht answered warily, looking the mage up and down. *"Will the dragons not sense this?"*

"Dragons are more limited creatures than you might think." Whist chuckled as he lifted one hand, showing off the ring still about one thumb. Whereas the jewelry had momentarily before been a heavy gold band, it was now almost black, and textured with sharp, cruel carvings. Observing them, Sureht—who knew nothing of magic—felt suddenly nauseous, like whatever spell was engraved into the ring was wicked enough to discourage even proximity to it.

"Dragon bone," the old mage answered the general's unasked question, turning his hand around and studying the thing for himself approvingly. *"Infinitely harder to come by than the common remains of man and elf. Allows for much more potent spellwork. You need not concern yourself with the High Chancellor and his 'primordial'."* Whist stated the title with a sneer. *"They are as blind to my presence now as they were in the council chambers, despite my appearance."*

"Be that as it may, I would prefer to see our business concluded sooner rather than later, mage," Sureht told the man, moving to stand on the other side of the desk from him to look down at the bundle of cloth. *"You said you had what I needed to conclude this charade. Show it to me."*

Whist smirked, but turned and reached for the cloth all the same.

"I must admit to curiosity, General," the old man said as he began unwrapping the object. *"When I was tasked with bringing about the end of your kind, I had not imagined to find myself such an influential ally."*

Sureht felt something squeeze at his heart at the question, but ignored it.

"There remains no such thing as 'my kind' anymore, mage," he said quietly, watching the man's hands work.

"But was it not my master who saw to that? I have to say I find your motives odd…"

Sureht swallowed, feeling his fists clench unbidden at his sides. *"Your Witch was only the beginning of the end. We are—*were, *rather—a people of war. We lived and died on the battlefield. If Sehranya was to be our destruction, then that would have been acceptable, terrible as such a close might have been. But no… It was what came after that ended the* er'endehn *of old, and we are better off joining our ancestors with the spirits than lingering as this pathetic echo of what we once were, cowering in a winged shadow…"*

"Two *winged shadows,"* Whist said with another smile, like he was basking in Sureht's fury. *"Your master has a master, now."*

"That beast is no master of mine," Sureht hissed.

The mage nodded this time, chuckling to himself. *"If you say so."*

Then he pulled the last of the wrappings away from the parcel, and Sureht had to forcefully stop himself from taking a step back at the sight of the thing.

Again, it wasn't the actual object that so sickened him. It was a skull, shaded the same near-black as the ring on Whist's thumb, and even to his untrained eye the general could tell it had once belonged to a dragon. It bore a long snout and large orifices where the eyes and ears should have been, and the clean ridges of curved fangs half the size of Sureht's finger would have been enough to go by alone. Separate from the whole, it might have been an impressive curiosity, if one to be disposed of before the High Chancellor realized such a thing was being kept within the walls of Ysenden.

Once more, however, it was the carvings that had nearly driven the general away from the desk.

In a mirrored pattern originating from a single, foul emblem chiseled into the crown of the skull, the markings poured outward. Not an inch of the bone was unblemished, down to the teeth themselves, and if he'd been brave enough to lift the thing Sureht suspected even the roof of the mouth would have been cut into. Like the ring, there was something about these symbols—these 'runes', he thought he'd once heard them called—that spoke of nothing but death and ill tidings to the general.

That was fine, though.

Death and ill tidings were exactly what Ysenden was in need of.

"This is it?" he asked after taking a moment to make sure his voice was steady, forcing himself not to look away from the carved dragon skull. *"This will be enough? It seems… small."*

Standing over the thing on the other side of the desk, Whist gave a dark laugh that was—for once—not the least bit amused.

"This will be enough," he assured Sureht, depositing the wraps beside the skull. *"It seems small because it is the skull of an infant beast, the only one the drey managed to drag away alive. I assure you, however, that it will not fail you."* He lifted his hand again to show off the ring once more as a reminder.

Sureht nodded slowly, not bothering to look up. *"And how do I activate it?"*

"As I instructed you before. Drench the sigil in blood—" Whist pointed to the larger emblem in the middle of the skull, taking obvious care not to touch the bone with his long finger *"—and it will awaken."*

"For how long?"

The old mage shrugged. *"Long enough. You have in your possession the only artifact of its kind, General. We did not exactly have the opportunity to test it."*

Sureht nodded again. *"Even a day or two would be sufficient, so long as the stage is set."*

"Ah, yes. To that end…" Whist reached into the pockets of Ryvus' robes, pulling out a small, square bottle that looked like it was filled

with water. *"The other thing you asked for."*

Without a word, Sureht held out his hand for the vial.

Whist relinquished it at once, smiling again as he did. *"I believe—as you say—this concludes our business, General. Place the skull as close to the center of the city as possible, and my master's weaves will do their part. We trust* you *to deal with the rest."*

"Your trust means nothing to me," Sureht growled, looking levelly at the man. *"Were this a different time and a different place, I would have struck your head from your shoulders the moment you showed your foul form to me, mage. I despise you. I despise you, your magic, and you spirit-cursed master. There is nearly nothing in this world I hope for more than to see you snuffed from existence."*

Whist shrugged, unperturbed by the menacing words. *"'Nearly', being the operative word. A common enemy will make allies of the strangest sorts. You might be surprised what kinds of friends my Queen has made, in these long years. You are not the only one to loathe the hand history has dealt you."*

Sureht felt like spitting at the old man, but held himself back. *"You have done your part. Now leave me, so that I might prepare for mine. When the time comes I will bury the skull in the middle sanctum, in the* yr'es, *and act from there."*

Whist bowed with mocking respect before turning and making for the door again. As he did, he waved his free hand over the dragon bone ring once again, and in the three steps it took to reach the room exit had transformed back into the tall, graceful figure of Yl'ah Ryvus.

He had just placed his once-again-feminine hand upon the handle when Sureht spoke up one last time, unable to help himself.

"Whist."

The mage looked over his shoulder, elven eyes almost politely expectant.

"What did you do with her?" the general asked, overcoming the

instinct screaming at him that he didn't want to know the answer. *"With the real General Ryvus?"*

The mage smiled cruelly. *"Dragons learn new forms through decades of observation and study. Our method is... more surgical."*

"Meaning what?"

"Meaning wearing another's actual flesh is easier than learning to recreate it."

And then, with that cryptic answer, Whist was out the door, letting it close behind him as he left, and leaving Sureht Syr'esh to fall heavily into the chair behind his desk, cursing the Witch, cursing the High Chancellor, and—most fervently of all—cursing himself.

CHAPTER TWENTY-EIGHT

"You've never lost a fight before, have you, lad? No... No, it doesn't seem so. Well, hear this: you are not the strongest. You are not the fastest. Chances are, you never will be. That's alright, though.

If you were the best, then what would there be left to learn?"

—CASSANDRA SERT, IRON WIND GUILDMASTER, TO A DEFEATED DECLAN IDRYS, C. 1057P.F.

Suffering from a nearly-constant case of deja vu was one of the stranger things Declan had ever experienced in his life. Odder still, the feeling of having been where he stood previously came not from his own memories, but rather from someone else's, adding to his muddled concentration. Despite everything—despite the cold breeze and the trees and the impenetrable grey of the now-darkening clouds that had ever-masked the sky since they'd left Ysenden two days prior—he kept seeing flashes of sunlight and a bright stone courtyard, like a ghostly scene interposed over the cleared patch of ground between the evergreens of the Vyr'esh that formed his *actual* surroundings.

Maybe it had something to do with the bare-chested elf ducking and weaving before Declan like dark water made solid, sword held by hilt and sheath at his back to solidify his handicap.

Seemingly impervious to the cold, Ciriak as'ahRen danced about the makeshift ring in silence as Declan did his best to strike the elf with the wooden practice sword the Lord Commander had surprised him with at the noon break their first day of the march, apparently having brought it along for just this purpose. It was their fourth time sparring like this, now, and the relative quiet of the "match" was echoed by the spectators, a good number of elves on break from their duties, along with Ryn, Bonner, and Ester as always. Lysiat, too, was present—she and her brothers having been the only ones of Colonel Syr'esh's command allowed to accompany the army after their request for exception had been allowed by as'ahRen himself—but Aliek and Tesied were either on sentry duty or helping the cooks distribute the march's evening meal.

Slashing horizontally at the Lord Commander's bare chest, Declan was unsurprised when the wooden blade was dodged with less than an inch of space between weapon and scarred skin. Unperturbed, he turned the cut into a spinning kick, hoping to catch his opponent in the gut since the elf had leaned back to avoid the blow, exposing his midriff. as'ahRen, of course, was far too quick for him, and twisted away so that Declan's boot caught only air. There would have been a time where such a miss might have left him flat-footed, but even the few spare weeks in Lysiat's care had carved Declan into a different kind of fighter, and he landed balanced even as his sword led the way again.

It didn't hurt, too, that Bonner had kept to his word and allowed him to start using a quarter of his corpomancy proficiency even in training, now.

Declan might have been mistaken, but he thought he caught a few mutterings of surprise from among the observing *er'endehn*, and he could just imagine Lysiat forcing down a smirk of pride from where she was seated with Ester, their backs to the trunk of a young pine tree. Ignoring it all, he kept after the Lord Commander, not letting up despite knowing it would take a miracle to land so much as a single blow on the elf. Ciriak as'ahRen, unsurprisingly, had proven himself a duelist of an ability unlike Declan had ever seen.

And that was without ever having actually *drawn his sword.*

It wasn't just the clear skill and discipline of the *er'endehn* that had been drilled into the Lord Commander as harshly as every dark elf. It wasn't just his body, carved—despite his age—into a lithe sculpture of corded muscle that rippled beneath countless scars with every motion. as'ahRen had something more, more even than Lysiat, and *far* more than Cassandra Sert had possessed. His eyes flew over Declan what felt like a dozen times a second, taking him in with a concentration that seemed both natural and yet acutely deliberate. His every move was never merely a response to Declan's actions, but rather a preparation for the next, like the elf could read the motions of the wooden sword two or three strikes ahead of time based purely on his opponent's stance and initiating blows. It felt, to Declan, like the Lord Commander never approached their practices as a mere combatant in a common dual, but rather as a general might treat a war, planning every decision with contingencies upon contingencies, until his enemy was rarely left with any surprises to offer.

It was at once disheartening and exhilarating to behold.

I've still got a long, long way to go, Declan thought to himself—not even for the first time in that single fight—going for a straight stab at as'ahRen's neck that he turned into a diagonal slash up at the side of the elf's head.

The Lord Commander dropped out from under it with the same elegance a tactful courtier might bow before a king.

For another ten minutes or so they kept on like that, going non-stop, Declan chasing the aged officer around their cleared circle in silence other than the panting sounds of his own breaths. Eventually even the Lord Commander started to breathe heavily along with him, and Declan drove himself harder, seeking to take advantage of the elf's fatigue if he could. He was careful not to let his slashes and cuts go wild, but he pressed them just the same, seeking more speed, more strength behind each blow. Even if he kept his promise to Bonner not to draw too much magic into his body, he could still push his limbs themselves to their limits. Declan swore to himself, as as'ahRen jerked his head to whip the sweat from his eyes, that he wouldn't stop until the elf gave up a point or *he* was on the ground gasping for—

Clack! WHAM!

As Declan's sword came down in a vertical arc, the Lord Commander brought his own weapon out from behind his back at long last, still holding it by the neck of its sheath as he snapped it upward. Declan's blade caught in the angle of the handle and cross-guard, but before he could even begin to retract it as'ahRen had moved to one side, dragging the wooden sword down and outward with him. As Declan's outstretched arm continued to descend, the Lord Commander brought his free hand up to take him by the back of the neck, then promptly drove a knee up into his gut. The air exploded out of Declan's lungs in a rush as he bent double.

And then he was flying, the elf—in a movement only possible by a body that possessed both immense strength *and* flexibility—twisting to flip him over the lifted knee and slam him to his back on the ground.

Declan coughed and wheezed, his whole body spasming under the shock of the impact as he lay on the frozen grass. Bonner had been kind enough to clear the snow and pine needles for their bout, but Declan wasn't sure he was grateful now, lying on the hard-packed earth. His vision spun, and he felt the weave of suffusion slip away as he lost himself for a moment, trying to regain his bearings.

When the dim glow of the canopy above finally stopped turning, he found himself looking up into a dark, bearded face that was nodding in what might have been approval.

"I've decided: you are quiet the terror for a human, Idrys," the Lord

Commander praised him, looking away just long enough to accept a shirt as an attendant—a small, slender elf woman in the white armor of the Chancellor's Guard—ran it over to him from the sidelines. "You might even make a match for some of our trainees, with skills like that."

"Y-you start training as soon as your kind can l-lift a sword," Declan croaked, unwilling to get up just yet. Somehow he'd managed to hold onto his practice weapon, and he brought the wooden blade shakily up in a mock salute to the Lord Commander. "W-wouldn't that make your trainees ten years old or s-so?"

as'ahRen smirked at him, having handed his sheathed weapon to his attendant so he could pull the shirt on.

"The average starting age is six, but you can do better than that." He looked to the woman at his side as he began lacing up the collar of the shirt. "What do you think, Mysat? Could Declan handle himself against a ten-year-old *er'endehn*?"

In answer, of course, the Guard—who Declan thought was a Major if he was judging the patterns in the gold accents of her armor correctly—stared at her superior blankly.

"Ah, right," as'ahRen muttered, looking a little abashed. "It's been so long since I've had the opportunity to speak common that I'm getting carried away."

As Declan finally decided to give sitting up a shot, the Lord Commander repeated the question in elvish, receiving a prompt—if flat—reply, which got a laugh out of the older elf.

"Mysat says that—"

"That I would do better starting with the unarmed infants," Declan finished for the Lord Commander, grunting as he used his practice blade to leverage himself to his feet. "Yes, I understood that." He turned and shot the petite major a glare that wasn't so much as acknowledged. "Any minute we haven't had for training, Ryn and Bonner have been forcing me to spend on your tongue these last five days, in case we get separated during the battle. Pleasantly, thus far I have only had the opportunity to better understand the insults that have been thrown my way."

"Oh she means nothing by it," as'ahRen told him, taking the sword from "Mysat" again and indicating that she was dismissed with a nod. As the major bowed and departed again, the Lord Commander started binding the weapon back to his belt, where it always hung unless they were sparring. "If anything I expect she's just loathe to give you credit. You have a knack for the blade I think most of my soldiers find alarming, given your… uh… heritage." He looked Declan up and down pointedly.

I would remind you that it was that 'heritage' that led you to request these fights in the first place, Lord Commander.

Declan and as'ahRen both looked around to see Ryn, Bonner, Ester, and Lysiat approaching together from the side of the clearing opposite where Major Mysat had departed. The commander looked like she was working hard not to beam as brightly as the yr'Essels both were, leaving only the dragon to take Declan in with a more-reasoned pride.

That was well fought. Even at a quarter of your suffusion, you got close a few times, I think.

Beside Declan, as'ahRen frowned.

"'A quarter of his suffusion'?" he echoed questioningly.

It made sense, Declan, realized, that the Lord Commander wouldn't know. Their last three matches—the midday and evening breaks of the previous day's march, as well as their earlier noon bout—had always had the old elf getting swept away on officer's business the moment their sparring was at an end. This afternoon, however, the army had halted early once they'd come within two miles of Erraven—not wanting their assault on the city to follow up a full two days at double-pace without reprieve—allowing as'ahRen to linger a little longer.

It was, surprisingly, Lysiat who answered the Lord Commander's question, and Declan's steadily-improving grasp of the tongue allowed him to catch most of it.

"It's my understanding that Declan has been limited by his teacher on how much he can strengthen himself with magic," she told the Lord Commander, motioning to Bonner as she did. *"For the purposes of training his body."*

The Lord Commander looked impressed, turning to Declan again. "I see. So that was hardly the best you had. Part of me wants to demand a rematch, now."

"Perhaps another time, as'ahRen," Bonner cut in before Declan could fervently agree on the spot. "I don't believe either of you has supped, and the evening grows late. I've no doubt the council will want to review our battle plan once again before we march at dawn."

"Bah," the Lord Commander grumbled in answer, though he did glance guiltily to the north, where the army proper lay beyond the scattered elves who'd lingered after the fight was done, likely hoping for another bout. "They can revisit it as much as they like, but unless our information changes there's nothing to adapt. The strategy was decided within the hour of Sen'Hev returning to Ysenden. The lot of them just want to feel self-important by spinning their wheels."

Declan and the others had been present for General Sen'Hev's account, the evening before their departure, so it was hard to disagree with the Lord Commander. She'd reported nothing overtly alarming, but it had still been a blow to every member of the council present—the spymaster Ryven had made her excuses through Syr'esh, as she'd apparently already immersed herself into the investigation of the Ysenden populace—that Erraven had indeed been overrun by Sehranya's wights. Sen'Hev had told them it had been trickier than expected to confirm at first, because the draugr appeared to have had a need to hide themselves woven into their Purpose. Even from up close the abandoned city had seemed like little more than an empty shell, likely hardly threatening to the exiles who'd flocked to the ancient seat of power with the expectations of starting life anew free of Ysenden's influence. Only when one of Sen'Hev's quickest lookouts had volunteered to approach the city more openly, in fact, had the dark elves confirmed the presence of the undead.

Then, however, it had been established without doubt when several hundred of the creatures had come pouring out of the stone and rubble to give chase to the scout, hounding the unit as a whole for more than a dozen miles before the general and her "eyes", as she called them, had put enough distance between them to shake the draugr.

"Be that as it may," Bonner responded diplomatically, "while *you* can afford to irritate the council, I'm afraid we cannot. You and Arrackes have left us with little option to plead our case to them directly, once this matter of Erraven is handled, so we cannot allow ourselves to fall out of grace with the generals."

Declan saw Ester leaning over to translate for Lysiat as the Lord Commander snorted at this.

"I would concern myself first and foremost with *obtaining* their grace before worrying about falling out of it, Magus." He motioned northward, towards the camp. "But as you wish. Lead the way, and let us see if my slinking off to trade blows with Idrys has risked your so-'stellar' reputation."

"Did we trade blows?" Declan asked with a chuckle, reaching back to brush dirt off the rear off his pants. "I seem to recall that match being less exciting than that."

as'ahRen smirked at him as Bonner indeed started making for the trees, followed closely by Ester and Lysiat. "I'm giving you credit for the attempt, boy. Take it or leave it."

"I'll take it!" Declan declared at once, earning a snort of laughter from Ryn as the three of them fell in behind the two women.

It wasn't a far walk to the encampment—Major Mysat had looked ready to rip the Lord Commander's head off when he'd suggested they hike to find a quieter spot outside the sentry ring—and even less time before the lights of the base were visible through the trees. Cresting a steep hill that had Declan, Ryn, and Bonner using stones and passing trunks to summit, the moonwing lanterns that supplemented the fading grey of the sun through the trees above came into view first, and half a minute later the lot of them had entered the camp proper and the bustle and boil that accompanied it. As ever, even the lowest ranked among the elves moved with impressive efficiency in and around each other, pitching tents, starting up the collapsible braziers to provide more light, and cooking and handing out the supper rations from beneath large, plain awnings of black cloth. It said something about the effectiveness and ability of the *er'endehn* that Declan didn't notice much difference between this war camp and the forward base that had hosted Colonel Syr'esh's two hundred men along the south edge of the Vyr'esh, weeks ago now.

Except, of course, for one stark contrast:

The sheer size of the place.

As they crossed through the alleys formed by the hundreds on hundreds of tents, whole contingents of soldiers on patrol split to let them through. It seemed, too, that with every passing minute the darkness beneath the trees was being chased further and further away, because where Syr'esh's command had borne dozens of braziers, the host around them was setting alight their *thousands*. The noise of the place was astonishing, too, the vastness of the woods not enough to swallow the shouts and the thumps of booted feet, and after a minute of walking and dodging moving elves, Declan could no longer look in any direction without seeing a sea of moving soldiers and erected tent tops. It was fortunate, actually, that it was their third day marching with Ysenden's army.

When they'd first laid eyes on the thirty thousand *er'endehn*, gathered and waiting in the massive ring of stone that had surrounded the *yr'es* of the city's middle sanctum, even Ryn had muttered a word of awe, while Bonner, Ester, and Declan had all stared in open amazement.

"*Lord Commander!*"

If the shouted greetings of the sentries a few minutes later had not informed Declan they'd arrived at their destination, the now-familiar shapes of the general's pavilions would certainly have done the trick. While only as subtly ornate as Syr'esh's had been, the tents were each about a half-again as large as the colonel's, and arranged in a wide, circular pattern around the largest swath of relatively-flat ground the soldiers had been able to find. Even then, however, they could not avoid the forest entirely, because a tree that had to be some thirty feet wide towered up from one side of the inner ring. As they passed through the dense sentry line and between the general's quarters, though, it was not this titanous evergreen that Declan and the others kept their attention on, having all of them now spent too long within the Vyr'esh to be much astonished by even this colossal specimen.

Rather, it was the High Chancelor's pavilion that everyone couldn't help but take in, no matter how many times they had done so before.

To call the space Arrackes' alone, of course, would have been unfair. While it did indeed house the dragon's sleeping and personal "chambers", it was also the host to the council's traveling war room, its massive partition forming the body of the three-part tent. As a result, the pavilion loomed larger and broader than that of any three generals' combined, though the gold gilding on black was still of the typical *er'endehn* subtlety. The only extra adornment, in fact, came in the form of the hammered brass emblem—about the size of Declan's body—that crested the peak of the center section, the sword and bow of Ysenden glimmering brightly in the growing light of the camp's fires.

Another dozen sentries—dressed this time in the white-and-gold of the Chancellor's Guard—saluted as'ahRen as the Lord Commander took the lead at last, passing Ester and Lysiat to wave off the soldier who'd stepped towards the massive entrance flaps of Arrackes' pavilion the moment they'd approached. Closing the last few yards, Declan started to make out the sounds of heated discussion from within, and when as'ahRen pulled open to lead the way inside, the voices rose proportionately.

An additional five days of near-nonstop lessons in the *er'endehn* tongue had indeed improved Declan's grasp of the language, but not so much that he could deduce anything valuable from the jumbled quips and arguments that filled the room the lot of them stepped into after the Lord Commander. The space was massive for a tent—reminding Declan of the circuses that popped up seasonally here and there throughout Aletha—with a lit brazier in each corner of the mat-covered floor to illuminate the dark interior. A trio of long, foot-thick struts of wood formed a central support, holding up the canvas high above them to jut through a hole out of which the smoke from the fires was being swiftly carried. In the middle of the space, around these posts, a circular table comprised of four rounded sections was covered in what looked like every map and architectural sketch Ysenden had held in its archives, ranging from altitude breakdowns to drawings Declan knew to be Erraven itself, both before and after its fall.

And, of course, over and around this gathering of information, the generals themselves stood.

It had taken some time—usually in the midst of his language lessons—but Declan had eventually learned the names of the council members by heart, and recognized most of the faces that turned to them as they stepped into the tent. Lessan Sen'Hev, the scout commander, was easily distinguished by her scowl, as was old Beh'lys Hayle, master of records, who had accompanied them to ensure the safety of the very documents now lain about the table. A few were missing—Sureht Syr'esh and the spymaster, Yl'ah Ryvus, were hunting for traitors in Ysenden, and the master of city development, May'lek ed'Vyn, had had duties to maintain—but for the most part all the rest were gathered, their expressions at the sight of the arriving Lord Commander ranging from frustration to placidity to relief. Sylak Ehst, commander of the archery divisions. Kest Dahn'Ys, responsible for provisions and sustenance. Even Kanon Vets, master of the medical and relief contingents, was present, having entrusted his hospital ward in the city to a handful of capable seconds.

And, black-red horns rising above all of them, Arrackes stood leaning over the closest part of the table with his back to all, head moving steadily left to right while he took in the maps for what Declan knew had to have been the hundredth time.

"General Sen'Hev, has there been any news?"

Declan barely caught as'ahRen's words, the Lord General's voice raised to be heard over the cacophony of the council as he strode forward. At the question, those officers who hadn't yet noticed their arrival looked around, and the arguments settled at once. As the scout commander turned to her superior to answer, Lysiat held Declan and the others back with a raised arm, motioning with a sign and a slight shake of her head that they shouldn't approach further without permission.

"*None, Lord Commander.*" General Sen'Hev's answer felt almost too-loud in the sudden quiet of the pavilion. "*No movement.*"

as'ahRen sighed, coming to a stop at the edge of the gathered generals, and Declan's still-limited understanding finally failed him when the elf answered even as he raised a hand to rub at his temples.

Fortunately, Ester was quick on stepping back to translate for him, as was her habit.

"Then would someone care to explain to me what the meaning is behind this uproar?" the Lord General had responded. *"We could practically hear*

the lot of you shouting at each other from the edge of camp. If there have been no developments, why are we gathering to debate once again?"

There was a moment of uncomfortable silence at this, with a few of the generals—most among those of Erraven blood, unsurprisingly—glancing at each other across the room.

Some are still not satisfied with the current battle plan, Arrackes at last spoke up, turning around as he did, the tinge of impatience in the old dragon's voice speaking to the fact that he, too, was tiring of what had become a nightly event since leaving Ysenden. *There are continued concerns of 'needless disturbance'.*

Had Declan thought it not wholly inappropriate, he would have rolled his eyes right along with Bonner, then, the mage never having been much for decorum. It was the same song and dance they'd played along to every time they met, with undoubtedly similar players involved yet again. Sure enough, Beh'lys Hayle seemed particularly unwilling to meet the Lord Commander's frown in that moment, apparently very suddenly taken with an outline of what Declan thought was the tree density around the Erraven ruins.

"How surprising," as'ahRen said dryly, deciding to give up on the old records keeper in favor of looking around at the rest of the generals. *"And disappointing. We march at dawn, and the great council of Ysenden is still bickering about old bones we won't even be seeing."*

"You can't know that." Useal Tehsts, the general in charge of overseeing the army trainees, was tight-lipped as she responded to this. *"We should not be assuming the draugr will come to us. If we are forced to take the city—"*

"We won't *be,"* the Lord Commander cut the woman off with a sharp look. *"We have said so a hundred times, and I tire of this insubordination."*

"According to the magus!" General Hayle had finally found his voice, seizing on the opportunity to glare at Bonner instead of either of his

superiors. *"According to his promises that this 'Purpose' of the undead cannot be changed. I still say we have misplaced our faith, if we are trusting in his words!"*

"A Purpose cannot *be changed,"* Bonner snarled in answer. *"It is a self-sustaining weave, just as much as a fireball or a blade of wind might be. To change it, one must extinguish such a spell and replace it with another, and we* all *here know, hopefully, what happens when a Purpose is removed from its host."*

A few of the younger generals—who had likely never witnessed the black fire that consumed the draugr in their final death—frowned ever so slightly, but before anyone could say more, Arrackes stepped in once again.

You begin to test my patience, General Hayle, the dragon growled, getting the old elf to tense and turn towards his Chancellor nervously. *By constantly questioning Bonner yr'Essel's word, you constantly question* mine. *Because I do not share the blood of the* er'endehn *I grant great leeway to this council—far greater than any in my position have before—but I* am *your High Chancellor by choice of the people, and my decision on this matter is final. We will follow the battle plan as it has been decided: surround the city, concentrating most heavily on the points of weakness, and let the wights come to us.*

"The fallen walls and the gates will require the most of our attention," as'ahRen agreed, splitting the crowded generals as he moved to approach the table, coming to a stop over it and pointing with a finger at the very map Arrackes had just been surveying. *"Sen'Hev and her scouts were pursued from the north-east entrance of the city, so we can assume to face heavy resistance there, which is why Master Ryndean and his companions will be supporting the High Chancellor and I at that point."*

In his mind's eye, Declan followed along with the plan, having seen the maps enough himself to have them practically committed to memory. Erraven was—or had been, rather—a city built as a perfect square, demonstrating the precision of the *er'endehn* in a different way to Ysenden's breathtaking design. The corners of the great walls that had surrounded the metropolis each pointed along a cardinal direction, originally broken up only by the massive, rising northeast and southwest gates that had looked impressive even in the sketches and more detailed maps Beh'lys Hayle had pulled for them all. There were other cracks in the defenses, now, the proud stonework having split and crumbled in several places after centuries without care, but Declan had to agree that the entrances would be the most likely points of egress, the timber of the gates having rotted away completely, according to the scouts.

Once the city is encircled wide, we will coordinate our approach together. Arrackes was continuing his summary, sounding tired of repeating the plan. *The draugr* will *come to us. We won't have to set foot within Erraven itself, you have my word.*

No one said anything for a moment, after this, not even the most outspoken of the generals looking like they wanted to disagree when the High Chancellor had just sworn on his honor. After a few seconds, Ester started to look around a little uncomfortably.

When she spoke, it was a simple enough question for Declan to follow on his own.

"*Now it's just a matter of* how *they'll come to us, isn't it…?*"

◆

The three ay'ahSel siblings together came to raise Declan and the others the following morning, rousing them an hour or so before the first light of the sun could be made out through the Vyr'esh. Declan started awake when Aliek pulled open the flap of the tent he shared with Ryn and Bonner, having slept fitfully despite the comfortable cot the dark elves had provided. He could have blamed the fact that he had gone to bed fully-dressed—donning everything he would need on the march but his actual armor in case they were attacked in the night—but the reality was it was nerves that had kept him tossing and turning from dusk to the pre-dawn, just as it was nerves that had him wide awake and leaping up at Aliek's waking word despite the lack of rest. Reaching down for the sword laying atop his folded furs and leathers on the floor—within easy reach of the bed—Declan had his weapon buckled on and his cuirass thrown over his head as Ryn or Bonner only just started to shake themselves awake.

Before tying the armor into place, though, Declan made sure—for the first of what would be a hundred times that morning—that his firestone still hung from the thong about his neck.

He had seen battle before, technically. Uprisings and rebellions the Iron Wind and the mercenary guilds had sometimes been called on to help quench, often in the parts of Viridian furthest from the al'Dyor's guiding hand. Sometimes, too, bandit camps formed large enough threats that they required a similar deployment to eradicate to the crown's satisfaction—or whatever other influential party had hired the sellswords of Aletha.

Still... The forces dispatched in those conflicts had only ever numbered in the hundreds at most...

Once he'd finished donning his leathers, Declan excused himself from the tent, stepping outside into the burning glow of the camp. Despite the lack of sun, the whole world beneath the trees glowed a somber orange, flickering here and there as groups of soldiers swept by the braziers as the army came awake. The building bustle had Declan amazed once again, and his worry redoubled as he took it all in.

A thousand wights. That's what they were facing...

Compared to the fifteen thousand spread out before him now, it seemed easy to consider the battle one of insignificant odds, but Declan knew better than that. Surrounding the city to make sure none of the undead were missed would spread the army thin, at least initially, and even if that wasn't the case the *best* possible outcome of the day would be that hundreds would die that morning, with no other way around it. Letting Ryn—and Arrackes, for that matter—torch the ruins from above had been an idea broached again in private, but with the internal peace of the dark elves teetering like a lit match on a keg of oil, it hadn't taken much to convince Declan the fallout of such a blatant disregard for the history of Erraven would be greater and far longer lasting than the deaths of the soldiers who would fall that day. It was infuriating, but unsurprising, at least once he'd wrapped his head around the fact that the dark elves—despite all their semblance of virtues and skill on the battlefield—played the game of politics just as deftly as the nobles of the Alethan courts.

"Still… You'd think a thousand bloody undead on their doorstep would get them to cool their heads a bit, wouldn't you?" Declan muttered, reaching up absently as he did to touch the firestone hanging over his leather breastplate again.

"Speak up, Declan. It's too early for mumbling."

At the groggy voice, Declan turned around in time to see Ester climbing out of the smaller tent nearby she had been sharing with Lysiat. The commander herself was standing with her brothers off to one side, talking quietly amongst themselves. They had been tasked by the Lord Commander with supporting Declan and the others that day, and it made him feel a little better knowing the ay'ahSels would be close by. He doubted much of anything would go wrong with Ryn, Bonner, and Arrackes in their main group, not to mention as'ahRen and his own growing power.

Still… The lives of his friends and companions weren't the ones Declan was worried about.

"It's not worth saying it out loud," he told the half-elf once Ester had come to stand beside him, looking her up and down as she surveyed the camp just as he had. She sported the same light leathers that had been gifted to her after the escape from the Mother's Tears, but in addition to her elven sword—a bit thinner and lighter than Declan's—and the gilded black bow and arrows slung across her back and hips respectively, she was also carrying a narrow helm of a familiar design under one arm, its long black plume trailing almost to the ground behind her.

"Where did you get that?" he asked, pointing to the helmet.

"Oh. Lysiat gave it to me." Ester glanced down at the armor absently before returning to scrutinize the encampment. "I'm sure Aliek or Tesied could find you a spare as well, if you want it."

"I'll ask," Declan agreed with a nod, following her gaze to take in the bustle once more. For a little while they stood like that, side by side, listening to the movement of the elves and Bonner's grumbled curses at the earliness of the hour from behind them. Eventually, though, Declan got tired of the silence.

"Are you ready for this?" he asked quietly.

Ester gave a low laugh.

"Gods above, no. But who can *really* be ready for this?"

"Fair point." Declan grimaced. "I was just thinking that even with the odds in our favor, this isn't going to be painless. If the wights attack the line as spread out as they can, casualties will be minimized, but if they only come out the gates or even one or two other places, we're going to be in for a fight until the army can collapse on the skirmishes."

Ester nodded slowly. "People are going to die," she said sadly, shoulders sinking a little. "So many people… Truthfully, it's a little hard to imagine, standing here now…"

"It won't be real until after." Declan was reminded then, that this was likely to be Ester's first *true* battle. "When you're standing among the fallen, keep your head, just like you would in the fight itself. There'll still be lives that can be saved, even after it's all said and done. Especially with your father around."

Ester nodded again. After another few seconds of silence, she turned to look at him.

"Don't do anything stupid, okay?"

Declan snorted. "Me? Never. You must be confusing me with someone else."

Without looking at her he could tell the woman was glaring at him, but that was the moment Ryn and Bonner decided to make their opportune appearance, ducking out from under the tent with a rustle of canvas.

"Ready, you lot?" Bonner asked as Declan and Ester turned to the pair. He was—as ever—unchanged from his everyday appearance, sporting nothing more than his multicolored robe and leather boots despite the frigid winter air. Even his hood was pulled back, revealing his bald head and braided beard, complete with a tense smile that made it seem like he was doing his best to inject his usual cheer into the morning. At his side, Ryn too was as he always was, black scales and golden eyes matching well with the hilt of the massive obsidian sword slung across his back, gilded in the same colors.

Before Declan or Ester could answer, footsteps at their back told them the ay'ahSels were approaching.

"Good, you're all up," Lysiat said tersely, face once more the stony mask of *er'endehn*, matching Aliek's and even Tesied's for once. *"Come. They're waiting for us."*

Wait. Ryn was looking around. *Orsik and Eyera. Where are they?*

Declan frowned at this question, turning himself. It wasn't uncommon for the warg to slink away through the trees in search of their breakfast, but now that he thought about it, it was far earlier than when they usually went hunting, making their absence strange.

It was Ester who offered them the surprising answer.

"They're already with the Lord Commander," she answered in common, dipping her head southward. "He asked me if he could borrow them last night?"

"He did?" Declan and Bonner asked together, mutually surprised.

Ester shrugged and nodded. "Apparently he was curious, so I introduced them and told him they could be bribed with meat."

"Ooooh I hope that didn't go poorly," Bonner muttered, brow creased in concern as he looked to Lysiat and switched into elvish. "*Commander, lead the way. And let's pray the Lord Commander still has both his hands when we get there...*"

The ay'ahSels glanced at each other in confusion at this, but did as they were told, turning to cut a clean line along the closest of the alleys, Lysiat with her twin swords at the lead, Aliek and Tesied with spears over mirrored shoulders right behind her.

It took them less than a minute to reach the southwest edge of the camp, the head of the march. Their nightly tents had been pitched close to the front line deliberately every evening, which—according to Lysiat—could be considered an honor, an acknowledgment of their ability. Only the most capable officers and their contingents formed the forward camp, trusted as they were to provide the greatest immediate defense in case of attack from the most likely direction of enemy assault.

Personally, Declan couldn't help but suspect there were some among the council hoping the wights would have fallen on them all in their sleep, but he had never voiced it.

Breaking away from the last of the tents, the relative quiet the seven of them stepped into after the surging activity of the battle preparations was almost eerie. The units who had the furthest to travel—around to encircle the far side of Erraven—were already lined up and awaiting their marching orders, and in the deepening dark of the failing braziers at their backs the elves seemed more like statues among the trees than any living thing. Indeed, as they pressed through the ranks, Declan touched his firestone again and summoned up a light with a thought, discomforted by the stillness of their surroundings. Had this been an army of men—even the most highly trained of the Vigil—the fidgeting and prayers to the Mother and Her Graces would have born with them a sense of need, of a desire to see the coming day through.

The *er'endehn*, instead, stood so calmly it was like each of them assumed they were going to die, and had no qualms with that concept.

Once again, Declan couldn't help but shake his head in amazement at the fortitude.

Not half a minute later, and deeper still into the night, they passed through the last of the waiting ranks, reaching the forward line in truth. Declan was relieved, as the gentle glow of his firestone brought a warmth to the waiting scene, to see that only a portion of the council was gathered here, the rest of them likely already dispatched to their own commands. Arrackes stood tallest in a tight-knit circle of the generals, listening to the scout master Sen'Hev speaking quietly at his left. To his right, as'ahRen stood in rapt attention, arms crossed as he listened.

Declan almost chuckled aloud when he found himself indeed breathing the slightest bit easier once he saw that the Lord Commander was, in fact, in one piece, and that despite the two large, white-and-grey shapes seated patiently on either side of the gathered circle.

"Eyera," Ester called gently as they approached, earning the attention of both wargs. "Eyera, come."

With a light bark of delight the beasts both came bounding over, the female to Ester, Orsik to Declan as he, too, summoned the male to himself. They bumped heads into expectant hands, pushing for rubs, which were doled out happily while Arrackes, as'ahRen, and the generals all looked around.

Ah, there you are. The High Chancellor was the one to speak first, and Declan looked up from Orsik's black eyes to see the old dragon approaching them. *I should thank you for lending them to us. I had my doubts, but I have to admit I felt better having them nearby.*

"You did?" Declan asked, not following.

It was the Lord Commander who answered, stepping between the generals too to nod a greeting to the group.

"You've got a smart pair of animals, there," he said in common, gesturing to the warg. "Master Ryndean told us we couldn't trust a dragon's senses when it came to the wights, so I thought a more conventional means of detection might come in handy."

Ah, Ryn sounded like he was the first to understand. *Between their noses and your ears, the draugr wouldn't be able to get too close without everyone being warned.*

Precisely, Arrackes said with a nod. *Wights can carry a complex Purpose. We know they'll leave the ruins when we advance, but there's no reason they couldn't have left earlier if forewarned of our approach. Even if Syr'esh and Ryvus have weeded out the treacherous elements from the city by the time we get back to Ysenden, we can't assume there isn't an agent among us, or in Erraven and capable of spying on us even now.*

"We know something about that, yes," Declan muttered, recalling the prickling awareness of Sehranya's eye as he kept petting Orsik between the ears. "Any news on that front? You were speaking with Sen'Hev when we arrived, it looked like?" He looked pointedly to the general, whose ever-present frown—already likely weighted at being left out of the conversation—only deepened when he looked at her.

"None." as'ahRen was studying the glowing firestone about Declan's neck with mild interest as he answered. "Just confirming. There's been no motion from within the city since she planted her forward scouts yesterday morning. They can't get too close, obviously, but they're near enough to make that call."

"That's only a good thing," Bonner said solemnly. "At the very least, even if there's *more* than the thousand wights waiting for us, they haven't been reinforced in the last day."

We were thinking much the same thing, Arrackes agreed, gesturing with a clawed hand to the soldiers waiting at their backs. *And we were just about to deploy the first wave when you arrived. They will have a half-hour start, which should have them in position around the south and west corners of Erraven by the time we reach our own.*

We're still taking the northeast gate? Ryn asked.

"We are," the Lord Commander confirmed with a nod. "And if it's all the same to you, Master Ryndean, we would have you all in the front line. We're expecting the heaviest assault on our position, particularly if the wights notice you and the High Chancellor. The advantage your group would be able to lend us might be lifesaving."

Ryn looked around at the others in question, receiving nods from Declan, Bonner, and Ester all at once.

We will go where you tell as, as'ahRen, Ryn told the old elf, turning back to him. *I only wish Arrackes and I could be of greater use, in these circumstances.*

The Vyr'esh has grown right up to the walls of the city, Arrackes explained, not for the first time. *I might be able to maneuver through the trees in my natural form, but you would have trouble, Ryndean.*

And dragonfire risks setting the whole of the forest ablaze, yes, Ryn finished for the lesser dragon, waving the rest of his reasoning away. *I am aware.* Then, though, his tone grew more serious. *If it's all the same to you and your council, I would tell you not to let us delay this day's events on our part any longer. See to your soldiers, High Chancellor.*

Arrackes smiled slightly, then dipped his head in respect.

Ciriak, call for the march, he said without looking away from his primordial. *The rest of you, start gathering your contingents. Second deployment is in thirty minutes.*

As one Sen'Hev and the other remaining generals departed to their duties, slipping by Declan and the others to make through the soldiers towards the camp again. In the end, only the Lord Commander remained by Arrackes, and as he watched Declan saw as'ahRen reach behind his back to pull out a long, black horn, polished to a glimmering sheen in the light of the firestone. Taking a deep breath, the old elf brought it to his lips, then blew out a long, low note that rang more quietly than Declan had expected, rumbling like the low wash of a distant sea.

"*Brruuuuurrrrrr!*"

To the ears of the *er'endehn*, of course, it was loud enough to hear for miles.

Thump. Thump. Thump. Thump.

With alarming precision and the brief shiver of the frozen forest floor beneath them with every step, the first wave began to move, splitting around Declan and the others to march either west or south with the intent to surround the city. The departure was swift even in the dark, and it wasn't more than three of four minutes before the thudding of boots—impossible to keep quiet by so many, even for the elves—vanished into the trees.

After that, it was only a matter of waiting.

It wasn't long before the rest of the contingents began to file up in replacement of the recently deployed, the soldiers arriving in scattered groups to form into their units without more than a quiet word from the lesser officers. Declan took advantage to ask the ay'ahSels—in still-broken elvish—after a helmet to compliment his leathers, but aside from that minor interruption they all stood and watched in relative silence as the army gathered. Even when Aliek returned from a brief departure to hand Declan a helm, the fit of the thing was too perfect to add much distraction after he'd pulled it on, feeling the black plume slip down his back as he cinched it tight under his chin. Twisting his head this way and that, Declan found his field of vision satisfactory, and he looked down as he pulled the blade at his hip half out of its sheath to study his reflection in the obsidian. Dark blue eyes set over a beard he hadn't trimmed in weeks stared at him through the slots of the black-and-gold armor, and he snorted in amused disbelief before slipping the sword back into place.

If you'd told me I'd be standing here one day..., he thought to himself, resuming his studying of the arriving army.

Within twenty minutes the rest of the elves had gathered, leaving the camp beyond the trees absent of all but General Vets and his medical corps, along with a hundred or so sentries to act as lookouts until the battle was through. Another brief wait—and one more quick gathering by Arrackes, as'ahRen, and the remaining generals—and a silent nod was exchanged between the High Chancellor and his Lord Commander.

"Here we go..." Declan heard Ester mutter from beside him, and for a brief instant he felt her hand take his forearm below the elbow, squeezing just tight enough to be felt through the rigid leathers. "Remember: don't do anything stupid."

Before Declan could respond this time, however, as'ahRen had raised the horn again, and the low, lingering note rang out for a second time.

"*Brruuuuurrrrrr*!"

In steady unison, they began to move.

The camp wasn't much more than two miles from the northeast corner of Ysenden, but moving carefully as they were through the dense, icy verdure of the Vyr'esh, it was a slow-going approach. The forest floor dipped and climbed, and icy streams cracked under the weight of a thousand passing soldiers. Without looking back, Declan could imagine the elven army moving like a black tide across the frost-strewn ground, around and about the gargantuan evergreens and along the natural valleys and hills of the land. It would have been an impressive sight to behold, he was sure, but between the still-limited light and his own need to look only forward, Declan left the view to his mind's eye. With every step—with every coordinated *thump* of booted feet at their backs—they drew closer to the fight, drew closer to the claws of the undead he knew would be waiting for them. Fear was absent, now—the draugr no longer horrified him as they once had—but just the same Declan's heart beat more heavily with every passing minute, leaving him to clench his jaw and march in silence beside his friends. Ryn, Bonner, and Ester strode at his sides, with Orsik and Eyera padding along just behind them. Arrackes and as'ahRen led the way, a pair of dark titans made small by the vastness of the woods, and what had been only their fainter shapes in the firestone's glow grew steadily clearer as the rising sun finally made its appearance through the trees behind them. It looked like it was going to be a clear day, boding well for all, and Declan forced himself to take in the forest as they pressed on, forced himself to enjoy the faint rays of red-orange light that managed to creep through the dense branches above. It helped ease the tension, helped ease the rigidness of his shoulders and the tightness with which he held onto the hilt of his sword with his left hand, having taken it up out of habit. Rather than the coming battle he forced himself to imagine what the Vyr'esh would be like as they crossed *back* through it after their victorious assault.

Unfortunately, he had only just managed to calm himself when Arrackes' voice interrupted his focus.

Halt.

There came snapped orders in all direction around them, and with exactly two more *thumps* of boots to ground the march went utterly silent again. All of a sudden, Declan could hear the wind through the leaves above them, as well as the distant *crack* of some branch or another breaking under the weight of fallen snow.

Then Arrackes spoke again.

Form!

There was a sudden surge of movement at their backs, and Declan turned with the others to watch the elves—originally organized in their marching columns—transition with practiced ease. Within ten seconds the individual contingents were gone, having molded into a single line, five-soldiers deep, that arched out into the lightening woods in what he knew would be a massive, precise circle. Those bearing swords stood at the forefront, after which two lines of spear-wielders had their weapons hefted at an angle upward, ready to drop them over their comrades' shoulders. Beyond this group, Declan saw the curved tips of bows, as well as arrows being drawn and nocked, visible through carefully measured body-length of space between each line of five, set in preparation for the constriction of the final approach.

"It seems it might be best if we take our places as well," Bonner said quietly, his voice still jarring in the silence.

"It would."

Declan turned in time to see Arrackes and as'ahRen approaching them together. The Lord Commander was donning a pure black helmet that might have materialized out of nowhere had Declan not caught a glimpse of the small major, Mysat, vanishing back into the lines nearby, and it was he who had spoken.

"The gate is just ahead," the old elf continued as he finished latching his helm into place. "Two hundred paces through the woods. We will see them soon enough. If you don't mind my presumption, I would ask Esteria to take the warg to the rear and act as local support. Master Ryndean—" he dipped his head respectfully to the dragon "—if you would stay close to the High Chancellor with me, the three of us will move about freely as needed."

Ryn looked hesitant, glancing at Declan uncomfortably, but Bonner held up any protest with a grim laugh.

"Declan and I can handle ourselves just fine, you damn lizard. In fact—" he looked to the Lord Commander "—can I assume you want us front and center?"

"If you think that's wise?" as'ahRen confirmed with a nod. "I have yet to see your abilities for myself, but I heard enough assurances from Colonel Syr'esh's command back in Ysenden to believe you two aren't exactly the soft-bodied mages my kind might like to imagine you as. If you could be our bulwark, breaking whatever tide comes at us, it would serve the battle well." He gestured to Lysiat and her brothers, motioning them forward. "Assuming that's agreeable, I will have Commander ay'ahSel and the sergeants acting as your personal support. I assure you you will be well defended."

"No assurances necessary," Declan said with a strained smile at the siblings, who stopped beside them to stand at the ready. "We know well what they can do."

"Not to mention Orsik won't want to come with me," Ester spoke up from the left, waiting patiently with one hand on Eyera, who had come up to sit beside her. With her other, the woman gestured beyond the lot of them as though to make a point. "He's more likely to stay with Declan. They're getting in the habit of finding each other in a fight."

Turning to follow her motion, Declan almost laughed at the sight of the male who—indeed—was standing almost expectantly not three feet from his back, hackles up and dark eyes lingering on the woods before them, in the direction of Erraven.

"Whatever you think is best," as'ahRen consented, turning to Declan and Bonner again. "We have a plan, then?"

"We have a plan," Declan confirmed as the mage nodded solemnly beside him.

"Good. In that case…" The Lord Commander turned to the ay'ahSels, switching to elvish to explain their protective assignment. The siblings snapped up a salute together to show they understood, earning a nod from as'ahRen.

Then the aging elf looked to Arrackes expectantly, and the old dragon didn't hesitate to give the order.

Begin the attack, Lord Commander.

The horn was in as'ahRen's hand again at once. He paused only for a moment, as though to steel himself, and Declan couldn't help but feel the slightest bit better upon realizing that even the greatest swordsmen of the *er'endhen* was not without his own unease.

Then the instrument was raised, and a third note rumbled through the woods.

"*Brruuuuurrrrrr*!"

None moved, waiting with baited breath. Once the sound of the horn had faded, a few seconds passed, lingering into five, then ten.

And then the response came, ringing out in the distance, answering dully from the far side of the city they couldn't yet see.

"*Brruuuuurrrrrr....*!"

Thump. Thump. Thump. Thump.

This time, as the army advanced, Declan was careful to step in time with the elves, participating in the diligent tightening of the thirty-thousand-sword noose. Though he and Bonner marched several paces ahead of the spear line, flanked by the ay'ahSels and with Orsik at their backs, to either side it was easy to see the endless circle of soldiers pressing inward, constricting inch by careful inch. Fifty paces into the approach, Declan drew his sword, reaching up as he did to take hold of the firestone in his left hand and pull it up and over his head, freeing its thong from the plume of his new helmet with a tug. Eighty in, and he'd wound the glowing rock tightly into his gloved fist, feeling the magics within pulse as he called on his corpomancy, pressing the spell evenly across his body. At once he felt stronger, faster, and he willed the power to take firm hold into his flesh and bones as they passed a hundred paces. Another twenty, and the relative darkness of the forest before them took on an unnatural texture at last, and Declan realized that what he was seeing was not the shadow and shade of the trees anymore, but the hewn surface of worn, black stone.

"Oh my..." Bonner muttered, apparently noticing the same thing, and Declan saw the old mage lift his eyes upward as they continued to near, and with good reason.

Despite the height of the trees around them, despite the fact that Ryn could have stood tall in his true form and not reached half as high as most of the lowest branches of the Vyr'esh, the walls of Erraven seemed to have no end, towering up and beyond the canopy of the evergreens.

Abruptly, Declan truly understood that Ysenden was not the only marvel the *er'endehn* had crafted in their time...

Then, though, he saw the gate, and his focus returned with a fervor.

It had been hard to make out at first, the linear cleaving of the stone that formed the city entrance camouflaging well with the rising trunks of the trees. As they crossed a hundred and fifty paces, however, the relief of the great gap within the darker defenses became clear, rising up into the branches just like the rest of the wall. It was fortunate that Declan had seen the sketches and maps, had already been aware of the marvel that was the gate. Otherwise, he might have been further astounded, unable to keep from gaping upward at the never-ending opening that he knew cut the black stone cleanly all the way to the very top, like a titanic blade had sliced the whole of the city in two. Instead, he was able to keep his eyes earthward, able to study the base of the entrance, through which a clear, blue sky was suddenly visible, along with the broken and crumbling ruins of what had once been a great bastion of the elves. After seven hundred years, nothing recognizable remained of the ancient city, not even when they came within thirty paces of the walls. Shattered stone was strewn across what might once have been a proud, cobbled road, now almost entirely swallowed by tall grass. Further into the city, half-blocking the sight of the far wall in the distance, the crumpled structures were piled high, forming a grim, rolling mound of weather-smoothed rock to stand monument to what once might have been. It should have been sad—and perhaps breathtaking—to witness, but Declan was too preoccupied in that moment worrying about what he *couldn't* see, rather than what he could.

Even as they passed beyond the thicker part of the forest, getting near enough the walls to strike them with a well-thrown rock, there wasn't a single sign of the draugr…

It wasn't wholly unexpected. Sen'Hev had said her scout hadn't drawn the ire of the wights until they'd been within ten paces of the gate, which Declan and Bonner hadn't yet breached. Still, it felt strange, and Declan couldn't help but mutter a silent prayer to the Mother above as his stomach tightened uncomfortably.

"Carefully, now…" Bonner said unnecessarily from his side, slowing down ever so slightly. Declan nodded just the same, checking on the stability of his suffusion briefly before drawing another weave into being on top of it, gathering heat into his clenched left fist.

It was a testament to their time together that, when his hand caught fire with a low *woosh* of flames, the ay'ahSels on either side of them didn't so much as flinch, while Orsik only growled in preparation at their back.

Thirteen paces. Now twelve. Now eleven… As they at last crossed the ten-pace mark, Declan could see clearly into the shattered city, taking in the ruins in more detail. He could at a glance make out a hundred different places where some nimble enemy might be hiding, ready to pounce, and he was glad for once that they had no intention of actually pressing *into* the walls. Still, though, they continued their approach, not stopping until they were within five paces of the start of the cobbled road poking here and there out of the grass.

As one behind them, the army halted as well, returning the day to its quiet once again.

For fifteen seconds they all waited like that, long enough that Declan eventually stole an uncertain glance backward over his shoulder. Ryn and as'ahRen stood with weapons drawn on either side of an unarmed Arrackes directly behind them, while Ester sat tall atop Eyera behind the archers, arrow nocked to her own bow. All of them were frowning, and theirs were only a few pairs of the hundreds of eyes trained on the empty gateway.

Turning back, Declan whispered sidelong to Lysiat, who stood nearest to him.

"*You hear anything*?"

The elf only shook her head slowly, tilting it as she did as though to listen. For a few seconds more, there was nothing.

Then she stiffened.

"*Something comes,*" she hissed, loud enough for everyone in the vicinity to hear.

There came a shout from behind, and Declan had to force himself not to look back again as he realized it was as'ahRen calling for what he thought was the archers to draw. Sure enough, the next order sounded out, and he recognized the urgent word "spears" even as the line arching out to either side of them seemed to shift downwards when several thousand polearms dropped in a wave. Declan didn't have time to think of how many arrowheads were pointed too close to his and his companions' backs, unfortunately, because in that moment he, too, made out the ugly sound.

Claws scraping against stone.

Holding his breath, he waited.

It was another few long seconds before the first of the wights finally showed itself, white-haired head crawling up out of the ruins to take them all in with empty eyes set in a dark, gaunt face. Its gaze seemed to sweep across what part of the line it could see from the other side of the gate, breaking slowly into a grin as it did, and it started to pull itself out of the hole it had been hiding in eagerly.

Then, for some reason, the thing met Declan's gaze, and it froze.

He didn't know why, but in that moment the earlier clenching of Declan's gut redoubled, tightening at the sudden stillness in the creature. He was only vaguely aware of the Lord Commander's order to "*Hold! Hold!*", too focused on trying to figure out where the sudden weight of fear had come from, dropping down on him to hang heavy across his shoulders.

The answer, unfortunately, came as the wight suddenly heaved itself the rest of the way out of the stone, displaying the ragged armor of a fallen soldier of Ysenden. Without pausing it threw back its head, chest expanding as though taking in a heaving breath.

And Declan knew.

"KILL IT!" he shouted, half-turning to look for Ester. "ESTER! KILL IT BEFORE IT—!"

Too late.

"SCREEEEEEEEEEEHHHH!"

The shriek the wight let loose in that moment was unlike any Declan had heard before it. It still carried the terrible, manic glee the undead always attacked with, but there was more to it, now, more layered in that sound. It was less a battle cry of any kind, and more—

"A call..." Bonner hissed in horror, realizing it too. "It's calling for something..."

Before Declan could respond, though, Aliek lifted his spear from the mage's other side, pointing with it.

"*There!*" the elf hissed before shifting his weapon slightly. "*And there! And* there*!*"

Sure enough, even as the terrible scream of the first wight faded into the trees around them, other shapes were stirring, clawing and crawling their way out of the rubble and ruins. As they watched, two, then ten, then fifty undead staggered to their feet, hungry eyes fixed on the elven army while still more of their ilk rose around them.

"The others," Declan snarled, willing the fire in his hand to redouble into a heavy blaze. “It’s calling the others.”

“Yes, but how many?!” Bonner had to shout as other, plainer screams started to rise up from the draugr.

“All of them!” Declan roared in answer, flinging his spell out in an arc of flames just as the wights began to charge.

CHAPTER TWENTY-NINE

The undead came in a single fluid wave, more and more pouring out of the broken remains of Erraven with every passing second. Declan's initial weave lit the ground beneath the gate aflame, but the fires only caught in the clothes and armor of the first lines, sending them shrieking to the ground to be trampled by the creatures that followed. There was a blaze of green light, and with a stamp of one boot Bonner turned the fifteen feet of frozen earth and grass before them to mud, discernible by the sudden sinking of the ground. More of the wights fell, splashing down to be engulfed in the sudden muck, and Declan sent out a second spell of fire in a cone over the space, setting alight to hair and flesh alike. Still, though, the others came, the shrieking screams of the draugr deafening, the beasts using the floundering bodies of their fallen like a bridge even as some of the corpses burst into black flames.

FIRE!

Arrackes' mind-speak rang clear through the noise, and with a physical blast of air from behind them Declan and the others experienced the terrifying feel of several hundred arrows missing their bodies and limbs by bare inches. The projectiles slammed into the coming ranks of undead, immediately sending several layers of the foremost wights into a black inferno, but the burning corpses were shoved aside and trampled on once again.

There was no time for a second volley before the creatures reached Declan and the others like a wave of living death.

An eruptive blast of heated force was all that kept Declan—and Lysiat at his side—from being overrun in the initial rush of bodies. His growing mastery of his pyromancy proved itself in the enormous energy that exploded outward from his left fist, sending a score of tightly-packed wights flying back. At his right, there was a *crack* of breaking earth, and a slab of the forest floor—now looking as hard as stone—rushed upward from beneath Bonner's feet to take his own part of the rushing line in the chest, bringing them all to a crushing halt. Almost at once, though, the pressure returned, and Declan only had enough time to draw up a second, lesser blast of power before the wights reached them.

Immediately, combat devolved into a roiling mess of claws and blades and fire.

His corpomancy pushed to its maximum, Declan felt twice as fast and twice as strong as he had ever before, standing his ground there with Lysiat. The woman's twin swords whirled in a dervish of destruction, and his single, heavier blade cleaved through limbs and heads and bodies alike. Despite the ferocity of these wights, these undead who had once lived as *er'endehn*, Declan was so far come from the man he had been when he'd *first* encountered the beasts. Then, he'd nearly lost his life battling a mere pair of them, and had required Ryn's assistance to end the fight.

He was no longer so weak.

The slashing of their bleached-white claws seemed less chaotic, less unpredictable, and Declan's obsidian blade worked a deft barrage of defense before him even as he wove flames into the onslaught, setting just as many draugr alight as he and the commander cut down combined. To his right, Tesied had taken a position, flanking Bonner opposite Aliek, the twins' long spears moving in mirrored blurs of lancing stabs and slashes. They were doing a fair job keeping the wights away from the mage, because Bonner looked to have had enough time to gather a more complicated spell in both hands, and Declan recognized the weave just in time to turn his head away and take a half step forward to mostly block Lysiat's view as well. With a roar, the column of manifested dragonfire blazed white, carving a path into the unending wights as it turned dead flesh and bone to ash. There were a dozen flashes of black flames mixed in, and that many again as Bonner dragged the spell sideways, then the magics guttered out to leave a charred cone of smoldering earth before them.

Almost at once, though, it was swallowed by twenty more bodies, the undead uncaring as their bare feet and worn boots alike blistered upon contact with the burning ground.

"So much for being 'the bulwark'," Declan ground out through gritted teeth as the wall of screaming corpses closed in on them once again, moving to encircle their little group. At his back, Declan heard the screams and tearing sounds of Orsik's destructive presence, shielding their rear, coupled with the steady *thuds* of what could only be a sharp-eyed Ester sending arrow after arrow into the undead the warg didn't manage to hold up. The wights, though seemed too intent on their target, the outpouring flood of them breaking like a rush to wrap around faster than they could be shielded.

Not until help arrived, at least.

SHING!

With the sound of screaming obsidian, Declan was suddenly aware of a large, dark shape standing almost back-to-back with him, supporting Orsik's efforts to keep them from getting surrounded. Ryn's great blade cut the wights down two or three at a time, and the dragon roared as he swung the weapon in one hand half-as-fast again as any human or elf might have managed with two. As though to echo this sudden arrival, there were a rapid series of the *whooshing* eruption of black flames from further to the right—close enough to hear the death wails of destroyed Purposes, this time—and Declan caught a glimpse of Arrackes and as'ahRen fighting side-by-side at Bonner's back. Together they defended the mage, the old dragon tearing through the enemy with bare, clawed hands, the Lord Commander a maelstrom of blades as his two swords made Lysiat's duel-wielding look like child's play.

What's more, they hadn't come alone.

Apparently the fact that the wights seemed to have only one target in mind had not gone unnoticed, because with a roar and the *crunching* of bodies striking bodies, Declan and the others were abruptly no longer a lone line. The *er'endehn* closest to them had collapsed inward, breaking their defensive positions, and all of a sudden a hundred black swords and spears were pressing in around them, cutting into the wights that had managed to ring them.

BLOCK THEM OFF! Ryn's voice thundered over the sounds of battle. *ON US! ALL WHO CAN HEAR THIS! COLLAPSE ON US!*

The words solidified Declan's suspicions as he ducked under a wight's slashing strikes, cutting its neighbor down even as he punched the offending creature itself in the gut, blasting it in two in a spray of fire. If the dragon was so willing to demand reinforcements, then there was no doubt they were indeed likely facing every undead that had been lurking within the ruins of Erraven. It had been stupid of them, he realized now, foolish of everyone—including *him*—not to have foreseen such a possibility. A thousand wights against the might of Ysenden might have seemed like grand odds, but if the Endless Queen could exact the right price from the equation, then the sacrifice on her part would have been worth it. He couldn't fathom why *he* was the first target—not when he stood shoulder-to-shoulder with the last primordial of the dragons, the High Chancellor of the dark elves, and the greatest living mage left in the world—but all the same he understood Sehranya's game, now.

And he had no intention of letting her win.

Drawing back his will, Declan trusted Lysiat and Tesied at his sides to shield him as he allowed his magic to converge, to weave again into a more-potent spell. It took a good four or five seconds, but his fist was aflame once more when he thrust it forward again, the *whoomph* of force blasting outward catching more wights than he could count this time. Tightly packed as the writhing mass of creatures were, very few were thrown off their feet this time, but the wall as a whole staggered back long enough to give them all a moment to breathe. Taking advantage of it, Declan dropped to one knee and scrawled the only rune he knew into the already-charred ground, drawing it as quickly and broadly as he could. He cursed as the mark of channeling came out imperfect in his rush, but it would do the trick, and the lines he'd made in the ground and soot flared red when he slammed the firestone wrapped about his palm into their middle, willing them into life. Pouring as much magic as he quickly could into the rune, he was rewarded as fire erupted from the earth before him, arching away in a dozen slashing patterns like lightning to rip and tear at the legs of the wights who had already recovered. As the creatures rushed forward again, trampling the emblem, the mark held, infused as it was with magic. It certainly didn't end the fight, but as Declan rejoined the battle he could tell there was a certain staggering to the onslaught now, just the smallest break in the constant wash of enemies as here and there flames bloomed throughout the horde whenever the weave caught in tattered clothes and worn armor.

"EXCELLENT, DECLAN!"

Bonner's shout came even as the mage let off another staggering spell, clapping his hands together before him in a gap the ay'ahSel twins had bought him. For once the ground didn't tremble, and it took Declan a moment of fearing the magics had failed before the nearest of the wight's screams took on a different tone, the hungry joy shifting into something angrier. When one of the draugr before him suddenly staggered, practically falling onto Lysiat's waiting blades, Declan looked down, then let out a harsh bark of laughter.

A thousand waving roots—like thin, snapping snakes—had come slithering out of the ground, and were actively ensnaring the feet and ankles of any undead who stepped within reach of them. Even better, the plants were catching fire as they whipped through Declan's weave, burning even as they climbed legs and dragged down the more unfortunate of the creatures. Together the two spells proved a devastating combination, the rate of the fight definitely slowing as the wights at the back of the group were suddenly forced to clamber and crawl their way over the stuck forms of their kind, not a few among them screaming as their bodies caught fire.

KEEP AT IT! Arrackes' voice roared over everything, the High Chancellor punching clean through the skull of one undead as he held another at bay by the throat even as he yelled. *BLOCK THEM IN!*

They were succeeding, Declan knew, were winning. As he cast a sheet of liquid fire over the writhing mass of creatures, he could see that the momentum of the wave was staggering.

Still... It wasn't without its costs.

The screams that echoed through the air, after all, weren't only the undead's. Though the mass of wights was clearly intent on getting to *him* for some reason, they appeared willing enough to strike out at whatever enemy was closest in the moment. Cruel creations that they were, they moved so quickly and with such ferocity that they sometimes threw themselves off the twisting forms of the rooted and burning, crashing down into the unsuspecting rear lines to rip and tear at everything and anything within reach. Even the sword-bearers of the forward line—collapsing steadily inward now on either side of Declan's group to bottle up the gate—were hardly going untouched, elves getting dragged into the throng of ripping claws left and right, or else falling screaming as the wights leapt at them from every direction. Even as he watched, cutting down three more of the beasts in as many seconds, Declan saw a half-dozen of the *er'endehn* fall, one particularly horribly when a creature threw itself at the women to take her by the throat in its teeth.

They would win at this rate, he knew, but they were going to pay a steep price.

And he wasn't sure they had to…

As more of the draugr erupted into red and black flames alike before him, falling prey to his and Bonner's combined weave, an idea began to form in Declan's head. It was a little bit mad, but any god looking down on the scene of the battle would have thought madness was the theme of the day already. White bone. Black blades. Red fire. Green magic. The insanity of the fight could barely have gotten more chaotic.

Barely.

He might have been wrong, but Declan suspected the Queen had made a mistake, and he was going to try to play on it. As he slashed the head of one lunging wight clean off, he called out to his left.

"RYN! CAN YOU GET ME IN THE AIR?"

As the elves had collapsed on them, bottling off the gate, the dragon and Orsik both had moved to flank Lysiat, fighting side-by-side next to the woman. He didn't answer for a few seconds, busy cleaving his great blade through the three necks of a trio of rooted wights, and only glanced around at Declan when the resulting explosion of black fire and death wails offered him a breather.

THE AIR?! his mental voice shouted back, sounding at a loss. *WHAT ARE YOU TALKING ABOUT?*

"I NEED TO GET HIGH!" Declan answered, blasting the upper body off a draugr that had been about to leap at Tesied on his right.

"ABOVE THE WIGHTS! I NEED YOU TO GET ME OVER THEIR HEADS!"

NO! Ryn answered as more of the creatures lunged through the black flames of their fallen ilk to press him once more.

"RYN! TRUST ME! IF I CAN GET IN THE AIR I CAN—!"

NO! I MEAN THAT I CAN'T*!* the dragon cut him off. *IF I TURN HERE, I'M LIABLE TO CRUSH EVERY ONE OF YOU, DECLAN!*

Declan cursed, realizing he was right. Ryn's transformations were explosive. He had seen once—in one of his rare dives back into Herst's memories—the dragon sending men screaming and flying as he erupted into his natural—and massive—state in the middle of a crowded ballroom. If he turned now, every being within several paces of Ryn—including Declan, Lysiat, Orsik, and Tesied—would be thrown off their feet in the best of circumstances, and pulverized in the worst.

WHY DO YOU NEED TO GET IN THE AIR, IDRYS?

The question that rang through Declan's thoughts came not from Ryn, this time, but Arrackes. Glancing to his right, Declan saw that that the lesser dragon was not looking in his direction as he continued to fight beside as'ahRen, though he'd clearly overheard the discussion.

"I THINK I CAN STOP THIS!" he shouted back without hesitating. "I THINK I CAN SEAL THEM OFF!"

HOW?

The voice came from both dragons, this time, and Declan didn't waste any words in explaining. When he was done, Arrackes turned his attention on Lysiat ay'ahSel, asking her—as the only relevant witness to the concept—if it was possible.

The elven woman shouted back a confirmation at once, too intent on the fight to spare any focus on anything but the cutting pattern of her blades as she worked to hold back the onslaught of the wights still hounding after Declan.

THEN LET IT BE DONE! Arrackes called back, and in the corner of his vision Declan saw the High Chancellor withdraw from the fight, letting a pair of sword-wielding elves take his place beside the Lord Commander.

"BUT RYN CAN'T TURN!"

NO, HE CAN'T! Arrackes agreed, having vanished into the line of *er'endehn* soldiers completely. *BUT* I *CAN!*

And then the dragon reappeared, sailing up and over the defensive line, having clearly taken a running leap and mustering up all the strength in his *rh'eem's* powerful legs.

Then, even as he arched down towards the writhing mass of wights, he began to change.

The Chancellor's transformation was, fortunately, no less abrupt than Ryn's were. What started as a rippling of his flesh turned into a rapid expansion outward, his black robes shredding into ribbons as his body grew and his limbs lengthened. Wings erupted out of his back, spreading wide and leathery, and his tail and neck both extended as his head widened and lengthened.

By the time he dropped among the undead again, Arrackes had taken the form of a fully-fledged dragon, and his landing shook the earth even as he crushed a score-and-a-half of the creatures under his bulk.

QUICKLY! The High Chancellor shouted, turning to Declan to send another fifty of the wights flying and screaming before he extended a great clawed hand towards him. *BEFORE THEY OVERRUN ME!*

His concern was valid, too. Despite his transformation, Arrackes looked only to be a little more than half of Ryn's size in his natural form, his grey scales streaked with the same dark red slashes that had marked his dragonling's figure. Even in the moment it took him to reach for Declan, several of the wights had leapt onto his sides, gaining purchase in the ridges of his scales, and started to climb.

Fortunately, it wasn't Declan's first time being carried so, and he didn't hesitate.

Taking hold of one of the lesser dragons claws as he sheathed his sword, he vaulted at once into Arrackes' narrow palm. The moment he shouted that he was secure, the dragon reared up, shaking off most of the undead clambering up his bulk.

The rest fell when he launched himself straight up into the air.

It was an advantage to his smaller size, Declan realized as the force of the momentum nearly flattened him within the High Chancellor's grip. Whenever Ryn had taken flight, it always required a running start. Arrackes, on the other hand, managed to get them airborne with nothing but one powerful leap and several great beats of his broad wings. They hovered for a moment, the impetus of the climb cut short as gravity took hold, and below them the massive gales of wind this caused sent wights and elves alike staggering. Declan saw Ryn take hold of Lysiat's arm to stabilize her as Orsik hunkered down on his other side. Bonner had a strong hand on each of Aliek and Tesied's shoulders, and as'ahRen looked to have found his footing after a forced step or two back. Beyond them, drawing the eye as she sat atop the contrasting white-and-grey back of Eyera among the army's footsoldiers, Ester had brought the hand not holding her bow up to shield her face, squinting upward with a half-stricken, half-furious expression.

Oh, she's going to kill me, Declan had just enough time to realize.

Then, with a twist of his body and a shifting of his wings, Arrackes shot out of their hovering standstill over the *er'endehn,* lancing off between the trees.

Declan's stomach flipped at the sudden change of direction, and he was glad they'd all forgone breakfast that morning in favor of a quick start to the fight. It came in even more handy when Arrackes demonstrated another useful trick of his slighter frame, managing a nimble loop around one of the nearest of the great evergreens of the Vyr'esh to come arching back about towards the battle again, streaking with all speed through the air. The dragon showed no intent of slowing down as he careened over his gathered soldiers—thousands on thousands of them now waiting to be of use as they'd come running from the other sides of the broken city—and Declan braced himself, focusing twice over on his suffusion as he realized what was going to happened.

With a *CRUNCH* of shattering stone, Arrackes hit the wall along the left side of the gate with all three clawed feet not being used to carry his passenger, massive red talons cracking into the black rock to find purchase.

Is this high enough?! the dragon asked urgently, looking down, no longer needing to shout in the temporary subdual of the fight his takeoff had caused.

In answer, Declan peered through the High Chancellor's scaled fingers.

"Yes!" he shouted, shoving himself onto his feet. "Keep me steady! I need both hands!"

They were nearly ten yards above the still-burning ground, upon which the wights not rooted down were quickly regaining their footing. As Declan unwound the firestone from his left hand, looping the leather thong over his head again for safekeeping, he watched and hoped, pleading to the Mother and the Graces that he had been right.

His gamble paid off almost at once.

With a unanimous shriek of irritation, the general direction of the horde shifted, all but the outmost lines of the pooling wights pulling back and away, fighting the tide of the still-coming others pouring out of the city. Those closest to the wall immediately leapt at it, bony fingers gaining little hold on the wind-weathered stone, but all the same several managed to start the climb upwards while others simply began clambering up and over their lower comrades' heads and shoulders, building a quickly mounting mound.

It was exactly what Declan had hoped for.

They needed to cut the enemy off, to keep them from streaming out of Erraven in an endless wave. If he could break up the onrush, then the press of the undead would lessen ten-fold, maybe even causing the remainder to scatter in search of other exits. Most importantly: the toll on the elves would decrease proportionally.

As arrows began to fire off from the back ranks of elven archers again, picking the ascending wights off the wall in quick succession, Declan brought both arms up, palms towards the pooling undead and already-enchanted ground beneath them, and began to focus.

He had intended—with the control he'd built up over his pyromancy in the last month—to draw from his reserves more carefully than the last time he called on a similar spell. In the tunnels beneath the Mother's Tears, willing his magic out of himself without the firestone as a vessel had been like opening the flood gates of a dam and pressing the water to move out faster and faster just the same. With the practice he'd put into controlling his weaving without a focusing element, he had expected that he would be able to manage much the same while still holding greater rein on his power.

Unfortunately, while Declan wasn't wrong about his improved manipulation, he failed to account for another aspect of his weaving that—it turned out—had grown equally in measure and demand.

Potency.

Where the roughened rock of the tunnels had taken time to heat and melt, the stone beneath where he and Arrackes hung began to glow almost the moment he let loose his will. The screams of the wights—some of whom had managed to climb to within five feet of the dragon's lowest foot despite the constant rush of arrows—turned hateful again as the flesh about their bone claws erupted into instant flame, sending most of the undead falling away. Declan was hardly finished, though, pressing the power further and more firmly as he drew it into existence, the stone of the gate under them turning orange foot-by-rapid-foot.

Then the unseen magics hit the ground, and the earth itself caught fire.

With a roar of rising smoke and heat an inferno exploded into instant being, feeding off the flames of the channeling rune Declan had left behind and the roots of Bonner's still-active trapping spell. It expanded, ripping out and into the city alike, consuming every corpse it touched, pulling them into the embrace of the flames like the drowning undercurrent of some great wave. As he poured his magic into the spell, Declan almost didn't notice the fires expanding too fast, too far, realizing only in the seconds before they would have engulfed the closest of the elves, the soldiers now scrambling away from the fight with yells of fear and surprise.

"N-No!" Declan managed to get out through clenched teeth, letting loose even more power to rein in what he'd already released. His control proved itself as the fires slowed significantly, but they still crept outwards, spilling over the last of the wights who'd made it out of the city. Declan feared, then, that he was about to enact the great horror of setting the Vyr'esh aflame, the *exact* reason Ryn and Arrackes had not let free their dragonfire.

Then, though, there came a blaze of blue light, and Declan felt the air—heated to the point of boiling—drop suddenly in temperature again.

With no noticeable sound over the roar of the inferno, a wall of ice some three feet thick began to materialize between the elves and the flames. It grew slowly, one yard at a time around the perimeter where the incinerated wights had stood, but it still outpaced the fire. Within fifteen seconds the army was safe behind the magic barrier, and Bonner—who had traced the frozen defenses into being with both hands from where he'd been standing at the very edge of the spell, grimaced as the strain of the act left him.

That was nothing, however, compared to what Declan was feeling.

As the stone of the wall beneath him and Arrackes began to melt, a corner of the gate sloughing off as molten rock, Declan felt the familiar—and unpleasant—sense of scraping the bottom of his reserves. Ignoring it—and the knowledge that Bonner was *certainly* going to yell at him later for this—Declan dragged his magic away, finding it easier now that they were limited by the physical presence of the ice wall. Like the tide rolling back out to sea, he exerted his control to press the weave through the gate and into the city, willing it to swallow as many of thc shrieking wights still gathered there as he felt his spells of suffusion being drained away into the pyromancy. His arms began to shake, then his legs a few seconds after. Before he knew it, Declan had fallen to one knee in Arrackes' palm, nearly losing his balance completely.

Then his vision began to darken, and Declan cursed himself.

"Well… shit," he muttered, fighting to keep his head up and the magic still pouring outward. "This wasn't part of the plan…"

As a heavy exhaustion pulled at him, dragging him down, Declan felt the weave begin to unravel. He battled it, of course, struggling mightily to focus, to will the wights he could still see through the gates to run, to flee. Strangely, there seemed to be fewer of them than there had been before, but he didn't recall seeing any of them make a break for the other parts of the wall, the cracks in Erraven's ancient defenses that would have given them another egress by which to attack from.

It didn't matter a moment later, though, when Declan lost the fight, feeling himself nearing the very last spark of his magics.

With an enormous effort he forced himself to stop, then, forced himself to release his hold on the wild weave. He retched as he cut himself off from the power, finding himself left with an emptiness inside his being he didn't think he'd had a the chance to experience the last time before passing out.

And speaking of passing out…

"Arrackes…" Declan said weakly, the black closing in around his vision.

… *Yes?* the dragon answered after a moment, sounding—for the first time—just the smallest bit stunned by what he had just witnessed.

"Catch… me…" Declan muttered.

Then he felt himself tilt sideways, off the dragon's hand, tipping out over the blazing hell that still raged below.

◆

Declan awoke to a sensation not unlike the feeling of his heart stopping. A keen discomfort—just short of pain—blazed outward from the center of his chest, tingling in a wave to first paralyze his lungs, then seize up his shoulders, neck, and abdomen. It continued to travel up his head and down his arms and legs, and only after it passed through his fingers and toes and faded from existence did he open his eyes with a desperate gasp for air.

A cold, blue sky greeted him, bright in the early morning sun. Contrary to the horrible sensation that had only just coursed through his body like fire, Declan could see his breath on the air, and he lay there panting for a good while before realizing someone was looking down at him, while others were talking nearby.

"Is he awake?!" Ester's desperate voice was recognizable even through a ringing in his ears. "Is he awake, Father?!"

The face of the figure directly above Declan came into focus, then, and Bonner's green eyes smiled down on him.

"He's awake," the old mage said before addressing Declan directly. "I thought we agreed you never wanted me to do that to you again, boy."

In answer, Declan only groaned, trying and failing to sit up. Immediately the familiar grasp of a strong, clawed hand took him by the shoulder, easing him into a sitting position, and he blinked blearily around to see Ryn on one knee at his other side.

Take it easy, the dragon said gently. *This is twice now you've pushed yourself into an arcane fatigue. You know it's going to take time to recover.*

That brought reality back a bit, and Declan lifted a shaking hand up to the middle of his chest, where he knew now Bonner's finger had likely been pressed only a moment before.

"Oooowwww," he hissed, feeling the phantom remnants of the injection of magic tingle down his back. "That *definitely* wasn't part of the plan…"

"A plan? So you're going to pretend you had a plan?"

Wincing at the cool tone with which the questions were asked, Declan looked up. Ester was on both knees by his feet, glaring at him with a combination of fury and relief.

"Er… Sort of?" Declan answered sheepishly. "Passing out wasn't in the program, though, I promise. That spell… It took more out of me than I anticipated."

"I'll say," came a rumbling voice from the right, and Declan turned his stiff neck to find Ciriak as'ahRen watching him from behind Bonner with a raised eyebrow. At his side, Arrackes stood silent, taken once more to his *rh'eem* and having apparently been fetched a spare set of robes from somewhere. He looked exhausted—they *all* looked exhausted—but no one seemed to have suffered any major injuries, and beyond the Lord Commander and his Chancellor an innumerable number of elven soldiers were milling about, looking to be patrolling the walls and searching the ruins for—

"Wait," Declan said abruptly, waking up fully now as he realized what he was seeing. "Hold on."

He supposed he should have guessed it at the sight of the sky, but he was obviously no longer beneath the cover of the Vyr'esh. On the contrary, he sat in a clear patch of grass not far from what could only be the crumbled remnants of part of Erraven, *inside* the city walls. Someone had taken his helmet off, too, his long hair sticking to the sweat of his forehead and cheeks as the winter breeze cut down from the open heavens above.

We won, Declan, Ryn answered his unasked question with a chuckle. *I would almost say* you *won, rather, but there was still some cleanup to be done after you decimated the wights.*

"After I… what now?" Declan blinked, looking around at all of them, not understanding.

Ester answered him with an angry punch to the bottom of one boot. "You burned them all to nothing, Declan," she hissed as though this *wasn't* excellent news. "Well, most of them. Nearly took us all, too—*and* yourself, at the end—but you burned them all."

This still didn't register, and Declan looked around blankly at the others. For the first time he noticed Lysiat ay'ahSel and her brothers standing not far away, the lot of them looking on as the commander petted a seated, panting Eyera and the twins held back a whining Orsik, who seemed to be trying to get to Declan. Unable to do more than blink at them, though, it was Arrackes who he finally turned to, Arrackes, who had borne witness most closely to his spell.

It's as they say, the older dragon told him tiredly, anticipating the question just as Ryn had. *I wouldn't believe it if I hadn't seen it myself, Idrys. Not in seven hundred years have I seen a human cast a spell of fire like that.*

The last would have been Amherst, Ryn himself agreed with a nod, still not having let go of Declan's shoulder. *I would know. You've come a long,* long *way, Declan.*

"Don't go giving him a big head, now!" Bonner cut in with a disapproving frown. "Herst—much less Elysia—could have cast that weave without breaking a sweat, not to mention controlled it better."

"Father, give him a break." Ester, despite her anger with Declan, was apparently just as ready to jump to his defense as she looked prepared to punch him in a much more delicate place than his foot. "Who knows how many more would have died if he hadn't done that!"

"I'm hardly criticizing him, Esteria," Bonner said, a little more gently this time. "I'm merely saying that he still has much to learn."

"Clearly..." Declan muttered, still not believing his years. "Can someone explain, though... I... What happened?"

"A rout."

It was as'ahRen who answered, white-red eyes taking Declan in carefully as he spoke.

"We estimate there were about five hundred left when you two—" he gestured briefly to the dragon beside him "—took to the air. After you were done—and Arrackes caught you—there weren't more than a third that number, and they came spilling out over what you'd left of the gate just like the rest of them."

Declan nodded, understanding as he turned to look past Ester. Beyond her, the gates of Erraven still stood, but a black, shallow crater was all that remained of the vestiges of the cobbled stone road that had led into the city. Indeed, it was still smoking, which told Declan he couldn't have been unconscious for too long.

"I guess a Purpose has its limits..." he muttered. "Did they keep after me, even after I passed out?"

They did, Arrackes answered this time. *Not a few of them burned their limbs to nothing trying to climb up to us. Once the ground cooled I ended up taking us back behind the army line.*

"There were so many spears by that point that they didn't stand a chance when they rushed after you," Ester finished for the High Chancellor. "I saw it all happen. They threw themselves on the blades like there was nothing more important than getting to you."

"I don't think there was," Declan said with a shake of his head. "I think Sehranya *knew* there wasn't a chance this fight would go her way, so she went for the win she could have. Why she went after *me,* though, I don't understand. Is it the Accord?" He looked to Bonner. "Does she think there's value in seeing me dead?"

The old mage frowned uncertainly. "… Possibly. As I've said, it seems doubtful *you* would be bound by the weave, though. You're descended from the *second* child of Igoric al'Dyor, and we're a fair few generations even from Herst…"

Then why? Ryn asked. *Why would is she so intent on seeing Declan dead?*

Bonner shrugged, obviously at a loss. "Haven't we been asking ourselves that for months now? It's possible Declan *is* connected to the Accord, which might explain it, but I'd have to examine the weave's vessel in Aletha to be sure. Even if he *is,* for some reason, he can't be as integral to it as Mathaleus and his family…"

"You think she perceives this Accord of yours as that much of a threat?" as'ahRen asked with surprising interest, looking between Bonner and Declan. "Sehranya?"

"She should," the old man answered with a huff. "I'll not have this argument again here, though, Lord Commander."

That would be for the best, I think, yes, Arrackes agreed, frowning at as'ahRen as though disappointed by the elf's question. *We have other matters to attend to, namely returning to Ysenden.*

"Of course," the Lord Commander said without looking at his Chancellor, eyes having come to a rest on Declan again. "If it's agreeable to all, however, I'd like a word with Idrys."

There was a general exchange of curious looks at this.

Regarding…? Ryn asked finally.

"The fact that his magic isn't the only area in which he might still see improvement," the elf answered.

Despite the cryptic response, Ryn appeared to get the message, because he pressed himself to his feet at once.

Bonner, there are wounded you should attend to, he said firmly, stepping around Declan to take the old man by the arm and pull him to his feet. *Ester, you come too.*

"Esteria may stay," as'ahRen countered, looking away from Declan at last. "If you would, in fact, send Commander ay'ahSel over as well. And her brothers."

Ryn nodded, then proceeded to start dragging away a protesting Bonner, who was shouting after why *he* had to leave when his *daughter* was allowed to stay.

Declan was about to ask the same thing, in fact, but then Ryn's passing of the ay'ahSels—and an obvious word of allounce from the dragon—had him immediately being barreled at by several hundred pounds of muscle, teeth, and dirty, matted fur.

"Ooomph!" he gasped as Orsik's broad snout slammed eagerly into his sore chest, flattening him back to the ground. From there, Declan could only laugh as the warg leapt and danced around his head, licking his neck and face energetically as he barked with excitement.

"Orsik! Off! *Off!* He needs to rest!"

Ester's concerned command had the animal pausing in his happy assault, just long enough for Declan to shove himself up again to safety. As he put a grateful hand on the warg's head, he looked around to see that Eyera had come to lay beside the still-kneeling half-elf, while Lysiat, Aliek, and Tesied were now standing at attention on Declan's left, opposite the Lord Commander. Only Tesied dared shoot him a wink that said 'glad you're not dead' before returning to his emotionless countenance.

as'ah'Ren didn't waste any time.

"Esteria, if you would translate for the ay'ahSels, I would speak in common for the time being." He waited then for Ester to climb to her feet and come to stand at the ready beside the dark elves before continuing. "Each of you all deserve praise for your acts this day. Idrys' goes without saying, but I think he would agree it's fair to assume he wouldn't have survived long enough to come up with the plan without the four of you watching his back." The Lord Commander paused a moment to let Ester turn his words, then kept on. "That being said, I have to echo Magus yr'Essel that there is much improvement to be made, on all of your parts. Criticism is for another day, I think, but there is never any time like the present to seize an opportunity to improve." He looked specifically to Declan. "I saw it. Your 'suffusion'. You fought with very nearly the speed of Commander ay'ahSel, and twice her power. What you need now is precision. Practice."

Declan felt something like anticipation pull at his throat, but he beat back the hope. No… It wasn't possible… Was it?

"As you may or may not know," the Lord Commander continued, "I oversee the training of the High Chancellor's Guard, ensuring that the best of our kind receive the highest level of attention. However, I have not personally trained any soldier of the *er'endehn* since Mysat."

Declan swallowed, now, not believing where this conversation was going.

Before them all, as'ahRen smiled, the expression at once warm and infinitely, unfathomably terrifying.

"I think—as proven by your acts today—and as a favor to an old, old friend," the Lord Commander met Declan's eye specifically, "it is past time I changed that. What say you all?"

There was a heavy moment of silence, Declan and Ester in disbelief until Aliek nudged the half-elf pointedly, asking for the translation her surprise had kept her from providing.

For the first time since meeting the siblings, the woman's words had each and every one of them looking utterly dumbfounded.

"*Sir…*" Lysiat's hesitant voice sounded like a child trying desperately not to shout for glee. "*Are you offering to… to train us?* All *of us?*"

In answer, as'ahRen's smile broadened, and the elation combined with the chill of fear redoubled in Declan's chest.

"Spirits protect you if you say yes, ay'ahSel."

CHAPTER THIRTY

Everything was taken from us, on that day. Well… nearly *everything.*

There remained, for most, nothing but the need for retribution.

—PRIVATE JOURNAL OF GENERAL LESSAN SEN'HEV, YSENDEN COUNCIL GENERAL, C. 1070P.F.

"G*eneral? They're expecting you.*"

Sureht Syr'esh started at the voice of the guard, looking up from where he had been staring at the reddened bandage looped around the dark palm of his left hand. The elf who had addressed him was one of two, she and her comrade standing at the ready beside the door, the both of them staring straight ahead despite having had to stir him from his musings.

"*Yes…*" the general muttered, still a little muddled, then more clearly again as he roused himself. "*Yes. Of course. We can't leave them waiting too long, can we?*"

The guards stayed dutifully silent as Sureht shoved himself up onto his feet. Standing there a moment, he let his fingers linger on the smoothed wooden surface of his desk, feeling suddenly nostalgic.

Once he left this room…

But the general shook himself of the doubt. Now was not the time for hesitancy. Stepping away from the desk a little too quickly, he strode towards the door of his office, straightening his tunic of fine, grey-and-red silks even as the guards opened the way and paired him, stepping out one in front, one behind. They, unlike Sureht, still bore their black-and-gold uniforms, on duty despite the festive intent of the evening, hands on the hilt of their single and paired blades respectively.

The guard commander's office was at the end of a narrow hall near the middle of Ysenden's heights, the path flanked by training chambers not unlike the upper sections of the city where the Chancellor's Guard trained daily. This late in the evening—and with the bulk of the army likely having rousted Erraven's draugr some time that very day—the spaces were largely empty, but Sureht found himself pausing again to listen, to take in the faint grunts of those few soldiers taking advantage of the night to spar in peace, appreciating the *clacks* and *cracks* of heavy wooden blades crashing against each other.

No matter what awaited him after this night, Sureht would miss those sounds, as well as the surge of pride that accompanied them.

Once again, however, he forced himself to turn away from the hall, taking in instead the true instrument of his plans.

Just to the right of his office door, a pair of timber barrels had been stacked one on top of the other, their surfaces marked and pocked with age. He had chosen the wine personally, pilfering the best from the council's cellars in the hopes that none would think twice about partaking that evening. Indeed, when he'd made the request, the quartermaster had been unable to stop himself from voicing his good-natured jealousy of the recipients.

It had been hard for Sureht to smile back.

Gesturing towards the spirits, the general addressed his guards. "*The medical wards are a ways, so we'll take a gondola down as far as we can and roll them from there. Can each of you see to a barrel?*"

With nothing more than a pair of nods the soldiers did as they were asked, working together to lower the top casket off the bottom, then tilting them both onto their side. Once they were ready, Sureht led the way down the hall, willing himself not to look back and take in the door of his office one last time.

Late as it was, the city was quiet, and so the three had little trouble making the half-dozen-floor descent. The incline of the spiraling ramp that encircled Ysenden was so steady that the barrels were never at risk of getting away from their handlers, and so it wasn't ten minutes before they'd claimed an elevator down to the lower levels, then rolled the rest of the way to their destination. The broad hall greeted them at last, cutting north into the wall of the mountain, crowned by a bleached-white timber crossbeam upon which the sword and bow of the city was painted in blue. Even from down the long tunnel Sureht could make out the faint sounds of celebration, and the general had to motion for his attendants—and their barrels—to lead the way into the medical ward.

He needed those last few moments, he realized, to steel his expression as much as his heart.

The shouting and laughter came from the very back of the ward, where a set of double-doors had been wedged open in welcome. Another pair of guards were stood at attention just outside the entrance, and they brought themselves up a little straighter upon catching sight of their commander, lifting heads that had been tilted slightly to listen to the celebrations.

"At ease," Sureht told the two with a smile once they were nearer. *"In fact, you're both off duty for the night. Come join us."*

"Sir?" the closer of the two asked, obviously taken aback. The general couldn't fault him. If a soldier of the *er'endehn* was given early reprieve once in a hundred years, it was a story to share in the barracks. Sureht knew as much, though, and already had his explanation ready.

"My son has at once managed to thwart Sehranya's first assault in centuries, and lost half of his command," he told the two sentries as his own guards paused with their barrels outside the door. Placing his hand on the shoulder of the closest, he smiled as broadly as he could manage.

"This is both a night to celebrate and to mourn, for my family and Ysenden both. I'll not have any soldier within earshot not participating." He managed a wink. *"That is an order."*

It did the trick, because the elf—a young spear-bearer likely not fifty years of age—offered back a tentative grin as he nodded. *"Then yes, sir. We'll be glad to join."*

"Good man." Sureht patted the soldier once before motioning all of them to enter ahead of him. *"Then in you go, all of you! You two—"* he turned back to his attendants, still bent over their barrels *"—see those to the middle of the room, then you are to join in as well."*

"Yes, sir." The pair managed to keep their pleasure better hidden, but the gleam of anticipation in their eyes wasn't missed by the old general.

He let them go by, watching with a heavy heart he hid behind his carefully-crafted smile before finally stepping into the room himself.

Not wanting to have given anyone reason to suspect anything was amiss, Sureht had left most of the festivities planning to his seconds, as he would have done for any other such event. Fortunately, they hadn't disappointed. The long room—ordinarily nothing more than one of the larger recovery wards—was lined on either side with some fifty beds, most of them still occupied by bloodied and bandaged residents. All of them to a one, however, were sitting up and smiling, talking with their seated and standing comrades that were the more-fortunate survivors of Kellek's command, the warm glow of more than twenty moonwing lanterns casting everything in a hearty air. Additional members of the unit stood in discussion around the long, food-laden table that ran up the center of the room, and there were others, too, the general saw, men and women who had the softer looks of residents of the city who'd long left their mandatory service behind. He was at once pleased and saddened to realize his seconds had seen fit to invite the families of the advanced unit. It hurt, for a moment, to watch the group's three or four children running about at play among the adults' legs, but the general felt a little better when he caught the pained expression of those partners, parents, and siblings of the soldiers who *hadn't* made it home.

Don't worry, he thought, taking a breath and striding deeper inside, smile still plastered on his face. *We will* all *be free of this charade soon enough.*

"Oh. General!"

The old elf looked around at the familiar voice, unable to keep the stone in his throat from forming as he caught sight of who it was who'd shouted out to him. The pressure of it turned to pain, watching as the broad-shouldered youth approached him excitedly through the throng.

Sureht had known, of course, that his son would be present. Of the entirety of the command, only the ay'ahSel siblings had been given leave to accompany the army south on the march towards Erraven, and then only because of their developing bond to the primordial and his companions. It still hurt, however, and Sureht had to work harder than ever to keep up his cheerful expression as Kellek reached him.

"*Son,*" he said by way of greeting, grasping an offered arm and taking his child by the back of the neck. "*You and I are not subordinate and superior tonight. Do not treat me so formally.*"

Kellek grinned. "*Yes, Father.*" Then he paused, frowning slightly as he reached up to pull the general's hand from behind his head, looking at the reddened bandage there. "*Did you cut yourself? When did this happen?*"

"*It couldn't be avoided,*" Kellek said with a shrug, trying to pull his wrist free of his son's grasp unsuccessfully as the colonel looked more closely.

"*Is this dirt under your fingernails?*" the younger elf asked, perplexed. Then, though, his smile was back, and he looked up again with a chuckle as he let go of the hand. "*Have you taken up gardening, Father? If Mother were to see such a thing...*"

"It couldn't be avoided," Sureht said again, forcing a cough out as he looped an arm about his son's broad shoulders, pulling him in to look over the room together. *"Now, did you need something? I can't imagine you'd rather spend the evening with this wrinkled old elf than with your command."*

It was a little cruel to remind the colonel of where they were, but Sureht wasn't keen on letting the young man's curiosity linger on his wound.

Sure enough, Kellek's face fell a little.

"I just wanted to thank you. It's rare for a member of the council to encourage such an event, particularly one outside our direct chain of command. My soldiers and I are grateful."

"Bah!" Sureht reached around with his other hand to pat his son fondly on the cheek. *"This is not a military celebration, boy. This is a father expressing his pride in his child, and his gratitude towards those who brought him home. What could be more natural?"*

"Well you're certainly taking your duty as a parent seriously, then." The colonel managed to grin again, gesturing towards where a space had been made near the very middle of the chamber for the two soldiers who'd rolled in the barrels now being righted and lifted onto the table. *"Is that wine you've brought us?"*

"The very best of it," the general admitted, pulling his son towards the food as he noticed more than one attendee eyeing the spirits hopefully. *"And in need of rescuing, apparently. That's to be for the toast, and I'm not sure we'll have enough as is given how many people have come out to celebrate."*

"I was told you asked your seconds to have as many people join us as was feasible," Kellek said with a chuckle, following dutifully. *"I say it's your own fault for not planning better."*

"How many people are *here?"* Sureht asked, releasing his son at last when the crowd parted for them, some nodding to him while others bowed respectfully as they stepped away.

"In all? A little more than two hundred, if I had to guess."

Enough, the general thought privately, reaching the barrels at last and giving them a quick once over. *More than enough.*

Fortunately, no one had yet noticed the new wax he'd had to apply himself, having broken the old stopper that had sealed the caskets for the last two hundred years only the previous day.

"Good," he said aloud after a moment, patting the closest of the barrels. *"No one's gotten greedy."* He turned to his son. *"Spread the word, would you? I'd like to make a toast, and I won't be having anyone without a glass in hand when I start. Not even the children."*

Sureht only snorted, then stepped away to do as he was told, shouting—to responding cheers—that all should line up to "partake of the council's wine!".

Sureht's seconds had already stowed the taps among the cutlery at his request, and so using the glass cups provided with the feast, it took fifteen minutes for drinks to be distributed throughout the audience, Sureht handing each one off himself, including to the bed-ridden. He had a word for all, of thanks to the unhurt, of encouragement to the injured, of sorrow to those mourning. They were coupled, of course, with him extracting a promise that none would drink until he was ready to toast the dead. As a result, by the time the last of the four youngsters had a small cup for themselves, the room had gone quiet, all eyes turning inward as the general poured himself his own glass from the dregs of the second barrel before holding it aloft.

More than two hundred arms lifted with his.

"I will not mince words," Sureht started strongly. *"As a member of the council of Ysenden, I first owe each and every one of you an apology. It is* our *failure that an enemy gained so strong a foothold within our lands,* our *failure that we allowed such a presence to exist without action."*

"You couldn't have known, General!" someone called from the beds along the west side of the room, hidden by the crowd.

"Sehranya took us all by surprise!" another voice echoed closer by.

Sureht smiled at that, hardening his will.

None need know it was not the Witch he was speaking of, after all.

"Be that as it may, it is still the duty of the council to defend the lives and ways of the er'endehn, *and the fact that there should be more of us present in this room is proof of our failure."* He took a steadying breath. *"I toast now. First, to those of you who have sacrificed blood and limb for your kind."* He scanned the celebrants before him slowly, meeting the eyes of every injured soldier he could find among them. *"Second, to those who fought with such skill and fortune that you have made it back to us unscathed."* Several of the unmarked soldiers dipped their heads in gratitude. *"Third, to the families and friends of those who did not return, and who I hope have found comfort and support among the comrades of your fallen."* Several reddened gazes met his gratefully, one or two cups lowering as suppressed gasps and sobs, hidden behind hands brought to faces and mouths, rang out in the quiet. *"And lastly, to our lost themselves. May we see them again among the spirits, and may they welcome us joyously and with open arms. To the gone!"*

"TO THE GONE!" those who could still speak echoed his final toast, and together every glass was lowered from the air and brought to eager lips, mirroring Sureht once again.

The general, though, did not drink, careful to avoid letting the dark liquid so much as touch his lips as he failed to stop himself from looking about the room. Some sipped and some guzzled, but within a few seconds all he could see had partaken, and almost at once the conversation resumed again, most generally around exclamations of delight at the flavor and body of the wine.

"I say it again, Father: I am grateful."

Sureht turned to see Kellek stepping out of the crowd again, glass half-empty in one hand as he smiled about at the chattering crowd.

"I have to agree, however, that the council is hardly to blame for any of

this," the colonel said, coming to stand before his father. *"There was little way of knowing that the Witch has risen again. My command was the most southern-pressing in a hundred years, and even* we *didn't have a clue until Lysiat and her brothers came stumbling out of the tunnels lacking most of their unit."*

"There is much we could have done, Kellek," Sureht said quietly, placing his untouched toast on the table behind him as he, too, took in the celebrations. *"Much we could have done a long time ago, to keep us from getting to where we are now."*

Kellek looked around at the general with a smirk. *"I don't follow your logic, Father, but perhaps in a millennium or two I will have garnered such wisdom."*

"Brat," Sureht managed to get out, turning a sad choke into a laughing cough just in time.

Kellek, though, was astute, and his brow furrowed slightly. *"Is everything alright? You seem a little… tense?"*

The general chuckled darkly. "*You have no idea, son. No idea. The history and pride of our kind rests on my shoulders, and I'm not sure if I'll ever be rid of that weight, in this life or the next."*

"Our… history?" Kellek asked, looking only the more confused.

That was the moment, however, that the first of them fell.

There came the *crack* of breaking glass from their left, then a dull *thump.* A women adorned in bright blue silks had collapsed, sprawling to the floor among the other elves, garnering gasps and shouts of alarm from those closest to her. Before anyone could so much as kneel down to check on her, though, a second cup fell and shattered, then a third.

And then, all of a sudden, people started to fall everywhere, and the screaming began.

"*What in the spirits?!"* Kellek yelled, whirling with the clear intent to rush towards the closest of the bodies, dropping his own wine as he did. He hadn't taken a step, however, when Sureht grabbed him by the arm and spun him around again.

Spun him around, and drew him in to the tightest hug the general had ever given his child.

"F-Father?" the young colonel stammered, clearly taken aback.

Sureht, though, only held him closer, squeezing his eyes shut against a hundred shouts of fear and the sudden stampede of would-be-celebrants headed for the door.

It didn't matter, of course. There were neither other patients nor caretakers in the hospital ward, and Sureht had seen to it that none of his guard or the borrowed ten thousand of the main army were posted nearby. He had faith, too, that the poison Gonin Whist had provided him with would act too quickly once it started to work, and sure enough he could tell by the *thump-thump-thump* that among those running for the hall, most weren't even making it out of the room.

And then, in his arms, Kellek began to sag.

"F-Father?" his son asked again, voice suddenly weak. *"F-Father? What… What did you do? What did you… do?"*

"What I had to," was all Sureht could answer with shakily, his composure finally breaking. *"What I had to, son. For the pride of our people."*

"Our… people?" Kellek whispered, his legs giving out so that the general was forced to ease him down until they were both on their knees. *"But… you're killing our… people…"*

And then he was gone, going limp in his father's arms, leaving Sureht to shiver and gasp in what he realized was a sudden, absolute quiet.

At last opening his eyes again, the general let his son down slowly, bearing him to the ground as gently as he could. Lifting his gaze, he looked around, his trembling redoubling at the sight.

A few of the elves had managed to make it into the hall, judging by the feet he could see around the corner of the door. The vast majority, however, had fallen where they'd stood, the life snuffed from them as though death had scythed through the room with a single sweep, sparing only Sureht. Men, women, even the children were still, sprawled out among the shattered glass of dropped cups and the red stain of leftover wine.

It was at once terrible to behold, and infinitely releasing.

At last, they would be free...

The general could have fled, then, could have risen and staggered from the room, even shouted for help if he'd seen fit to. Instead, however, he did not move, kneeling beside the corpse of his son, one hand on Kellek's chest to wait.

As promised, he did not have to be patient long.

Not half-a-minute after the last echoes of the terrified screams had faded from the stones of the hospital ward, something in the air changed with the faintest passing *thrum* of sound. Sureht could not place what it was exactly, but the shift was present, if ethereal, like a distant ringing in one's ears. It felt like the aura of the world as a whole had been altered, the clean, warm air brought in by the carefully crafted ducts hidden in the walls and ceiling suddenly chilly. If he'd had a mind to try, the general might have realized he could see his breath all of a sudden, but his vision was blurry behind the watery veil of tears of relief and regret alike.

Just the same, he did not miss when the first of the bodies began to stir.

It was, expectantly, the woman in the blue silks, the first to have fallen. Initially her movements were abrupt. A jolt of an arm. A spasming of the body. Then, though, there came the tearing sound of flesh, and the elf's fingertips split open as bone grew violently outward, forming cruel, bloody claws. For a second or two more she lay there, still again.

And then, at last, as the other bodies began to twitch and twist around her, the woman began to rise.

Sureht did not have to watch to know what he would see, did not have to take in the standing corpse to know the woman's eyes would be colorless orbs, now. As she found her feet, he heard the rattling sound of unsteady breathing, the body learning to work again as the Purpose's corruption—instilled by the rune-craved dragon skull he had buried among the trees of the *yr'es* far below them—was completed. The general drew his own, shaking breath, seeing the other forms begin to rise as well, one after the other after the other.

And then, under his hand, Kellek moved.

Whether he had simply been too absorbed in the horrifying scene to notice the change, or if his son's transition had merely been more seamless then the others, Sureht would never know. All that mattered to him was that by the time he looked around, the young elf was sitting up, pale eyes fixed on his father, bony claws scraping wickedly at the stone. For a moment, the two of them only stared at each other.

Then Kellek's mouth twisted into a horrible, hungry smile.

Sureht let out his last breath in a hissing laugh.

"It couldn't be avoided."

With those final words, the former Lord Commander of the fallen city of Syr'hend closed his eyes, not even having the time to yell in pain before the wight that had been his son found his throat with its teeth.

EPILOGUE

"Then everything I know and love will have already burned to the ground, and there will be nothing left for me to lose regardless."

—High Chancellor Arrackes to Declan Idrys, c. 1076p.f.

Sitting on her black throne, the Endless Queen waited. She was not impatient—time, after all, was eternally on her side—but she *was* eager. For once her fool of an apprentice seemed to have seen her plans through to perfection, and she struggled not to smile as she absently stroked the crystal speaker's charm that hung about her neck with the desiccated fingers of her right hand.

She would wait. She would wait as long as she needed to.

Fortunately for her, word arrived even as she thought this, the charm glowing a faint blue-pink, the only true light that ever saw the inside of her throne room.

My Queen, Gonin Whist's voice whispered gleefully within her head. *Ysenden has fallen.*

Then, with that simple statement, the charm dimmed again, leaving the chamber to its shadows once more.

For a long, long time, the Endless Queen did nothing, allowing herself to bask in the glory of this distant victory. She had spent weeks obsessing over the weave they had handed to the traitor Syr'esh, had sacrificed the dragon's skull that had been the one great remaining gem of her gathered materials. With no liche, a charm to raise the dead as they fell had been the best she could manage, provided at great cost.

And now, every ounce of that time, effort, and sacrifice was proving itself worth it.

At last, the Queen smiled, death-dry skin flaking from her jaws and cheeks as she did. Dropping her right hand from around the charm, she reached instead a little deeper into the ancient folds of her tunic, finding the untarnished gold necklace that hung about her neck there. Pulling on it, it was but a moment before the simple chain came free of her clothes.

The chain, and the meticulously crafted silver ring that hung from it, the hilt of the twin swords that formed its band holding in place a single, flat black gem.

"And so—" the Endless Queen hissed gleefully, taking in the faint lines of the stag's head and shield etched painstakingly into the stone "—I succeed where you had failed, Sehranya…"

THANK YOU ALL!
PLEASE READ!

Once again we find ourselves here, and once again we are absolutely flabbergasted by that fact. That you—yes you, the wonderful, brilliant example of a human being reading this right now—SO much for your support, and we genuinely hope you enjoyed the book!

On that subject, a few notes:

First: **Please, please, *please* consider rating and reviewing *A Blood of Kings* on Amazon, as well as any of your other favorite book sites**. Many people don't know it, but there are thousands of books published every day, most of those in the USA alone. Over the course of a year, a quarter of a million authors will vie for a small place in the massive world of print and publishing. We fight to get even the tiniest traction, fight to climb upward one inch at a time towards the bright light of bestsellers, publishing contracts, and busy book signings.

Thing is, we need all the help we can get, and that's where wonderful readers like you come in!

Second: If you want to join Wraithmarked Creative's growing community, be sure to jump into the conversation at:

• The Wraithmarked Creative's private readers' group on Facebook, where we geek out about magic and nerdy things.

• The Wraithmarked Patreon, where you can get early art, early access chapters, and whole books months in advance.

Regardless of whether or not you choose to review, reach out, or support us elsewhere, thank you again for taking the time to read *A Mark of Kings*.

All the best, and stay amazing
Bryce & Luke

Made in the USA
Las Vegas, NV
27 October 2021

33082243R00271